DATE DUE

APR 1 7 2008	
MAY 1 2008	
MAY 1 3 2008	
MAY 2 0 2008	
JUN – 3 2008	
JUN 1 7 2008	
JUN 3 0 2008	
Sept 22	

VIE FRANÇAISE

VIE FRANÇAISE

Jean-Paul Dubois

Translated from the French
by Linda Coverdale

Alfred A. Knopf New York 2007

THIS IS A BORZOI BOOK
PUBLISHED BY ALFRED A. KNOPF

Translation copyright © 2007 by Alfred A. Knopf,
a division of Random House, Inc.
All rights reserved. Published in the United States by Alfred A.
Knopf, a division of Random House, Inc., New York, and in
Canada by Random House of Canada Limited, Toronto.
www.aaknopf.com

Originally published in France as *Une vie française* by Éditions
de l'Olivier, an imprint of Éditions du Seuil, S.A., Paris,
in 2004.
Copyright © 2004 by Éditions de l'Olivier/Le Seuil

Knopf, Borzoi Books, and the colophon are registered trademarks
of Random House, Inc.

Library of Congress Cataloging-in-Publication Data
Dubois, Jean-Paul, [date]
[Vie française. English]
Vie française / by Jean-Paul Dubois ; translated from the
French by Linda Coverdale.
p.   cm.
ISBN: 978-0-307-26287-5
I. Coverdale, Linda.   II. Title.
PQ2664.U28435V5213 2007
843'.914—dc22   2007015678

Manufactured in the United States of America
First American Edition

To Louis, my grandson
To Claire, Didier, my children,
and Frédéric E.

"You're the grandpap, aren't you? Grandpaps are special people around here."

And the child's miniature body did adhere to his chest and arms, though more weakly than the infants he had presumed to call his own. Nobody belongs to us, except in memory.

—John Updike

Man is smaller than himself.

—Günther Anders

Contents

VIE FRANÇAISE

CHARLES DE GAULLE

(January 8, 1958–April 28, 1969)

AND my mother fell to her knees. I had never seen someone collapse so suddenly. She hadn't even had time to hang up the telephone. I was at the other end of the hall, but I could hear every sob and see her whole body shaking. Her hands seemed like a pathetic bandage over her face. My father went over to her, hung up the phone, and then he collapsed as well, sinking into the armchair in the front hall. Bowing his head, he began to weep. Silent, terrified, I remained motionless at the far end of that long hall. By not approaching my parents, I felt as if I were buying time, protecting myself for a few more moments against the awful news that I could guess at anyway. So there I stood, teetering on the edge of grief with my skin on fire, studying with a watchful eye how quickly calamity can spread, and waiting for it to overwhelm me in turn.

My brother, Vincent, died early on the evening of Sunday, September 28, 1958, in Toulouse. The television had just announced that 17,668,790 French citizens had finally approved the new constitution of the Fifth Republic.

Neither my father nor my mother had taken the time to go vote in the referendum. They spent the day at the bedside of my brother, who had been operated on for appendicitis complicated by acute peritonitis. His condition had taken a turn for the worse the previous evening, and around midday, he had lost consciousness.

I remember that the doctor on duty had spoken at length with my parents to prepare them for an outcome that he now felt was inevitable. During that discussion I had remained sitting on a chair out in the corridor, wondering what they could be talking about, behind that door, that I wasn't supposed to hear. I thought about my brother, about everything he would have to tell me when he came home from the hospital, and I was already envious of the status this heroic survivor would enjoy over the next few weeks. At that time, I was eight years old and Vincent barely ten, a modest difference that was in reality quite important. Vincent was a giant of a boy, a perfectly proportioned child who seemed built to lay the foundations of a brand-new world. He was surprisingly mature for his age, and would patiently explain to me the ups and downs of the adult world, protecting me all the while from those same vicissitudes. He was the most popular boy in school but did not hesitate, when he felt he was in the right, to stand up to a teacher or to our parents. And so, in my eyes, he was a colossus. When I was with him, I felt sheltered from life's troubles. Even today, forty-six years after his death, when I think back on our childhood, he is still the same towering figure, so beloved and admired.

When my father rose painfully from his chair and came toward me, he looked like an old man. He seemed to stagger, as if hauling some invisible burden behind him. I watched him come closer and somehow knew that he was going to tell me that the world had come to an end. He laid a hand on my arm and said, "Your brother has just died." Without any consideration for my father's anguish, without showing him the slightest sign of affection, I rushed into Vincent's room and grabbed his chromium-plated metal coach pulled by six white horses. This toy, or rather, this souvenir, had been brought to him from London two years earlier by our uncle, a shifty sort of person, short and unpleasant, but a great traveler. The object doubtless came from an ordinary souvenir shop near Buckingham Palace, but it was so heavy, and shiny, and the details of the carriage—in the lanterns, the wheels—were so precise, and the high-stepping horses exuded such power, that to me it was a talisman, and if my brother had not already been an exceptional child, this object would in itself have endowed him with an aura of supreme prestige. Vincent never let me borrow the coach and team, claiming that they were too fragile and I much too young to play with such a thing. Sometimes he would set it on the floor in the living room and tell me to lay my ear against the parquetry. "Don't move," he would say. "Don't make a sound, and close your eyes. You'll hear the horses' hoofbeats. . . ." And of course, I did hear them. I even saw the team flash by me in full gallop, with my brother as their bold driver, perched atop the sparkling carriage as it rocked on its springs. Then I would vaguely sense that I was at the very heart of childhood, that world we nourished with our vital energy, day after day. The child is father to the man—and I wanted to grow, to grow up, faster, and stronger, like this princely brother, this cavalry master.

At the moment of his death, my first reflex was therefore to despoil him and seize the object. To steal it. With the feverish usurpation of a treacherous heir. I must have been afraid that Vincent would carry that coach off into the grave. Perhaps I was hoping, through that sacred and forbidden possession, to acquire a share of his glory, his legitimacy, and to become an older kid at the very least bold enough to plunder the dead and whip stolen lead horses into a trot. Yes, in the hour of his death, I robbed my brother. Without remorse, without regret, without even shedding a tear.

My name is Paul Blick. I am fifty-four years old, an awkward age that hesitates between two perspectives on life, two contradictory worlds. With each passing day my complexion shows my age a little more. I take Norpace and Inderal for my arrhythmia, and like everyone else, I have stopped smoking. I live alone, I dine alone, I'm growing old alone, even though I do try to keep in touch with my two children and my grandson. Despite his youth (he's going on five), I sometimes recognize on my grandson's face not just some of my brother's expressions, but also that confidence, that serenity Vincent displayed as he went through life. Like my brother, the child seems imbued with a peaceful energy, and to meet his gaze, so bright and curious, is always unsettling. For Louis's fourth birthday, I lifted the coach down from the top shelf of the bookcase and set it in front of him. He examined it for a long time—the wheels, the horses—without touching it. Not the slightest bit entranced, he seemed rather to be taking mental inventory of its every detail. After a moment, I told him that if he laid his ear to the parquet, he, too, might hear the sound of hoofbeats. Although skeptical, Louis did crouch down, and in that posture, gave me—for a fleeting second—the joy of glimpsing my childhood go galloping by.

Vincent's funeral was a dreadful experience and I can say that from that day on, despite our efforts, my parents and I never managed to constitute a real family. After the service, my father handed me my brother's Kodak Brownie Flash camera, never imagining that this object would later change my life.

Vincent's death amputated part of our lives and some of our essential feelings. It changed my mother's face so profoundly that within a few months she looked like a stranger, while her body shrank, wasting away as if consumed from within. Vincent's disappearance also paralyzed all her gestures of tenderness, turning this previously affectionate woman into a kind of distant and indifferent stepmother. My father, once so lively, so talkative, walled himself up inside silence and sadness, and our formerly exuberant family meals now resembled suppers served for so many graveyard statues. Yes, after 1958, happiness abandoned us, singly and collectively, and at the table, we left it to the television announcers to fill our hours of mourning.

My father had just bought a TV set of varnished wood in February or March of 1958: a Grandin, equipped with an iron-cored choke allowing us to tune in the single channel stingily available in France at the time. This newfangled item had made my brother and me extremely popular at school, especially on Thursday afternoons, when we invited our friends to come watch the latest episodes of Rusty, Rin Tin Tin, and the adventures of Zorro, but we reached the pinnacle of our success that summer, with the dazzling performance of the French soccer team at the World Cup matches in Sweden. During the afternoon, when the events were broadcast, the living room of our apartment resembled the packed stands of a stadium as we all followed Remetter's tackles, Vincent's deft footwork, Fontaine's shots at the goal, the dribbling of Kopa and Piantoni. I can still recall with uncanny precision the details of the 5–2 match between Brazil and France in the semifinals in Stockholm: the tartness of the lemon sodas; the sickeningly sweet cherry pound cake; the grainy black-and-white image that occasionally—heart-stoppingly— began scrolling up the screen; the slatted shutters we closed to block the glare of the late-afternoon sunshine; the suffocating heat of that dramatic, shadowy interior; my brother's booming voice urging the team on; the flurry of goals; and then, gradually, the shouting dying down, hope slipping away, and the living room emptying out almost reluctantly until only my brother and I were left, off in a corner, exhausted, disappointed, completely crushed. A few days later, in the finals, Brazil would trounce Sweden 5–2, and France would beat Germany 6–3 to take third place. I don't remember a single thing about those last two events. Probably because they were now simply soccer matches, untouched by that unique grace of the afternoon when I had supported my brother in his support of France. And after so many years, despite all that we forget throughout our lives, in my memory that little island is still safe and sound, a tiny, radiant territory of shared fraternal innocence.

That was the last summer I spent with Vincent. Soon his place across from me at the dinner table was taken by de Gaulle. What I mean is, the Grandin TV set was put behind the chair where my brother had sat for ten years. I saw this change as a usurpation, especially since the general seemed to spend his whole life inside the TV, and I quickly came to detest that man. His conceited profile, his kepi, his lighthouse keeper's uniform, and his haughty bearing all bothered me, plus I couldn't stand his voice, and I was absolutely convinced that the distant general was actually my grandmother's true husband. Her other half, her natural counterpart. They had a certain arrogance in common, plus a taste for severity and order. A woman of another era, my grandmother was for me the archetype of ugliness, meanness, bitterness, and treachery. After my brother's death, and for reasons that were never revealed to me, she left her imposing house to come spend every winter in our apartment, where she commandeered the master bedroom, which looked out over Square Saint-Étienne. During her stay, I was absolutely forbidden, without exception, to enter what she referred to as her "apartments." The widow of my paternal grandfather, Léon Blick (a landed proprietor, as one said in those days), this woman commanded her family like a brigadier. Toward the end of the 1920s, Léon went AWOL several times by abandoning that barracks life for Tangier, where he would live it up for a month, gambling at the casino. His returns home were always tumultuous, it seems, with my grandmother meeting him each time at the front door backed up by a priest, to whom the poor man was obliged to confess all his North African depravity then and there. That was Marie Blick: harsh, strict, bad-tempered. And Catholic. I can still see her during those winters in Toulouse, transfixed in front of her fireplace, endlessly saying her Rosary, her head always covered with a mantilla. From the hall, through the half-open door, I would watch her almost pray the skin off her lips. She was like an implacable machine, wound up tight, with a single goal: the salvation of lukewarm souls. And while she was at it, she would sometimes sense my heathen presence: I would glimpse the iceberg glint of her gaze and feel my blood run cold, yet I remained petrified, unable to flee, like a rabbit in headlights.

Marie Blick had vowed undying hatred to Pierre Mendès-France, the Jewish prime minister who had negotiated the French armistice with Ho Chi Minh in 1954, but she reserved her fiercest curses for the Soviet Union, homeland of the bloodthirsty and the godless. The slightest allusion to that nation during the evening newscast would literally hypnotize her. But one man in her rogue's gallery outshone all others, a man we sensed she would happily have strangled with her bare Christian hands: Anastas Mikoyan, chairman of the Presidium of the Supreme Soviet of the USSR. My grandmother took a wicked pleasure in massacring his name by calling him Mikoyashhh, dragging out the last syllable with a hiss. Whenever she saw this apparatchik on the TV screen, she would strike the floor a few times with her cane, draw herself up like a creaky automaton, fling her napkin dramatically onto the table, and always grumble the same phrase: "I will withdraw to my apartments." Reinvigorated by this transfusion of hatred, she would then set out down the long hall, and we'd eventually hear her door slam shut. In her lair, the waltz of the Rosaries would resume. I recall having tried for a long time to discover why Mikoyan, that little man in a black hat, could trigger such outbursts from Marie Blick. When I asked my father one day, he smiled vaguely and said, "I think it's because he's a Communist." But Khrushchev and Bulganin were Communists, too, yet they never merited my grandmother's wrath for Anastas.

Although I was never a member of the Party, I believe that in her pantheon of despicable creeps, Marie Blick assigned me a spot well ahead of Stalin or Bulganin, right up there with the infamous Mikoyashhh, for she addressed me and treated me with a similar disdain, which became more pronounced after my brother died. In her eyes, Vincent had always been the sole Blick heir. He was the image of my father, and although still young, had already shown signs of a stern maturity. As for me, I was just a weedy offshoot, a spermatic leftover, an ovular error, a moment of divine carelessness. I resembled my mother, in other words, a different family, one that was poor, very poor, not from these parts, from up in the mountains, in fact.

Until 1914, my maternal grandfather, François Lande, was a shepherd. He lived high in the Pyrenees on a sunny slope of a pass known as the Col de Port, which at the time could truly be called the ends of the earth. One could even say, in a way, that François lived on the moon. So much cold, so much snow, so much solitude. It was on that rugged terrain where the sheep could barely keep their footing that the Great War came looking for him. Two gendarmes climbed that summit shrouded in mists to deliver his travel orders. François, who lived in the south at the top of the world, wound up in the north in a trench six feet deep. He did what he had to do, got his share of horror and poison gas, and came home, broken in body and mind and old before his time. At first he did try to go back to his mountaintop, but the mustard gas had done its job. He and his moth-eaten lungs ended up in the suburbs of Toulouse, where my grandmother Madeleine bought a pushcart and began selling fruits and vegetables. As for François Lande, he stayed home, looking after his bronchi and jumping out of his skin every time the doorbell rang. He never answered the door, ever convinced that gendarmes would return to drag him back to the front. I saw him crawl under his bed one afternoon when someone knocked on the door. A moment before he'd been dandling me on his lap—and then he had changed into some kind of terrified little rodent. I remember my grandfather as a tall man, quite thin, always wearing a black cape and gripping his iron-shod shepherd's staff. He didn't talk much, but there was a great gentleness as well as a constant alertness in his face. He seemed both afraid and aware of that outside world he sometimes observed from afar, through the window curtains of his room.

Shortly before my grandfather's death, in 1957, my mother took him one Sunday to the top of the Col de Port. He and I sat side by side during the trip and I don't recall his saying a single word throughout the entire ride. Once the road started to climb, however, and fold into hairpin turns, François showed a growing interest in the landscape, the houses, this old world he was seeing once more and doubtless for the last time. His eyes seemed to glitter with a savage animal joy. He rediscovered the frigid summits, the indescribable odor of high altitude, the light in the sky, the scents and colors of the earth. When the road ended, he got out of the car and set off up the path to a familiar mountain ridge, holding my hand. I had no idea where that man was taking me, but I could feel his warm hand squeezing mine. He said something like "In good weather all the sheep were over there, on that slope. And my dog, he would always wait for me near the path." I think he was talking to himself, seeing through things to their former life, gazing at the virtual horizon of his memories. Because that day, in the places he was showing me, all you could see was the static procession of chair-lift pylons at a fledgling ski resort. Then, I clearly remember that François Lande sat down stiffly on the ground, hugged me, swept his hand across the entire landscape, and said, "You see, child, that's where I came from."

And so that is where I came from, too, partly. Young as I was, I could certainly see that on the Blick side—I mean my grandmother, the general's "spiritual" wife—there was little enthusiasm for an alliance with such modest mountain folk, let alone for the produce-peddling of my grandmother Lande. Marie Blick tried for a long time, it seems, to dissuade my father from marrying my mother. There was no question of consenting to such a lopsided union. The eldest Blick child deserved better than the daughter of a crippled and half-crazed shepherd. The families did not attend the wedding, and aside from my mother, no Lande ever met a single Blick except my father. When she addressed my mother, Marie Blick always used this condescending formula reserved, at the time, for undesirable daughters-in-law: "My child, if you do not train these boys from their earliest years, you'll never be able to control them later on." "Don't forget, my child, when you go out, buy only Melba toast for Victor, I believe he has gotten fatter." When she was living with us, Marie Blick made a point of speaking to my mother as if to her female house servants, in her own home. I think my grandmother is the only person I ever really hoped would die. And for a long time I was angry with my parents for not putting that woman in her place, but it's true that in those days it was quite normal to stoically endure being tortured by one's elders, even when they were monsters.

After Vincent's death our life lost all semblance of one, and for two months every year, when my grandmother was in residence, it became sheer hell. In addition to lashing out at the chairman of the Presidium, Marie Blick bullied my father about his weight, criticized the family meals, and forbade me to talk at the table or to leave my seat without permission. Whenever I broke one of those rules, she could never restrain her angry reaction, tapping her foot and saying sharply to my father, "My poor Victor, you have raised this child like an animal. One day he will make you shed tears of blood."

Much later, I heard a strange story. Toward the end of his life, my paternal grandfather, Léon Blick, suffered from a condition akin to Alzheimer's that made him lose considerable mental ground. Not only was he forgetting everything, but he also grew inclined to offer large sums of money to certain of his farmworkers on the pretext that "the land belongs to those who work it." Anyone but my grandmother would have considered this argument a sign of common sense and seen in these repeated gifts the marks of a generous spirit on the part of a rich landowner open, at the end of his life, to progressive ideas. But Marie Blick saw in her husband's behavior only the final spasm of his serious illness, and she succeeded in having him committed.

Flattened by the psychiatric hammer blows of the time, surrounded by raving lunatics and alone in the world (my grandmother forbade her children to visit their father), Léon Blick fell rapidly into a decline, and ceased speaking for a year before slipping gently into death.

Meanwhile my grandmother, who was then far from being an old woman, began regularly seeing another man. He was, she said, a kind of trusted overseer of her business affairs and supervisor of the tenant farmers. In reality, despite her professions of piety, Marie Blick, like other women, sometimes needed sex.

After the death of Léon Blick, things went on as before for a few months, until this new friend took it into his head to acquire my grandfather's gun. Always careful to keep her finances separate from those of her lowlife lover, Marie Blick relinquished the family firearm to him at a price that is still remembered as even more indecent than all her libidinal eccentricities. Swindled but happy, the lover went home and proceeded to clean the weapon. No one knows how or when it discharged. The sweetheart was simply found lying on the floor, his face destroyed by a volley of lead shot, Léon Blick's gun still in his stiff hands.

I missed Vincent. Two years after his death, I still could not resign myself to his absence. I needed to know that he was by my side. As for my parents, they had their work, of course, and they continued to eat meals together and to sleep in the same bedroom. But they no longer seemed to hope for anything, either individually or as a couple. I sometimes felt as though the world were advancing all around us at a brisk pace, while we stood still, dazed by our pain.

After the Second World War, with financial aid from his family, my father bought a five-story parking garage with spiral ramps. He named the business "Day and Night," and opened a Simca dealership on the ground floor. He sold and repaired Arondes, Arianes, Trianons, Versailles, and a few luxurious Chambords. I couldn't tell you anything today about what Victor Blick thought of those four-door sedans or motor vehicles in general, because I don't believe I ever heard him talk about automobiles at any time in our family life. Except, perhaps, in 1968, when it came time to choose my first car, which obviously wasn't a Simca, but a 1961 Volkswagen 1200 Beetle.

My mother, Claire, hardly ever talked about her work as a proofreader. Once, and only once, she briefly explained to me that she corrected the grammatical and spelling errors of journalists and authors who were careless about the usage of the subjunctive or the agreement of past participles. You might consider that a relatively repetitive and peaceful task—hardly a stressful one, in any case. You would be wrong, though. A proofreader never rests. A proofreader must always ponder, wonder, and, above all, worry about missing a mistake, an error, a barbarism. My mother's mind was never at peace, so compelled was she, at all hours, to verify the proper application of a rule or the validity of a correction by consulting a small mountain of books dealing with the particularities of the language. A proofreader, she used to say, is a kind of cheesecloth employed to filter out linguistic impurities. Yet, never satisfied by her biggest catches, Claire Blick was haunted instead by those tiny slipups, that sediment of inaccuracies constantly swarming through her mind. She often rose from the table in the middle of supper to go check something in one of her encyclopedias or specialized reference works, merely to quell a surge of anxiety or lay some niggling doubt to rest. Such behavior was not specific to my mother's character. Most proofreaders apparently develop this kind of verificative mania. Their occupational hazard is the endless quest for purity and perfection.

Seen from the outside, Victor and Claire Blick seemed like a couple well attuned to the optimism of those times of full employment and economic renewal, when electrical household appliances were appearing everywhere. Yes, my parents were just like all those men and women bursting with energy and hope, but in fact they were only two hollow logs snagged in a fast-flowing river. Every day at the same time, they watched this new world in labor, listening to its groans, but they sat stony-hearted before its long procession of atrocities. The fate of the Belgian Congo, the machinations of Joseph Kasavubu and Moïse Tshombé, the death of Patrice Lumumba—my parents found such things as boring as the fluctuating stock price of the Upper Katanga Mining Union. Sitting before a television set that spewed unbridled mayhem and seemed to have been left in charge of my education, I never stopped praying for my brother to appear and reclaim his seat at the table, so that we could finally turn that Grandin off, let life come back, and all pick up our conversation again right where a postoperative complication had interrupted it on September 28, 1958.

The war in Algeria, like so many other events, remained a distant abstraction, images from another world that simply flitted across the convex screen. During 1961, however, we were often awakened at night by the noise of explosions that shook Toulouse. These disruptions organized by the OAS—the Organisation de l'Armée Secrète—affected every neighborhood and preoccupied the citizenry, but although we definitely heard the loud detonations and may even have seen certain things, we did not discuss them at all. Not even when the silence of our noon meal was disturbed by the concert of car horns along the Allées François-Verdier honking out the slogan *Al-gé-rie fran-çaise*. Three short, two long: the Morse code of the French forced to leave their Algerian colony. And we never said a word when the post office near my father's garage was blown up with plastic explosives.

Our Christmas dinner in 1962, on the other hand, was quite a talkfest. It took place in the home of my grandmother Marie Blick. The entire family was there, except, of course, for Madeleine Lande, the socially unacceptable greenmarket retiree, and my grandfather François, who had died some years earlier of his pulmonary troubles. Madeleine and the doctor had found him curled up under his bed, lifeless but still at war, terrified by the stubborn ghosts of two gendarmes intent on taking him into custody and then off God knows where. This time, François Lande had eluded them for good. He was buried where he belonged, up on that summit he had once called home, not far from the indifferent parade of ski-lift pylons.

Well, that Christmas meal was one I will not forget. I was twelve, and the world itself hardly seemed much older than that to me. That year, you would have thought the family had gathered, not for a holiday meal, but to argue about the "events." That was the delicate term for the Algerian war. The Blicks ran the gamut of opinions held throughout the country at the time. First, my grandmother: a Pétainist at heart, lately returned to the Gaullist fold, a staunch Christian who was anti-Communist, anti-Mendès, and anti-me, a woman who did not like to wait between courses at the table and who couldn't have cared less about the situation in Algeria, that ungodly place forever lost to Christendom. My aunt Suzanne: my father's eldest sister, a close copy of her mother, anti-Mendès, of course, anti-Semitic on occasion, anti-me at all times, and eternally nostalgic for a white and French Algeria. Her husband, Hubert: an uncanny ringer for the tough-guy actor Eddie Constantine (but with a Provençal accent), a former militiaman, a veteran of Indochina and a bygone world, who was rumored to have briefly returned to active service in the OAS. My second aunt, Odile: an English teacher at the Lycée Pierre-de-Fermat, an anti-colonialist with reasonably Socialist sympathies, who was living with Bernard Dawson, a divorced sports reporter (a rugby expert) who made no secret of his leanings toward the French Communist Party. Among the rest of my relatives, I will mention one of my cousins, Jean, ten years older than I was, the unlikely son of Hubert and Suzanne, a hybrid who admired Elvis Presley and the anarchist Mikhail Bakunin, a nice kid who would die in a car accident a year after the student demonstrations of May 1968, of which he was a harbinger.

My parents? Faithful to what they had become after Vincent's death: silent, pleasant, polite, obligingly present, yet, at the same time, completely absent.

Before the meal, my grandmother insisted on saying one of those prayers only she could come up with, an interminable grace that pissed off everyone, starting with the extreme right-wingers, who could hardly wait to attack the earthly pleasures of the table.

They bore down on the seafood, the Sauternes, and the goose liver before deciding the fate of Oran, Algiers, Tlemcen, and Saïda. Hubert raised his glass.

"Merry Christmas to all the independent niggers. Still, it's weird to think we're no longer at home out there."

Dawson did try to explain that Algeria had not always belonged to France and with the colonial era past, it was time for independence.

"You sound like that other son of a bitch."

"I trust, Hubert, that you do not have the general in mind when you say that. Not in front of the children."

"But Mother Blick, everyone—even the children—knows that your general is a real bastard, that he betrayed a people and a country and had those who defended it shot."

"Just what do you mean by that?" demanded Dawson.

"I mean that he had true Frenchmen executed: Roger Degueldre, Claude Piegst, Albert Dovecar, Bastien-Thiry—those names mean anything to you?"

"You're talking about members of the OAS! Three of them were murderers, and Bastien-Thiry tried to assassinate him!"

"No, actually, I'm talking about real patriots."

"You have a singular notion of that word, Hubert."

"You know what, Odile? Screw you, you and all your Commie-Socialist crap."

"Hubert, I won't have you speak to my daughter like that. Think of the children. Control yourself."

"I've been controlling myself for almost twenty years, Mother Blick—twenty years of people telling me, one way or another, to shut up. No matter what Odile thinks, I've always been on the side of my country and the flag. Whether during Marshal Pétain's time or at Dien Bien Phu. Who did you think was fighting off those slanty-eyed bastards while you were all having yourselves a nice comfy Christmas, huh? And in Algeria, if not for the OAS, who would have kept those peasants of the Front de Libération Nationale at bay?"

"You know how many victims your OAS racked up? Two and a half thousand Frenchmen and more than twenty thousand Muslims!"

"Sure, Bernard, keep spewing that same old Party propaganda. But let me tell you something. It's not twenty thousand but forty thousand, sixty thousand burrheads we should've taken out when they started cutting them off and stuffing them in our mouths. You can't preserve an empire if you're not ready to fight terror with terror."

"Really, Papa, you're the world's biggest fascist."

"Who asked you, you little jerk?"

"Hubert, please. He's your son. And it's Christmas Eve."

"You're right, Mother Blick. I apologize."

"What Hubert means is, all this business of self-determination has opened the floodgates. You'll see that at this rate, soon we won't be at home here in our own country. Besides, isn't that true already? I mean, who could have imagined a day when our minister of finance would be named *Wilfrid Baumgartner?*"

"Meaning what, Suzanne?"

"Oh please, Odile, don't play dumb, and stop making such a fool of yourself in front of everyone for the umpteenth time."

"So you think *I'm* the one being ridiculous? Have you been listening to yourselves for the last hour, you and your husband, waving the flag and going on about burrheads and kikes, as you call them at home? You think you're still in Vichy?"

"Ah, Vichy, here we go again!"

That was when my father rose from his chair, gently placed his napkin on the table, and said, "I'll go get the turkey."

When he returned, bearing the platter in front of him with the cook's help, the tension between the two sisters had subsided. France has always found reconciliation around a roast fowl. Exasperated by his parents' Pétainism, my cousin Jean was standing by the window, smoking a cigarette. Such lapses in etiquette were guaranteed to drive my grandmother crazy. She began to fume discreetly as a prelude to venting her anger. Tapping the floor three times with her cane, she exclaimed, "Young man, come to the table immediately, if you please!" Spoken with all the nastiness and imperiousness she could muster, the words serrated by her clenched teeth cut Jean to the bone.

It was also on that Christmas Eve in 1962 that my grandmother did something truly despicable, even for her. We had made it through the dessert, Indochina, Algeria, Vichy, how well my father's Versailles V8s were selling, the comfort of Renault's Frégate Transfluides, the sturdiness of the Peugeot 403 Cabriolet, the superiority of a good Pomerol over any Saint-Émilion, the pathetic season Stade Toulousain—the local rugby team—was having, Schultz's career with the Toulouse Soccer Club, the children's future, vacations in Hendaye on the Bay of Biscay, and the inevitable stories about maids and cleaning women pilfering as never before. It was on this last topic that my grandmother weighed in. She had, she announced, an infallible method of assuring the honesty and loyalty of her servants: "I give royal tips so that they genuflect." Suzanne and Hubert tittered nervously, almost as if farting. Everyone else, I think, felt embarrassed. While the cook was clearing the table, pretending not to have heard a thing, my grandmother sat in seeming innocence, probably counting the silver.

The Old Lady died the following summer, during our holiday on the Basque coast, so we had to rush back from the beach to contemplate the ingratitude of that face once more before it decomposed. We had hardly arrived at my grandmother's house when Aunt Suzanne, who had taken charge of arrangements, urged me to give the deceased one last kiss. The idea of pressing my lips to a corpse made me sick. My aunt led me over to the body, which lay in the center of a room already as dark as the tomb, with all the curtains closed. The sweetish smell in the air was a mixture of white flowers, burning candle wax, and—I was pretty sure—already decaying flesh. Feebly illuminated in death, Marie Blick's face was even more terrifying than it had been in life, a final concentration of every base emotion. Noticing that her eyes were not completely closed, I imagined that through the slit between her waxen eyelids this wretched woman would continue, from beyond the grave, to supervise the slow evolution of the genes she had passed on to her descendants. Faced with this spectacle, I felt my body stiffen and my stomach heave, while my aunt's hand at my back pressed me forward toward the earthly remains of "the general's wife." Seized with a sort of gastro-intestinal panic, I imagined a teeming mass of slugs already at work beneath the sheets, exuding a flood of excremental fluids with odors that were already leaking through the thin layer of skin. A thousand snakes began to writhe in my own belly, and suddenly I felt them ascend to my stomach, up my throat, into my mouth, and spurt shockingly onto the immaculate sheet covering the deceased. Everyone interpreted this spasm as an expression of my deep grief, which earned me special treatment during the funeral. And so, to spare me further emotional distress, they excused me from the rites at the cemetery and the descent of the coffin toward what I dearly hoped would be hell.

All through those ceremonies and days of mourning, no one shed the tiniest tear. Dressed in black, everyone wore a grave expression, but there was not the slightest trace of sorrow on those faces already scrutinizing one another as rivals in inheritance. As always, this distribution reawakened the full range of private jealousies, selfishness, and unacknowledged vileness at which the petty bourgeoisie excels. Finally, after some discreet negotiations, the two sisters—the Socialist and the Catholic reactionary—slyly allied themselves for the sake of the loot and despoiled my poor father, who now had a deep and legitimate cause for sorrow. He saw the maternal fortune pulled out from under him, his only inheritance (grudgingly bestowed) the run-down family house. He continued to sell Simcas, but this fresh blow, on top of the loss of his eldest son, snuffed out whatever tiny spark of life might still have flickered in him.

Such was my family clan at the time: unpleasant, out-of-date, by turns reactionary and revolutionary, and terrifically sad. In a word, French. Yes, my family resembled our country, which, having overcome its poverty and shame, felt lucky to be still alive. A nation now rich enough to despise its farmers, to make laborers of them and build them absurd cities of functionally ugly apartment blocks. Meanwhile, automobile transmissions were adding a fourth gear, enough to convince the entire country that we had gone into overdrive.

Growing up in that France wasn't easy. Especially for a shy adolescent trapped between Charles de Gaulle, on the one hand, and his prime minister, Georges Pompidou, on the other. Furthermore, it was unthinkable, in matters sexual, to expect the slightest guidance, the least scrap of information. Deprived of the knowledge and experience of an elder brother, flanked by uncommunicative and overwhelmed parents, I had to entrust my initiation to a kind of jolly voluptuary, a complete nutcase who was amazingly imaginative, capable, and fiendishly perverse, without scruple or inhibition, and blessed with remarkable health. David Rochas was a year older than I was and—doubtless—several lifetimes ahead of most human beings on this planet.

It was at the age of thirteen, and probably somewhat later than my peers, that I discovered on my own (and thanks to Victor Hugo) the principle and technique of ejaculation. I had been confined to my room that Sunday to read and summarize a few chapters of *Les Misérables*. Like all boys my age, I was constantly bedeviled by a deep current, a violent tension that endlessly roamed my lower abdomen. To calm or attempt to control that chronic excitement, I used to grasp my appendage and fiddle with it mindlessly, like an impatient traveler jiggling his foot. It was both pleasant and horribly frustrating. And then Hugo came along, with that endless reading assignment, on that blessed Sunday. This time, in the full throttle of the erection (the simple mechanics of which I understood perfectly), occurred a most brutal, mysterious, and archangelic phenomenon, with its dazzling emission of liquor and that terrifying and radiant sensation of sweet electrocution. Like a transfigured pilgrim, I realized that I would now live only to experience this shiver again and again, that everyone on earth was busy chasing this *frisson,* and that it made the world go around, caused famines, wars, and was the real engine driving the survival of our species, in itself justifying our existence and encouraging us to stave off tirelessly the hour of our death. So, from Hugo on, like a real *misérable* in the eyes of the Catholic Church, I jerked off like a maniac, as escape from that deadly little country of mine. I beat off to female TV announcers, mail-order catalogs, newsmagazines, advertisements with girls perched atop tires—in short, any picture at all showing me some bit of feminine flesh. That's when David, if I may put it this way, took my future in hand.

If you can imagine what the Italian actor Vittorio Gassman looked like as a boy, that was David Rochas. His face expressed an excitable virility that was a touch obtuse, yet masterful. He went to my school and played scrum half on our rugby team, while I played fly half, which meant that during our matches, our fates were closely linked. On the field, David became a bundle of energy, a kind of madman who led his pack with noisy brio. After the game, it was worse. Never stopping or holding still, he always preferred action, giving the impression of a soldier in the field, constantly on maneuvers. The only problem was that all this resilience, this dynamism, was devoted to the satisfaction of almost insatiable sexual needs and obsessions. Never, in my entire life, have I met anyone else with such an appetite, or so enslaved by such drives, his body seeming tortured in perpetuity by that seminal vapor seething inside him. He was a kind of spermatic volcano with permanent fumaroles bearing witness to the danger of a sudden eruption. Agitated, dancing from one foot to the other, he constantly kept one hand in his pocket. When I asked him about it, he replied, "I keep the beast on a short leash." Sometimes he would leap abruptly from his seat and pace around the room, grimacing and heaving angry sighs. Grabbing his dick through the material of his trousers, he would mutter with accents of mingled regret, anguish, and fury: "Fuck! If my mother were pretty, I'd screw her!"

His mother, it must be admitted, was no prize. With her husband, she ran a sizable real estate agency on the Boulevard de Strasbourg. The more I frequented the Rochas household, the better I understood the unusual predilections of their only son. Aside from a marked taste for flashy cars and showy furniture, this couple was remarkable for the flaunting of their insatiable lust. In their apartment, Monsieur and Madame Rochas were continually brushing against each other, cajoling and caressing each other, and kissing. Although a neophyte in these matters, I felt certain that such displays went way beyond the norms of other couples I knew when, right in the kitchen, I would see Michel Rochas grab his wife's ample breasts and thrust his purple little tongue into her mouth. Sometimes it was Marthe who would ostentatiously slip her hands into her husband's pockets while he was knotting his tie. And they acted as though their conduct were the most natural thing in the world. I thus began to understand the source of my friend David's turgescent torments.

Although only a year older than I was, he was vastly superior to me in all respects. Familiar with the fundamental principles of life, David read the great works of philosophy while the rest of us had only just discovered the origins of pleasure and the comic-book adventures of Akim and Battler Briton. He smoked complimentary cigarettes distributed by Air France and lent us old copies of *Paris-Hollywood* movie magazines that were falling apart but still graphic. This weird kid just fascinated me. Sometimes he would show up with *Die Welt* or the *Frankfurter Allgemeine Zeitung* under his arm, unfold his newspaper, and pretend, for an entire hour, to read the news in German. I have no idea why.

One evening in his room he was striding up and down, with "the beast on its leash," when I saw him suddenly push his desk against the wall he shared with his parents' bedroom next door. Then he turned out the light, placed his chair upon the desk, and with catlike grace, climbed this arrangement to reach a small oval window set in the wall. As he crouched, his profile faintly illuminated by the lamps in the next room, I could almost see the quivering muscular tension in the face of this transfixed predator. He signaled me to join him, and that was when I discovered the cause of his distress and excitement. Michel and Marthe Rochas were coupled together, one inside the other: he behind her, humping like mad, his hands fiercely gripping the plump flesh of her rump; she on her knees, uttering little cries in cadence, her face turned toward the rear, her eyes shining and alert. Their son hauled out his tackle and began to masturbate. Yes, bracing himself against the ceiling with one hand and laboring away with the other, wincing and puffing, David Rochas was jerking off to the sight of his father fucking his mother. Even though I'd written off God and religion after the death of my brother, at that moment I felt that I was witnessing what in Catholicism would fall within the purview of mortal sin.

By frequenting the Rochas house, I had learned not to be shocked by anything anymore. I would barely notice when David's mother sometimes opened the door to me dressed in negligés worthy of those arousing pages of *Paris-Hollywood*. Actually, there was not a jot of calculation, provocation, or exhibitionism in that woman's behavior. That's simply how she was, free in her ways and comfortable with her body. Well ahead of her time, she seemed to have made her peace with sexuality and its taboos. It was a different matter for her son, who lived in real physical torment and may also have experienced moral distress. For although David was our guide in many respects, he was no less inept than the rest of us at going up to a girl and getting anywhere with her. As soon as things heated up—in every sense of the word—the high priest of onanism proved himself just another lowly worshipper from afar.

His discomfiture never lasted long. As proof I can attest that he never displayed the slightest hint of contrition when he confessed the truth to me about his experiences of "penetration." On this subject I ought to say that David Rochas's inspiration preceded by six years the lubricious inventions of Alex Portnoy described by Philip Roth in 1969.

When David Rochas opened his apartment door to me on that spring afternoon in 1963, he had a strained and stormy look in his eye, and his jaw muscles, twitching like pigeon hearts, seemed to express annoyance at my arrival. I had obviously come at a bad moment. He let me in and before I could utter a word, he said, "Go wait for me in my room, I'll be with you in five minutes."

As he hurried off toward the kitchen I noticed he was wearing a little apron around his waist. In contrast to his nervous nature, David's room was a veritable den of tranquility: pale almond wallpaper, blond wood furniture, Scandinavian-style bookcase in perfect order. The room was so neat that you would never have imagined that this Zen enclave was the lair of an eccentric and hyperactive adolescent. But when David returned, he was a different person: calm, relaxed, almost smiling. His electro-convulsive twitches and tics had vanished, in any case. He went over to the window and opened it wide. Leaning on the sill, he looked out at the sky while constantly slipping his hand into his trouser waist. He felt his genitals, then sniffed his fingers, like a terrier picking up a scent.

"Damn, it stinks of garlic."

"What, your hand?"

"No, my dick. My dick really reeks of garlic. That damned roast."

"What roast?"

And then David Rochas, fourteen years old, a ninth-grade student (in the A track: French literature, Latin, Greek) at the Lycée Pierre-de-Fermat, told me that for almost a year he had been plunging up to the hilt into all the beef roasts that Mme Rochas, his mother, had ordered prepared and larded twice a week from M. Pierre Aymar, the head butcher at the Boucherie Centrale. David explained his procedure in a quiet, composed voice, rather as a cook might give you a recipe.

"First I take it out of the fridge an hour or two ahead of time, you see, so that it can warm up to room temperature. Then, I take a reasonably large knife and make a cut, right in the middle of the roast, dead center. Not too wide, either, just enough. Then, I put on the apron, and I drop my trou, and have at it. Except that my fucking mother often sticks the roast full of garlic. If I rub against a clove, my dick stinks for two days."

What a vision: my best friend, scrum half and future captain of our school rugby team, standing in his kitchen, knife in hand, reaming with a voracious and ardent dick the family roast—expertly prepared from a prime cut of beef—to be served that very evening with green beans and scalloped potatoes dauphinois. I knew the meal well. I had eaten it several times at the Rochas family table.

"You fuck your mother's roast beef?"

I couldn't stop repeating that, torn between hilarity and panic by this sensualist and his necrophilous libido.

"You fuck your mother's roast beef?"

I didn't dare ask him the burning question, the one that would have sprung to the mind of any rational being. No, I did not have the courage to ask him if the Don Juan of chuck, the Lovelace of tenderloin, actually came in the beef roast. Doubtless I already knew the answer. There he stood, smelling his garlicky fingers and smiling like a Neapolitan Lothario after a one-night stand. Then, remembering his guest, he turned to me and said, "You want to try?"

I never stayed for dinner at the Rochas apartment after that, and my relationship with David, although still fraternal, became less intimate with the realization that my friend lived in a world to which I had no access, a singular and terribly lonely universe, a libertine principality where freedom and transgression had no meaning because nothing was forbidden or impossible.

Not too long ago, I saw David Rochas again. He looked like a Norwegian banker with a fondness for Scandinavian beer and Riga herring. He told me that he was divorced, that he had married a young woman whom he had gotten pregnant, and that he worked in the personnel department of a semiconductor company, a subcontractor for a large firm. He never mentioned our youth and seemed no more eager than I was to rekindle our former friendship. Suffice it to say, he seemed to have mastered his demons, the "beast" demanding the leash no more, his mother no longer its obsession.

What good would it do now to talk about school, that purgatory of adolescence? In those days, education was strict, austere, inflexible. One was obliged to learn. At all costs. Learn everything—and its opposite. Greek, Latin, German, English, the knotted climbing rope, the geology of Hercynian folds, Pico de la Maladetta (a major summit in the Pyrenees), Mont Gerbier-de-Jonc (a volcano in Ardèche), Ovid, *Dicunt Homerum caecum fuisse, The Song of Roland,* $ax^2 + bx + c$, When one verb immediately follows another the second verb is in the infinitive, *How old are you?,* the Battle of Fontenoy in 1745, Cardinal Richelieu, *begin, began, begun,* Plato's cave, *"hic, haec, hoc,"* the isosceles triangle, *Ich weiss nicht, was soll es bedeuten* (Heinrich Heine), $a^3 + 3a^2b + 3ab^2 + b^3$, tarsus, metatarsus, *Ideo precor beatam Mariam semper Virginem.* There was no fooling around.

At that rate, we were soon old before our time. But one still had to learn, and learn on a forced march: learn to eat without putting one's elbows on the table, learn to swim on one's stomach, back, side, learn to stand up straight, learn not to pick one's nose, not to answer back, learn to keep quiet, to control oneself, in short, as they said in those days, "learn to be a man." Strangely enough, that education took a turn through England, a nebulous and initiatory territory where every young middle-class citizen was supposed to perfect his first or second foreign tongue (an appendage he was quick to stick, upon crossing the Channel, into the mouth of the first available girl in London). And so, around the age of fifteen or sixteen, we already had our eyes glued to the Folkestone cliffs, eager to meet at last these promisingly cheeky Anglo-Saxon birds we'd heard so much about.

You have to imagine France in those days: a gray or navy blue Peugeot 403 upholstered in short-nap velvet, with de Gaulle at the wheel (holding it with both hands), Yvonne at his side, her handbag on her knees, and us, all of us, in the backseat, enduring the nausea of those Sunday outings, and the dizzying boredom of an already outmoded future. With Paul VI pontificating on his balcony and Pompidou—our hopeless prime minister, the eternal gofer of the Fifth Republic—playing on his accordion. Yes, all of us in the back, with the windows open only a crack to keep us quiet without letting in too much fresh air. France was like those rather stiffly designed station wagons, those four-door sedans owned by notaries or state employees, dreary things driven in stately moderation by a Catholic general always ready to shift down through the gears and who lived, the rest of the time, in our Grandin television sets. I'm talking about a place that today has vanished more completely than Atlantis, a country with woolen mattresses, where mailmen rode yellow mopeds, where olive oil was sold from big vats and glass bottles required deposits, a country where there was nothing shady or scandalous about paying for a car in cash, which didn't come from illegal revenues or profits hidden from the tax authorities but from long years of saving. The salesman would fill out the order form and the buyer would reach into his jacket pocket, pull out several wads of folding money fastened with straight pins, count out those bills as big as restaurant napkins, and conclude the deal. Yes, that's how you bought a car, or a gas stove, or even a house. With imposing colored sheets of paper as crisp as crackers. Sometimes my father would come home from work at the end of the week with the receipts, more loaded down than a Wells Fargo stagecoach. On such evenings, I'd wait until everyone was asleep and discreetly swipe a few small bills from the bonanza of all that loot.

After the va-va-voom of the V8s, the delusions of grandeur and gracious living, things at Simca had settled down to more modest ambitions. For instance, instead of Chambords, Versailles, and Beaulieus, my father now sold the more prosaic-sounding 1000, 1100, 1300, and 1500 models. Although the sign over the façade continued to gleam "Day and Night," there was something as yet imperceptible in its light that hinted, somehow, that one era was ending in France, and that another—as yet indefinable, fragile, like a scent just beginning to emerge—was in the air.

As for me, I launched my personal revolution during the summer of 1965. On the advice of my language teacher, my parents agreed to send me for an entire month of education to the bosom of a sinister family on Atwater Street, in East Grinstead, an utter hole about an hour south of London.

My hosts were the Groveses: James and Eleanor Groves. They jabbered constantly (but as Beckett said, "To speak up—isn't that already the first degree of companionship?"), drank bathtubs of gin, and stank permanently of perspiration. They drove a two-door Borgward that looked bizarre from any angle. Aside from their penchant for alcohol, and perhaps even because of it, the Groveses were extremely mellow people who understood perfectly that a French boy on vacation might sleep elsewhere than in East Grinstead as often as he liked, providing that he remembered to look the right way when crossing the street. Even today I am infinitely grateful to those malodorous alcoholics for having allowed me to discover, for a whole month, what some people search for in vain all their lives: not just sex, love, and rock and roll, but the utter joy of being oneself.

For the first time, I really felt as though I existed. I was experiencing a permanent intoxication that steeled me for epic boldness, talking to girls, walking along with my arm around their shoulders, kissing them, caressing their incredible breasts, slipping a hand beneath their intimidating skirts and, whenever fortune smiled at me, finally feeling that too brief electrocution that made you a man and allowed you, when the time came, to go back home again with your head held high. During those thirty exceptional days without a family or a country, I sizzled with the same vitality a butterfly must feel when it bursts out of its chrysalis.

During the day, I hung around the Carnaby Street area or else near an old bowling alley tucked away near Piccadilly, and in the evening, I tried to sneak into the rock nightclubs or rhythm-and-blues joints scattered around Soho. There were three outstanding events that marked the summer of 1965, and when I think back, I figure that, really, the gods of East Anglia were definitely with me.

For those times when I decided not to go back to East Grinstead, the Groveses had advised me to sleep over at the home of their friend Miss Postelthwaith, a charming woman with one of the most comfortable beds I have ever slept in. Lucy Postelthwaith possessed the sleek elegance of those women in midlife who have never lacked for anything. So refined were her manners and upbringing that she avoided embarrassing me with her Oxford-accented English and addressed me essentially through smiles and gestures, the way the nationals of old colonizing countries do when they try to communicate with "the natives." I quickly felt at home in that cozy apartment where no one ever asked me anything. Some mornings, Lucy would prepare a Continental breakfast and bring it to my room. One morning, she entered to find me naked and—boiling with stupid adolescent sap—using her incredible mattress as a trampoline, which at each leap sent me practically headfirst into the ceiling. Completely unfazed by this spectacle, Lucy simply set the tray down on the chest of drawers, settled into an armchair, and encouraged me with a broad smile to continue my exercises.

When I had run out of breath, she pretended to applaud and gave me what I took to be a compliment in which figured the word "spring." I was convinced that she was congratulating me for *my* "spring" (unless she was worried about her mattress). Our game quickly became a habit, and each time I stayed over, Lucy Postelthwaith would bring the breakfast tray and I, like a little soldier obeying regulations (and treating his dingus to some fresh air), would entertain her for a good five minutes with the gymnastic display of my bouncing balls, which Lucy always observed with the same heartfelt smile. Sometimes, just to be nice, she would slip a dozen pounds into my pocket. I already imagined myself, a sprightly and precocious young man, enjoying the career of a successful gigolo.

My second experience was more troubling. One afternoon, at that bowling alley I mentioned before, I met a French girl, a little older than I was and also engaged in the same language-immersion racket. She was a rather common girl, solidly built, a devoted chewer of gum (the pinkish variety), and noticeable mainly for her intimidating bust. She was wearing a clinging little Shetland wool sweater and a wraparound kilt. I no longer remember through what circumstances we wound up in one of the last rows of a movie theater that was showing an American film starring David Niven. We had known each other for barely two hours and yet we were necking as though our lives depended on it. While I kneaded her imposing chest, she gave me a hand job of thrilling proficiency. I felt a school of rainbow trout wriggling in my pants and, eager to delay a finale that I sensed was imminent, I tried to forget these delights by concentrating on the adventures of David Niven—a ploy that failed me dismally. I exploded well before our hero could light the fuse of the dynamite with which he had been fiddling for some time. It was then that my companion slipped her hand behind me and began to stroke my loins, massaging me just as she chewed her gum: relentlessly. I couldn't believe a woman had ever done that to a man in a movie theater. No more than I could imagine that her second finger, wily and alert, would sneak between my buttocks and in a split second, pop right into my asshole. No one had ever told me that women could do such things—or that men could get off on them. So, breathless and wide-eyed, I sat up in my seat like a jack-in-the-box (my famous "spring," no doubt). Once the shock of surprise had worn off, I took the girl's hand and gripped it in mine, more to ward off another attack than to show her any particular tenderness. And while the film dragged on, I was thinking that the only guy in the world who could make a girl like her happy was my friend David Rochas.

Sinika Vatanen was nothing like those other two women. She was simply the sweetest, loveliest, most graceful girl on earth. She had green eyes and long black hair, was a native of Tampere, Finland, and she, too, was abroad to perfect her English, which was already quite good. After meeting on the shingle beach of Brighton, we had promptly decided to spend our lives together without even discussing it, for such things are immediately obvious when you are fifteen years old.

We had loved each other from the first and would of course remain inseparable unto death. We lived like that for a whole week, lying on top of each other, inside each other, beside each other, in each other's arms. When she caressed me, I felt as if I were gliding over water. We used to walk along the piers that reached out into the sea. I had forgotten my parents' faces, my brother's death, the existence of the Groveses, and even my vaulting awakenings in Miss Postelthwaith's guest bedroom. I was now simply Monsieur Vatanen, the toast of all England, lover of the most gorgeous woman in the world, that incredible seducer from Toulouse who at the age of fifteen had already experienced life to the fullest, from morning "springing" to anal probing, with a detour through vaginal roast beef. I was that M. Vatanen, leaving his family, his country, abandoning his studies, to live in the northern latitudes of snow and ice by the side of this unique woman whom he would love and protect to the end of his days. Much later, in a book whose author I have forgotten, I read, "Being truly at ease means never feeling compelled to give oneself completely." Those few words reminded me immediately of Sinika Vatanen. They paid her greater homage than I would ever have been able to do.

Our affair ended in the simplest way: she took the ferry to Finland, and I took another to my country. As soon as I got home, I told my parents of my decision to go live in Tampere. They suggested that I take a shower before sitting down to dinner. I wrote to Sinika for three or four months. She sent me poems and some pictures of herself. Then, one day, she sent a snapshot of her dog, which looked like some kind of old plush banana. I cannot tell you why the sight of that animal transformed my feelings, but in an instant, the most beloved, gentle, and beautiful of women left my heart and life forever.

Still, I was on my way to becoming a man, with all that that implies about learning to compromise one's dignity. In any case, I persevered with my boring studies while listening to the Rolling Stones, Percy Sledge, and Otis Redding, as France tried to make the best of a third and even a fourth Pompidou administration. Thanks to rural political demonstrations down in the Midi, a slogan with a certain rustic friskiness was becoming popular: "Pom-pi-dou, pump-o'-shit, pump-o'-*sous*!"— the *sou* being that old-time five-centime coin so dear to the peasant's thrifty heart. As for de Gaulle, he still lived in our TV sets, which now went by the name of Téléavia, Ducretet-Thomson, or Grundig. He would say things like *"La mano en la mano,"* "Long live free Québec," "Europe from the Atlantic to the Urals," or "The Israelis are a strong and confident people." The longer I listened to that man, and watched him stride through crowds wearing that park attendant's kepi of his, the more he seemed to be living on another planet, addressing the imaginary inmates of an abandoned zoo. In those days, kids used to call their clueless parents "dodos" or "old fogies." Well, our *líder máximo*, the father of a gerontophilic country, had simply become a kind of psychopathic mummy wrapped in khaki. What else can I say? Perhaps this: for his sorties, the general had exchanged his former presidential Simca Régence with its imperial tail fins for a Citroën DS with a chassis by Chapron. A change much regretted by my father, naturally, for while he was certainly a republican, he was a car dealer to the core.

I have no idea where I was and what I was doing when John F. Kennedy was assassinated in 1963. On the other hand, I remember perfectly the family meal on October 8, 1967, when the television announced the death of Ernesto "Che" Guevara. It was, I believe, the first time that the picture of a man's corpse was broadcast at the dinner hour with such nonchalance. I recall the images of that bullet-riddled body, lying on exhibit before the cameras to prove to the world that the guerrilla fighter had definitely been killed, but also to emphasize that the path of revolt was a dead end. There was a clear desire to instruct, a warning, in that display. Those images joined many other instances of military arrogance, other barbaric episodes and coups d'état. A current of rebellion was stirring throughout the West. This wind of sedition, as yet fitful and capricious, was swirling up out of our tiny lives, often arising from insignificant things, little individual depressions, family disagreements, cultural or educational dissension. The growth of political consciousness was still hesitant, but the new generation no longer wanted to wear crew cuts, or get dragged off to church, or live a cut-and-dried life. A generation that truly was a million miles away from its parents. Never before in history, no doubt, had there been such a deep and brutal break in the social continuum. The year 1968 was an intergalactic voyage, a much more radical epic than the modest American space conquest that merely envisioned taming the moon. Because what was at stake that May was nothing more or less than the simultaneous departure of millions of men and women—without a concerted plan, or special budget, or training, or führer, or caudillo—toward a new planet, another world, where art, education, sex, music, and politics would be free of the narrow-minded norms and codes forged in the rigors of the postwar period.

What led to these upheavals? Franco's garrotes, the assassination of Martin Luther King, the smugness of princes, the general's kepi, the crypto-fascist politics of Tixier-Vignancour (Marshal Pétain's defense lawyer), the plague of the clergy, the mustiness of our schools, the vise of morality, the condition of women, the absolute power of the intellectual elite, the *Torrey Canyon* supertanker disaster, the arrogance of Giscard d'Estaing (already!), Pompidou and his Gauloises Bleues cigarettes, the kidnapping and murder by French policemen of Mehdi Ben Barka (a leader in the movement to oust the French from Morocco), the Vietnam War, Vatican II, plus my father (with his slick patter about his shitty Simcas), my mother (and her neurotic silences), my aunt Suzanne (with her demands for order, a bit more army, lots more church, and above all, respect), her husband, Hubert (sinking into his snooty alcoholism and racial hatred), Odile (the former Socialist converted to Giscard's constantly shifting rhetoric), and even Dawson, the sports reporter defeated by bitterness, a Communist reduced to parroting the Party lines of the central committee congresses.

At eighteen, very few of us that spring were hip to the ideological subtleties of the movement. The more political among us claimed allegiance to the Situationists, a libertarian group that gained prominence in May 1968. But the vast majority followed the line of the student revolutionaries Daniel Cohn-Bendit, Alain Geismar, and Jacques Sauvageot, and we knew nothing at all about the "First Proclamation of the Dutch Branch of the International Situationists" signed by Alberts, Armando, Constant, and Har Oudejans. As for me—in contrast to the Situationist strategist Guy Debord, who wrote at the beginning of the '60s, "Victory will belong to those who learn to sow disorder without loving it"—I adored a good mess. Mess for mess's sake. Making a shambles of the street the way you smash old toys. Cutting ties and breaking rules in a last childish temper tantrum. Mess in its invigorating and uncontrollable guise, an almost fluid messiness that seeped into all the cracks in society, living off its own energy, blowing the fuses of factories and families, flooding that flat land, a mess that rose with the swiftness of a galloping horse or a flood tide and put to flight those government ministers in three-piece suits who figured out, a little late, that you cannot negotiate with a tidal wave.

On March 22, while students in Nanterre were occupying their university administration buildings, I, in Toulouse, was slipping behind the wheel of my first car, a 1961 *perlweiss* Volkswagen equipped with two bumpers, a six-volt battery, and a convertible canvas roof. A used car from the dealership garage, with seventy thousand kilometers on it and my father's seal of approval. He had supervised the overhaul, and when he solemnly handed me the keys in his office, he said something like "I hope this car will drive you to the bac"—in other words, to success on my baccalaureate exams. A perfect example of my father's humor: concise, minimalist, ominous. Then he added, slipping into a more professional tone, "In my judgment, it's a first-rate vehicle." He adored that qualifier and used it at every opportunity. A car could be first-rate (of course), but also a meal, a movie, an outing, a rugby game, an argument, or even an idiot. So, I had a "first-rate" car, a fantastically liberating toy, a rocket to freedom. Whenever I accelerated and heard the whirring of the fan cooling the four little cylinders, I felt not only in control of something much bigger than I was, but also, more important, in complete command of my life at last, thanks to that Bakelite steering wheel. My movements on March 22 were thus devoted to a tour of the city, a few kilometers on the open road, and a homecoming as triumphal as that of Jason bearing the Golden Fleece.

I owe the student rioters more than I can ever repay: I owe them my pompous and farcical baccalaureate degree, served on a plate by a social class I saw shaken to its core for the first time. I have never liked teachers. I am not one of those repentant types who render belated or even posthumous homage to this or that former teacher who supposedly gave them a leg up in life by enlightening them about the beauties of literature and the charms of science and the humanities. All the educators I ever encountered—schoolteachers, professors, assistants, hapless substitute instructors—were nasty, underhanded, out-of-it demagogues and cowards, full of themselves, keeping a tight rein on the weak while currying favor with the strong, and forever addicted to that maniacal love of classification, humiliation, and elimination. Instead of places in which to learn and grow, I saw schools and universities as triage centers dedicated to filling factories and offices according to the demands of society. And so in that lucky springtime, when I (a born dunce, an utter ignoramus) was given the chance to throw this ignorance into the faces of those trembling *kapos,* I swore that whatever happened later, I would never deny the blessed grace of those times. In 1968 it was impossible not to obtain your baccalaureate degree. Stripped of its written sections, the ordeal was reduced to a wary hand-shake between teacher and student, the former automatically congratu-lating the latter for the brilliance and concision of an oral exam that had sometimes never even taken place. For once, the petty customs officers of knowledge were forced to relax their vigilance, abandon their zeal, and let pass the dregs of those smugglers whom in happier days they had delighted in dutifully questioning, inspecting, and turning away. With my head held high, I appeared before a panel of examiners who showered me with extravagant praise. Like a rugby team at my back, the pack of student insurgents pressing onward had just shoved me across the university goal line.

Furthermore (aside from the shivers of joy I felt at each of those astonishing get-togethers), it was thanks to those oral exams that I real-ized how everything in the life of a society was determined by its power structure. If there were enough of us to reverse the reigning force field, yesterday's bloodthirsty vultures would instantly and as if by magic turn into a flock of simple sparrows.

At home, that May was a month like any other: sad, silent, dreary. In spite of all the strikes, my father left for work every morning to sell his quota of Simcas, while my mother attempted to straighten out the sub-standard prose in her daily assignment of literary mishmash. Around the family table, we never discussed what was happening in the streets, the merits of the demonstrators' grievances, or the government's posi-tions. Except, perhaps, for one comment my father made about some pictures of people barricading gas depots: "This time I think they've gone a little too far." In his opinion, gasoline was more sacred than the blood of God. Without gas, no more cars. Not everyone in the family was so restrained in their commentary, and I remember in particular one explosive dinner toward the end of that May. My parents and I now lived in what had been my grandmother's house, and the table had been set up outside in the garden. In the warm evening air, beneath the ridiculous colored lights my father had strung in the branches of the chestnut tree, two irreconcilable clans had swiftly squared off. The first group included the fervent Gaullists: my impossible aunt Suzanne, her ex-Socialist sister, Odile (still a teacher), and some friends of theirs, the Colberts, splendid specimens of former collaborators freshly converted to Realpolitik. On the insurgents' side, naturally, were Cousin Jean, an early supporter of Cohn-Bendit; his father, Hubert, a ferocious anti-Gaullist who supported what he called "the worst-case scenario" in hopes of bringing down the general; Dawson, distrustful of the leftists but clinging to the shifting line of the Party; and myself, with my sup-posed diploma, the Last of the Mohicans, full of vim and vinegar. As always, my parents were silent hosts, turning a deaf ear to the argu-ments. Until the moment when my mother, exasperated by Aunt Suzanne's pontificating on the respect owed to material success, inter-rupted her to calmly quote the marquise de Montespan, mistress of Louis XIV: "The grandeur of a destiny arises as much from what one refuses as from what one gains." Everyone sat flabbergasted. I do believe that it was the first time since my brother's death that my mother had spoken up like that in public.

"Society wouldn't get very far on that sort of doctrine," sputtered a flushed Colbert. "It's perfectly obvious where we're currently heading in the hands of those who are, precisely, refusing to accept the system."

"Absolutely," Suzanne chimed in. "In life, everything is up for grabs. Everything. And if you don't take it, someone else will, so . . ."

The extreme intellectual vulgarity of that woman reduced every-thing to the simple idea of property and accumulation. Without listen-ing to what my mother had said, she had heard only the word "refuses," a concept she found frankly blasphemous. There followed a lively dis-cussion of covert political manipulation, during which Jean attacked the alienating laws of the "system" and his father theorized with his cus-tomary deft levity about the word *chienlit*—"bed-shitter"—which can also mean "havoc," which de Gaulle had famously condemned in May 1968.

"It's definitely an expression a fucking drill sergeant would use."

"Hubert, will you ever manage to complete a sentence without using a single rude word?"

"My dear Odile, ex-Socialist, neo-Gaullist, and future—what, Chabanist? Pompidouist? Radical-Socialist Edgar-Faurist?—let me tell you something: a native of Vichy like myself—since you like so much to remind us of that moment in history—who has had to take it so often and so deeply from your beloved general, is certainly allowed in turn, every now and then, to call him a fucking drill sergeant, no?"

"Well, I agree with my sister," announced Suzanne. "I think de Gaulle has perfectly defined the problem: we have reached the time for reform, perhaps—and I'm saying *perhaps*—but certainly not for havoc."

And that's when I made a remark that albeit light on political substance was inarguably in tune with reality.

"Yes, but the point is, actually, that that's just what we like: fucking havoc."

Everyone looked at me as though I'd cut a tremendous fart. Gently stroking one eyelid, Suzanne turned toward my father to sigh, in an aggrieved tone, "As Mama used to say, my poor Victor, I do believe that child will make you shed tears of blood one day."

Perhaps my aunt had just displayed a certain gift for premonition, in the light of what was to happen four or five days later.

The movement gradually lost momentum. To make sure he had the army behind him, de Gaulle was preparing to visit General Jacques Massu (the "victor" of the Battle of Algiers) at the French base in Baden-Baden, while the Right was sprucing up for its huge march, and gas, the Holy Grail of the masses, was flowing back into the pumps. Every evening, however, more or less spontaneous gatherings of demonstrators would set up barricades and tangle with our riot police, the CRS. The confrontations in the streets of Toulouse, although less spectacular than those in Paris, were nevertheless numerous and brisk. Not yet in college, I didn't belong to any little political group and was hanging around those chlorine-washed avenues of uprooted paving stones like a solitary tourist. There were often clashes on the Boulevard de Strasbourg and the Boulevard Carnot, really violent affairs. To the sound of gas grenades, the CRS would charge in a herd, sending the more impressionable demonstrators fleeing into narrow side streets while the die-hard anarchists held their positions staunchly, retaliating with paving stones and Molotov cocktails. It was just impossible to stay on the sidelines of such contests without eventually joining the insurgents.

In my case, I chose to swell their ranks at a most unusual time and place, to say the least. That evening, two or three barricades had gone up on the Boulevard Carnot, and the CRS had responded with increased fury. Stunned by the gas and the din of the explosions, we had fallen back toward the Place Jeanne-d'Arc, a stone's throw from my father's garage, and the paving blocks of the square had been swiftly pried up in readiness for a new police charge. At around ten that evening, after many small skirmishes, the CRS had launched what they hoped would be a definitive assault.

Go figure what went through our heads that night. Who knows why, but we held our positions instead of dispersing into the neighboring streets, and we fought back so fiercely that it was the attackers who beat a retreat. In their hurried confusion, a group of CRS soldiers entered the busy street where Victor Blick's Simca dealership was located. Seizing their chance to turn the tables for once, those rioters familiar with the local geography led a charge against that isolated group of soldiers, who made the mistake of taking refuge behind the support pillars of the building housing my father's business. That was how I came to be hurling paving stones at the CRS—and especially into the plate-glass windows of my father's dealership, windows that shattered thunderously one after the other, like the pounding of the Atlantic against the boulders of a jetty.

I must admit that during this siege, part of me was yelling at the mob, "Stop, stop, this is my father's garage, he's a nice guy who just sells Simcas to workers getting ready to go off on vacation!"—while another, less forgiving part of me was going even crazier and shouting one of Raoul Vaneigem's Situationist slogans: "When your conscience despairs, attack the status quo!"

The next day, I wasn't brave enough to accompany my father to the garage and pretend to share his sorrow. I simply listened to the report he gave later that evening of the destruction, which he described, as was his wont, quite calmly and in measured terms.

Along about mid-June, the government decided to ban the most radical leftist groups, the police evacuated student protesters from the Université de la Sorbonne and the Théâtre de l'Odéon and cleared the nation's streets, Renault voted to return to work, and most of the nation gave the general a resounding vote of confidence.

Two months later, the Warsaw Pact brought Czechoslovakia to heel, and France detonated its first H-bomb. Everything was returning to normal and yet, nothing would be the same. I enrolled in the sociology department of the fledgling Université du Mirail in Toulouse, and began preparing myself for a new life.

On April 28, 1969, rejected by a referendum he himself had confidently demanded, de Gaulle resigned all his offices. As my family sat together before the television, following with only modest interest the results of that election, my father abruptly raised his hand as if to grab something passing in front of him, and then collapsed across the table, felled by his first heart attack.

ALAIN POHER

(First Interim, April 28, 1969–June 19, 1969)

WITH its cranes, heavy equipment, and countless little cubical buildings, the Université du Mirail rather resembled a seaside resort under construction: a small town, inexpensive, geared to the masses (but not close to any seashore), hastily thrown together to absorb the prodigious spontaneous generation of students that appeared in 1968. In sociology, the first new degree-accredited discipline to emerge from our recent seismic shift, life was sweet, attendance optional, and leftism de rigueur. The most right-wing professor in the entire department belonged to the French Communist Party. The others were Trotskyites, anarchists, or Maoists who loathed one another and waged stealthy battles to promote the preaching of their particular dogmas in these new leftist chapels. Preoccupied by their wrangling and their subtle ideological jousts, those intellectuals lavished on us credits for which we naturally could take no credit at all.

My father was slowly recovering from his health problems and now spent only a few hours a day at the dealership. Throughout those difficult months, he never asked me for the slightest help, or ever suggested that one day I might take over for him at the helm of Day and Night. He had probably guessed that my plans were tending in an entirely different direction. Actually, I hadn't the faintest idea what I was going to do.

In a way, I was apprenticed to life, open to everything, motivated by the blind and febrile egoism of youth.

At home, life was becoming more difficult. The oppressive atmosphere there was in sharp contrast to the brash enthusiasm of the leftist debates that went on all afternoon in our classrooms. When I went home, I felt as if I were a prisoner under evening house arrest who, after an ordinary day of freedom, must return to his cell at night. My parents must have known how bleak and emotionally stunted our home life was, for they made no protest when I hurried through the meal and abandoned them, sometimes a bit abruptly, at the supper table.

After I passed both my baccalaureate and driving exams, my physical appearance changed. Let's say that I grew tougher, more virile—if that word ever had any real meaning. I now sported a mustache, a tentative beard, and most impressive shoulder-length hair. I fancied myself the very image of a libertarian student beholden to no god, master, or job, but poised at the forefront of modernity.

I therefore had only one thing on my mind: leaving home at last to live the truly avant-garde existence I deserved. Now and then I managed to hook up with a girl in the back of my Volkswagen, on a narrow, uncomfortable seat that simply fueled my desire for a place of my own as soon as possible.

Everything else went on its merry way. With de Gaulle gone, Alain Poher served briefly as our head of state and even tried, during his short stay, to convince the country that he could be more than an interim leader. He declared himself a candidate for president, but a man born in 1911 in Montboudif, in the *département* of Cantal, a former director of the Rothschild Bank who garnered just over fifty-eight percent of the vote, sent Monsieur Poher straight back to his senatorial lair.

GEORGES POMPIDOU

(June 20, 1969–April 2, 1974)

THE army: that was my obsession in those days. I had decided early on and for all time that no matter what it cost me, I would never wear a uniform. Even for one hour. And there was no question of claiming to be a conscientious objector, which in those days meant accepting a kind of *Untermensch* status in the forestry service, where for twenty-four months (instead of the regulation twelve) you were ordered to polish tree trunks. My rejection of the army would be total; my assault, frontal.

Nevertheless, after receiving my call-up notice I went to the induction center at the barracks in Auch for the "three days," during which you endured a medical exam, including a palpation of the testicles and a battery of tests intended to evaluate your IQ. Those three days, which usually lasted only thirty-six hours, were crucial for anyone opposed to military service. Either you joined the slim and envied contingent of the "exempt," or you were classified as an ordinary private and thus condemned to a year of relentless shit. To avoid being pronounced "fit," some prospective inductees actually tried cutting off a finger, drinking whole pots of coffee at the last minute, or even faking insanity. Sometimes the examining physicians were confronted by truly arresting clinical pictures hitherto unknown to medical science: guys drooling greenish gunk concocted from foaming agents, for example, or vomiting a mixture of mercurochrome and soap. Other men were so steeped in caffeine or more powerful stimulants that they could neither sit nor stand still, and trotted around the office as they answered the doctor's questions. A minority played the simulated homosexuality card, a high-risk ploy that might land you directly in one of the disciplinary fortresses that France still maintained in Germany.

A thick winter fog enveloped the city and the barracks that first day. It was before sunrise, and all the soldiers had been up for some time, busy with essential tasks like raking the gravel in the courtyard, saluting a limp flag, raising and lowering rusty barriers, shouting crazy orders, and terrifying big silly boys by glaring at them with bleary alcoholic eyeballs.

I had parked my Volkswagen right outside the front gate, where I knew it was ready to carry me far away if things went badly. Just inside the guardhouse, I was ambushed by a tall, lanky fellow with a tiny head, who shrieked at me in a falsetto to *get a move on!*

I crossed a small courtyard and entered a building in which all the windows were clouded with steam. Waiting for me behind the door was an African colossus, who promptly screamed into my ear.

"On the double, strip and hit the shower!"

"But I just took a shower."

"Shut your face or I'll shut it for you!"

Next on the program:

1. What eats a sheep? a) a goat. b) a wolf. c) a shepherd.
2. What does a boat do? a) It rolls. b) It flies. c) It floats.

Getting most of fifty such pertinent questions correct did not qualify you to be a lieutenant general. However, it did allow you to join certain so-called elite troops, such as the navy's special forces or the paratroops. You had to be very careful when being pointedly sarcastic in your replies, because claiming that a shepherd might be greedy enough to eat a sheep or arguing, after five years of college, that battleships can fly in formation could easily get you sent to the frozen plains of Germany to join other wiseguys.

Shortly before noon, a career soldier gathered us in the courtyard before leading us into a huge mess hall that smelled of both dog food and industrial-strength detergent. It was a penetrating, fairly nauseating odor enlivened by the effluvia of the noon repast: slices of beef with Brussels sprouts au gratin in a kind of gummy white cream sauce. The sight of the vegetables and especially the meat riddled with garlic cloves made me feel sick. I imagined a kitchen battalion of David Rochases, swords drawn and pants down around their ankles, briskly tenderizing those regulation roasts.

"Are you gonna eat that?"

At every table in the world, there is always someone endowed with a prodigious appetite who compulsively cleans his plate while keeping a constant eye on everyone else's. At the first sign of anyone dawdling over the meal, the hungry eater—no doubt driven by ancestral instinct—tries to snag the potential leftovers.

"Are you gonna eat that?"

It was a little guy with glasses, who reminded me of those pink and featherless baby birds, their beaks wide open, constantly clamoring for a morsel. After dispatching the meat in three mouthfuls and gulping down the gluey sprouts, he burped daintily, like a child.

Two or three hundred guys in underpants. Holding slips of paper. Waiting, in a sort of gymnasium, to unveil their complete anatomy to an army doctor who behaved more like a veterinarian. Inspection of the teeth; hearing and eye tests; palpation of the balls and other glands. To relieve his boredom, perhaps, or because he really found it funny, the doc on duty allowed himself a few lame wisecracks when he hefted our genitals. Ah, army life . . .

The evening's entertainment was on a par with the day's activities. Five-thirty p.m., mess. Six-thirty, movie. Nine-thirty, lights out. At six o'clock, continuing my fast, I was lying on my bed in the barracks reading a magazine. Three or four others had also preferred to abandon the meal for their beds. After a few minutes, a soldier with a rugged face burst in and yelled, "Everyone downstairs! Compulsory movie!"

I could understand that the showers were compulsory, just like the medical exam or those multiple-choice tests. But a movie?

"What's the film, Sarge?" asked a guy at the far end of the dorm.

"*Any Number Can Win*, croot. And guess what—your number's up!"

And then, something inside me slammed shut. A kind of security measure like those motion detectors.

"I've already seen the movie. I'd rather stay here."

"I'm not asking you what you'd rather, I'm ordering you to go downstairs with the others."

"I said I'd stay here."

"Hey, Gina Lollobrigida, with your pretty curls—what's your game? You want to jerk off in peace, is that it?"

I didn't answer, I didn't move, I hardly even breathed.

"Get off that bed, you self-fucking faggot!"

This noncom had quite an original repertoire of insults.

"Where d'you think you are? At the beauty parlor? Getting your nails done, you mother-pounding monkey? Get your butt out of that fucking bed and join the others downstairs."

"No. I'm not going anywhere."

"Look what we've got here, a queen of assholery! You dick-licking fuck, I'm going to send you down those sucking stairs with a boot so far up your ass you'll choke on it!"

Pouncing on me, he grabbed my hair with both hands, and dragged me off the mattress.

"So you don't want to go to the movie, you scumbag bastard!"

I struggled to stand, but he slapped me so hard that I tumbled to the edge of the staircase, where a kick in the stomach left me winded. Shoving me like a bale of hay, the noncom pushed me down the stairs. I bounced along like a third-rate stuntman, trying desperately to minimize the damage, but by the time I reached the bottom of the first flight, I was missing two teeth. My right cheek and eyebrow were hamburger.

"Get the picture, turd sucker, or do I have to help you down the rest of the way?"

I tried to stand up, if only to face my attacker with a minimum of dignity, but I no longer had any arms or legs or breath. Two broken ribs were stabbing me in the sides, and I barely noticed the small group gathering around us.

I heard something like "goat-poking ass-wipe"—and then my vision faded, my tormentor's voice grew slurred and distant, and I closed my eyes without realizing what a priceless favor that—to borrow his phrase—"self-fucking faggot" had just done me.

I spent the night in the infirmary, checked on every fifteen minutes by the doctor on duty and a draftee assigned to the medical corps. In the morning, after wriggling like a worm to sit up, I discovered a scary stranger in the mirror—the face I would have to live with for the next few weeks.

At around noon, I met the commanding officer in his office, a large, sunny room on the top floor of the main section of the sprawling barracks. The colonel was about forty with an erect bearing, a clean-shaven face distinctly etched with deep lines, and a natural authority untainted by the slightest vulgarity. He spoke in a calm, clear voice, pronouncing each word almost as if he were snipping it out with shears.

"Monsieur Blick, I assure you that I am quite distressed at what happened last night in my unit. Your patent insubordination is no excuse for such excesses. I noticed in your file that you were a student at the Université du Mirail in Toulouse, were you not?"

"That is correct."

"May I ask you, Monsieur Blick, the nature of your feelings toward the military?"

Although I had no idea where he was going with that or what he really wanted from me, I did feel that my injuries and the misconduct of his subordinate would allow me, for the moment, to have the upper hand.

"I don't have to answer that question."

"You see, Monsieur Blick . . ."

The colonel seemed to have the habit of beginning a sentence while looking you right in the eye, then doing an abrupt about-face before continuing to speak with his back to you. Suddenly ignoring your presence, denying your existence, in a way, he thus appeared to be addressing an imaginary interlocutor outside the window.

"You and I are in a position that allows us a certain latitude of action. So be nice, don't spoil our discussion by adopting an aggressive and overly intransigent posture. Let me rephrase my question: Would you find it agreeable to be exempt from military service?"

I could now guess at the bargain the colonel was hinting at: I would not file a complaint against his noncom, and in return, the army would strike me from its list.

"In exchange for what?"

"I don't think that we can really talk about an exchange. Let's just say that the misbehavior of someone in my command now places you in a position to demand legal redress from this institution. Any condemnation of said institution—always a problematical affair—would still not release you from your obligatory national service. On the contrary, I would even say, insofar as orders would obviously be given, at the time of your induction, to offer you ample opportunity throughout your full twelve months to discover the breadth and depth of possible duties during the period of conscription. As certain assignments are particularly uncomfortable and austere, I would understand perfectly if, because of some philosophical or political convictions, you were to choose this courageous option."

"Otherwise?"

"Well, let's say that we could arrange to agree that you unfortunately slipped and fell on the stairs on your way to last night's movie screening. In that case, obviously, our insurance would cover all your medical expenses and would compensate you in accordance with their contractual rates. As for the army, which, when necessary, knows how to be compassionate and generous, it would remove you permanently from the national service list. That, *grosso modo,* is what our transaction might resemble. Although less chivalrous than the first solution, this option has the advantage, on the other hand, of bringing you greater personal comfort."

And that is how I got to go home three hours later, soundly thrashed but freshly bandaged, released from my duties, albeit delicately humiliated. Observing the time-honored formalities of an armistice, the colonel and I met once more in one of the mess halls to sign our respective documents with a flourish: my less-than-glorious statement about my "accident," and his certificate of exemption, valid even "in time of war when, while the conflict lasts, you will be assigned to a civil service."

Implicated in March in the squalid Markovic murder case, Georges Pompidou went on to be elected president of the Republic three months later. After eleven years in the barracks, France was about to be managed like a mom-and-pop store. And our sprightly prime minister (from *grand bourgeois* Bordeaux, to boot) was hardly the man to change that: Jacques Chaban-Delmas seemed to me at best like an irritating tennis player adept at returning easy lobs so as to look good and last as long as possible. In any case, he had neither the stature nor the sensitivity to contemplate the pertinence of these words addressed by a black worker to his white boss as early as 1956, in the newspaper *Présence Africaine*: "When we saw your trucks, your planes, we believed you to be gods; and then years later we learned to drive your trucks, soon we'll learn to fly your planes, and we realized that what interested you the most was making trucks and planes, and earning money. What interests us is using those planes and trucks. Now you are our blacksmiths." It was the same with our own lives: we spent our youth forging them, then bargaining them away for measly salaries, but we never really used them, we never wound up at the controls of our own "personal" trucks and planes. And those who thought otherwise were either Chabanists or completely out of it, which came to about the same thing.

Late in the spring of 1969, my cousin Jean died in a car accident on the winding road of the Col d'Envalira, in the principality of Andorra, where he had gone to spend the weekend with his girlfriend. She had been thrown from the vehicle, whereas Jean had been literally cut in two by the sheet metal of his little Austin. The police and insurance company reports did not establish with any certainty the cause of the accident, which a first document ascribed to excessive speed, while a different expert concluded that the brakes had failed.

My parents were hit hard by this untimely death, which, in its suddenness, reminded them inevitably of the brutal loss of their own child. True to herself, my aunt Suzanne organized the funeral, the ritual death announcements, the thank-you notes, with all the coldness of those whose gift it is, under any circumstances, to hold themselves aloof from sorrow. Hubert, however, was crushed at the loss of this son he had probably never understood, but had deeply loved. Unlike his wife, he recovered a part of his humanity through his loss, and drew closer to my father, shaking off forever his rancid hatreds and his nostalgia for the good old days.

At the beginning of May 1969, I met a girl a little older than I was, a beauty built to last and to make men dream throughout eternity. Marie was quite different from the other women of that moment. Fashion then favored those who were thin, of average height, with small breasts, but Marie was all curves, with a bust that was ample but in perfect proportion to her height (just under six feet, which was almost a disability in those days), and she stirred up male hormones wherever she went. When I walked into a café with Marie on my arm, I felt as though I were honking the horn of a red Ferrari. This made me hugely self-conscious, but it was rather gratifying to notice that other men tended to walk softly in her presence. She had a way of looking at them that said "Don't even think about it," as Americans like to say.

Marie worked as an assistant in the office of a dentist who anesthetized his patients with laughing gas or—in a nod to the counterculture— treated them to a session of sophrology: mind-over-matter meditation in front of an aquarium full of exotic fish that ate one another. Sometimes I would wait for Marie outside the office, and after going out to dinner we'd end up in the small apartment she rented facing a canal, along the Allées de Brienne. I envied her that private space, and I admired the autonomy she enjoyed. Marie was a stunning woman, but to me she was first of all the incarnation of independence. She often said, "You've got time, you're still young. And besides, you're lucky to have parents who can support you and pay for your studies." She had never had that chance. Sterilizing surgical instruments or cleaning spit sinks was not a vocation. Marie's parents, both workers, had had six children, whom they kept in school as long as the law required before launching them into life, allowing natural selection to take its course. The most enterprising had survived; the others, three boys, had joined the police force and the army.

Compared with the hard knocks Marie had known, my upbringing was spoiled, protected, and privileged, which sometimes made me uneasy. Still, she entranced me, especially when she would announce, for example, in a tone that brooked no argument, that she was paying the restaurant bill. Or when she suddenly felt like buying me an expensive Shetland wool sweater. She was generous, uncomplicated, with a fundamentally sane outlook. To her, politics was an activity reserved for retirees or snobs, a diversion halfway between stamp collecting and golf. Taking an interest in men who never took an interest in you was time-consuming, she said, and Marie had too little spare time to waste it arguing about things that never went anywhere anyway. She preferred (by far) to make love, an objectively subversive and fortifying activity, and one that was in any case highly recommended by my anarchist and Situationist pals.

How shall I put this? Marie impressed me in daily life, but I must admit that in bed, she intimidated me, and sometimes even petrified me. We were the same height and yet, in her arms, between her long legs, beneath her magnificent breasts, I felt like a child, a clumsy kid playing naively with his nurse's titties. During our frolics, she turned me this way and that as she pleased, as though we were living on the moon and I were weightless. But whenever I tried to do the same with her, it was a massive catastrophe, a muscular debacle. And yet, Marie wasn't fat, far from it. She was splendidly built. At the time, in addition to my athletic insufficiency, I was inexperienced enough to believe that it was my duty to show her that as a male, I, too, could heft my partner like a barbell.

When I bared my soul—once again, unwisely—on this worrisome point to David, he displayed his customary delicacy and indulgence, settling the problem definitively: "Girls like that, they're like American cars. As long as the road is straight, things are fine; as soon as it starts to turn, you wind up in a ditch."

During that third week in July, the road, as a matter of fact, was turning every which way, while Marie and I were heading down the side of Jaizquibel, a little mountain that divides Fuentarrabía from the working-class neighborhoods of San Sebastián in Spain. The Volkswagen was humming along, while at the foot of the deep green hills, the ocean was giving off the briny scent of holidays and happiness. We had put down the top, Marie had her feet up on the dashboard, and the sun was patiently nibbling its way along her lanky legs.

"I like your tibias," I told her.

"My tibias? How can anyone like tibias?"

"They are fantastically sexy bones."

"Sexy, tibias? Now you're into bones, is that it?"

"In general, no. But it's true that yours are really outstanding. Incredibly long and straight. And then your smooth skin, gleaming over them . . ."

She nodded gently, like a kindly psychoanalyst, then ran her hands beneath her calves, stroking her legs as though she were rubbing lotion into them, and asked me, "How long before we get to France?"

France was right there, on the other side of the Bidassoa, that narrow river running between Irún and Hendaye. At the border crossing, the customs officials had us open the forward trunk of the VW, and after a cursory glance into the backseat, not neglecting to check out Marie's legs, they waved us on.

The station at Hendaye was always crowded, for that was where travelers had to change trains, the track widths in France and Spain being different. In the summer one could thus see French tourists in polyester shorts mingling on the train platforms with Spanish workers lugging heavy suitcases, fleeing Francoism to try their luck in Toulouse or on the plains of southwestern France. While waiting to change trains, most of these migrants wound up in nearby restaurants, which all advertised on large blackboards *calamares en su tinta,* squid cooked in their own ink—succulent, tender, tasting faintly of iodine, and served in steaming little ramekins.

It was Monday, July 21, 1969, and all the newspapers were covering only one story: that night, two Americans named Aldrin and Armstrong were going to walk on the moon. More modestly, Marie and I were walking along the endless beach at Hendaye, where the coolness of the late-afternoon breeze occasionally made us shiver with pleasure. Out on the open water we could see tuna boats heading for port. Far from gaping mouths, ugly cavities, dirty dressings, and threatening forceps, Marie seemed—with her wind-tousled hair and sun-burnished skin—to be happy and relaxed. Receptive, open to life's possibilities. Sometimes, when she took a deep breath, standing there facing the salt spray, it was as if she were storing up all the power of nature.

Clinging to the hill, the bungalows of the motel dug in on the summit, although the last few units looked as if they were letting go, slipping gradually toward the abyss beyond the cliff. When night fell, a sea wind came up and wrung the necks of the tamarisk trees, bringing clouds and some showers. Marie and I spent the evening in bed watching television. What were we expecting from a lunar adventure that barely concerned us? All that outer-space suspense, those emotions launched into orbit—the whole thing left me cold, whereas Marie couldn't have been more absorbed by each news bulletin, almost as if her happiness and much of our future depended on what was going on up there. She kept talking about the third astronaut, Collins. She had heard that he would not be leaving the command module: if everything went well, Armstrong and Aldrin would do their moon walk, while Collins remained in lunar orbit. To have gone through all those years of preparation, endured the intensive training, taken those insane risks, just to stay inside the module, parked like a taxi, while the others discover the supreme lightness of being, dancing endlessly on the sidewalks of the moon . . . Marie could not accept the sacrificial fate assigned to Collins, a victim of inconceivable cosmic injustice.

Stretched out by Marie's side, I was mesmerized by the TV's bluish reflections glimmering on her skin. From time to time, a thin haze of sleep veiled my eyes, and I would sink for a minute into a kind of amniotic fluid in which sounds reached me only in faint snatches. Propped up on a small pile of pillows, however, Marie was closely following the expedition, which was scheduled to reach its goal at around three or four in the morning.

"Do you realize that on the moon you're six times lighter than on earth?"

What I realized was that it was late, and that I was feeling more and more of those prickly sensations that always announced or accompanied my erections. I realized that three guys in deep-sea diving suits, whose faces you never saw, were busy completely fucking up the night

I'd been getting ready to spend with a spectacular girl. Making love on the moon with Marie would have been child's play, even if up there, according to the same laws of gravity, happiness probably didn't weigh that much at all.

"Do you know how fast Apollo traveled toward the moon? Twenty-four thousand miles per hour! At that speed, they said, you could reach Paris from New York in less than ten minutes! Can you imagine that?"

I signified my assent with a sort of primitive groan that could mean almost anything. My mind was floating on the edge of sleep, while my dick, in tune with the world and knowing perfectly well what *it* had in mind, was filling its ballast chambers. In such moments of diminished consciousness, I would often see Victor's face again, solemn with concentration as he carefully put away his toy coach. Or else his radiant smile when he managed to score a goal in soccer. It was a little as if, taking advantage of my drowsiness, my brother were slipping through the cracks of time, rising from the depths of my youth, and like a bubble of life, bringing oxygen to my memory. I wondered how my brother would have handled Marie and if he would have been able to lift her in his arms, defying gravity. He was the big brother. He would have known how to solve that kind of problem.

"Did you hear that? The LEM is going to set down at around three o'clock, and if everything's on track, Armstrong will come out right afterward."

I had to last until then. One of these days some jerk somewhere in the world would come along and ask us where we were on the night when men first walked on the moon. Confined within our respective lives, we would then be able to remember that we were lying next to each other ensconced in that protective bed, in that Basque motel where certain rooms near the cliff seemed ready to give up and slide gently into the ocean.

Marie lit a cigarette and began to blow smoke rings. The smell of blond tobacco, with its fragrance of cinnamon and honey, roused me from my torpor.

"You're blowing smoke rings again."

"Does it bother you?"

"No, but when you do it in public, I think it's a little vulgar, which isn't like you."

"You can be so uptight sometimes."

That was, to me, the worst possible reproach. Because a libertarian could not be uptight. Never, ever.

"I'm not uptight at all, but when people in a restaurant see you blowing smoke rings, they can't help thinking that you're bored with me and that's why you're killing time like that."

"You are so touchy and arrogant. And how twisted to think people who've never seen us before would imagine stuff like that because of my smoke rings. Do you even know why I blow them? Because I read somewhere that Charlie Chaplin announced he'd leave a quarter of his fortune to the first person who could blow seven concentric circles while he watched."

She launched three perfect wreaths toward the ceiling, but the fourth, after a promising start, disintegrated in some invisible turbulence. Marie stubbed out her cigarette, drank a swallow of sparkling water, and slid down between the sheets. The warmth of her belly and the silkiness of her legs provoked a fresh irrigation of my penile tissues. The touch of her body and the coolness of her fingers were keeping me hopelessly earthbound, which meant more to me—especially that night—than anything in the world.

"Now you have to do me like never before, so I'll remember it all my life."

I rolled on top of her and held her tight. She was so eager to be happy that she began to moan before I'd even gotten started. I was tucked into the very deepest of pleasure's pockets when I heard Marie say, "Something's going on."

"What's going on?"

"I think they went outside. I saw something move by on the screen."

That's how it goes. While I dreamed of us launching together into bliss, she, rigidly vigilant, was keeping a cold eye on the TV. After listening to the announcer for a moment, she detached herself from me with unseemly haste and jumped out of bed to go turn up the sound.

"The images we are seeing are extraordinary. Barely one hour ago, the LEM set down in the Sea of Tranquility within four miles of the designated landing spot. And now, at three fifty-six a.m. Paris time, on this July 21, 1969, for the first time in the history of humanity, a man has just set foot on the moon."

Sitting naked on the edge of the bed, fascinated by events on the screen, Marie seemed to be mentally xeroxing every moment. As I watched the gray screen and listened to the lyrical commentary, I thought about how Marie had preferred the spectacle of other people's happiness to the pleasures of our bodies. Lying on my back, with an invisible weight crushing my chest, I felt as never before how gravity rules the Earth. While I was reflecting on the asynchronism of emotions and desires, Marie said, "Can you imagine how Collins feels?"

She was brimming with compassion for that odd man out, but I was Michael Collins, too, that orphan, that guy waiting in the taxi for the rest of the planet to finish playing with the stars so that he could get back to his normal life. There was one difference between us, though. Behind the porthole, to pass the time, Michael must have been thinking something along the lines of "When bodies fall in a vacuum, they are subject only to gravity, which is presumed constant along the entire trajectory. The trajectory is vertical. The fundamental relationship is described in the equation: $m\ddot{z}=mg$, with z being the altitude."

"Do you think those guys will be able to return to Earth without any problems?"

"Marie, I'm cold and I'm tired. I really hope those guys make it back home, but now, be nice, please turn the sound down and let me sleep."

"You can sleep while those two walk around on the moon?"

"Yes, I think that I can manage it."

"Would it bother you if I kept watching?"

Nothing would have bothered me more, but I said, "Not at all," and even sat up to kiss her on the mouth. Then I lay down again, holding my genitals as if I were cradling a bird in my hand.

Maybe there's something strange about me, but in the same way that Sinika's dog had flash-frozen my feelings and libido a few years before, that interminable Basque night on the moon abruptly estranged me from Marie. I tried to put up a good front until the end of our vacation, but it didn't take a genius to figure out that my appendage was now dragging its feet as it went halfheartedly about its job.

At the beginning of the following summer, I decided to leave home. A three-months' contract as a temp and the prospect of a position as a study-hall monitor when the fall school term began would allow me to move into my own place sometime in October.

When I told my father about my decision, he simply replied, "I understand." In his language, that meant "I won't say that I'm happy to hear this, but in your place, I'm sure I would do the same. No one can live very long in a family like ours." He started to walk off toward the garden, then turned to ask me, "Have you told your mother?"

"No, not yet."

"Don't say anything to her. I'll take care of it."

Then he took his pruning shears and like a busy neighborhood hairdresser began trimming the new growth on the boxwood shrubbery. He was now spending most of his time beautifying his little yard, not obsessively, but with real affection. Things had changed a great deal at the garage, unless it was really my father who had changed. He said that the dealership had been reduced to an unmanageable old colony, a territory on the verge of independence that he still visited occasionally, of course, but the administration of which he had entrusted to a kind of young proconsul who governed a bit too harshly, according to what my father had heard, and who in his opinion would not last long in the Simca empire, which was already in decline.

As for me, I was getting into harness as a salaried employee for the first time, working in a semipublic firm in charge of the paperwork for the paid vacations of construction workers. There were some thirty of us who examined the pay slips and reports of work stoppages due to bad weather that were submitted by contractors. We had to record these hours of unemployment on special forms, write in the worker's name, add up a few figures, and determine the correct amount to be paid out. It was a job like thousands of others: one link in an administrative chain, a relic from another century, just a crummy job that nibbled away at your life—a sort of little salaried cancer that didn't kill you, just paralyzed your happiness every day. It was actually funny that our job was figuring out how long other people's vacations would be. I knew that I would be stuck for only a few months in that compartment hermetically sealed off from the world; the majority of the employees had already spent most of their lives there.

After my brief stay in that office, I began to suffer from a strange tic that has bedeviled me ever since: my mind becomes involuntarily fixated on a proper name that I can mentally repeat, almost unconsciously, for days, weeks, months, and, in some cases, even years. Sometimes, when I become aware of that rumination, I feel compelled to say the person's last name out loud, as if to prove to myself that this endless loop is real and that I am not crazy. What's even more ridiculous is that the names are usually those of little-known athletes, names that became lodged in my memory against my will years ago and are now suddenly imposing themselves on me. I can remember, for example, endlessly repeating "Zaitsev," who played defense or wing on the Soviet hockey team in the 1970s, I think. I was also fond of saying "Hoegentaler," the name of a German soccer player. Over the last few years, I've been invaded by brand names like "Jonsered" (chain saws), "Gorenje" (electric household appliances), or "Ingersoll" (compressors). This tic, a discreet compulsive disorder, can go off at any moment against my will, during times of sorrow as well as joy, and although nothing shows on the outside, those stubborn, insidious mantras settle into my head like a skipping record: "Jonsered-Jonsered-Jonsered-Jonsered . . ."

The man in charge of my department at the agency was named Azoulay. He was about forty, with a nasal voice and the terrible accent of a Frenchman born in Algeria, a bully who liked to throw his cologne-doused weight around. His office smelled like lemon-scented Lysol, and whenever I went there my eyes watered as if I were trapped in a smoky forest fire. When he was in a bad mood, Azoulay shouted orders at us from his office; the rest of the time, he addressed us as if we were animals in a zoo.

His sole reason for being was to make other people pay for his disappointments, losses, and inadequacies. Doubtless already a mean bastard back in Oran, Azoulay had become a real son of a bitch in Toulouse. A maniac for law and order and rules. The very rules that France had not respected in Algeria, well, Azoulay and his big mouth were going to teach them to the French, and in particular to his favorite target, Éric Delmas, a weary man, prematurely worn out, with age spots on his hands and a face as shiny as an old suit. Delmas wore shirts with collars so big that they dwarfed his scrawny neck and emphasized his frailty. Homing in on this weakness, Azoulay enjoyed tormenting his underling: "So, M'sieur Delmas, you got thinner overnight? Careful! If you keep this up, your bones will start to go!" Or, "M'sieur Delmas, it's so windy out—don't forget to tie some bowling balls to your feet!" Azoulay would shout those things from inside his little aquarium, with his squawking crow's voice, so that everyone in the department—as happens in departments everywhere—could hear and laugh complacently at the boss's pathetic jokes. For my part, I tried to be nice to Delmas, but he had become so used to persecution that he seemed almost embarrassed, even upset, whenever anyone paid the slightest kindly attention to him.

One morning, seeing Delmas drop his phone receiver and burst into tears at his desk, I thought of my mother on the day she learned that Vincent had died. There was a common root in their abrupt pain, a kind of suffering that struck too quickly to allow the hanging up of a telephone and permanently burdened you with a telescoped picture of existence. After observing the scene from afar, Azoulay left his cage and approached his prey.

"Trouble, M'sieur Delmas?"

"I'm going to have to leave. . . . My daughter has just gone into a coma. . . . That was the school . . . they said . . ."

"I'll tell you what they said at that school—they said, this M'sieur Delmas, he's always got a good reason for leaving early! Really, M'sieur Delmas, you're always halfway out the door, hey? All right, go on, but I want to see you back here at two p.m. sharp, got that?"

Lost in the confusion of his panic and his tears, the other man was putting his things away as clumsily as a schoolboy being sent to see the principal. I had never seen a grown man behave like that. The raw suffering of Monsieur Delmas was unbearable. Azoulay? After loitering briefly in the center aisle, he strode back to his fishbowl with the air of a smug study-hall monitor.

Unable to work all that morning, I was angry with myself for not having intervened during the incident. I was the only person who could have done so, the only one who could stand up to Azoulay, because I was a temporary employee, and he couldn't hurt me. Instead of intervening, however, I had silently stood by.

At precisely two that afternoon, Delmas was seated dry-eyed at his desk, pen in hand, checking over his contractors' notices of work stoppages due to inclement weather. His daughter was doing better, and had regained consciousness. That was the important thing. The rest didn't matter. The telephone hadn't rung. He hadn't picked it up. Nothing had happened. Nothing.

This mute, stifled epilogue released something inside me, maybe a knot of fear, or of anger. I stood up and went to beard Azoulay in his den. He looked up in surprise.

"M'sieur Block, I don't believe I heard you knock, did I?"

A swarm of tiny black dots danced before my eyes, my heart was thumping wildly, and my words stuck in my throat like cotton batting.

"I asked you a question, M'sieur Block. That door, there: Did you knock on it, or not?"

Like a furious bear, I raised my arms and slammed both fists down on his desk with all my strength. The noise impressed even me. The blow shook the desk, the floor, and the flabbiest parts of my boss's greasy face. In hindsight, I believe that I should then have let loose a terrible primitive bellow, a grizzly's roar, and stalked off without a word. Instead of which, probably jarred loose by my desk-pounding prowess, words poured from my mouth.

"Listen to me carefully: the next time you make the slightest comment to Monsieur Delmas, it won't be your desk I'll punch but your face."

Meanwhile, I shoved under his nose those fists that had just rattled the room and, I could tell, his self-confidence as well.

"What's come over you, Monsieur Block! You startled me, a moment ago."

"Blick."

"Blick? What's that mean?"

"My name is Blick, not Block."

"Well, M'sieur Blick, so, what do you think you're doing?"

"I'll tell you again: while I am working here, you will speak respectfully to Monsieur Delmas. And this evening, before you leave, you will apologize to him."

Leaving Azoulay's office, I slammed the door so hard behind me that all the windows were still rattling when I got back to my desk. Expecting some dreadful reaction, all my colleagues were staring at their boss, who brought his pen to his lips for a moment, sucked on it like a thoughtful student, and after seeming suddenly to resolve his quandaries, got back to work.

At home that evening, and for the first time in a long while, my mother took a lively part in the conversation, joking with my father about the new Model 1100 Simcas and asking how I was finding my first month as a wage earner. I talked to her about alienation, eyestrain, backaches from sitting still too long—but not a word about my run-in with Azoulay. She shared some of her singular opinions about work with me and then, with the suddenness of a bird taking wing, vanished into the kitchen. When she returned, I looked at Claire Blick and saw a woman still young, attractive, lively, and full of wit, despite the wear and tear of life. While pouring herself a cup of decaffeinated coffee, she said to me, "Listen, this afternoon, I read something written by Alain, the philosopher, which—who knows why—reminded me of you: 'The appetite's doing fine; the laundry gets done, and life smells good.'" Coming from my mother, that "reminder" sounded like a compliment.

I finished my trimester at the Building Trades Paid Vacation Agency without any problems. Azoulay was no longer bothering Delmas. As for me, he seemed literally to have erased me from his field of vision. So that my stay at the agency would not have been in vain, I took sly delight in fiddling with the balance due on numerous work records, thus offering extra bonuses to laborers slaving away out at construction sites. Azoulay was unquestionably on to what I was doing, but—might makes right—I was convinced that my grizzly display had taught him that discretion was sometimes the better part of valor.

On the other hand, my outburst had not had the same effect on my colleagues. It hadn't made me popular, brought me any support, or earned me any sympathy. Broken and exhausted, Delmas was beyond such feelings. As for the others, perhaps they resented my having involuntarily shown them that their real enemy was not so much Azoulay as their own cowardice.

On my last day at work, everyone left without saying good-bye to me. Azoulay was the last to go, and he paused for a moment by my desk.

"M'sieur Blick, well, the thing is . . . Concerning those supplementary hours, ahem, on the inclement weather work-stoppage notices. I wanted to let you know that I was obliged to correct everything, and to write a report to management. So you mustn't hesitate to go pound on their desks, you know, if they send for you, okay?"

A few days after my summer job was over, I received a letter from the Department of Education informing me that I had been assigned to a position as monitor in a high school in a distant suburb of Toulouse. This time, the prospect of even a modest but stable salary made me feel I was actually getting somewhere. I could start looking for a studio apartment, or something a little larger to share with other students. In those days, it wasn't necessary to produce five years of pay stubs, six medical certificates, a security deposit of seven months' rent, eight bank statements, nine copies of any extant police records, and look like a trust-fund kid—all just to find an apartment. In fact, the owners of old and somewhat run-down apartments often appreciated the tenancy of happy-go-lucky university students, who weren't fussy about their living conditions and enjoyed the pleasures of independence more than mere creature comforts.

In finding such lodgings, I had an ace in the hole. The Rochas real estate agency, although it specialized in sales and high-end properties, maintained in addition a rather solid roster of rental units available to students. Marthe Rochas absolutely insisted on keeping up this low-yield segment of the business, which she saw as a long-term investment. To her, a college student represented a consumer in embryo. That badly dressed, long-haired medical student in the shaggy Afghan coat, timidly pushing open the agency's front door, could be tomorrow's hottest rhinoplastic surgeon. And if she put up with that mop of hair for the moment, it was only in order to scalp the unsuspecting client in the future. Marthe Rochas was as greedy for money as she was for sex. Everything was there for the taking, the principal sum as well as the small change, and there was no time like the present, and no profit too small. Michel Rochas, for his part, was less avid. He conducted business like those nonchalant vacationers who drive along with an elbow out the window. In the whole time that I had known him, the only expression I'd ever seen on his face was that peaceful gaze, the relaxed smile of the sexually satisfied mammal. Marthe in her industriousness even displayed some aspects of the chronic and undifferentiated agitation that marked her son. In her eternal gray suit that smartly defined her waist, she resembled the hardworking bees of summer, bustling from file to file, extracting nectar that she seemed to be storing on her hips, which had become more curvaceous with the passing years.

For three days, David's mother took me under her wing to show me a dozen apartments ranging from the bachelor studio, a single-cell alveolus appointed along the discouraging lines of the lowest common denominator, to the bourgeois apartment graced with oaken woodwork, chestnut parquetry, and lofty ceilings with rosettes of plaster meringue.

I decided to narrow my search to an apartment spacious enough to house three or perhaps even four tenants. Such a community, so intellectually stimulating, offered the enormous advantages of providing ample companionship as well as dividing up the rent.

Informed of my preference, Marthe told me to meet her at five that afternoon on the fourth floor of a cheerful building on the Allée des Soupirs. "The Lane of Sighs": What could be more romantic than beginning life as a bachelor at such an address? Surely the tenants would be noble souls in shining armor, languishing in the company of a few visiting ladies in search of eroto-chivalrous adventures. The *allée* in question—which led to the Canal du Midi, constructed by Louis XIV—did not really deserve its tranquil name, however, since the sirens of a nearby firehouse would have drowned out any sighs.

That day, Marthe Rochas was wearing a heavy perfume, outrageously floral, with a hint of amber or cinnamon, a scent suitable for the evening, even the night, with deep, intimate notes that would linger even into sleep. Marthe Rochas hadn't waited for such late hours to surround herself with that heady fragrance. I followed in her sizzling wake, listening to her heels clacking on each step of the stairs with that Spanish je ne sais quoi, that flamenco verve, that inviting familiarity.

The apartment was laid out like a fan: four bedrooms opening onto a vast and vaguely hemispheric living room that rather resembled a big scallop shell. The main windows all gave onto a large and shady courtyard, promising cool breezes in the summer.

"You won't find a better place."

There was nothing professional about the way she said that; indeed, her voice was tinged with something like nostalgia. You sensed her envy of the young people who would live here and their excitement when they would move in, that feverish time when everyone is eager to begin a new life with the intoxicating feeling that from now on, anything can happen.

"I'm sure that you've already chosen your room."

She was standing with her shoulders back and one leg slightly turned out, the foot almost at a right angle, as though she were a ballet dancer at rest. Her crossed arms lifted up her bust, gently swelling behind the neckline of her white blouse.

"You're going to be happy here. I can feel it."

So could I. The slanting light of the setting sun filled the room with an atmosphere of protective intimacy barely ruffled by faint noise from the street. Sometimes simply walking up a few steps and crossing the threshold of an unfamiliar place will bring you to the captivating heart of another world, where everything you wanted, thought, and believed a moment before turns suddenly upside down.

In this topsy-turvy universe, where what is false is always a moment of truth, Marthe Rochas, wife and mother, director of a real estate agency, became once again the woman I had seen through that small oval window in her son's bedroom wall: available, submissive, yet avid and imperious, working her rump while her offspring, his eyes glued to the window, reaped the benefit of her example by spilling his own seed.

Marthe Rochas went over to a window, as if to watch some pigeons take wing, and placed the palm of her hand, with the fingers slightly apart, against the edge of the sash. Without any sign from her, I came closer. The old parquet floor creaked, as if to warn me at each step to be careful. When I was right behind her, near enough to brush against her, I froze, clinging like a swaying Métro rider to the last handhold of my conscience. She was the one who came to me, simply, without turning around, without looking at me. She stepped back, pressing her buttocks against my abdomen, rubbing against the part of me I could no longer control. And with both hands firmly pressed against the window, she arched her back and murmured, almost hoarsely, "You're not there. . . ."

This mysterious statement panicked me. I was there! Definitely. She could say what she liked, but I was applying myself to her with no less precision than her son once employed to skewer those roasts. With the same exaggerated movements I'd seen in tawdry films, I grabbed her forcefully. Then with a throaty little laugh of satisfaction, she seemed to say, "Atta boy, all right, now you're there." This modest assent thrilled me, and a low-voltage shiver coursed along my spine.

"Don't rush, we have plenty of time."

Without turning around, she slipped her hands inside my pockets to explore the contours of her new toy, and I suddenly felt as if I had shot to the surface of the ocean after a long, breathless submersion. No woman had ever fondled me through cotton cloth with that much savoir faire. I had never imagined that such treasures of the senses could be lurking in my pockets. When she finished her preliminary examination, I realized—without having even noticed that subtle unbuttoning—that my pants were down around my ankles. That woman had the buttocks of the devil and the fingers of Houdini. With an elegant, almost affected gesture, she raised her skirt, lowered her panties, and led me to the precise place she had chosen. As I entered her, I remembered how she had appeared that distant evening to my adolescent eyes: hoisted on the dick of Michel Rochas and looking behind her with exaggerated attention, like a driver trying to parallel park. Yes, that was it: looking at you like that, as if you were a stretch of curb, a kind of obstacle, Marthe Rochas seemed at such moments to be busy parking herself.

"A little to the right, that's it."

And now she was guiding me, directing the maneuver. The driving lesson continued, the pleasure somewhat spoiled by her constant barrage of directions, which I could not help taking for so many criticisms. As we advanced into the unknown, her requests became recriminations, demands that grew more imperious, more explicit.

"Keep going, don't stop whatever you do. . . . Stroke my nipples . . . and my clitoris. . . . Not like that . . ."

Marthe Rochas had her habits, her requirements, a strict MO, with a checklist I was obliged to follow. Soon overwhelmed by performance anxiety, I felt like a novice pilot facing an instrument panel that was far too sophisticated for me. Lights were flashing, the controls were no longer responding, the situation seemed to be getting out of hand. I had been reduced to a flustered and helpless automaton, reacting haphazardly to a confusing blizzard of signals.

The moment arrived when I no longer knew what was up or down, left or right, cause or effect, vice or virtue. Sensing my distress, plus the characteristic rigidity of preorgasmic tension, Marthe Rochas did try to head off the catastrophe with one last injunction.

"Not now, no, not yet!"

She could have said "Not already." Or "Not like that." Or "Not so quickly." She chose "Not yet." And thus was I made to feel as if I had fallen from a dizzying height through a hostile and icy atmosphere, while my companion pouted in childish exasperation. I'm sure that I told her how sorry I was, that I had no idea what had gone wrong. But Marthe Rochas seemed not to hear my excuses, and as if uncoupling herself from a trailer or some other deadweight, she stepped away from me, with awkward finality.

"We'll have to forget about all this immediately. Nothing happened in this apartment. Are we quite clear about that, Paul?"

We were. Marthe Rochas had already swallowed her brief disappointment, forgotten that unsatisfactory detour, and moved on to other things. Her clothes and general appearance presentable once more, she recovered her professional demeanor.

"What have you decided about the apartment? Are you taking it?"

While pulling up my wretched pants I replied yes, and I knew that it would be some time before I could erase the memory of my clumsiness and walk casually across that room.

We parted with a handshake in front of the building. She headed back to the agency with a determined step, leaving me standing there for a moment, watching passersby come and go. I took a deep breath and reflected that I now lived on "the Lane of Sighs."

It was at that address, a few months later, that Round-Up was born, a whimsical and laid-back rhythm-and-blues group I started with a few of my roommates. In its various configurations, this ensemble lasted five years, stretching to as many as nine members in its more extravagant periods. I was the only one who led a reasonably normal life: I got up in the morning, I slept at night, ate at more or less regular hours, and maintained what could be called sociable relationships with other human beings. My fellow band members might exhibit one or more of those characteristics, but no individual ever managed to combine all of them.

After a very short period of initial discovery, Round-Up (four of us in its first incarnation, the nucleus) set out to conquer the clubs and private parties. We offered an impoverished repertoire of pieces generally performed with three chords, our ignorance of the rudiments of music, to say nothing of our technical inadequacies, keeping us far from the harmonic sophistication of anything by an Otis Redding, a Stevie Wonder, and still less a Curtis Mayfield. We were—and what's more, we remained until the end—pitiful musicians, with no talent but plenty of gall. We didn't have to answer to anyone. To us, music was a highly subversive activity, the continuation of the revolution by other means. In fact our rehearsals were often given over more to hashing out politics than music, and we took more pleasure in trashing the "system" than in finding the proper tempo. That didn't keep us from playing all over the place in god-awful clubs and the homes of individuals too kindly or tone-deaf to know better.

So, when invited to provide the music for an evening wedding party, we would perform a few sets and play recorded music during our breaks. Although we despised the institution of marriage, we had agreed to behave ourselves and keep mum about our distinctive views. We hadn't, however, allowed for Mathias. He was a terrifying saxophonist who allied the emphysematous wind of a Fausto Papetti to the raging delirium of the most way-out avant-garde, a fringe-group Maoist with kung-fu tendencies and a radical revolutionary who considered any impulse of affection to be a "neurotic capitulation." In his world, men should approach women only during the summer months, to work in the fields and help out with the harvest. The sexes needed to realize that their raison d'être was not reproduction, but collaboration in building the dictatorship of the proletariat, a dictatorship evidently favorably disposed toward the martial arts and Selmer saxophones. With his stentorian voice and puny physique, his strange bowl-cut coiffure, and his obsession with *katas,* the formalized sets of martial arts moves and techniques, Mathias sometimes gave the impression of being assembled from disparate elements picked up on different continents.

When, mike in hand, one of the wedding guests introduced us that evening and announced the first number by Round-Up, he could not have imagined how much malevolent energy he had just released. Before we had even attacked the first note, Mathias went up to the mike and, raising his fist, shouted, "Marriage is the most dishonest form of sexual relations—that's why it enjoys the approval of those whose conscience is pure! Nietzsche . . ." In the ensuing stunned silence we tried a rather sloppy blues in E-A-B. Crowds are pretty forgiving, and we received a smattering of unearned applause. While records of more reasonable melodies spelled us for a bit, some guests even came up to debate or have a glass with us. They were genial people, who'd innocently gathered to have a pleasant time and wish a couple a good start in life. Their questions were mostly pleasantries: What did we do for a living? Had we been playing together long? Where had the name "Round-Up" come from? I found no compelling way of explaining that the band's name was in fact the name of an herbicide that had lodged itself for months—right before Ingersoll—deep in my maniacal brain.

Just when we were about to tackle our second number, Mathias, who had never seemed this scrawny and aggressive before, grabbed the mike again: "Marriage is the legal form of prostitution, the notarized arrangement of morally approved pimping aggravated by—" This time, Mathias didn't get to finish his quotation: the father of the bride, a sprightly quinquagenarian crammed into a suit jacket that probably hadn't fit for years, now stepped up to wrest the mike away. Feeling victimized by an attempt to limit his freedom of expression, Mathias struck his absurd combat pose and inflicted on his supposed attacker a *mawashigeri* that may even have been reinforced by an *osotogari*. In any case, our host went flying upstage, collapsing into the percussionist's stand of cymbals. The crowd then surged forward and latent loyalties were declared, staked out on either side of an imaginary line supposedly representing the border between good and evil, reactionary attitudes against the will of the people. In the melee, we took a lot more blows than we dealt out, before being expelled like foreign bodies, driven off by chair-wielding guests.

"What the fuck got into you?" asked the least damaged soul among us.

His nose and upper lip already swelling, Mathias replied through a mouthful of blood, "It wath nethethary."

"What?"

"He said it was necessary."

"That's great. And can you tell us how we're going to get our instruments back now?"

It took several days and the intervention of kindly intermediaries to recover our possessions, which had suffered severe reprisals in the meantime: the guitar strings had been cut, along with the power cords of the amplifiers and keyboards, and the heads of the congas and drums sliced to ribbons.

Three years after '68, we were still full of piss and vinegar from the movement, and hadn't noticed that the Man from Montboudif had returned the country to the fold and its citizenry to work.

In those years, what could possibly have connected the France of a Georges Pompidou and prime ministers like Chaban-Delmas or Pierre

Messmer to the slapdash universe of a Mathias, champion of invective, the "Little Red Book," and kung fu? For that matter, what could connect most of us to that president straight out of the Rothschild Bank and his seconds, a former mayor of Bordeaux and an ex-minister of overseas departments and territories? Absurdity, perhaps, and ridicule, as on the occasion (in late '74 or early '75) of our brief and humiliating concert at the legendary Blue Note, which in a way marked the end of Round-Up.

You have to imagine what the Blue Note meant to us: a kind of consecration, the culmination of all our years of apprenticeship. We were finally going to play black music in the quintessential black nightclub frequented only by a black clientele. We were nearing our goal at last. We owed that booking to Hector, one of our three guitarists, who also happened to be a disastrous soloist and a coenesthepath (the flamboyant archetype of the hypochondriac). Hector was stricken every day with a different dreadful disease, the symptoms of which he would describe to us in detail along with his slim chances of surviving another three to five years. Strangely, these afflictions were not cumulative, since regularly, inevitably, and magically each morning, the new illness would drive away the old one. Whenever we pointed out to him the unlikelihood of this phenomenon, he would pitch a fit and expound upon divers politico-nonsensico theories whereby the liberated patient had to escape his condition of *nonawareness* to take his system in hand and challenge the senseless privileges of the medical elite. The physical body, he used to say, no less than the social body, must be in permanent revolution. At least once during every concert and rehearsal, Hector would wince and hold his sides, chest, or belly, set down his guitar, and walk unsteadily offstage to nurse his agony. Sometimes he didn't even bother to wander off and would collapse right in front of us, on his knees, a tiresomely repetitive spectacle of his successive death throes. Like those bad actors riddled with bullets who drag themselves endlessly across the desert, Hector just couldn't stop dying.

Much later, I wondered if Hector had used his imaginary pathologies to con the owners of the Blue Note into giving us a gig through some incredible emotional blackmail. I imagined him telling the manager of his boundless admiration for Curtis Mayfield and Malcolm X, then remarking to him that he played in Round-Up, but that unfortunately, all that wouldn't last much longer; yes, he was seriously ill; no, he preferred not to talk about it; he had but one regret: never having played at least once at the Blue Note before leaving this world. What? It was possible? He'd look into it? Really? I knew that Hector was cracked and twisted enough to try something like that, throwing himself into it with all the conviction of the condemned man he really thought he was.

We arrived at the club at the end of the afternoon to set up and run a sound check. The drummers, the eternal twins from hell, were taking drags like there was no tomorrow. The grass had the pungent smell typical of fresh leaves still impregnated with all the plant's molecular properties. We took a wicked pleasure in smoking our pot in public, an extra tingle of depravity. I had planted a few stalks in the family greenhouse, where they flourished like nobody's business. Informed of my gardening, my mother was kind enough to water the grass regularly in my absence. My father, who had listened to his own father's tales about visiting some dark opium den in Tangier, considered my horticultural efforts mere child's play, although I suspected him of testing the effectiveness of my produce a few times.

The stickmen drummed away. Hector would go off every ten minutes, to vomit, he told us (the disease of the day was some kind of hepatitis), returning with damp hair and grandly swallowing a few antispasmodic pills. Mathias changed the reed in his Selmer, the guitarists tuned up, and I tried to untangle the mess of cables connecting the chorus and phaser pedals. For that special evening, I had borrowed a Hammond organ with a rotating Leslie cabinet. At right angles to that instrument was a Fender piano, on which I set my old Moog synthesizer. Even today I can precisely recall every detail of those instruments, which I could identify simply by their smell. Depending on how they're made, keyboards give off different odors: some smell of neoprene, others emit fumes of soft solder as they heat up, still others smell of varnish and particleboard with a scent like licorice. That afternoon, however, blown out by the weed puffing of the two guys on the skins, my nose was in no condition to undertake such subtle analyses.

Having apparently recovered from his hepatic problems, Hector left us at around seven o'clock, suffering this time from "a fit of epistaxis"— a small run-of-the-mill nosebleed he described as an uncontrollable hemorrhage requiring the urgent intervention of a medical expert.

Cured, bandaged, tuned up, and seriously high, we were onstage at ten that night, ready to launch into our first number, Hendrix's "Castles Made of Sand."

From the opening measures, I felt that something was happening, something hitherto unthinkable, unforeseeable: we were playing well. Let's say that we were respecting the tempo without blowing the chords or shredding the melody. In that magical place, we were touched by a kind of grace, even though our initial cohesion did have a tendency, as the set continued, to come gently undone. We were the first whites to play the Blue Note, the first whites to be *recognized* by blacks. Was there ever a sweeter dream of fusion? In the middle of a piece by Wilson Pickett, the name of which I've forgotten, the stage suddenly went completely dark. The lights were still on in the rest of the club, however; the bar glittered enticingly, and the club's sound system had kicked in when our amplifiers had gone silent. The audience—it was always crowded at the Blue Note—had moved out onto the dance floor as if nothing had happened, as if we weren't there, as if we had never played a note. Panicking, rushing feverishly to get back to our set, we felt around in the dark onstage, trying to check our connections. After a moment, the owner's assistant came up to us.

"You can pack up now."

"Pack up what? We barely got through five numbers before the power failed."

"There was no power failure."

"What do you mean, no power failure?"

"The boss decided to pull the plug on you."

"He shut off the electricity?"

"That's right. And now you've got to clear the stage, fast. Sorry!"

Like docile ghosts, we silently unplugged everything and carried our instruments to the van waiting outside. Lugging our stuff, we tried to slip among the club's customers, who just sneered at us.

Right before we left, I thought I saw Hector near the bar, getting a dressing-down from a big black guy in a suit who must have been the owner. When he joined us in the van, Hector was pale and holding his stomach, but as usual, we paid no attention to his imaginary ailments. He did try to tell us something, but couldn't get the words out. Then he leaned over and threw up.

That must have been toward the end of 1974, when I was getting ready to leave the apartment on the Allée des Soupirs, having decided that I had fully explored the glories and miseries of communal life. In a little over four years at that address, my roommates and I had already buried two presidents of the Republic: Charles de Gaulle, who died of a ruptured aneurysm (November 9, 1970) and Georges Pompidou, who succumbed to Kahler's disease (April 2, 1974). Always anxious to nourish his neuroses, Hector had written those names, dates, and causes of death in big black letters with a felt-tip pen on the inside of the bathroom door. We were so used to his harmless madness that I don't think any of us ever asked him why he made those latrinesque inscriptions. We simply accepted that every day, when we sat upon the throne, we would have no alternative but to read his morbid notations.

There were four of us sharing that space: Mathias, the implacable saxophonist; Hector, the incurable guitarist; Simon, the highly improbable bassist; and me, the sensible pianist. Three of us were students with part-time jobs that allowed us to live in peace and pay the rent. Simon Weitzman was the exception. He said he was studying medicine, yet he never set foot in an amphitheater. Unbelievably enough, Weitzman claimed to be an Arab, a member of the Moroccan royal family and the nephew of the Moroccan minister of the interior. In blithe disregard of said claims, he spent his days playing cards, hanging around the racetrack, concocting complicated swindles, and stealing furniture from university premises. Our armchairs came from the student lounges of the Université Paul Sabatier. The chairs and two big tables in the kitchen were originally the property of my old alma mater. The strange metal bookcase attached to the wall by our front door had been lifted from the Institut des Études Politiques adjoining the Faculté des Sciences Sociales. That was how life went: we'd go to bed one evening in an empty apartment and awaken the next day, thanks to a descendant of the Prophet, with a living room crammed as full as Ali Baba's cave. Simon would then light up a cigarette and fix us with a bright eye glittering with malice and glee. Physically, Weitzman was the image of the Algerian revolutionary Houari Boumediene, a resemblance, given the political and racial climate of the time, that was not to his advantage. Simon, however, lived in a world well beyond such contingencies. Intelligent, pragmatic, adapting instantly to every situation, he improvised his life in the heat of the moment. He borrowed or swiped whatever came to hand, from happiness to a pair of skis, a woman's bike, or leatherette armchairs. Simon was not a thief. He was simply unfamiliar with the concept of ownership. To him, the world was a communal pot into which everyone could dip according to the needs and desires of the moment. He was certainly aware of rules, customs, prohibitions, but he preferred to ignore them with elegant Mediterranean disdain and the engaging zest of a rowdy child.

At night Simon received visitors. Quiet guys you sometimes encountered in the hall, in the early hours of the morning. They all left a trail of mystery and stale tobacco. At that time, anti-Franco demonstrations and violence were on the rise. Homemade bombs were planted in front of the Spanish consulate, not far from the main police station and the Palais Niel, which housed army headquarters. The frequency and intensity of these nighttime explosions increased, while across the border, the caudillo continued to order the execution of political detainees, who were garroted.

Simon and Mathias had linked up with some militants from various small groups fighting actively against the Franco dictatorship. Basques, Catalans, and anarchists from the Confederación Nacional del Trabajo paraded through the apartment. In spite of his suspicious background, his vaunted family ties with the Moroccan dictatorship, and his reputation as a bicycle thief and pillager of offices, Simon rapidly became our visitors' sole interlocutor. The rest of us spoke much better Spanish than he did and had more extensive political credentials, yet he was the one who inspired confidence and was considered a worthy representative of the international struggle. Often our guests even preferred to shut themselves up in his bedroom to talk, which affronted us. Our jealousy reached a crescendo one evening when Simon announced in the middle of dinner, "It's going to blow up tonight."

"What's going to blow up?"

"The consulate."

"What do you mean, the consulate?"

"I'm telling you the consulate's going to blow up. That's all."

"And how do you know that?"

"I just know."

At two that morning, an enormous explosion shook the entire neighborhood awake. No doubt all thinking the same thing, Mathias, Hector, and I shot out of our bedrooms and found Simon sitting in a chair, smoking a little cigar with the relaxed air of an Englishman on holiday.

"How did you know?"

He gave me that con-artist look of his, raised the cigar butt to his lips, and blew a few smoke rings that spiraled upward. Then, more enigmatic than ever, he slipped into his overcoat and headed out the door. Without looking back, he tossed us a simple "Good night, guys."

In those days I was working out in a distant suburb as a monitor in a high school named after Marie Curie. The principal of this school and its more than four hundred pupils was humanly pathetic, intellectually deficient, and professionally perverse. There was, in the coldness of his visage, something reminiscent of the flabby features of Benito Mussolini. Edmond Castan-Bouisse ran his school like a battleship. Sole master at the helm, he lorded it over a few conspicuously cowardly and submissive ensigns, lined up along the first gangway, while all the bosun's mates and apprentice seamen were jammed into the engine room. In other words, Castan-Bouisse was a flaming asshole, a self-important halfwit puffed up and reinvigorated by the defeat of '68.

I had arrived there in 1970, the year he decided to whip things back into shape and inflict on pupils and teachers alike the outrageous new regulations he'd cooked up in his Formica-paneled brain.

Marie Curie was one of those schools that had lost prestige after its student body was transformed by an influx of essentially rural children who had previously attended smaller schools scattered throughout the *département*. Most were the sons and daughters of farmers, while the rest came from families of modest means living in cheap housing built on the outskirts of towns. Castan-Bouisse detested what he called that "impossible clientele." He did not understand why the department of education should have assigned him, the Champion of Rules and the Guardian of Virtue, to such a rat hole. With his savoir faire, his war experience in the Resistance (loudly contested by his detractors), and his expert knowledge of Latin and Greek (absolute rubbish, according to those who should know), he deserved to direct a lycée of distinguished reputation. Instead of which he was surrounded by a hostile, rustic, and almost barbarian population, as he put it, and backed up by a bunch of incompetents more interested in unionizing and fornicating than in the inviolable precepts of secondary education.

"You do not intend, I would assume, to keep your hair that long?"

That was the first thing Edmond Castan-Bouisse said to me. He knew neither my name, nor where I came from, nor what studies I was pursuing, nor whether my brother was dead or my parents alive, but he had already settled the most urgent question once and for all.

During my entire time at Marie Curie he had to live with that mop of hair, which he found unbearable to look at. My mere presence upset him so much that I could hear his teeth grinding in the silence of his office. Affixed to his door was an enameled plaque in Gothic letters: MONSIEUR LE PRINCIPAL. It was easy to imagine that the style of lettering had been chosen specifically to intimidate the rural populace, browbeat the humble teachers, and enhance the aura of this implacable suburban dictator.

"In addition I will ask you not to be familiar with the students, who for the most part have not received an education that would allow them to understand subtle distinctions in relationships of authority. You will therefore limit yourself to applying our regulations to the letter and to advising me of the slightest breach in their observance. And . . . your hair . . . as soon as possible, of course."

With his right index and middle fingers, he mimicked the snipping of a pair of scissors along the flank of his own already well-advanced baldness.

. . .

Life" at Marie Curie was a kind of three-dimensional hell. On the lowest stratum, I had to endure the uproar of pupils who had understood perfectly that I was not a guard dog but a pet who wished them no harm. At the top, the kaiser needled me constantly for my leftism, my lack of authority, and my exuberant locks. As for the teachers, stagnating at the midlevel of my troubles, they took dutiful pains—and in some cases, pleasure—in echoing Castan-Bouisse's reproaches, sometimes even piling on their own.

In this scholastic cesspool, only two little tribes gave me timid support and comfort. First of all, there were the three Communist teachers, members of the National Teachers' Union, against whom Castan-Bouisse had been waging tenacious war for years. In private or with his minions, he referred to this trio as "the Bolshies" or "the Russian front." And now my arrival had reinforced that trio, if indirectly; by drawing the fresh ire of the top brass, I allowed the Reds to catch their breath a bit, reorganize, and target specific operations against a principal now engaged in hostilities on two fronts. Before every vote of the school's administrative council, the "Stals," as they were also called, would try clumsily to flatter and bamboozle me, assuring me, for example, that I was their "objective ally."

The second group that didn't actively plot against me were the adulterous lovers. They represented a not inconsiderable percentage of the faculty, an interesting professional subcategory. The sympathy they showed me was easily explained: in their extraconjugal activities, they all felt that they were committing the irreparable, transgressing the sacrosanct school regulations, and like me, constantly flirting with the disciplinary board. Infantilized adults, both terrified and excited by their puny depravities, they now felt secretly in league with the "revolutionary" world I represented to them. They tried to convince themselves that lying to their mates, brushing against each other in the teachers' lounge, fondling each other between classes, and fucking every other Wednesday were so many acts of political emancipation and liberation. They saw themselves as the vanguard of a new sexual disorder marching against the lockstep of a normative and castrating society. Every other Wednesday I lent out the keys to the apartment on the Allée des Soupirs, where a couple of them could moan to their hearts' content for a few hours. They had little time to spare for their hanky-panky, since their respective spouses, also full-time teachers but of the punctilious sort, strictly observed the time-honored dinner hour.

Several times a week, I might also happen to drive one or another of these illegitimate couples to school in the morning. They would show up at the apartment at around seven-thirty, climb into the back of the Volkswagen, and make out for the entire ride. Sometimes they even wound up unpresentable, and like an indulgent taxi driver, I'd have to pull over before arriving at the school so they could fix their hair and straighten their clothes. In spite of these efforts, their flushed cheeks and rosy, swollen lips betrayed them.

After a few months, I became so much a part of their private lives that they no longer felt the slightest restraint in front of me. I'm thinking in particular of that English teacher who would clamber into the Volkswagen to join her waiting lover after classes were over and tell him, lifting her skirt a little, "I'm already all wet." This she would say in her naive-and-retarded-adolescent voice without any embarrassment at all, as though I were a vaporous abstraction, a servant left over from the ancien régime: blind, deaf, and dumb. The next morning, however, as soon as classes began, this moist Madonna was quite capable of curtly ordering a student to leave the room simply for chewing gum in class. I don't care how miserable their sex lives were: such grandiose hypocrisy, confounding inconsistency, and wretched need to penalize their pupils just astonished me.

I spent almost four years in that debilitating and petty world where the worst was always yet to come. As time passed, all those people seemed to become fossilized in their respective roles in relation to a brazen Castan-Bouisse, who methodically tormented the little labor camp of which he proudly claimed to be both *kapo* and protector. One morning he arrived at his office to find the word *"Heil!"* written on his door with a black felt-tip. The incident swelled to such proportions that it led to a quasi-public polemic about his so-called Resistance past. I don't know what Castan-Bouisse did during the war, but it couldn't have been worse than the lousy combat he waged in peacetime.

When summer vacation rolled around in 1974, I left Marie Curie, never to return. On my final day, Castan-Bouisse turned up just as my last class came to an end.

"You're leaving us today, Monsieur Blick? You know what I think of you, so I will spare you the usual 'You will be sorely missed' and so on. Here, no one will miss you except, perhaps, all those bratty little monkeys who next year, I hope, will face a more conscientious and less permissive monitor. Do you take drugs, Monsieur Blick?"

"On occasion."

"I knew it. Definitely. 'On occasion' your dilated pupils are a textbook illustration of mydriasis."

"I have to go now, Monsieur Bouisse."

"Castan-Bouisse, if you please—you are still in my school. And I will ask you not to use that condescending tone with me."

That man's language reminded me of my late grandmother Marie Blick: their words revealed the same constant battle to control the hatred struggling inside them, like an angry mastiff on a leash.

"One last question: It was you, wasn't it, who wrote that German word on my door last year?"

"You mean *'Heil'*?"

"That's correct."

I took one last look at that little gauleiter: so soigné, tightly buttoned into his gray suit in hot weather and cold, always perfectly clean-shaven. Despite his constant and determined effort to project an image of virility, there was something ambiguous, even feminine about him. It was easy to imagine him as a devotee of saunas and men's toilets.

"No. I did not write anything on your door."

"Listen to me carefully, Blick. I know it was you. I know it the way I knew that you take drugs. So I sent a report about all that to the Department of Education. A detailed report. I fondly hope that this file will follow you wherever you go and that it will prevent you from enjoying a career in our national educational system, should you ever contemplate entering such a profession someday. Now get the hell out of here."

. . .

That summer was particularly hot and dry in the southwest of France. My father had turned the garage over to his young deputy and now often stayed at home, where he spent most of his time taking care of his garden, which had become a splendid museum of greenery. In a few years, he had managed to transform an arthritic old yard into a wonderland of marvelously varied things. Some of the shrubbery seemed to flow in stretches of seamless green alongside pathways, while other bushes wrapped around elms and cedars like thick fur collars. Pruned, thinned, finally relieved of their dead branches, the palms, chestnuts, acacias, mulberries, and Judas and plane trees came into their own. And everywhere, linking clumps of trees and bushes with solitary shrubs, lay a carpet of lush, velvety, exquisitely even grass, regularly trimmed by a lawn mower of English manufacture that left ruler-straight wheel tracks we could still see days later.

Much more than a hobby for my father, this garden was a kind of cure for his heart problems, his ultimate reason for being. And it is always at such times, when we believe that we have finally achieved happiness and fulfillment after years of effort, that the unforeseen occurs to lay us low, trampling us, our work, and our dreams.

It was the drought that laid waste to my father's last small square of life. A drought of overwhelming intensity and duration. That year, the spring rains had been sparse: almost no precipitation in April or May, and none at all in June. July was a permanently running blast furnace beneath a sky so despairingly blue that by mid-month the authorities established water restrictions. The watering of crops was regulated in the countryside, and no one was permitted to pump water from the now stagnant Canal du Midi. In Toulouse, washing cars, filling swimming pools, and above all watering gardens—whether public or private— was forbidden.

My father, a loyal citizen and law-abiding to the core, scrupulously obeyed the restrictions and let his putting-green lawn turn yellow. Then came the turn of the most vulnerable bushes to broil slowly in the sun. Next were the trees. The cherry trees withered and shed their leaves as if it were November. Day after day, an entire world was sti-fling. The earth cracked open while roots vainly sought the slightest moisture in the soil.

In the evening I sometimes visited my parents and would have coffee with my father. We'd sit out in the garden, where we could hear leaves falling. When they hit the ground, they made a tiny metallic noise that never failed to pinch my father's heart.

"Everything is parched. The whole place is dying."

When August arrived, he decided to defy the law and began water-ing at the base of his trees every night. He set up several hoses that he moved every fifteen minutes. He moved quickly, like a bicycle thief, afraid of being caught acting against the public good. He tried to assuage his remorse by explaining that watering at night limited evapo-ration and so he was returning to the water table much of what he siphoned off. He managed to deceive himself like that for an entire week, at which point his guilty conscience no longer had to worry: the pumps began to suck air. The aquifer was dry.

Over the following days, my father spent his time listening to weather reports, hoping to hear that the barometer was falling. In the evening, he went out onto the terrace to gaze at the sky and watch heat lightning in the distance.

Big thunderstorms arrived toward the end of the month. I was with my father when the first downpour began. We went outside to breathe in that singular smell of damp earth. The swirling air was full of myriad plant smells suddenly released by the storm. In the garden, huge rain-drops clattered down on the carpet of dry leaves like lead shot.

"I never imagined that it would all end like this one day. The grass will be green again in a week. But it's too late for everything else. All the rain in heaven won't ever bring my trees back to life."

France had a new president of the Republic; Richard Nixon had just resigned; the world was prey to all sorts of wars and conflicts—and yet, that evening, nothing seemed sadder to me than to see my father, a gentle and enlightened monarch, wandering at the edge of his lifeless and lonely kingdom.

ALAIN POHER

(Second Interim, April 2, 1974–May 27, 1974)

BEFORE my father endured the caprices of the heavens that summer, I suffered, in the spring, the attentions of a demented dentist. His name should have warned me: it was Edgar Hoover, like the director of the FBI. Hoover was Marie's boss. I had kept up a desultory relationship with Marie, and ever since the Man on the Moon episode we had called each other occasionally to exchange news about the little events in our lives. So when a dreadful pain began to gnaw at one of my molars, I naturally turned to her for help. She arranged an appointment that very day with Hoover, a hulking giant of indeterminate age with a serious five-o'clock shadow. Furthermore, a kind of black fleece curled out of the collar of his smock, leading to visions of a chest and back thickly covered with fur. Hoover suffered from the illness common to those of his profession: he talked all by himself. He sat you down in the dentist's chair, asked you where it hurt, and as soon as he began to treat you, launched into an excruciatingly dull monologue about, say, a sports event, the doings of some celebrity or other, Watergate, the coming presidential elections in France, or his opinion of Alain Poher. Hoover, I knew, had also been Marie's occasional (yet jealous) lover for more than two years. I knew about their relationship, but I just couldn't see how those two could wind up in the same bed. I could not picture that hairy, abrasive lump jiggling between Marie's silken legs, or that sandpaper chin scratching her porcelain bosom. But that's what Edgar Hoover did.

Marie had also confessed to me that ever since his wife had run off with his partner, the dentist suffered from some kind of chronic clinical depression that he treated in the American fashion, before he closed his office every afternoon, by breathing a few puffs of laughing gas, which he sometimes used as a light anesthetic. That was his way of facing the rest of the evening and what he saw as the permanent failure of his life. Marie had often come upon him lying in the treatment chair with the mask over his face, his eyes rolled back, sucking in euphoria-inducing nitrous oxide, his professional tipple, his cannabis in a can.

"That's where it hurts, when I apply pressure: there, right?"

Hoover seemed to be an aficionado of pain. Especially when inflicting it. You'd have to be blind not to notice the joy that twinkled in his eye when, with the simple pressure of his index finger, he let loose a vicious cataclysm in your jaw. Those sadistic thrills must have been what enabled him to hang on until the critical moment of his gaseous Happy Hour.

"I'm going to give you some antibiotics, and in five or six days I'll kill the nerve. That *is* where the pain is, isn't it?"

And lightning shot through my mouth once again.

Marie had made the mistake of talking about our past affair. As soon as I set foot in Hoover's office, I sensed that he didn't like me.

Marie did not live with Edgar Hoover. She had kept her apartment, where she still slept several times a week. That evening, no doubt stimulated by the circumstances of our reunion, we wound up at her place, where, as was her wont, she gave me a glimpse of happiness and sent me flipping all around the bed. My tooth, in the meantime, kept throbbing, and even more painfully, thanks to the pounding of my heart and the intensity of my desire.

In the morning I began my antibiotic treatment. One hour after I took the first capsules my entire penis began to itch violently. The itching then gave way to a disquieting burning sensation. By noon my dick had taken on a quite colorful and frightening aspect. The skin was covered with vesicles: big, disgusting, and painful blisters that I was sure were brimming with infectious germs. I had no idea what this putrid disease was, and it didn't seem possible that Marie could have infected me with such a venomous, virulent, and fulminant *alien*. Wrapping my tool in a huge wad of gauze, I rushed to a dermatologist, who took one look, diagnosed a local pigmented erythema—an allergic reaction to antibiotics—and predicted that it would take forty to fifty days to clear completely.

I lived like that for almost two months, with my poor penis skinned alive and mummified in a smelly sausage of petrolatum gauze bandages. And my tooth, released from the antibiotics, was back doing St. Vitus' dance. I kept going to see Hoover, but nothing helped. The painkillers he prescribed allowed me to doze through the night; I dodged the shooting pains the way one leaps over puddles. Whenever I consulted him, he never failed to shove his fingertip into the most inflamed part of my gum.

"That's where it is, huh? It reaches all the way into the upper jaw when I press here, right?"

After treating himself to this pure moment of sadism, he would fetch his tank of nitrous oxide, plop the mask over my face, and open the valves wide. Then my lungs would fill with a cloud of happiness as volatile and artificial as the real thing. I remember that each time, before he put away his tank, Hoover would sneak himself a whiff, like someone polishing off a guest's glass. When I rose from the chair, I always felt as if I were living in a tipsy world where nothing stood up straight, and I even had to lean to one side to pass through all the crooked doors in the office. Whenever I ran into Marie in the hall, I would give her a friendly wave, but I was so cerebrally disadvantaged that she had already vanished into the treatment room with another patient by the time my hand began to wiggle.

I came almost daily to consult my specialist.

"The abscess has gotten bigger. And since you can't take antibiotics, I'm going to have to operate. You're not allergic to anesthetics, by any chance?"

Once again, Hoover had asked me that question with the particular intonation of the true pervert. The more consultations I had, the more convinced I became that this neurotically jealous man was making me pay through the teeth for my relationship with Marie.

"Open wide. It's going to hurt when I stick the needle in, but the pain should go away soon."

The gorilla had me in his hands. Standing next to him in her face mask, Marie assisted in his malpractice. She could see inside my mouth and discover all its imperfections, and even look into the folds of my tonsils. I knew that from then on, she would have a clinical and surgical image of my oral cavity. The thought made me cringe.

"*Chérie,* give him a little gas."

In front of all his other patients, Hoover was formal with Marie and called her mademoiselle. When I was there, he preferred the more affectionate term, doubtless to affirm his status as the dominant male. Well, *Chérie* gave me a good dose of nitrous oxide. Then *Chérie* put a retractor into my mouth, tucked cotton sponges into my cheeks, aspirated my saliva, wiped off a few trickles of blood, and while Hoover was torturing my benumbed gums, I thought about what *Chérie* had recently been up to with my penis, that poor organ now disfigured and condemned to convalescence, swaddled like a Chinese spring roll. Hoover crammed into my mouth whatever was at hand, carelessly shoving the instruments in the way you load a station wagon for a morning's fishing jaunt. And he talked, chirping away relentlessly.

". . . Obviously the presidential elections will be different this time around. You remember Barbu bursting into tears, I don't recall which year that was, and Ducatel, who began his first speech with 'Let me introduce myself: Louis Ducatel, inventor of the tube of the same name' . . . *Chérie,* there . . . Aspirate . . . So really, this time, with René Dumont, the famous ecologist, and that woman, whose name escapes me at the moment, we're heading for . . . *Chérie,* fix me a new injection and slip him another hit of gas. . . ."

With his fiendish cocktails and his depraved use of painkillers, he had me in his power, controlling me and using his mysterious procedures to inflict extraordinary dental pain and wounds that he alone was then able to treat with his shots, his apothecary jars of capsules, and his tanks of gas. In two weeks, Hoover had managed to knock out my genitals and turn me into a submissive drug addict unable to distinguish between the platforms of candidates anywhere on the political spectrum, from Left to Right, and above all, unable to honor or even go anywhere near *Chérie*.

VALÉRY GISCARD D'ESTAING

(May 27, 1974–May 21, 1981)

HAVE never voted. That's a principle to which I hope always to stay true. So far, I have resisted every temptation, all well-reasoned arguments or specious pleading, every attempt to make me feel guilty, to unsettle, pressure, or blackmail me, and I have clung to the single canticle in my modest breviary, convinced that ever since '68 a loathsome bunch has rigged our elections. So in my own modest way, I have tried to have nothing to do with them. That might not seem like much to certain deep thinkers, but the crystalline purity of that concise resolution had always suited me just fine. It would not be appropriate here to go into the grounds for my decision; I will simply say, to flesh out my preamble, that I never, throughout my life under this ongoing Fifth Republic, encountered a single candidate campaigning for my vote to whom I would cheerfully have entrusted the keys to my car, let alone my country—in short, a fellow with whom I would have liked to spend a week's vacation or even just go fishing. On the evening of May 19, 1974, however, when I heard that Giscard d'Estaing had been declared the winner with a 1.62-percent lead (barely 424,599 votes more than his opponent, who was unquestionably a bourgeois in Socialist's clothing, but in every way the lesser of two evils), I spent an uneasy hour steeped in the melancholy of realizing that I had done a bad thing.

If I have hardly mentioned the progress of my studies in sociology, it's because they seemed like a long and easygoing session of physiotherapy. After four years of showing up, I had not written one sentence, handed in the shortest paper, passed the tiniest test. The instruction was more along the lines of a general assembly than a course of lectures. And if a few of the professors had ever tried to practice their profession, however discreetly, they would probably have wound up in a reeducation camp, in a factory, or out in the fields, so that they might learn the basic rules laid out in Raoul Vaneigem's Situationist treatise *The Revolution of Everyday Life*. At the end of each year, the administration would simply give us our credits. There were no exams and no supervision. There was no need to fill out any forms or fulfill any requirements for the bachelor's and master's degrees handed to us automatically. Even our presence in class was not obligatory. All we had to do was sign up at the beginning of the term and float along, dropping in from time to time to show that, on occasion, "Dialectics can break bricks." Classes consisted of endless ideological and strategic confrontations among Situationists, Maoists, Trotskyites, libertarians, members of the Parti Communiste Marxiste-Léniniste Français, and a few precocious autonomous radicals, partisans of armed struggle. The teacher assigned to babysit us was silent, unobtrusive, and attentive as he completed his training by taking notes on this perpetual ferment of ideas.

I would be at a loss to explain why the election of Giscard d'Estaing upset the organization of this perfect world, but within a few weeks the atmosphere had changed completely. The administration (had it received orders? did it fear an inquiry?) began to tighten the reins. The professors perked up, and the assistant profs started fiddling with their minuscule powers. When the exams of 1974 came around, the faculty stipulated that we hand in a paper for each of our accredited courses. There was as yet no question of verifying the extent of our knowledge, but still, we had to swap these paper tokens for our diplomas, as if we were buying them with play money. We saw this as a pronunciamento, an unthinkable bid for power, and at many general assemblies everyone argued about this return to intellectual elitism. The most radical among us proposed a "physical" solution to the problem: beating up a few teachers and sacking the administration offices. Others, more reformist in spirit, advised going immediately on strike and mobilizing all the universities.

What had so far been only a jolly student rumpus turned into riot and insurrection thanks to a suicidal assistant teacher named Breitman, who decided on his own—we never found out why—to challenge us directly. He taught the most despised of all subjects, statistics, and as a member of the Parti Communiste Français, to our way of thinking he was a far-right militant. He wanted us not only to turn in individual papers at the end of the year, but also to take an actual exam to prove our mastery at calculating margins of error and other statistical fantasies.

Neither a twisted ideologue nor a shrewd tactician, Breitman belonged to that relatively unsophisticated category of rather embittered teachers whose psychological rigidity leaves them ready to seize up at the slightest conflict, while Breitman's political opinions and fidelity to the Party reinforced his unwillingness to compromise. In each of his classes, he was sharply challenged to explain his decisions and his attitude. He would then collect his things and leave the classroom without a word. After a month of such behavior, we resolved to intimidate this maverick and drive him back into the herd. Three of us went to his home at dinnertime. When he opened the door, his face clouded over immediately.

"What do you want?" he asked stonily.

"To talk things over."

"What things?"

"Can we come in?"

"No."

Jesús Ortega, the least patient among us, kicked the door so hard that it slammed against the wall and knocked down a picture.

"Don't pull that shit with us! We said we came to talk things over!"

"There's nothing to talk about. You're not at the university here— this is my home! So get out!"

At the very instant Breitman stopped speaking, Ortega's wide-open hand landed with a dry smack on his face. And the instant after that voluptuous slap, we were all sitting on the sofa in Breitman's living room like old friends.

"Okay, Breitman, listen up: this cowboy business of yours, it's finished, over, got that? We don't even care what's gotten into you lately. Tomorrow you'll tell everyone you've changed your mind and you'll be giving us credits for your course like always. Or else."

"Or else what?"

"Or else we'll beat the crap out of you and set fire to that jalopy of yours."

Breitman seemed to grow more compact where he sat, gathering up the last molecules of his courage the way one prepares to meet the shock of an oncoming wave. Without looking at us, with his head pulled down between his shoulders, he said, "Tomorrow I'll say the same thing I've been saying all along: you must all take the exam. There will be no exceptions."

Jesús Ortega slammed his hand down flat on a low table, breaking the glass in two with a noise like a zipper closing.

"Fucking Communist!"

I was taken aback, and in spite of our numerical advantage, I vaguely sensed that Breitman was winning the contest.

Ortega paced up and down the living room yelling, "Fucking Commie!" as the walls seemed to close in around us. Breitman was hardly older than we were, but we were merely buzzing insects, while he was the very incarnation of the reality principle, deeply rooted in the materiality of the world.

"You've got until tomorrow, Breitman. After that, we'll nail you."

Ortega kicked the sofa in a rage and stormed out. We heard the sound of breaking glass in the hall and then, nothing. I said something like "You'd better think about all this."

Breitman looked up at me: his face was livid, his eyes glittering with fury.

"Get the fuck out. All of you, get the fuck out of here!"

The next day, and for the next two weeks, the campus was in chaos, just as in the glorious May days of 1968. Demonstrations, strikes, clashes with members of the Union Nationale des Étudiants de France, looted offices, overturned cars—the fission of the Breitman core was going nuclear, so the university shut down for ten days to restore some order to the premises and some calm to the situation.

When the university reopened, we found that Breitman had not budged: he was still a stubborn Communist and more determined than ever to verify with professional zeal our statistical aptitudes. An agreement was reached with the administration: Breitman could carry out his intention of assigning us all grades, but no matter what those grades were, the university pledged to grant us that course credit according to the custom of the ancien régime. That is how I received my due and left that madhouse where I had been a boarder for five years. I was twenty-four years old, with a grotesque diploma in my pocket and a skewed vision of that darkling world. The Americans were about to leave Vietnam, Pinochet had taken over in Santiago, Picasso was dead, and my young life looked to me like one of his Cubist paintings.

Ever since my brother's death, I have gone through difficult periods when I fall prey to feelings of failure, abandonment, and loneliness. In that autumn of 1974, I had a similar impression of great emptiness while accompanying Marie home one evening, when she told me in a toneless voice that she was pregnant by Edgar Hoover. One flaw in her birth-control protection, one moment of forgetfulness or carelessness had sufficed to allow one of the millions of that hairy odontostomatologist's spermatozoa to get the better of the chalaza, nucellus, funicle, and tegument of Marie's ovum. The last thing in the world she wanted was for the dentist to know about her condition. He was her employer, she said, and she did not want him for a husband, or father, or even for advice or moral support in her anguishing predicament. So she had called me. So that she would not be going alone into the institutional-green examination room of the doctor who had told her to bring towels and, above all, cash.

Dr. Ducellier was one of those practitioners whose willingness to risk performing abortions was not rooted in any particular wish to help women in distress. Like most of his confreres, moreover, Ducellier charged a prohibitive fee. He was a middle-aged man who seemed permanently exasperated by his short stature and always walked on tiptoe. One large swath of eyebrow cut his fat face in half over two tiny marbles (close together and of a startling blue) that looked everywhere but into your eyes. Ducellier wore a short-sleeved smock that bared his muscular forearms, the arms of a weight lifter, stuffed with steroids and used to working with forceps. His specialty, however, was neither gynecology, nor obstetrics, nor surgery. His practice was in the more prosaic realm of legal medicine and medicinal expertise. He was essentially hired by banks and insurance companies to check out the liver and kidneys of board members or entrepreneurs applying for bank loans or guarantees.

When we'd climbed the stairs to the doctor's office, I had noticed that Marie, impassively toting her little gym bag, had already embarked on her painful and lonely trip, one of those dangerous expeditions during which a woman inevitably loses part of herself.

"Who are you?"

"You want to know my name?"

"No, what is your relationship to her?"

"Her friend."

"That's all I see here, monsieur. Everyone who sits where you're sitting is a friend. What I want to know is whether you are the best friend or the 'bed friend,' so to speak—the progenitor, in other words."

Ducellier was entertaining himself. Like all crooked doctors, he openly despised the men and especially the women who paraded through his office. It was clear that in some confused way, he felt cast in the role of father, judge, and censor. This pitiless benefactor would cut to the quick to root out vice, and put you through the mill doing it. Money ruled his life, but it was something else, something more suspect and disquieting, that guided his hand.

"No, I'm only her friend."

Sitting next to me, Marie remained expressionless, her bag at her feet, while her hands, waiting one atop the other, kept each other company. It took me a moment to discover why her face was different: she wasn't wearing makeup. She had come here without any artifice, stripped of the desire to please or to appear other than she was. For the first time, I was seeing her truly naked.

"It's just your bad luck: in a month you would have been able to take advantage of the new law. But it wouldn't be wise to wait, and in any event, I gather, you'd be beyond the permissible period by then. You've been pregnant how long, you said?"

Marie replied in a choked voice, weakly gasping out her words. His face a mask of indifference, Ducellier continued his routine.

"You have the payment?"

He counted it calmly, flipping expertly through the bundle of bills, like a meat wholesaler or a car salesman. All labor deserved remuneration, and at some point money changes hands. That's all.

"Fine. Madame and I will go to my examination room, and you, monsieur, I will ask you to be patient out in the waiting room. If you leave to run an errand, ring three short times when you return so I'll know it's you."

Ducellier rose and gestured for Marie to precede him. Before she'd taken even three steps, he stopped her with a touch on her arm, and pointed to her bag.

"You're forgetting your towels."

Slowly, life was teaching me its rules, showing me its priorities, pointing out the invisible boundaries between the world of men and the world of women. I knew that at that moment, Hoover was wearing his mask, inhaling his bottled elixir, lying in his chair with his legs slightly elevated to help blood flow to the brain. Marie, well, she was stretched out on an exam table with her legs spread and her feet in stirrups, while that beady-eyed man slipped all those cold things into her. In that businesslike brain of his, did Ducellier think he was giving her her money's worth? I had nothing to do with the whole affair and nothing to do in the waiting room, yet my mind was filled with muddled thoughts and feelings about fatherhood. My chest felt heavy with a nameless distress, and I remembered the night of the lunar landing, when Marie and I had mysteriously gone astray from our trajectory of love. I remembered our conversation about Collins, the third astronaut who had made that entire voyage for nothing, who had never left the capsule. I told myself that the same thing was happening to Marie's fetus. It had also made a long journey, through a palpitating universe of the infinitely small, only to find at the end of that crossing an impassable door and a porthole through which, like Collins, it could no more than glimpse a world it could hear, and feel through vibrations, but where it would never set foot.

When Marie emerged from Ducellier's exam room, her face was pale and drawn and her hair, damp with perspiration, was sticking to her forehead. I asked Ducellier to call a taxi.

"Don't worry, there's a taxi stand down on the street."

The job was done, and now he was anxious to see the last of us. Perhaps he had scheduled another appointment and didn't want his patients to run into each other.

"In theory, everything will be fine. If there is a problem, call the doctor whose phone number I gave you."

"You won't be seeing her again in a few days?"

"No. You must never come back here. That's it. And now I will say good night to you."

Going down those dimly lighted stairs, we could feel his sharp eyes watching us until we reached the very last step, when we heard his door quietly close.

I stayed the night in Marie's apartment. She shivered with pain and loneliness. After a heavy dose of pain medication, she finally fell asleep, holding my hand.

For a few days, that visit to Dr. Ducellier continued to stir up strange things inside me, as if the accumulated sediments of my life had been violently disturbed. Those muddy waters dimmed my vision, enveloping my mind in a swirl of memories in which the dead jostled the living, and the shouts of children shattered the silence of stones.

One morning I drove for a half hour in the direction of the Pyrenees. The plane trees along the road formed a green vault worthy of the loftiest cathedral. Once all the roads in the south of France were like that, shaded with glorious foliage. Travel used to be fun, a kind of pleasure outing before an afternoon nap.

It was the first time I had returned to the small country cemetery where Vincent was buried. I didn't know why, but Marie's abortion and the ensuing turmoil had led here, to the edge of this slab covering my brother's bones. I tried to picture his skeleton, the shape of his skull, the state of his teeth. What had happened to his hair, his nails? What was left of his clothes? And his diver's watch, watertight to a depth of thirty feet, with its fluorescent hands and watch face—had it survived all that time six feet under? Refusing to be swept away by a flood of sorrow, my mind threw up phantom dikes of conjecture about Vincent's remains, but those flimsy ramparts gradually collapsed beneath the weight of tears welling up from the depths of our childhood.

I have never prayed. Or understood why people go through the pretense of kneeling and supplicating when there is no one listening. I've never prayed, or truly believed in anything. I see life as a solitary exercise, a journey without a destination, a voyage across a lake whose waters are both calm and foul. Most of the time, we float. Occasionally, our own weight drags us down beneath the surface, and when we touch bottom, when we feel the nauseating slime of our origins, then we feel an ancestral fear, like tadpoles wriggling their way toward death. A life is never anything but *that*. A study in patience, and the bottom is always a bit muddy.

I was sitting on the tomb, quite close to my brother. We were together again at last, side by side, as in times past. I could speak to him, tell him that his departure had set us all into free fall. If he had stayed with us, Papa would doubtless have kept his garage and a stronger heart. Mama would have continued to talk, to laugh at the dinner table, to wear bright colors. And I, at night—I would not have been so scared of drifting down to the bottom of the lake. I told my brother that I had always loved and admired him. I spoke to him of our childhood together, of all that he had meant to me: a reassuring older brother, a humming speedboat carrying me along toward life and adulthood. I told him that I was sorry about the horses and carriage. I confessed to him that I had often daydreamed about wearing his watch on my wrist. Before leaving, I explained to him that I would have liked to hear his opinion, at least once, about what I had made of my life.

I read his name on the gravestone. Our name. The one that made us inseparable. I'm perfectly aware that this pious wish is hopeless, but I like to think that my brother, somewhere, is watching over me.

On my way home from the cemetery, I stopped by Marie's apartment. She seemed in good shape and had already gone back to work a few days earlier. Casually, the way she often concealed her real feelings, she chatted about all sorts of trivial things, carefully—and understandably—avoiding any reference to the visit to Dr. Ducellier, but at some point, I made the mistake of wondering about the future of her affair with Hoover.

"Do you know what Louise Brooks used to say?" she asked, after a moment's pause for reflection. "That you can't fall in love with a nice guy. Because the only guys you really love are bastards, and that's just the way it is."

The tip of my tongue went automatically to the still tender crater left by my tooth, which Hoover had finally pulled. I was devastated by what Marie had just told me. Her words had come crashing down on me like some castrating fatality. And even today, sometimes, they still weigh on me.

Anna Villandreux's dazzling beauty, and above all, the way we met, only gave new luster to that disquieting theorem.

In the presence of the woman who was to become my wife, I often experienced the strange phenomenon that affects compasses as they approach the pole. And for a long time, she had only to look at me to shake my defenses, my principles, even my deepest convictions. Anna possessed nothing like Marie's imposing and majestic figure, but her face bewitched you with a regal reserve that nevertheless betrayed an indefinable seductiveness behind the calm of her hazel eyes.

We met one evening at a private party given by Cruise Control, a band whose members were all rich kids with long, shiny hair. They were basically a bunch of good guys who were eternal students, trying to put off their entry into adult life for as long as possible. Apparently immune to angst and materialistic attachments, most of them seemed completely carefree, gorging on earthly pleasures and taking full advantage of the sexual smorgasbord of those times. Anna was the girl-friend of the lead guitar, an occasional musician condemned too young to the grind of studying pharmacolgy. He was a good-looking boy with something feminine about the cut of his jaw, and fingers that looked as long as spider-crab legs. When he was cranking out chords, he seemed awkward, like a clumsy tennis player, always on the brink of disaster, but managing at last to pull off some really fine work. In addition to his talents as a soloist, Grégoire Elias had a reputation as an insatiable womanizer. With undeniable chic, his pals had nicknamed him Zipper.

I think I distrusted Zipper from the first moment I saw him. To me he was a seducer of that cavalier, well-heeled variety so completely bereft of political consciousness, for whom women are a distraction on a par with car racing, slalom skiing, and golf. As soon as I laid eyes on Zipper, I thought of Louise Brooks and Marie. He was the perfect incarnation of Marie's proverbial bastard, whose overweening demands women love so much to satisfy.

I don't remember a lot about that evening, or the people at the party, or the quality of the music. My only real memory is of Anna's face: red lips in a perfect oval, and the eyes of a fawn, planets with dark reflections that always seemed to conceal the unfolding fate of the world. Her neck was slender; indeed, everything about her body was so slim and delicate that you felt she must somehow be above the ordinary laws of gravity. Anna was wearing a dress I will be able to draw until the day I die: a sheath of black jersey that clung flawlessly to her aristocratic derrière and blooming breasts, with their sumptuous nipples you would never associate for even one second with any nutritional function.

From a purely esthetic point of view, Anna Villandreux and Grégoire Elias were a perfect couple. And if you considered their long-range prospects, the practical combination of their family assets and professional aspirations seemed to guarantee them a life of ease. The Elias clan was a vast medical archipelago, in which each island possessed its own specialty and systematically referred its patients for further consultations to the most important radiology and diagnostics center in the city, a facility owned and directed by the family patriarch, Simon-Pierre Elias. And so the tribe lived in a closed circuit, regularly bleeding a captive clientele held in weary submission by an endless succession of modern ailments. Grégoire was both the black sheep for having dropped medicine for the less demanding field of pharmacology and therefore the previously missing link as well in that unbroken chain of medical exploitation. Once in place, he would prove the ultimate racketeer, filling the prescriptions written by his elders. With him, the system would come full circle.

The Villandreuxs did not belong to any dynasty. First-generation petit bourgeois without the advantages of any family network, they had only their industry and determination to rely on. Jean Villandreux was a pragmatic man, down-to-earth, and full of life. A man of firm opinions, he had no patience for abstraction, profiteers, idlers, and leftist ideas in general. With equal savoir faire, he ran a prefabricated swimming-pool company and a weekly national sports magazine that concentrated on soccer and rugby. Far removed from a world she considered too masculine, Martine Villandreux had started out as a general practitioner but for the past fifteen years had been performing plastic surgery in a clinic specializing in nose jobs, breast remodeling, and face-lifts. She had passed on her luminous beauty to her daughter, and her face now bore the invaluable patina that comes from life's tiny wrinkles of disillusionment.

The Villandreux and Elias families moved in the same universe, even though their respective planets clearly did not possess equal gravitational pull. On that evening in early spring, however, unaware of such subtleties and knowing nothing about these accomplished families, I had eyes only for their paired offspring: Anna, a stunning apparition, and Zipper, whom I wished dead, then and there, as he was attempting a solo by Santana. From that day on, I devoted my whole life to spending time in their presence. I had to approach them, infiltrate their circle, gain their sympathy, become a familiar figure. When I look back on that period, I see myself as spiderlike: patient, resolute, blind to the world, focused on my task, spinning the innumerable threads of my amorous web.

Through constant application, a certain artfulness picked up during leftist debates, and the ultra-laid-back style of the times, I found myself adopted before the spring was over. With Grégoire, of course, I talked music. He had conventional taste of a stupefying mediocrity, waxing sincerely enthusiastic over dreadful groups like America, Ash Ra Tempel, Pink Floyd, Kraftwerk, and the inexcusable Jethro Tull. There was no sophistication, not the slightest coherence in his choices. Frankly, he had the taste of a jukebox. Aside from music, he loved skiing in winter, sailing in summer, sports cars, and, all year round, girls who would put out. Long weeks of observation had led me to believe that Grégoire did not love Anna. I mean not really, not enough to lose any sleep, much less cut off his own arm. Anna was on the same footing as an MGB cabriolet, Kastle skis, a Fender guitar, and the band Yes. She was one of those accessories that make life sweeter, more agreeable. In Grégoire's mind she wasn't exactly an object, but certainly the best thing he had found on the market to stroke his ego. He rarely showed her any affection, treating her instead more like a good pal whose breasts he sometimes enjoyed contemplating while downing a martini. Anna and Grégoire formed one of those make-believe couples who are photographed in front of an exemplary villa or in an English convertible. They seemed to exist only in the illusion of representation, like a trick of the light.

Concentrating on her professional future, Anna seemed satisfied with that minimal mode of life and a boyfriend devoid of mystery. Grégoire was so transparent and predictable that Anna was guaranteed complete control. She had inherited her father's ambitious spirit, and she never hesitated to tackle the world head-on. Anna was two years older than I was and already had a degree in economics. She had one more year to go in law school, and was working as a legal intern.

The longer I studied them, the more convinced I became that Anna had no real affinity for Grégoire Elias and that there was no reason for her to keep seeing him. If I had been blessed with even a glimmer of lucidity, I would have quickly figured out that she had no reason to be interested in me either.

During the summer Elias spent a few weekends at the seashore with his group of friends and fellow musicians. Grégoire and entourage went from place to place, depending on the season, like a flock of geese. Anna hated that kind of migration and preferred to stay in Toulouse. She lived with her parents, even though she had the keys to Grégoire's place and sometimes stayed there several times a week. That apartment looked out onto the stately trees of the Jardin Royal, a princely and peaceful view in the very center of a city so busy that it always made you feel as though you were late for an appointment. I had been a guest many times in the vast living room furnished with Knoll armchairs and sofas, where Grégoire liked to give parties for his friends in Cruise Control. Parties with the requisite sex, drugs, and, unfortunately, insipid music. The ritual never varied: about thirty guests, alcohol, a tajine or platter of couscous, background music, people talking through mouthfuls of food, sophomoric dirty jokes, a little grass or coke to put color in everyone's cheeks, clothes that gradually become a burden, guests pairing off in ever more illicit combinations, multiple couplings, free-trade zones, and then that period of slackening off when people peel themselves apart, their skin still damp from something more like dazed bewilderment than contentment. I saw all sorts of things on those evenings: fucked-up guys slamming doors on their own dicks; drunken girls peeing into the sound hole of a guitar; Grégoire himself going down on girls strapped into amazingly realistic dildos. One of the guys in Cruise Control even jerked off his dog, who'd been prepped with a hefty slice of the signature house dessert, hash brownies.

Although she did breeze through one time, Anna avoided these gatherings, which she clearly recognized as vulgar frat parties for retard musicians. It didn't bother her at all that Grégoire was the host and a prime mover of these affairs. And he was quite open about amusing himself like a soldier on leave. He laughed all the time. It was only natural. You had to have *some* fun. Anyway, that's how he was brought up.

Whenever I was there, I always had the vague fear that Anna would drop by unexpectedly and catch me in the living room on all fours like a she-wolf, suckling (from my single and turgescent "breast") a classics teacher high on hashish and the Philistine delirium of Jethro Tull. There was really no reason for me to worry or feel such convoluted guilt, but somehow I felt as if I were cheating on Anna.

That was a strange time. Most of us went through it like an undiscovered continent of unlimited freedom, vast unknown territories existing only for the pursuit of unrestricted pleasure with no holds barred. We were offered an unprecedented adventure, a profound upheaval in the relationship between men and women, stripped of all religious trappings and social conventions. That implied a rejection of monogamy, an end to the concept of bodies as property, the abolition of jealousy, and also, why not, a fair shot at hedonism for the workers of the world.

Toward the middle of the night, when he'd shot his wad and nothing mattered anymore, Grégoire Elias would come collapse next to me to chat, since there wasn't much time left to kill. I intrigued him. As he put it, I was the only leftist he knew. We tried to talk politics a few times, but that was a superhuman effort for him, like pushing an enormous granite boulder with his forehead. He stumbled over basic concepts, floundered among the tiniest abstractions, and always gave up in the end, trotting out his magic formula: "You say that now but tomorrow you'll wind up like everyone else."

Talking about music was no picnic either.

"You hear that? It's so cool with my new amp—a Harman Kardon, two hundred watts, with Lansing speakers. All new everything, even the cables. Can you tell the difference?"

"The sound's good, but the stuff you listen to! Might as well use an old Teppaz."

"I don't get what bugs you about what people like. You've got really weird taste. I mean, you're the only guy I know who doesn't like the Beatles."

"That's just how it is."

"Still, shit, the Beatles . . ."

"Their stuff's too tricky, too English, it puts me off."

"Hey, wait a minute, you can't say things like that. Tell me again the names of the guys you like, you know, so I can see. . . ."

"Curtis Mayfield, John Mayall, the Isley Brothers, Brian Eno, Marvin Gaye, Soft Machine, Bob Seger."

"But who are they? Fuck, I've never heard of a single one of them. I'm sure that if you asked anyone here they'd say the same. I'll tell you something: music isn't complicated. You put your coin in the machine and if the whole room isn't dancing in thirty seconds, it's 'cause it's shit. Did you get yourself sucked off tonight?"

What could I say? I was in his apartment, on his designer leather sofa, steeped in his hashish oil, stuffed with Oriental pastries, and in love with his girlfriend. I felt as never before how hard it is to share good moments with people who neither think nor see the world as you do. I was becoming convinced that there could be political disagreements between a man and a woman that were much deeper and more irreconcilable than any incompatibilities of personality. And yet there I was, madly in love with a right-wing girl, from a right-wing family, who fucked her wealthy right-wing boyfriend several times a week.

Anna grew more lovely with each passing summer day. As the sun brought out her southern beauty, her skin glowed like polished chestnut wood. We were seeing each other more often, and it wasn't unusual for me to tag along on her errands while Grégoire was off doing something athletic. I enjoyed those consumer hikes. I loved walking with her and watching her buy things. Her way of trying on shoes pleased me, and so did her way of paying, of always refusing to take her receipt. And of course we had to hurry along, without wasting time, even if we didn't have much else to do. Occasionally we had a drink on the terrace of a café, and I would watch her arm muscles rippling softly in the sunshine, or tiny beads of perspiration pearling at the base of her throat. I hadn't yet dared share with her my theory about tibias, but hers were striking, as elegant as the prow of a sailboat, and they took my breath away whenever I allowed myself a look at her legs.

At such moments, Grégoire Elias had never existed and neither had the sexual revolution. Anna was mine, all mine, and I had every intention of keeping her by my side like that for the rest of my life.

After leaving my job at Marie Curie, I had moved out of the apartment on the Allée des Soupirs and returned to live with my parents until I found new employment. Physically diminished by his health problems, my father seemed to have shrunk into himself, and his face was much changed. When he went upstairs to his office, he looked like an old man climbing the last steps of life. His mind was still alert, however, and he was philosophical about the mounting failures of his worn-out body. When we ate together, my father never complained about his health. On the other hand, he never failed to remind me of something that in the last four years had become a constant worry to him.

"Do you realize that I'm going to die without ever seeing the apartment in Torremolinos except in a photo?"

The apartment in Torremolinos. That story went back to 1971. On the advice of his young garage manager, my father had acquired a small apartment in Spain that year, in the resort town of Torremolinos on the southern tip of the peninsula, hard by the Strait of Gibraltar. A wise investment, "gilt-edged," my father kept saying during all the months that preceded the signing. He had bought the place in the blueprint stage on the strength of a guarantee to recover his investment in ten years. The underlying principle was simple: you invest the capital sum; the developer then builds the apartment while retaining the right to rent it out for his own profit eleven months out of the year for ten years; in return, he undertakes to pay you 10 percent of your initial investment every year. At the end of the contract, you are therefore the owner of an apartment that has cost you nothing. My father seemed delighted with the ingenuity of that arrangement, a financial magic trick, the quintessence of equitable business. Although he examined the deal from every angle, he couldn't find a single flaw, not one hitch, with the interests of both parties safely preserved. I did not share his enthusiasm, however, and had even come within an inch of scuttling the transaction.

For reasons of inheritance, the apartment had been put in my name, which placed me in an almost untenable position. How could I advocate plastic bomb attacks on the Spanish consulate, demonstrate against executions by garroting, consort with the most radical anti-Francoists, and at the same time "invest" in Iberian real estate—a veritable golden goose for the generalissimo—the sum of *un millón veintiuna mil quinientas cincuenta pesetas,* the total cost of the eighty-four square meters of apartment 196 in Tamarindos 1, a building right on the beach of that impossible Costa del Sol? Although my father insisted at length that this was just an investment and that deep down, he felt as I did, I couldn't bring myself to share his hypocrisy. It was only at the end of a long campaign during which my mother deftly used my father's ill health to force my hand that I agreed to lend my name to this scheme, which I found increasingly repellent.

On the day the papers were signed, I felt that I'd made a Faustian bargain. The representative of Iberico, the real estate company, was treating me as though I were some ally of the regime. Every page of the contract began with: *"La Sociedad Financiera Internacional de Construcciones y Don Paul Blick, de nationalidad francesa, mayor de edad, estudiante, natural y vecino de Toulouse, con domicilio Allée des Soupirs . . ."* El señor Peña Fernández-Peña, the company's agent, was a caricature of the mealymouthed Iberian front man. With his slicked-back hair and rectangular tortoiseshell glasses, he could just as easily have been a maître d' in a Spanish inn or the director of surveillance and information in an office of the Guardia Civil. While I was signing the last pages of the original document, he was talking to me about copies that would be sent to me later by a certain Don Alfonso del Moral y de Luna, the senior managing partner of the firm. And it was then, on the very last page of the contract, that I discovered the name and address of the notary chosen by Iberico to endorse all these transactions: Carlos Arias Navarro, Calle del General Sanjurjo, Madrid. Arias Navarro. I couldn't believe my eyes. I was doing business, practically in the flesh, with one of the most influential ministers of the caudillo.

I never dared tell that story to anyone, and until the whole business ended in 1981 in the most outlandish way, it almost made me feel as if I'd been a collaborator. And so, despite my father's periodic lamentation over this distant investment he would never lay eyes on, with its inaccessible beach of white sand, his whining never aroused the slightest compassion in me. Especially since at the end of that summer in 1975 I was preoccupied with finding a quiet job, nothing fancy, a temporary position whereby I could earn a living for a year or two. It was Anna who came to my rescue by mentioning me to her father. He happened to need a replacement for one of his sports reporters, who was about to retire. Jean Villandreux soon met with me in his office on the Allées Jules-Guesde, a luminous cocoon paneled in blond wood and connected to a small room done up in extravagantly virile decor. Published every Monday, *Sports Illustrés* was a national weekly magazine devoted mostly to rugby and soccer. For a small fortune, Jean Villandreux had bought this periodical from its founder, Émile de Wallon, the legal owner since 1937. Still printed in large format on maize-yellow paper, *Sports Illustrés* was one of those immutable publications unaffected by anything—wars, progress, prosperity—and that new generations find exactly as their predecessors have left them. You could put it on your night table, set off on a ten-year voyage, and upon your return, pick up reading right where you'd left off. In *Sports Illustrés,* nothing, except the final scores, ever varied.

"Are you a sports fan?"

"Soccer, but especially rugby."

"Have you played?"

"Yes, both."

"Actually, I don't really need a specialist, more a jack-of-all-trades. Someone who can dash off a report in the stadium on Sunday, then come back to the office to record the scores sent in by our regional correspondents, as well as revise their articles. And when I say revise . . . Have you already written for a newspaper or a magazine?"

"Never."

"You think you could do this?"

"Frankly, I don't know."

"Sociology, right?"

"That's it."

"Nothing to do with sports."

"Not a thing."

"My daughter tells me that you're clever, so let's say that we'll try this out together. You come here Sunday morning, the managing editor will explain the work to you, and he'll assign you a match to cover that afternoon. We'll see each other again here on Monday at noon. Your name's Block?"

"Blick."

Jean Villandreux spent at least two hours every day at that office. He adored the atmosphere of this magazine impregnably cushioned against all the jolts and upheavals of the outside world. When he had bought the firm, he'd known nothing about the press, its rules, laws, or rhythms. He loved sports, however, and more than anything, he loved sports gossip: the bickering among players, the rumors about trades, the pressures on coaches, the secret salaries, the doping scandals, the groupies trailing around after the star players, and the club presidents, too, who led wild lives of yachts and Ferraris behind their laconic public images. Villandreux did not belong to that small world of well-paid muscularity, but he enjoyed being able to watch it through the porthole of his office. It was a welcome change, in any case, from the stressful business of building swimming pools.

"You know my daughter?"

"Fairly well."

"Seems you squire her around when Grégoire isn't there."

"That's about it."

"What do you think of Elias?"

"He's somebody who skis in winter and sails in summer."

"Ha-ha! I like that. Right on the button. In other words, a real asshole."

Leaving his office, I had the feeling that I'd scored some points. I had not yet spoken to Jean Villandreux about my salary, but if only to hear the boss comment like that about my rival, I was ready to work for free.

That Sunday I turned up bright and early at the newspaper, feeling like a man about to have a first go at parachute jumping. My five years of university had not prepared me for this. I knew a lot of phrases such as "The political regime governing any human society is always the expression of the economic regime at the heart of that society" (Kropotkin), but they wouldn't help me describe a sliding tackle or figure out who was offside.

Louis Lagache, the managing editor, a man of old-fashioned courtesy, used the formal *vous* with his subordinates, called them all "friend," and deployed a large and erudite vocabulary with a casual ease that belied the popular image of off-color newsroom slang.

"So you are the gentleman recommended by our director. Welcome to the club, friend. I trust that you will be the Golconda we have long awaited."

"What's a Golconda?"

"I mean a diamond in the rough, friend, a kind of unpolished carbuncle."

I didn't dare ask him what a carbuncle was. I had too much to learn before my first assignment—which fact seemed lost on Louis Lagache, who burbled on endlessly.

"Do not worry, friend. We'll have a word in a little while to settle any petty practical matters. And of course, heavens, do not forget that the important word in *Sports Illustrated* is . . ."

"Sports?"

"No, friend, no. Illustrated. At our paper, the key word is *illustrated*. Never forget that what readers of magazines such as ours love above all else are images of victory, photos of heroic effort, pictures of exploits. Writing the little scribbles wound around those snaps is never more than an effort of modest silkworms spinning legends, captioning clichés. Have I made myself clear?"

Lagache insisted on using fancy language to speak of simple things, as if floating above the hurly-burly of sports journalism. I would later learn that behind his mannered façade he was a consummate professional who could rescue desperate situations and wax eloquent about games he made it his duty never to attend. When I asked him one day how he had acquired his expertise, he tossed off a jaunty reply.

"That entire little world is so predictable, friend, and the events as repetitious as the conventions of theatrical farce: people come, go, enter, leave, doors slam, lovers pop out of closets. Mind you, I do not believe that this routine is the prerogative of the sporting universe. One finds this misoneism in every socioprofessional milieu. What I think, friend, is that man, even of the muscular variety, is still a little fellow."

Lagache was the only one of the editorial staff to see the world with such detachment. Most of the others were intensely involved with the vicissitudes of the sporting market, constantly analyzing trends and events. The soccer specialists, by far the most obsessive, religious scribes of endless statistics, tracked the performances of players after every game, and then spent hours debating which eleven should join the lineup of the "Team of the Week."

Sports journalism, and journalists in general, never enjoyed much standing in my family. I will never forget my father's consternation when I told him that after five years of higher education I had decided to work as a reporter. Rubbing his eyes, he murmured, "I would even have preferred that you join the police."

After two weeks of apprenticeship, I signed on at a decent salary to spend my weekends in damp half-empty stadiums. Sometimes I followed the teams on the road. Sharing the lives of professional soccer players—or simply traveling with them—is a depressing and even noxious experience. When not on the field, and not in training, those guys take naps and play cards. They may have superpowerful bodies, but they have the interests and private lives of infants. And they quickly marry carelessly peroxided blond nurses, whom they suckle like nice little boys before going to sleep (and sleeping late), while the wife keeps an eye on the career: pushing a ball around.

It was hopeless to try having a serious conversation with guys raised in the cult of the strong, silent sports star: winners or losers, gifted or unlucky, they relied solely on the twenty-five words or so issued to them by the training centers of the Rugby Federation. The coaches were no better: when their teams lost, they always managed to make themselves scarce. In victory, they strutted through the halls like roosters in Lycra (emblazoned with the logos of the club's commercial sponsors).

I hated locker rooms after the games. "Every defeat has something to teach us" or "I think we're turning a corner now." At such moments, feeling curdled with shame, I knew exactly what my father had meant about joining the police.

At *Sports Illustrés* there were reporters who specialized in whipping up crises—cunning investigators, wily, insinuating hypocrites capable of starting major conflagrations with a single nasty paragraph. They'd go see one team, then the other, fanning sparks here, adding tinder there, just to publish daily reports on the effects of their meddling, and disagreements that should have been settled in private over a glass of wine wound up as headlines or sent to arbitration.

"Did you think, friend, that journalism was a noble activity engaged in by gentlemen with virtuous motivations? You know what the poet

Paul Valéry used to say: 'I am an honest man, which means that I approve of most of my actions.' All my men are like that: convinced—like most reporters, in fact—of the validity of their malfeasance."

Although today I find it difficult to remember exactly what Louis Lagache looked like, his voice—composed, rather deep, beautifully modulated—continues to rumble along inside me like an endless, distant thunderstorm. Listening to him all those years ago, I felt as if I were in the presence of the last relict of a vanished time, a blasé survivor whose quintessentially French wit was deployed solely to iron out the ugly creases of daily life.

In two months so many things had changed in mine that sometimes I had the uncanny feeling of spying on someone else's existence. First there had been my job at the magazine, so unexpected and unlike me; then the new, almost too sophisticated apartment I had just moved into; and above all, Anna's unlikely and abrupt decision to move in with me.

In one evening she had left Grégoire Elias, loaded most of her belongings from her parents' home into her tiny Morris, and moved them to my place. As someone who endlessly ponders the repercussions of moving a single pawn, I have always been fascinated by those natures capable of deliberately provoking a domestic earthquake, repudiating a settled existence with a few words, emptying out a closet, moving from one house to another, changing beds, partners, habits, sometimes even opinions, and doing it, as the ancient Aramaeans said, in less time than it takes a nanny goat to kid.

Elias had been sent packing. A sudden, unexpected, immediate expulsion. His case had been decided in an instant. He was there, and a moment later, he was gone. Along with his MG, his boat, his Docksiders, his Harman Kardon, his Lansings, his Vox, his Fender, his Lacostes, his Jethro Tull, and his pharmaceutical aspirations. What terrible thing had he done to fall from grace? As far as I know, nothing in particular. As I heard later, he'd been his usual self that evening: rich, cheerful, playful, but also rude, crude, lewd, and a boor. This cocktail, formerly the secret of his success, had proved fatal. Anna's character, I would discover, resembled those infinity pools her father built, and like those solid constructions, she could placidly take the massive pressure of a great deal of resentment, but when the critical threshold was reached, the entire reservoir overflowed in all directions. And that evening, unaware that he was approaching the danger zone, Grégoire Elias had simply gone for his usual little dip.

Taking advantage of Elias's absence during the five days leading up to that breakup, Anna and I had hardly left each other's side. Immersed in a kind of sensual intoxication, we had taken complete inventory of our talents and tastes, a frenetic experiment we conducted in Grégoire's empty apartment. Being with Anna on those premises, unencumbered by their detested owner, his entourage of jerks, and their frightful music, was a slightly perverse and definitely exciting exercise—a succession of suns and moons beneath which I was kneaded, manipulated, licked, swallowed, caressed: a dazzling voyage of one hundred and twenty hours during which I felt as if a shaman were slipping butterflies with incandescent wings into my chest.

It all seemed to happen outside our control. We hadn't planned a thing. Chance had merely arranged for the tectonic forces that work in "the darkness within" to finally bring to light the loving conjunction of our continents. When he returned and slipped his key into the lock, Grégoire Elias had no way of knowing that behind the door waited a rigged trial, a kangaroo court that would consign him, summarily, to the limbo of brazen vanity.

Living with Anna was as simple and pleasant as biking down a long shore road on a summer afternoon, with life humming softly in your ears and a breeze caressing your face with the scent of new-mown hay. Hours and days tiptoe smoothly by, and at night, when you open your eyes, you have that precious feeling of having found your place on this earth.

I was slowly discovering Anna's real character, a complex, protean geography, where paths along the heights are flanked by chasms that take your breath away. There was so much more fragility, sadness, and generosity in the eyes of that woman than in the indifferent gaze of the courtesan who had floated along in the boisterous wake of Grégoire Elias. From the moment we began living together, I don't believe we ever discussed him again, or even mentioned his name. It was almost as though he had never existed.

The first crack in this enchantment appeared on November 20, 1975. Driving home from *Sports Illustrés*, I heard on the car radio that Franco had died. I was overjoyed. I remember passing a stream of exiles driving slowly along the Boulevard Carnot, honking out their excitement and waving black-and-red flags. I detoured past the Spanish consulate, where a crowd rejoiced, clapping their hands and singing Catalan songs. For more than thirty years, tens of thousands of Spanish Republicans and refugees in Toulouse had been waiting for this moment.

When Anna came through the front door, I could hardly contain myself, delighted with the news I had to tell her.

"Did you hear? Franco is dead!"

"So?"

I felt as if I'd been dropped into a void, swinging at the end of a rope that might break at any moment to send me plunging down among all the caudillo's black souls. All she'd said was "So?"—and my world collapsed. Elias might have said the same thing. Elias and all the hangers-on who lounged around his apartment. "So?" I understood with a jolt that the emotional and carnal ties that bound me to Anna had blinded me to our profound incompatibility. We belonged to parallel universes. We hadn't been breathing the same air, or sharing the same atmosphere. Leftism was my theology, while she ranked politics somewhere down with macramé. My lousy eighty-four square meters way off in Spain gnawed at me every night, whereas her family business shamelessly sold pools to the loveliest homes on the Costa Brava. I was still reading the theoreticians of revolution; she subscribed to glossy business magazines.

Only a king-size bed was a level enough field on which to reconcile our differences. On that modest surface we let our bodies take over, and they acquitted themselves quite well, working as allies for as long as the tournament lasted, then leaving each contestant to compare, in silence, the relative merits of bourgeois fellatio and left-wing cunnilingus. But were thirty square feet of high-density latex a large enough base for a loving, meaningful relationship? In spite of my laid-back ways, I had a deep craving for stability in those days, a desire to love only one woman—and for as long as possible. I even had a detailed model for the ideal companion: a girl who would look like Sinika and think like my brother, Vincent; someone who would love me and also bring me to my senses whenever I began going off track; a person with whom I could play, putter around, smoke some weed, sleep out under the stars; someone to whom I could tell the sacred story of the toy coach and speak about the haunted apartment on the Allée des Soupirs, and with whom I would never feel the burden of being alive. Or the fear of dying alone.

But with just one little word I tumbled back down to earth and understood that in reality I was in love with a Giscardian bourgeoise, a fierce free-trade advocate, a selfish economist (of admittedly exceptional beauty) for whom Guernica would never be anything but a provincial town in Biscay Province, famous for its foundries in the Mundaca Valley.

I don't believe Anna noticed my dismay. And why would she? After all, from her point of view, "So?" was a perfectly neutral response.

"You know, I've got a problem with the car," she added. "If I accelerate too fast, the engine starts skipping, as if there weren't enough gas."

"I'll go down and have a look at it."

"Now?"

I'd grabbed the chance to leave the room, concentrate on something else, and forget what had just happened by taking a serious hit of heady gas fumes. I spent a good hour in the cold semidarkness messing around with the platinum-tipped screws, spark plugs, and even the fuel pump of the Morris, the fenders and underside of which were showing the first nibbles of rust. When I went back upstairs, I found Anna lying on a sofa reading a biography of Adam Smith.

On the pretext that this economist had begun to write *An Inquiry into the Nature and Causes of the Wealth of Nations* in Toulouse in 1765, Anna had chosen this father of liberalism as a guru whom she used to justify all the excesses of modern capitalism. She much admired the optimism of this Scot for whom the market was a self-regulating entity, thanks to the natural equilibrium of supply and demand.

"If you want to understand Smith," she would tell me, "you must accept his position that there is nothing wrong in fostering private interests, since they all eventually wind up converging toward the general good."

By virtue of these axioms established more than two centuries ago by the venerable Scotsman, Anna Villandreux, following in her father's footsteps, was preparing to make a fortune, and consequently (she sincerely believed) to fill our national coffers.

At the office the next day, no one mentioned Franco's death. Except Louis Lagache, who was delighted to engage me on this subject as soon as I walked in.

"Did you notice, friend, how promptly that little Spanish king jumped into the bedroom slippers of power? These aristocrats are unbelievable. Indestructible, really. They remind me of bacteria flash-frozen by history, spirochetes put to sleep but capable of springing back to life at the slightest warming of the atmosphere."

"What are spirochetes?"

"If I were to say spiriferous brachiopoda instead, I don't suppose that would get us anywhere. So let's say a fossil genus of Paleozoic bivalve mollusks having a shell with two spiral appendages at the hinge. Getting back to our subject, have you read that unforgettable article claiming that this Monsieur Franco carefully kept all his nail clippings in tiny silver boxes? We were familiar with the talent for tyranny displayed by this antediluvian specimen, and now we discover that the lout was also an onychophage. . . . You smile, but you say nothing. Sometimes you intrigue me, especially when you affect that little air of not giving a fig about what anyone says to you. See, right now, one would need to be clever indeed to divine what you're thinking. In any case, friend, I shouldn't imagine that you'd be shocked by what I've just said. You are too young and your hair is too long for you to love dictators and respect kings."

"You know, you're the only one at the magazine who doesn't use the informal *tu* with me."

"I have always detested the professional use of *tutoiement,* a rather grubby familiarity that insists that the members of a trade guild throw aside the most elementary courtesy in the name of I don't know what good fellowship."

"While I think of it, have you decided which game I should attend on Sunday?"

"When you consult the schedule board you will see that this Sunday, you will remain here. You will be in charge of organizing and rereading the rugby pages. That will give you a change from the little soccer sodomites. And you will spend the day inside, where it's warm."

Now that I was living with his daughter, Villandreux had been avoiding me. He no longer called me into his office to joke about Elias, share the latest backroom gossip, or ask me how I felt about Lagache and if I understood everything he said. The two men maintained a strange relationship of mingled fascination, envy, contempt, and a very masculine form of affection. Villandreux possessed the wealth, but felt impoverished in the face of his employee's erudition and efflorescent vocabulary. And while Lagache was a master wordsmith, he was chronically broke and often reduced to participating in the humiliating "petty cash" ceremony. Clinging proudly to his dignity, he had resisted this ritual for many years until, driven by necessity and an immoderate fondness for the track, he had joined the queue like everyone else, holding out his hand and saying, "Thank you, Monsieur Villandreux."

The "petty cash" was a small wine gift box of white wood, kept stuffed with five-hundred-franc bills and locked in the executive secretary's wall safe.

Every week Villandreux would meet with the seven department heads of *Sports Illustrés* in his elegant office. He would ask his assistant, Marianne, to bring the little treasure chest, and in accordance with their respective merits, he then parceled out hefty weekly bonuses to his "seven mercenaries," as he called them. With the money changing hands openly, it was an embarrassing moment for all the recipients. What had they done to merit such largesse? What were the criteria of

excellence? In what way had the less well rewarded failed? The partici-
pants in that ceremony had long ago given up asking themselves such
questions; they now simply disguised their uneasiness, took the money,
and thanked their eccentric and generous boss, who somehow managed
to arrange things so that at the end of the month, everyone's bonuses
added up to about the same amount. But in that case, why not just give
all these department heads the same official raises? This would have
made the accounting department's work easier, of course—while de-
livering a heavy blow to the boss's ego at the same time, however, and
that ego was quite sensitive to its erectile position.

Whenever he noticed me, Villandreux would wave casually. Anna
had made the mistake of picking me up at the office two or three times,
which was enough for the entire editorial staff to begin thinking of me
as "the guy fucking the boss's daughter." I could understand that Villandreux, usually a monster of tactlessness, might cling to his personal
conception of acceptable protocol, and he had probably concluded that
his image as a benevolent proprietor would only be tarnished through
association with a supposedly libidinous underling whom everyone
assumed had landed his job thanks to his "magic wand." This being the
case, Villandreux, so attuned to office scuttlebutt, had no reason to seek
my company.

A strange dinner party reestablished more cordial relations between
us. Anna's parents had insisted on inviting us over on the first of January, the day after a New Year's Eve that had clearly left its mark on the
faces of our hosts. With their pasty complexions and woozy eyeballs, so
telling of nights beclouded by sex, alcohol, or other substances, Martine
and Jean Villandreux still seemed to be slightly intoxicated, as if by a
delayed-action drug. They barely touched their rosy goose liver, a few
Arcachon oysters, and some broiled swordfish. Toward the end of the
meal, perhaps somewhat restored by the bracing marine protein, Jean
Villandreux warmed to the occasion, even placing a hand on my shoulder
to ensure my complicity while he gleefully skewered my predecessor.

"Tell me, Paul, does Anna talk a lot to you about Adam Smith?"

"Very little."

"That's a good sign. When my daughter's fed up with a fellow she bombards him nonstop with Adam Smith. I've noticed that, right, Martine? Toward the end, with Elias, it was Smith morning, noon, and night."

"Papa . . ."

"What, it's not true? When you came here that's all I heard, Smith this, Smith that. Of course, I must admit that with Grégoire the choice of conversational subjects was limited. That guy was a real calamity."

"Papa, will you please cut it out?"

"You know what I said to your mother when she told me you were going out with him? 'Elias? Alas!' Jacques Goude, who knows the family well, told me that Grégoire was an even bigger jerk than his father, who'd already acquired a reputation as quite a large one."

"Papa . . ."

"But Paul's the one who really nailed that idiot. The first time we met I asked him what he thought of Elias. And you know what he said? You remember, Paul? 'He's a guy who skis in the winter and sails in the summer.' Anna, one day you'll have to explain to me what you ever saw in that dope."

"Jean, you're becoming downright rude."

That was Martine Villandreux. Her voice sleek with fatigue. A cigarette poised at her manicured fingertips. Her bangs falling negligently over her forehead. One strap of her black dress slipping off her shoulder. She was unbelievably disturbing. Without a doubt the most sensual woman I've ever known. Dripping with languor, her face delicately etched by time, her body sheathed in a few curves, Martine Villandreux outshone the innocent perfection of a daughter twenty-five years her junior. That woman exuded an erotic power as strong and unmistakable as the scent of freshly cut grass. On that rocky New Year's Day evening, all I wanted was for the father to go off with his daughter and leave me alone with the mother. Then I'd watch her finish her cigarette. In her mouth, I'd taste the flavor of moist tobacco. And there wouldn't be much to say. She would walk away, to the bathroom, leaving the door wide open. I would follow her. She would take off her panties, sit down on the toilet, and release a stream of urine. Hearing the faint sound of that waterfall, I'd close my eyes. With the humility of a pilgrim, I'd kneel down and slip my bent arm up between her legs, and with my hand clamped on her crotch, things would loosen up. Tongues would explore all possible holes, licking everything in sight. There would be no more front or back, face or profile. Mouths would be full, plus hands, throats, and anything else available. The skin of grappling bodies would stretch in different directions, channeling runoff like pagan gargoyles, and all sorts of liquids would trickle down inside of thighs. Words would ride to the rescue. They would slip into ears with reptilian stealth. She would murmur, "I'm sucking my daughter's favorite balls." And then we would be surrounded by that sacrilegious glow, that gratifying feeling that our treachery had not been in vain. Next it would become impossible to tell the difference between human postures and the positions of dogs. This clash of flesh would exude the marine odors of life, as the spindrift of cum lubricated the last orifices. Teeth would bite into skin. He would plunge in up to the hilt, digging his own grave, and she would lead him to the brink of his downfall. And then, since he'd come all that way, he would topple into that unctuous gulf where so many others had perished before him.

Afterward, simply wipe up a few traces of memory . . .

And none of that would ever have existed.

"Do you enjoy working at the magazine?"

Martine Villandreux clearly couldn't have cared less about my answer or my involvement with *Sports Illustrés*. She was simply pretending, in spite of her hangover, to be interested in her daughter's new boyfriend. Without even giving me time to reply, moreover, she turned to her husband.

"You haven't given the children their presents!"

"What presents?"

"Jean, you're impossible. The ones on the chest, out in the front hall."

"They're for them?"

Nothing very original. A costly fountain pen for me, an exorbitantly expensive pair of boots (and a fat check) for Anna.

"Happy New Year to you both."

Martine Villandreux kissed us efficiently and the whole thing was over before we knew it. Then, as suddenly as a popping champagne cork and without any preamble, Jean Villandreux launched into an unexpected critique of the general inadequacy of Giscardism, that "bastard branch of de La Tour-Fondue," the family name of Giscard's great-great-grandmother.

"You should never trust guys who claim to be descended from Crusaders via brand-new stepladders. Do you realize that here we are in the twentieth century with a president of the Republic—and let me repeat that word, republic—who married a woman named Anne-Aymone Sauvage de Brantes and called his two daughters Valérie-Anne and Jacinthe? With such airs, I shouldn't be surprised if one day this country votes for the Left."

No one felt up to commenting on that abrupt outburst of civic indignation. Jean Villandreux poured himself a glass of Pomerol and drank it in little sips with his eyes closed. After a bit more small talk, everyone quickly decided to go to bed. The mother with the father, and the daughter with me.

For a long time I was troubled and embarrassed by the physical attraction I felt for Anna's mother. Whenever I was with her, I picked up her sexual vibrations, which were particularly in tune with my own, but this reception turned to static later that year, in the middle of the summer, when something important happened.

When Anna told me that she was pregnant, I felt as if a high-speed train had just rocketed by me. When the moment of fear had passed, a pleasant warmth flooded my body: all the muscles at the back of my neck relaxed, and joy of a whole new kind (sizzling, impetuous, a little anxious) introduced me to the very first feelings of paternity. The weak-kneed father that I was took the mother-to-be in his arms . . . and sensed her coldness, her distance, almost—even—her absence. She told him that this was a catastrophe; he did not understand why. She repeated that she was not ready, that she could not keep the child. He said nothing, even though he knew what all that meant. He had already carried the gym bag and the clean towels. At night he had held Marie's hand. And during the day kept track of the painkillers. But this time, he knew it would be much, much worse. Because the father was not Edgar Hoover.

For a week Anna swung between periods of doubt and moments of certainty. Whenever she wavered, she had good reasons to justify her confusion. I could understand that. It was more difficult for me, however, to accept never really being consulted when she mulled over our future and that of the child. She didn't much care about my thoughts on the matter, for she was thinking above all as an only daughter, bent on protecting her territory from any intrusion. Well, the baby and I, in a way, were obtrusive, even unwelcome guests. Perhaps this was happening too early in a shared life, but I found nothing terrible or frightening in the situation. I loved that girl, she was expecting a baby, I was the father, and a decent monthly salary would allow us to raise the child.

Toward the end of July, in one of her mysterious changes of mind, Anna decided to keep the baby and immediately became a doting expectant mother, enthusiastically and almost fanatically preaching the capitalist advantages of a family and the benefits of maternity. I clearly recall that her decision to forgo an abortion was taken on the day of the execution of Christian Ranucci, the last man to be put to death in France. A few days before that twenty-eighth of July, 1976, Giscard had met with lawyers who pleaded for mercy for Ranucci, who had been condemned by the press rather than by any evidence against him. In the end Giscard had refused to give any indication of what he would do. And on the day of the execution, the president had simply let the hours tick by.

Giscard never gave in. Never picked up his telephone. And Ranucci's head was cut off. This member of the petty nobility, who had bent over backward to "raise" the name of d'Estaing, took his place in history as the last president of the Fifth Republic to allow a prisoner to be guillotined. That July evening, while the television was describing the circumstances and precise time of Ranucci's death, the man who had been elected by majority vote to be our head of state seemed to me a pathetic creature, a contemptible human being. I have never since been able to see his face without thinking of that execution, and suffering an acid reflux of memories.

Anna was two months pregnant when we told our respective families. My parents welcomed the news with as much happiness as they could feel. Stunned, my father saw me in a new light, both tender and skeptical. Only yesterday I'd been a lonely child pushing Dinky Toys around the bedroom carpet, and here I was now with a woman on my arm, in line for the unbelievable title of paterfamilias. I knew that many contradictory feelings and ideas were racing through Victor Blick's mind. In that centrifuged chaos there were probably images of a triumphant Vincent, the Day and Night garage, my mother in a summer dress, me coming home from school, the scribing needle of an electrocardiograph—a whole past, all jumbled together. When the wind died down, he would have to sort through all those bits and pieces, arranging them in order of importance to make space for the anticipated new arrival, the new Blick who would make me a father. But for the moment, Victor Blick simply gazed at me with fond incredulity.

Although she had been emotionally mutilated by Vincent's death, my mother was stirred by the echo of an age-old joy, a feeling from far away, an ovarian shudder dating back, perhaps, to the time when she was pregnant with her first son.

Throughout our visit, Anna was her sole preoccupation. It was obvious that in my mother's eyes, Anna alone carried the keys and the treasure of life. And so my mother showed great gentleness and consideration, allowing herself, it seemed to me, a moment's reprieve from her usual constricting routines. For once, there was nothing to correct, nothing to find fault with, nothing to regret or to cry over. The coming child was the first new thing to reclaim her from her past and let her glimpse a possible future devoted to life.

As for the Villandreuxs, they took the news much less calmly, and Anna's mother, initially dumbstruck, was obviously hard put to hide her hostility. She had certainly had something else in mind for her daughter: a different start in life, better prospects, and a more suitable partner, naturally. Someone from her circle, for example, who would have gone skiing in winter and sailing in summer, like a less disastrous Elias. There seemed to be two Martine Villandreuxs. There was one who appeared to be a reasonably emancipated woman, a blooming creature of liberal convictions who was capable, you felt, of seducing, loving, and openly tasting all the pleasures of life. And there was the other Martine, constrained by conventional Catholicism, hemmed in by the stinginess of bourgeois principles, armed with all the pompous clichés of petty conservatism, a stern, austere, unforgiving woman given to wounding comments and mean-spirited remarks. Faced with this second Martine, you were continually amazed that such a perfect face and inviting body could house so black a soul.

When Martine Villandreux realized that we intended to keep the child, she launched a flank offensive, the consequences of which I had not anticipated.

"And when are you planning to get married?"

In 1976 the world was still old-fashioned, conventional, covertly controlled by religious morality. A child was expected to have an officially recognized mother and father bound together in a time-honored fashion.

"We have no intention of getting married."

Although I'd spoken in a normal tone of voice, without the slightest edge of insolence or aggression, those few words provoked a violent reaction from Anna's mother.

"If you wish to keep this child, that is your business, but I will ask you to behave like responsible parents. A marriage is indispensable. And the earlier the better."

Anna's mother sprang out of her chair and left the room without even looking at her daughter. In a gesture of cowardly solidarity, her husband followed her, giving me the little smile of masculine complicity that often meant, in their milieu, "Women are slaves to their hormones."

Martine Villandreux's brutal attitude and intransigent responses were meant expressly to drive a wedge between me and her daughter along my bias against matrimony. She knew that Anna was psychologically incapable of dealing with family conflict, no matter how slight. That's how Anna was made: the very idea of a disagreement with her parents could plunge her into despair. She was as quick to surrender at the first sign of discord with them as she was to assume the most combative posture in her relations with the outside world.

During the ride home, Anna was already suggesting that marriage "wouldn't be the end of the world, after all, because what difference would it make, and why shouldn't we make our parents happy?"

"I have no intention of making your mother happy by going through an absurd, empty ritual."

"In other words, you're upholding your sacrosanct political principles? You know what? You're as stubborn as she is, and just as unfair."

"What's that supposed to mean? And how am I being unfair? Excuse me, I still have the right to oppose marriage without turning into a savage."

"Anyway, you're always against everything. Your leftist prejudices distort the way you see the world and everyone in it. You have such bizarre reactions."

"What are you talking about?"

"Nothing."

"You're accusing me of bizarre reactions, and I'd like to know what you mean!"

"Well, for example, the day I came home and you told me Franco had died, you were as excited as if you'd just won the national lottery. I call that a bizarre reaction!"

Martine Villandreux had achieved her goal. She had succeeded in injecting her venom between the tree and its bark, between a mother and father. And to advance her rancid scheme of marriage, she had even managed to resurrect the old caudillo from his tomb.

The rounder Anna's belly grew, the more my determination weakened. I clung to my principles like an exhausted mountaineer hanging on a rope, but I was slowly losing my grip. I didn't want to make Anna miserable, or complicate her pregnancy, still less to give my son a bad first impression of his father. I asked only one thing: that I be allowed enough time to capitulate with dignity, and submit with honor. They refused me even that. The affair had to be organized with unseemly haste, and Anna's mother was happy to tell me why.

"You seem surprised that I'm asking you to hurry things along, Paul. Have you no idea of the urgency of this marriage? Can you imagine our embarrassment—and especially Anna's!—if she were to arrive for the ceremony with a huge six- or seventh-month belly? It's a simple question of respect. Sometimes your reactions are truly bizarre."

That day, instead of capitulating to the remodeling of my life, I should have pushed Martine Villandreux over on her sofa, stripped off her finery, and humped her like a Hells Angel. I should have heeded David Rochas's old precept: "If my mother were beautiful, I'd fuck her." I think that would have straightened us all out.

Two weeks later Anna's parents and mine met over dinner. (I forgot to mention that in the euphoria of her victory, Martine Villandreux tried to make her daughter agree—behind my back—to a brief religious ceremony before the event at city hall. The firm refusals of both Anna and her father foiled that plan.) The formal and pretentious dinner was at the Villandreuxs' house. The elaborate table display reminded me of those May Day parades in the former Soviet Union, when the regime would trot out all its hardware and missiles to bully the curious and, above all, to astonish the yokels. I knew Martine Villandreux. I knew she was capable of such baseness. The vermeil dinner service reflected the gleaming silverware, while the crystal stemware set rainbows sparkling in the stoppers of the carafes, and even the knife rests, carved from slabs of Iceland spar, added one more touch of refinement to the setting. Meaning no harm, my parents made no response to this massive deployment of dining artillery. Their life had slowly withdrawn them from the whirl of parties and receptions, and they had long ago forgotten the prideful codes and rules of such petty table games.

Fortunately, Jean Villandreux discovered in my father a first-class interlocutor on the subject of cars. Unlike other topics of conversation, mechanics has the federative power to draw men together, quickly making of them partners or accomplices in luck or misfortune. They have all, at one time or another, had to deal with planetary gears, gaskets and sleeve valves, steering knuckles and master cylinders. These dilemmas create invisible male bonds among drivers victimized by fate. My father expounded his private theory about the decline of the Simca company, and a captivated Villandreux listened as reverently as if granted an audience with the founding father of the firm. My mother had no such luck entrancing her partner in conversation; the aridity and marginality of her work carried no luster in society. After inquiring as a pure formality about the nature of her guest's profession, Martine Villandreux launched into a long self-serving speech on the virtues of plastic surgery, which she saw as a second Women's Liberation, an emancipation allowing every woman to take full possession of her body. The illogical stupidity of her reasoning brought to my mother's face that faraway look and faint smile I knew only too well. Claire Blick was no longer there. She had left that table of vanities and futile ostentation. In that chair sat her double, a lifeless shell as dark as an empty tomb. I imagine that at such moments, my mother must have been dreaming about a life she might have shared with another family in another world. Martine Villandreux, however, continued busily attending to this one. With her dazzling appearance, stylish toilette, and blooming complexion set off by a few jewels, she was simply overwhelming, and quite clearly in command of this family council. In spite of all her charms, however, she seemed increasingly vulgar to me, imposing herself on everyone through this display of wealth, success, elegance, and beauty. Next to her, with her drab clothes, intense silences, and modest and enigmatic smile, my mother seemed a polite lady's maid. While we were having dessert, our hostess made a blunder that brought tears to my eyes. This happened unexpectedly during a turn of conversation that seemed innocent enough. Anna's mother was talking about her daughter growing up as an only child, and explaining how much she would have liked to have had another baby. Fiddling idly with her hair, she turned to my mother and asked, "From what I hear, Paul had a brother, didn't he?"

She said it the way she said everything else, tossing words into the conversational flow, without thinking twice, without imagining for a second that those words could tip the enormous weight of sorrow that had remained in unstable equilibrium over our heads for eighteen years.

Asking that question in the past tense was already an answer in itself. What exactly did she expect? That after two decades of silent bereavement my mother would dredge up moving memories or relate the circumstances of Vincent's death? Was she hoping that Claire Blick would describe her son as he once was: affectionate, generous, loyal, courageous, sturdy, industrious, good-looking, endearing, the owner of a silvery coach and a Kodak Brownie Flash camera? Our entertainment director's question was answered by an uneasy silence. We served ourselves a little more dessert, and the reassuring tinkle of small spoons against the silver-gilt porcelain plates comforted the mistress of the house with the idea that, in painful circumstances, the most important thing is to remember that the show must go on.

When we got home, I let Anna go off to bed while I spent some time alone with my brother's coach and Brownie Flash. I looked at the street for a long time through the viewfinder of his camera. And the simple fact of placing my eye in the center of that frame, where he had so often set his own, made my heart weep.

The visit to city hall really made me feel that I was doing something inexcusable, and I prayed that no one—especially none of my old friends—would see me in that café-waiter's getup. During the worst moments I also imagined that Anna, eager to spring on me one of those silly surprises popular with Anglo-Saxons, had invited my old band Round-Up to provide the music, and I could see them onstage in full formation, unable to play a single note, staring at me as if they'd seen a ghost.

Fortunately, only a few members of my immediate family had been invited to that sad affair, and anyway, they were completely outnumbered by the Villandreux contingent. Their social status but also their taste for grand display had led Anna's parents to throw an incredible party intended to impress everyone. All the Villandreuxs' relatives, friends, and acquaintances were there. Jean had even summoned—which is not too strong a word—the entire editorial staff of *Sports Illustrés*. I suppose that for all those smiling journalists, I was now "the guy who managed to fuck, impregnate, and marry the boss's daughter." Glass in hand, and weaving just a wee bit, Lagache came over to congratulate me.

"Friend, you have an absolutely charming wife, and I wish you all the happiness an honorable inhabitant of this planet may expect. Do you know that I myself was once married? To a sort of termagant pythoness who daily predicted the end of the world and our happiness."

"And did she turn out to be right?"

"In a way. One morning at breakfast, fed up with hearing her obliterate the future like that, I rose and quite calmly, without a word, punched her in the face. Of course I immediately turned over a new leaf. Forgive me, friend, for speaking to you of such woeful exploits on a day like this, but I do believe that this excellent Glenfiddich is making me drunk."

Executing a graceful about-face, Lagache swayed his way off through the crowd to rejoin a few précieuses who were already in ecstasy over his convoluted vocabulary. In this aspirationally princely decor, Lagache unwittingly played to perfection the role of the impertinent courtier.

Abandoning her innumerable friends, Anna came over to sit next to me for a minute.

"What are you thinking about?"

"Oh, I don't know. All this, all these people moving around, dancing, talking . . ."

"Do you think we'll be happy?"

"How should I know?"

"You seem sad."

"It just isn't a very jolly day."

She understood perfectly what I meant. In the end she was embarrassed to have imposed this farce on me when I disapproved of such playacting. She had found me sitting amid this world that was not my own, silently bent under the burden of social conventions. Would we be happy? It was a question for Lagache's ex-wife.

Anna drew her hand across my face, as if to thank me for having accepted all this for her, for having proven that I was *really* marrying her for love. Would she have done the same for me? This time, only she knew the answer to that mystery.

In certain respects, that evening embodied everything that had begun to bother me, and still does, about living in my country. As the novelist Emmanuel Bove had written about something entirely different, it was obvious that "an epoch was coming to an end, and that another would begin, but one necessarily less beautiful than its predecessor." The long period of nonchalance, freedom, and happiness ushered in by May 1968 was definitely over. People had put away their illusions, hitched up their pants, stubbed out their joints of THC, tossed back their hair, and returned to work. Entrusting its concerns to a calculating kinglet who sought the common touch by faking a passion for the accordion, the country had tricked itself out in silly clothes and bought even sillier "attaché cases," which supposedly concealed within their heat-molded frames the essence of twentieth-century power, whereas in reality, without admitting it to themselves, people were secretly dragging around their shame and misery at having shrunk back into their little selves.

Raymond Barre, Giscard d'Estaing's last prime minister, was already theorizing over the merits of "austerity" and wrestling with the unions when my son, no doubt taking advantage of the confusion, decided to come into the world.

When we first met, I found him rather ugly and unfriendly. Eyes closed, puffy lids, a pug face, a no-neck conehead, and fists clenched in fury. When the nurse pointed him out to me in his cradle, she just said, "Seven pounds ten ounces," the way they announce the fighting weight of a boxer before a match. Those numbers became so embedded in my brain that even today, when I catch sight of my son during one of his visits, I sometimes think, "Hmm, here's Seven-pounds-ten-ounces." We named him Vincent. Actually, I'd never for a moment thought of naming him anything else. And neither had Anna. When I told my mother about Vincent's birth and she learned his name, she burst into tears, hugging me as if I'd been her only son. With a look on his face that I hadn't seen since my early childhood, my father said simply, "Vincent Blick. That's nice, that's very nice." After charming the Blicks, Seven-pounds-ten-ounces made such a hit with the Villandreuxs that all the tensions built up during the critical marriage process were forgotten. Watching all those adults leaning over him and acting like idiots singly or en masse, I reflected that births (like deaths, by the way) have the strange power to unfreeze hearts and wipe clean the overloaded slates of the past.

A year and a half later, when my daughter, Marie, was born, I was able to verify the justice of my observation. Marie seemed as instantly delighted to enjoy the subtly oxygenated atmosphere of this planet as her brother had been reluctant to join the club, brandishing his fists in a foul mood. With her blond hair, Atlantic-blue eyes, and her way of smiling at each admirer, she was like those English girls on holiday in the south of France who are enchanted with everything. I had a daughter. I was bursting with pride. A daughter. The most beautiful gift life can offer a man.

It was Anna who had decided to have another baby so soon. In order, I think, to fulfill as quickly as possible her promise to herself: not to have an only child. Like me, she had doubtless suffered too much from familial solitude, that endless and disappointing childhood spent staring at oneself.

Although the roles would soon be reversed, I noticed that for the moment, Vincent and Marie were educating their mother, teaching her to distinguish the essential from the secondary, to choose substance instead of appearance, being instead of seeming, and a baby bottle instead of Adam Smith. The honeymoon did not last long. Anna was not naturally attracted to the maternal role. She adored her children, but the temptations of the outside world and the urge to get busy making her fortune grew daily more pressing. Especially since Jean Villandreux, eager to devote himself entirely to *Sports Illustrés*, had offered her a chance to run Atoll, his swimming pool company, which no longer interested him at all now that he owned a magazine and had tasted the pleasures of press barony. For Anna, this was an opportunity to put her diplomas and abilities to the test. Before she had even accepted her father's offer, I knew the list of her goals by heart: increase the earnings of an already flourishing company by 10 percent a year; face up to fifty or so managers and workers just waiting for her first misstep; revamp the catalog to introduce new models; and launch a whole line of hot tubs and Jacuzzis, which were quite popular in America. I felt that Anna had been waiting for this chance for years. It was as if, in her mind, all the dossiers were already prepared, negotiated, budgeted, and entered in an accounts-receivable ledger. Although she had never once set foot in the offices of Atoll, she talked about her new role, discussing the strengths and weaknesses of the company as if she were its founder.

Anna was suffering from a disease that was rather widespread during that Giscardo-Barrist era: *entrepreneurial fever,* characterized by an uncontrollable need to create a supplementary cell inside the free-trade honeycomb. One's own little nest in the Great Everything. This desire to work, build, advance, imagine, and produce generally brought on a remarkable swelling of the ego and a violent crisis of self-confidence. Anna had all those symptoms, so I wasn't surprised to see her slowly withdraw from the three of us to plunge into the whirlpool bath of her father's business.

That brutal immersion completely changed our way of life. Within a few days, the woman I loved and with whom I shared the sweetness of being alive gave way to an administrator railing against powerful unions, disorganized employers, taxes on profits, unmotivated personnel, and the mandatory benefits required by the state. These upheavals led me to a decision I'd already been mulling over for some time: to quit my stupid job and devote myself to my children. And raise them in peace and quiet. Like an old-fashioned mother.

I had the feeling my decision suited everyone. Anna immediately felt let off the hook for neglecting her babies. Jean Villandreux seemed relieved not to see me hanging around the halls of *Sports Illustrés,* his new full-time domain. As the head of Atoll, Anna earned a very comfortable salary, so I could devote myself to my new job as stay-at-home father with a clear conscience.

I loved those years spent with Vincent and Marie, those seasons lived outside the world of work and adult preoccupations. Our lives were made of walks, naps, and afternoon snacks of gingerbread that had the flavor of innocent happiness. Since I anointed and powdered them, I knew every little corner of my children's skin. I recognized the dominant elements in their scents: an animal note in the boy, a vegetable one in the girl. With a hand behind their necks in the warm bathwater, I supported them as they floated like that, serene in their little niche of the world, as if they were back in the womb. Then I loved to dress them in clean, sweet-smelling clothes, and in winter, put them to bed in warm pajamas. Marie would quickly fall asleep, gripping my index finger in her little hand. Her brother would cuddle against my forearm and let his big dark eyes gaze unfocused into the distance, so that even before he fell asleep, he seemed to be dreaming.

My days passed in the completion of simple, repetitive chores—mostly housekeeping—in which I couldn't help seeing a certain nobility. When Anna came home, dinner was ready and the children in bed. My life resembled that of those model wives in American sitcoms of the 1960s, impeccable and attentive women whose purpose in life seems to be helping the alpha wage earner relax after the fatigues of the daily grind. The only things missing in my case were the full skirt and high heels. As for the rest, like my transatlantic sisters I served a scotch to the tired entrepreneur while feigning interest in her managerial complaining. Sometimes she asked me how my day had been; "Normal," I would reply, and that adjective—albeit minimal and hard to pin down—seemed to satisfy her meager curiosity. After finishing her drink, she would put away a few files and, like any good father, go kiss the children good night as she tucked the blanket around their shoulders. While I set the table, she would glean a bit of news from the television before asking me what was for dinner. When the menu met with approval, I was rewarded with a "Wonderful!" ringing with impatient appetite. When my offerings failed to please, I had to be content with "Don't go to so much trouble, I'm not very hungry tonight." That was my life: domestic in every sense of the word. No matter how removed I was from the affairs of the world, and as paradoxical as it may seem, I realized that I was living much more intensely on this earth than Anna was, for though she always claimed to do everything from her heart, she never really left the little basin of her emerald green pools. And so, from the balcony of our big new apartment I watched the hours pass and the world turn. I noticed the death of a pope, and discovered, one morning, that of Mao Zedong. (The east is red, the sun is setting.) The *Amoco Cadiz* spilled its guts into the ocean, and the radical fringe pillaged

Fauchon, the expensive gourmet food store in Paris. Revolution broke out in Iran, while here and there people were beginning to talk about the magnificent diamonds given to Giscard (who at first denied receiving them) by his friend Jean-Bédel Bokassa: emperor of the Central African Republic, kleptocrat extraordinaire, and finally, cannibal king. And Jacques Mesrine, the "Robin Hood" bank robber who had become an embarrassment to the French government, was ambushed at a traffic light, and gunned down the way you wouldn't kill a dog, his body riddled with bullets in an execution-style killing.

All those events, no matter what their importance, were shoved into the background when Anna came home from work. She couldn't help it: every day she rehashed for me the lead stories of the "Atoll Gazette," which always involved attempted putsches in the joint production committee, water-cooler pronunciamentos, union revolts, and power plays by the government agency regulating social security payments.

Even though it was becoming ever clearer to me that Anna and I were drifting apart, I was happy to live like that with my children and a woman whom I still loved in spite of herself. I had taken advantage of all my free time during the day to return to an old passion of my childhood: photography. I have always loved that silent activity, so solitary and discreet. When I was a teenager I would go off with my father's Contarex to photograph (preferably) the world of minerals and vegetation—in fact, everything that didn't move. Freeze-framing stillness fascinated me.

I had an impressive collection of pictures of fruits, vegetables, trees, and ordinary stones, and to me, each still life was radiant with energy. I worked exclusively outdoors, surrounded by nature, skimming my shots from the disorder of the world, from what chance and the seasons brought my way. Back home, I developed my films and printed my pictures in a little photo lab I'd set up in a dressing room adjoining the bathroom.

It was my father who initiated me in the mysteries of the darkroom, where, in the glow of a safety light (he used a sodium lamp), I developed the films before printing the pictures on paper. The first time I saw my father produce an image with silver salts in the developer and then fix it in a hypo bath, I really thought he was a magician with super-natural powers. And I truly believe it was that magic trick that gave me my love of conjuring images out of nowhere. Of re-creating bits of the world on my scale. Pagan snapshots, fragments of life both unmoving and extraordinarily close to my conception of humanity.

The more I think back on it, the clearer it seems to me that it was this moment of mystery and grace between a father and his son that made me what I later became.

The year 1979 was drawing to a close. I would shut myself inside my little closet every night while Anna and the children slept and, cut off from everything, I would print the images I had taken during my walks with Vincent and Marie. I did not yet know it, but by living that life of seeming aimlessness, I was forcing the hand of fate.

I had lost track of my former friends from the university and the apartment on the Allée des Soupirs. Whenever I thought about them and all the time we spent together, I felt that vague, indescribable nausea that accompanies secret betrayals. And yet, aside from a less than glorious marriage, I had nothing to be ashamed of. Supported by a small business firm, tied down by my little family, isolated, out of touch with political currents and fringe groups, I certainly wasn't a model revolutionary activist anymore. I no longer belonged to that exultant margin of society. I had joined another category of human beings of (more or less) goodwill, guys not worth much, perhaps, who don't believe in anything, but who nevertheless manage to get out of bed every morning.

Two or three times a month, Anna gave dinner parties at home to which she invited two childhood friends and their husbands. Laure Milo, a sexy young mother with a luscious rear end, was in the same profession I was: she was stalwartly raising her children with a kind of bracing good humor. Her companion, François, an engineer at Aérospatiale, worked on the wing units of Airbus projects. After completing his internship, Michel Campion had joined a clinic renowned for its expertise in cardiac surgery and neonatal care. Brigitte, his wife, devoted her time to many sports and a great variety of beauty treatments ranging from manicures to Rolfing to highlighting by biocosmeticians specializing in capilliculture. The combined skills of all these specialists, however, could do nothing for Brigitte Campion's problem: she was devoid of charm and elegance, and no matter how you looked at her, she resembled a rumpled little man. The Campions had a child who was never seen, about whom they rarely spoke, and who was usually entrusted to the care of Michel's mother.

These dinner parties always began the same way: the women would join me in the kitchen to chat about recipes, family, and children, while the men had a drink in the living room talking shop with Anna. I often wondered how Brigitte and Laure thought of me. Was I a complete man to them, or some hybrid being, a mutant, concealing beneath a masculine appearance a distinctly feminine motherboard? If I had to say, I would have allowed that I saw myself as a fish out of water, often sad, increasingly tired, and beginning to resemble, as things dragged on, a dead fish.

During those dinners, Anna was transfigured. Among friends, she left behind all pressing worries, professional masquerades, and balance sheets to become radiant once again. Even though I'd had nothing to do with that transformation, I was happy to rediscover for a few hours the girl I had fought hard to take away from Elias.

That evening we were all still at the table when the telephone rang. It was my mother. Her voice seemed to come from another planet.

"Your father has had another heart attack. The EMS ambulance is taking him to the hospital. I have to hang up now. . . . I'm going with him."

From then on, every moment of that evening is engraved in my memory. The Murray Head album *Between Us* that was playing in the background. The mingled odors of perfumes and tobacco. The reassuring light cast by the lamps scattered around the room. The strange look on everyone's face as they stared at me. The noise of a long, impatient honk from a car horn out in the street. Anna saying "What's wrong?" And the conviction, as deep as a stake driven through my heart, that I would never see my father alive again.

When Anna and I arrived at the coronary care unit of the Hôpital Rangueuil, my mother already looked like an old woman. She stood leaning against a glass partition, her arms tightly crossed over her chest, shivering in the blast of an invisible winter. When she saw me, she nodded tenderly at me, as if to say "Don't rush, there's no point anymore."

My father was behind the glass panel, lying on a hospital bed. He had that same relaxed expression I recognized from when he would take a nap on summer afternoons, with his mouth a bit open and his jaw slightly sagging. He had an IV line, and various leads connected him to a monitor. Anna was trying to comfort my mother, the cardiologist was checking the dials, the medical apparatus was emitting short beeps, and everything seemed under control, and yet, imperceptibly, my father was slipping away from us.

Toward midnight the doctor came to explain to us the extent of the damage "Monsieur Block" had suffered. My mother listened to him, too dispirited to bother correcting his mistake. And when he said, "Go home and rest, Madame Block—I'll see you tomorrow, when I hope I'll have better news for you," she acquiesced without a word. The suggestion suited her. Most important, she felt that he had implicitly assured her that there would be a tomorrow, and that Victor Blick would not pass away like that, alone, without seeing anyone again, in the middle of the night. With such a promise, she would accept, without flinching, to be called Block—now, tomorrow, and if necessary, for the rest of her days.

As I drove my mother back to her house, I was convinced that we were coming to the end of our time as a family and that my father would die. What bothered me was that I felt like the only one who knew this.

I stayed with my mother. She had a cup of tea, spoke with me for a moment about Anna and the children, then went upstairs to bed, exhausted, and slept like a stone. Downstairs, prey to anxiety, I tried to pass the hours pacing in the living room or walking in the garden. My mind was full of incoherent images and jumbled thoughts. My brother and me in the car with my father. My grandmother spitting out her "Mikoyashhh." The photograph of Sinika's dog. My grandfather Lande on top of the mountain. Michael Collins gazing out at the moon. The furtive eyes of Dr. Ducellier. The starry night sky during the great drought. Me, throwing cobblestones at the windows of the family business.

Throughout that long night I also recalled my father during his glory days, when he captained that enormous galactic ocean liner that seemed to watch, "Day and Night," over the city. He was the one who had come up with that unforgettable sign. (Today the garage is long gone, of course, but the inhabitants of Toulouse still orient themselves in reference to that invisible landmark, which remains rooted in the minds of several generations of townspeople.) Behind the glass panels of his office, with his double-breasted suit and his Esperaza fedora, he looked like a character in one of Jacques Tati's gentle, eccentric films, someone brimming with confidence, clinging to his prerogatives, but humming with a childlike joy each time he got to fiddle with the levers of the modern world. The cars drove in and out in a ballet of squeaking tires on the gleaming red metal ramp. A stickler for cleanliness, my father insisted that his establishment look more like a maternity hospital than an oil-and-lubrication center. His greatest pride was that no odor of hydrocarbons would ever taint the air of Day and Night. His shop foremen saw to this so well that every drop, every leak, every spill was immediately wiped up with a rag. My father bought enormous bales of old cloth cut up for just that purpose. I don't know why he called the Simca P60 models Pedros, but I remember perfectly that he, who hardly ever talked about cars, began at one time to explain, emphasize, and insist that the Simca 1100 was, from a technical and esthetic point of view, the acme of front-wheel drive in modern times. With an almost biblical tone, in a voice of priestly certainty, he always ended his homily by saying, "And you will see: the Simca 1100 will be copied a hundred times, imitated at the very least, but never equaled." That pompous speech was no spur-of-the-moment inspiration and had nothing to do with any talent for improvisation. Like an epic poet of automobiles, one day he had gone off somewhere to compose his "Ode to Simca," I was sure of it.

The nights that precede the death of a father are always feverish and confused, strange, unreal, peopled with unexpected phantoms and chaotic recollections. The flames of memory dance in all directions, giving off light, pushing back the implacable advance of darkness hour after hour. Torn in so many directions, you wind up no longer knowing what you truly wish for: death, because it will end the agony, or simply a little more life, because you never know. . . .

That night we knew: the call came at five o'clock. The voice on the telephone said things simply. The heart had stopped beating. All efforts to resuscitate were useless. The cardiograph, silent. Take your time. He's here. Waiting for you.

And my mother, torn from her night, dressing with a traveler's haste, rushes down the stairs and slams the car door as if to cut all ties with this world. She wants me to drive faster, says that we might still get there in time, weeps as she begs I don't know whom to do God knows what, asks about Anna whom she'd just seen a few hours earlier, worries about the children, curses the telephone, speaks of my father for the first time in the past tense, climbs painfully out of the car, goes down the long hall clinging to me, enters a dimly lighted room, approaches the gurney, looks—insofar as she can—death in the face, and out at the end of an invisible pier, abandoning all resistance, slowly collapses, clutching my father's hand in hers.

I stood there for a moment, motionless, seeming to wait for something or someone. Then I stepped forward and I kissed my father. I kissed him from far away, as if I barely knew him. His skin was so cold.

Leaving the hospital, I went directly home. The first glimmer of daybreak had just appeared. Anna was still in a deep sleep. I sat down in the kitchen with a glass of club soda and burst into tears.

By 1979 Simca's days were numbered. My father did not live to see the Simca emblem vanish from what became the Talbot 1100.

FRANÇOIS MITTERRAND (I)

(May 21, 1981–May 7, 1988)

NEVER had so many things to tell my father as during the months following his death. I would have liked to explain my absences, my moments of indifference toward him, my silences, the way I hadn't appreciated his handling of his business and his difficult family. I would have liked to ask his advice, tell him about my problems with Anna and the children, and hear what he really thought about what I'd done with my life.

I'd had no idea how much my father's death would change my life and the way I saw things. With him gone, I was not a son anymore, and I became physically conscious of my share of singularity. I was no longer the younger brother of the incomparable Vincent Blick; instead—which was just as intimidating—I was, as Sartre said, "a man made of all men, who is equal to them all and worth any one of them." As for my mother, she began a downward spiral of vague anxieties that all reinforced one another. She often worried, for example, that she would not have enough money to take care of her too big old house, and it was to ease this fear that I suggested that she sell the apartment in Torremolinos.

Such a move would be doubly profitable: I would both help my mother and rid myself of a morally burdensome inheritance.

Shortly after Franco's death, the Iberico Company had gone belly-up in a resounding international bankruptcy that sent Carlos Arias Navarro to prison for embezzlement. The reckless use of accommodation notes had led the former government minister and his associates to sell the same apartment to several clients, and they had pulled this wretched scam hundreds of times. But a trip to consult the public trustee's office in Madrid confirmed that I was the sole owner of apartment 196 in Tamarindos 1. All I had to do was put the place up for sale and go cash it in for its weight in pesetas. In a way, by acquiring this modest asset, my father had aided the Franco regime and then become—quite involuntarily—one of those little dominoes that in falling would help bring down an entire system.

Toward the middle of May in 1981, I received a phone call from my real estate agency in Torremolinos telling me that a client in Madrid wished to purchase the apartment at the listed price. All I had to do was come sign the sales contract in the local notary's office. To put this trip in context, I should mention the rather sorry economic climate in France in those days. The nation's old conservative demons had caught up with the country, and the election of Mitterrand had caused a precipitous decline in the worth of the franc, a 20 percent loss in value on our stock exchange, and the flight of capital that galloped day and night toward all our national borders. And there I was, lightheartedly driving off to Barcelona in my old Triumph, a capricious little English cabriolet that had a vague resemblance to a fish, plus sloping headlights and a frowning radiator grille that made it seem permanently grumpy at having to drive around. I had decided to go as far as Catalonia, where I would fly to Málaga via Iberia Airlines.

I remember the hopeful atmosphere of my springtime flight to southern Spain in the light-filled cabin of that Boeing, and my feeling of well-being, the thought that things were changing and would work out for the best. Planes have always had an analgesic and euphoric effect on me, perhaps because of the relative lack of oxygen, unless flying at an altitude of twelve thousand meters is what gives me that intoxicating illusion of being released from all earthly cares.

Sitting relaxed in my seat, leaning my head against the little window, I mulled over our weird recent election that had ended in the theatrical exit of Giscard d'Estaing: rising from his chair after addressing the nation on television, he had walked offstage, leaving the French to face the fear of emptiness. Flying along between heaven and earth, I thought about the man who had openly renounced the world of the living and been replaced by that man of inexhaustible greed, who had chosen to inaugurate his era by visiting the illustrious French dead in the Panthéon, long-stemmed red roses in hand. I did not like those people, still less their public display of paltry emotions and meager visions.

From the apartment balcony, I could almost glimpse the coast of Morocco and the far edge of my father's dreams. That evening I tried to be his eyes, to show him what he could never see. When the management company had failed, the building had begun to deteriorate. The spacious marble lobby no longer hummed with the activity of concierges and deliverymen. The aluminum clocks set to the time in the great capitals of the world had been stilled. The luxuriant interior plantings were dusty and dry. These proud spaces where people met and walked were now almost deserted. Yet the air was incredibly pleasant, and the southern wind smelled sweet. I had an appointment the following day at noon in the law office of Consuelo y Talgo. Everything seemed perfect. Looking out at the sky, I thought about my father's life, and drifted gently off to sleep to the restful sound of the sea.

Consuelo looked like Talgo, unless it was the other way around. In any case, they both looked more like mescal-soaked Mexican bandits than Andalusian lawyers. And their office looked like them: dirty, disorganized, improbable. Located on the third floor of a truly repulsive building, it consisted of two rooms packed with incongruous objects rarely found in a law office: a motorbike frame, an old kitchen fridge, a hot plate sitting on some loudspeakers, a brand-new racing bicycle, a plastic trash can full of oranges, and empty beer and soda cans lined up absolutely everywhere. The file folders on the warped shelves looked like old laundry set out to dry.

From the corner of his eye, Consuelo watched Talgo, who looked askance at me. In addition to the odor of burned tortilla, there was a general smell of suspicion in that office. The place stank of fraud.

"Señor don Blick, pray take a seat."

"The buyer hasn't arrived yet?"

"Actually, señor, the buyer will not be coming. He telephoned us yesterday: he has been detained in Madrid."

"Do you mean to say that you've brought me here for nothing?"

"Absolutely not. Our client has appointed my associate, Señor Talgo, as his proxy, and Señor Talgo will represent him during the transaction."

"Do you have this in writing?"

"Actually, the document was only drawn up yesterday and will not be delivered to us for two days yet. But that does not in the least prevent us from signing the sales contract today."

"And what about the payment?"

"Señor Talgo will give you a check."

"A check from your law firm?"

"No, a personal check."

With his lopsided face and those canine jaws sporting a grim smile, the lawyer—if he ever did actually get anywhere near a law school—reeked of forgery, abuse of the public welfare, embezzlement, improper solicitation of legacies, influence peddling, and a hundred other foul deeds. Something told me that if I accepted his proposition, I would never again see Talgo, or Consuelo, or the keys to the apartment, or my title deed (so exceptional for my sole ownership), or maybe even my family. I would disappear as if by enchantment, leaving my children orphaned and my mother ruined.

"I'm sorry, but this is all highly irregular: the buyer is not present, there are documents missing, and you are proposing to pay me with a personal check."

"It's true, our client's unfortunate change of plans has affected certain things, but our current proposition is entirely legal."

"Perhaps, but under these conditions I will ask you to pay me the sum due for the apartment in cash."

"In cash? But señor, we don't have such a sum available here in the office!"

"Well, then, bring it here this evening or tomorrow morning."

"Have you considered the exchange control? You cannot take that much money out of Spain without declaring it to customs officials."

"I'll take care of that."

"Give us a moment, señor."

Francisco Talgo and Juan Consuelo left the room with a conspiratorial air. I had quickly figured out that the client in Madrid had never existed and that Talgo was buying the apartment for himself. Why had the two men concocted such a story when it would have been so much simpler to tell me the truth and do things the ordinary way?

As I watched the partners return, I reflected that few men in the legal profession anywhere in the world could beat these two at scuttling like crabs, oozing treachery, and emitting so many bad vibes.

"The sum will be ready tomorrow morning, señor," Talgo said, the two standing side by side, trying hard to smile. The next morning, Consuelo obsequiously turned the pages of the official documents while Francisco Talgo and I appended our signatures. Trying to seem relaxed, Consuelo chatted aimlessly about the weather, the cultivation of oranges, the influx of German tourists along the beaches. I paid no attention to his ramblings until he asked me a more personal question.

"Are you returning to France along the Atlantic coast or from Barcelona, señor?"

The previous day, without really knowing why, I had lied to the two lawyers by telling them that I had come down from Málaga by car. Feeling suddenly paranoid, I became convinced that those two bastards were going to sell me out to the customs officials once I'd told them where I would be crossing the border. Not only would they be revenged for any inconvenience I had caused them, but they would also collect a bounty for informing on me.

"I'll be returning through Madrid, Burgos, and the Basque country."

"A lovely region, señor, truly lovely."

When Talgo opened his attaché case and stacked up in front of me a veritable fortress of pesetas, I realized that I'd gotten myself into a serious fix. How was I ever going to carry all that money? I had no luggage and no time now to go buy some, because I had to get to the airport.

Consuelo and Talgo watched me leave the way one would step back from a booby trap.

The Boeing left on time and I barely made it on board. Padded with paper money, bundled in bills, I was armored in currency. I'd stuffed it everywhere. In the pockets of my trousers, shirt, jacket, raincoat, in the linings of my clothes, around my waist, and even in my socks, wrapped around my ankles. During a few fleeting bursts of euphoria, I rejoiced to think that I had prevailed over those two sleazeballs, escaping alive from their den of thieves. An instant later, I would be awash in anguish, afraid that I'd been conned, or scammed by some mathematical sleight of hand in the exchange rate. Bathed in perspiration, my hands clammy and trembling, I shut myself in the toilet to hastily recount the small packets of my loot. Or rather, of this money that would relieve my mother of her most pressing worries.

When I slipped behind the wheel of my car in the parking lot of the airport in Barcelona, I must have looked like one of those disaster survivors who grin beatifically at everything in sight, grateful to their rescuers and ready to love the whole world until the end of time. I turned the ignition key and my ancient Triumph's six cylinders rushed headlong into the throes of combustion. Another few hundred kilometers and my mission would be over. On the highway leading to the border crossing at Le Perthus, it occurred to me that while French capital was fleeing abroad in all directions during that May, I must have been the sole French citizen plotting to bring money *into* the country.

This comical predicament then veered into the grotesque. About twenty kilometers from the border, the engine began making a strange metallic gargling that ended in a sharp crack—followed by utter silence. For a moment the Triumph seemed to glide serenely above this problem, but, overtaken by reality, it slowed inexorably to a stop in the emergency lane. The timing chain had just snapped. A full day's work—if you had all the pieces on hand *and* if the crankshaft and valves had survived this devastating breakdown. Even before I went to call a tow truck from the roadside emergency telephone, my first reflex was to collect the many bundles of pesetas I had concealed in the glove compartment and the side pockets of the doors and hide them again in all the pockets of my clothes. I was just finishing that operation when I noticed a Seat pulling in behind me: the Guardia Civil had arrived.

The proceeds from that apartment were cursed: Spain and Catalonia were making me pay a high price for that familial collaboration! Since those two policemen would definitely find it strange that I crackled like an old newspaper whenever I moved, they were going to frisk me, and I would be locked up in the worst prison cell on the peninsula along with Arias Navarro and other elderly brutes of the regime. The policemen, however, were neither curious nor suspicious, and they even asked me to remain inside my car while waiting for the tow truck. They had turned on their whirling emergency light to alert other drivers and sat smoking quietly in their Seat, which filled up with a thick blue cloud as the minutes ticked by. That close to the border, it was a French garage mechanic from Perpignan who regularly took broken-down vehicles in tow, and when he arrived, he simply winched up the Triumph without even looking under its hood. He asked me if I wanted to ride in the truck cab with him, but I elected to stay in my car. We crossed the border without even stopping, taking the road reserved for service vehicles, and the driver dropped me off at the railway station in Perpignan, telling me to call in two days for news about the Triumph.

I left for Toulouse at about ten that evening. I remember a nightmarish trip in a train crowded with rowdy, red-eyed soldiers who staggered from compartment to compartment in a miasma of beer and urine, flashing their yellow teeth as they screamed obscenities. The curse was clearly still in effect. Moving as little as possible, terrified of attracting the attention of the savage horde, I tried to sweat silently, muffled in my mantle of money.

Early the next morning, I arrived at the bank with my pesetas neatly packed, this time, in a small leather suitcase. When I opened it, the branch manager could not repress a nervous twitch of his upper lip. I never suspected that this almost imperceptible tremor betrayed the intense jubilation of the predator who has just realized that his prey is now doomed.

"It is rather unusual, in these times, for our customers to bring us money from abroad."

"I know."

"Even if your gesture is, let us say, patriotic, nevertheless, this importation of currency is an infraction of the exchange control regulations. You should have arranged for an interbank transfer."

"I know, but that was impossible, I had no choice."

"We can, of course, deposit these pesetas to your mother's account, but you should understand that technically, this operation will incur some fees and that in consequence, naturally, we will not be able to apply the true rate of exchange."

"What are you saying, exactly?"

"Precisely what I just told you: you will lose in the exchange transaction."

"How much?"

"I must first consult our foreign currency department, but I will have an answer for you by early this afternoon. For such a sum, I must obtain approval from Paris."

At three o'clock, the branch manager ushered me into a small room connected to his office. Like some absurd traveler or foolish immigrant, I still had my precious little suitcase by my side.

"I do not have very good news, Monsieur Blick."

"Meaning?"

"Given the present political and economic circumstances—which are, as you know, somewhat unusual—the manager offers to deposit this money at today's rate of exchange, minus ten points."

"What does that mean, ten points?"

"Ten percent."

"Ten percent?!"

"That is correct. Ten percent less than today's rate of exchange."

"But that's a huge amount! And it's illegal!"

"I am aware of that. However, so is what you are asking us to do. No bank will offer you a better deal, even if you can find one that will agree to change this money."

"What are my alternatives?"

"Fraudulently return these pesetas to Spain, deposit them in a Spanish bank, and legally transfer them to your mother's account."

"Wait a minute—do you know what you're saying? I would risk getting arrested as a currency speculator in Le Perthus for illegally exporting from France this *Spanish* money that I fraudulently imported from Málaga two days ago."

"That is correct."

"You've got a real nerve. I will discuss your proposal with my mother and give you her answer tomorrow. I don't care for your way of taking advantage of the situation."

"I can understand your point of view. On the other hand, what I find hard to fathom are the reasons that led you to bring such a sum into France illegally rather than to effect an interbank transfer that would have cost you nothing."

Those reasons were named Juan Consuelo and Francisco Talgo. Two little lawyers. Two scruffy crooks. But wasn't this calm and well-dressed banker, fiddling with figures in his discreetly elegant office, really more frighteningly dishonest than that outlandish pair of Andalusian rascals?

My mother, who was not fond of either numbers or negotiations, accepted the bank's proposal with enthusiasm, delighted to recoup a good part of that wayward money too long exiled in Spain.

Two years later I learned that the bank representative who had so adroitly brought me to heel had been fired because of several instances of malfeasance, but I never discovered if the episode of my mother's money was among them.

Although 1981 marked my failure as a smuggler, it was also the year I began a career in photography. The children had grown and were now in school, but I continued to take care of them while attempting to work in my spare time. Jean Villandreux's connections helped me land some jobs, a few series of abstract photos in color that were used as packaging designs.

I took pictures during the day and disappeared into my little lab at night to develop and print them. My new schedule meant that I hardly saw Anna at all anymore, and we had to hire someone to fill in for me with the children at times. Vincent and Marie were intrigued by this new development, for they were used to having their father around, a masculine presence constantly available to wash sheets, iron pajamas, prepare snacks, and dry their tears with motherly aplomb.

After encouraging me for years to live like a nanny, now Anna wanted me to abandon my housekeeping and persevere with my photography. She even voiced a decided opinion about my work: technically, it was all above reproach, but it had no connection with the real world and was singularly lacking in life. Although I had always found my wife's smugness and unshakable convictions exasperating, I had to admit that in this case she was not completely wrong. It would have taken a clever eye indeed to find the slightest trace of human activity in my Ilford or Agfa negative storage boxes. I photographed only things in the plant and mineral worlds, whatever was motionless, fragmentary, partial. Sometimes I even settled for pure abstractions, content to capture the iridescence of a point of light or the depth of a shadow. Through her criticism, I could clearly see the direction Anna wanted my work to take. She would have liked me to be a news reporter with sensitive feelers, a Witness Without Borders boldly reading the world's entrails, snapping shots of everything that moves, changes, quivers, stirs, leaps, runs, parades, pretends, shakes, falls, is born, whimpers, wails, gets bored stiff, and dies. What Anna Villandreux really wanted was to see me work for *Paris Match,* when I sometimes found it hard just to leave the house.

Anyone looking at my photos might have thought I was living in a universe where life as people commonly know it had simply disappeared. Although those many images showed things rather than beings, however, I felt that each one, in its modest candor, its refusal to *seem,* inspired a kind of peace, gentleness, and even goodwill. I did not know it yet, but everything that Anna complained about in my work would soon provide the impetus for my success.

When I think back to that time, I tell myself that Anna and I were almost like neighbors. We were living in a foolish way, but on good terms with each other. Her apprenticeship was over, and she ran her business like a prizewinning horsewoman whose graceful form disguises her steely expertise. Anna had quickly sized up the firm and the true nature of its employees. Unconcerned about treading on anyone's toes, she had gradually stepped up the pace of production and investigated new export markets. In no time she had transformed a quiet family business into a sort of frenetic ballroom where everyone whipped around the dance floor. And of course productivity had followed suit: a 6 percent increase the first year, another 9 percent the following year, 12 percent the next, and the rate had been steady ever since. Her new hot tubs and Jacuzzis were molded out of moiré plastic in colors and textures that resembled casino chips and plaques. It was all in hideously bad taste and sold like hotcakes. You'd have thought that all France and southern Europe were saving up every sou just to treat themselves to the privilege of splashing all day long in one of Anna's dreadful bubbling cauldrons. Although Anna was quick to pass scathing judgment on a wide range of subjects, she was unable to bear the slightest reservation about the quality or the esthetics of her products, a sensitivity I had occasion to measure once again when she handed me her new spring 1983 catalog.

"It's not bad, huh?"

"Frankly?"

"What do you mean, 'frankly'. . . ?"

"You want me to tell you frankly what I think of it?"

"Of course!"

"It's not great. I mean, not the sort of thing I like. The materials, and especially the colors."

"What's wrong with the colors?"

"This metallic green, the shiny blue, and this yellow with an orange sheen—all these brilliant pigments, they're really . . . odd."

"Since when have you had an opinion about hot tubs?"

"Since you asked me for one."

"You're right, I don't know what possessed me to show you these things, when you're such a pure esthete."

"Don't get so upset, it's ridiculous."

"You want me to tell you what's ridiculous? Your attitude, that's what! Your shitty little leftist attitudes are ridiculous! You make fun of what I do, you don't care how hard it is for a woman on her own to run a business like mine. The competition, exports, the exchange rates, market pressures—you're so far above all that!"

"Anna . . ."

"The only thing you care about is not growing up, acting like a child with your children, and escaping responsibilities. Me, every day, I have to fight to provide a living for sixty-three people! Excuse me: sixty-four— I forgot about you."

"Nice touch."

"That's just how it is! Not to mention your precious leftist coalition that devalues the franc twice in one year, taxes companies like nobody's business, and creates a surtax for the rich! So pardon me if under these conditions I make hot tubs in poor taste that just happen to sell well and earn us a living!"

"Haven't my photos been contributing a little bit for a while now?"

"Your photos . . . You're talking about your photos. . . . You want me to tell you what I think about your freeze-dried pictures?"

"Thanks, you just did."

Anything to do with Atoll was completely off-limits: the kidney-shaped pools of the Riviera Line, the Epurator diatomite filters, the Excellence pumps, the absurd Balloon bubbling cauldrons—it was all *terra sancta*, untouchable. The slightest criticism—even the tiniest reservation—about any of these products was a personal attack on Anna, a challenge to her life, her work, her abilities, Adam Smith, and even our fading marriage, which languished like our sex life.

Anna was drowning her libido in the shoals of her Atoll, while I was parking mine in Laure Milo's warm bottom.

The after-school pickups, birthday parties, free afternoons, movies, school vacations, and all the other activities we'd shared so many times had quite naturally brought us together. Laure felt as lonely as I did in those days because her husband had the same committed relationship with aeronautics as Anna had with recreational bathing. François lived only for his wing units and shared the obsession common to all the other salarymen in his corporation: to someday seize dominion in the skies from Boeing. "Toulouse first, Seattle second!" The corollary to that patriotic axiom was that he spent his spare time entranced by the curvature of his airfoils instead of the curves of his wife. During Anna's weekly dinners he kept trying to convince us that the heart and soul of the European consortium of Airbus Industrie was in Toulouse, and no-where else: "Right here is where we develop, design, and assemble the planes. They take off from here, all of them, from the Concorde to the Airbus 300. The other countries that participate are just subcontractors. If you want to understand how Airbus really works, that's the one thing you always have to keep in mind." If at that moment François Milo (project coordinator of God-knows-what tail unit or leading wing edge) had unglued his eyes from the heavens and peeked more humbly under the table, he would have noticed the mother of his children fondling my privates. On certain days of the week, while our kids were in school, Laure had taken to dropping by my darkroom. We'd shut ourselves up in this protective dungeon and fuck to the health of the consortium and the Jacuzzis as well, fuck for all we were worth, stifling in that tiny space, twisting and turning, mingling our intimate odors with the harsh smell of the hypo. Wrapped around each other like that in the yellow light of the sodium lamp, grappling in high gear, we must have looked like a giant squid busily devouring itself.

I haven't worn underwear since I was little. Those superfluous gar-ments have always bothered me, and I just don't like the feel of them. I will never forget Laure's erotic thrill at discovering that modest quirk of mine, which symbolized to her a kind of sexual availability that promised a complete change from her conjugal routines: "You know François—prudish as a monk. Underpants? If he could, he'd wear three pairs!" Going through life without underpants seemed to her the height of licentiousness, the apogee of debauchery and lust. She'd never met a man so free.

When sufficiently aroused, Laure lost all sense of restraint in what she said, releasing a torrent of libidinous steam kept under pressure for far too long. Some things she said made me shiver with pleasure, and some truly gave me goose bumps. Her buttocks, as I've already said, had been designed by an engineer as much obsessed with aerodynamic perfection as her husband was. Nothing, not one mole, not the tiniest crease, marred the exquisite beauty of that out-of-this-world derrière. All Laure had to do was lean on the edge of the enlarger and lift up her skirt, and the sky was the limit.

Neither one of us was given to postcoital Jesuitical contrition. No regret, no remorse, no guilt. Just pleasure, a pleasure that was only salutary and had no bearing on our spouses. Beyond the confines of our little haven, the lives we knew by heart were waiting for us, but in that darkroom, that principality of ecstatic fucking, amid the silver salts and still lifes, we abandoned ourselves like two solitary travelers coupling frenetically with strangers.

I have often been struck by the determination with which reasonable, intelligent, and educated people contrive to derail their sex lives by remaining faithful for decades to mates who are just as brilliant, talented, and affectionate as they are, but subject to social and hormonal clocks entirely unsynchronized with their partners' lives. And despite such incompatibility, these out-of-synch couples flounder grimly, mired in frustration, denying the obvious. While François Milo was energetically selling medium transport aircraft to Aer Lingus, Laure was dreaming of cunnilingus. And yet the two of them continued to live in that mute and asexual no-man's-land where they raised their children, watched television, went on vacations, and bought family-size cars on the installment plan.

Fucking Laure was an activity as natural and exhilarating as running headlong across a field. I didn't know it yet, but those pleasant romps were gently leading me toward the comfy paddock fate had in store for me. Once more, benevolent chance took the form of Jean Villandreux.

After handing his company over to his daughter, my father-in-law had taken firm command of *Sports Illustrés,* undertaking an immediate and energetic renovation of a magazine that had seemed set in stone since its creation. This upheaval deeply shocked the editorial staff, who could not understand how a swimming-pool manufacturer, a hitherto lackadaisical boss, could abruptly disfigure a national institution. Officially, nothing justified these changes except management's halfheartedly expressed and rather vague desire to modernize. The truth was much simpler: Jean Villandreux was bored silly. The sports banter that had temporarily amused him no longer enlivened his empty afternoons. What he wanted now, what he needed, was action.

He began by attacking the color of the magazine's print stock, a yellow that he resolved to turn white in one weekend. Next he changed all the typefaces, the page setting, and the entire layout. Before each change, he summoned me to his office, laid the various mock-ups out on his desk, and asked me to pick one.

"Tell me what you think, Paul."

"Why are you asking me? You know I don't have a clue about publishing."

"Perhaps, but you've got a good eye. All photographers do, and yours is first-rate."

Jean Villandreux had a while back anointed me "the guy with a good eye," a kind of visual guru. The photographs that so irritated the daughter filled the father with admiration, leaving him openmouthed before the image of a couple of trees or three wet pebbles.

"We're changing the typeface at the end of the week. Which do you prefer? Garamond, Times, or Bodoni?"

"Maybe Times."

"I knew it. I was sure you would pick Times."

He immediately called the production manager to inform him that from then on the magazine would be printed in Times.

"By the way, how's Anna?"

"She's fine."

"Full of complaints about the employers' tax or her files on export-subsidy claims, I suppose? You must admit, she's done wonders with Atoll. And yourself?"

"What about me?"

"How are you? You look a little tired. You're starting to look like all those guys getting a little something on the side. Ha-ha!"

"I'm okay."

"Seriously, Paul, I might have something for you. A job. A big one and quite interesting."

"Here, at the magazine?"

"No, in Paris. An editor friend of mine is planning a book about trees, a very special project, I believe, one species per page, deluxe, the whole bit, you know what I mean. I spoke to him about your work and he seemed really interested. He'd like you to call him."

"That's nice of you. It's only thanks to you that I'm starting to get anywhere with my photos."

"Anna's supportive in her way?"

"As you know . . ."

"I do indeed: she's getting to be more and more like her mother."

Along with my "good eye" I had a pretty good ear, and this last remark was no compliment. I had heard Jean Villandreux complain bitterly more than once about his wife, betraying the vague resentment or frustration of a disappointed and neglected man. As for Martine Villandreux, time and age seemed to have no hold on her: she was as alluring as ever, her figure and youthful complexion still turning heads. Even I sometimes still felt brief bursts of desire for my mother-in-law, and tortuous fantasies of sodomy would bedevil me in the half-light of my darkroom.

"Why don't you and Anna come to dinner tonight? I'd like that."

I had no doubt that Martine Villandreux had a lover, some intern or young plastic surgeon with whom she occasionally assuaged her midlife crisis. I had once surprised her most awkwardly in her office at the clinic in circumstances that were anything but professional, even though there had been nothing explicitly improper, more a certain steaminess in the atmosphere, flushed cheeks, a palpable sense of embarrassment and the interruption of something that had just happened or been about to. Although Martine Villandreux had immediately regained her composure, her partner—whose face I can't for the life of me recall—panicked like a child and darted between us as swiftly as a rainbow trout. Before he vanished out the door, however, I'd had time to notice his exuberant erection. My mother-in-law then stared pointedly at me, and in her magnificent eyes I saw every possible variation of resentment and contempt. It was clear that her husband had experienced this wounding treatment well before I had. Perhaps he endured it every evening.

Martine Villandreux's outrageous egotism and unquenchable desire to dominate others allowed her to project a sangfroid sometimes indistinguishable from utter indifference or callousness. One evening when Anna and I had been invited to dinner at her parents' house, her mother came home late and in a rage.

"I'm so sorry, but I had a problem at the clinic. I lost a patient."

"What do you mean 'lost'?"

"Are you doing this on purpose, Jean, or what? Lost, all right? Lost, lost!"

"You mean she died?"

"Yes! She died!"

"What happened?"

"The idiot came in for a breast reduction. I operate, everything is fine, and then she goes into V-fib. The anesthesiologist goes crazy and calls the cardio, but by the time the guy gets there, her heart has stopped. Flatlining, it was hopeless."

"Good Lord . . ."

"Then I had to break the news to the family. All the others had beat it, naturally. The husband couldn't understand what had happened, and he started to ask me suspicious questions. Finally I had to take him aside and just speak candidly to the poor guy: Listen, when your wife has heart trouble, you do not let her have cosmetic breast surgery! Period!"

"So what did the guy say?"

"Well, what could he say? He started to cry. I just hope it doesn't all end up in court. The last thing we need is to give the insurance company an excuse to hit us with some huge rate increase."

From that moment on, I couldn't get Jean Villandreux's remark about Anna out of my mind: "She's getting to be more and more like her mother. . . ."

Anna certainly was like the times we lived in: insolent, greedy, anxious to possess, to have, to show off, to behave as if history were truly at an end. Well before Fukuyama, my wife was developing a thesis that reduced the world to a sort of acritical mass necessary only for regulating the currency exchange rate and raking in collateral profits. During the eighties, you had to be dead not to have any ambition. Money had the aggressive and truly noxious smell of toilet deodorants. All those who couldn't stand the stink were asked not to interfere with those who could. Swiftly won over by the perks of the business world, the Socialists and their friends would display the traditional fervor of converts as they slipped into the domain of industry, infiltrated the financial sphere, invaded the halls of power. Finally my wife began to say good things about them—a sure sign. Hadn't they chosen Laurent Fabius as prime minister, and managed to clean the Communists out of the government? "France is gradually recovering her human face," my mother-in-law would opine, piling it on. Such were my country and the family whose lives I shared.

My mother was slowly turning into an old lady. She continued to correct and return the work of all sorts of writers who, through ignorance or carelessness, grew ever more heedless of proper usage. She who had always worn her heart on the left did not understand my mistrust of the Socialists. Although I did not yet know it, she was nursing a passion for François Mitterrand that would eventually become all-consuming.

His name was Louis Spiridon, like the winner of the first Olympic marathon of modern times, and he directed the "luxury book" department of a major Parisian publishing house, where he glided along the narrow hallways as if floating on a cushion of air. He spoke to his authors—as well as to printers, booksellers, and distributors—with great civility and equanimity. Any relationship with Spiridon had to be civilized: he belonged to that race of men bred to rise above character defects, discourage misbehavior, and dampen disagreements. As a good friend of my father-in-law's, he welcomed me warmly. One thing did intrigue me: Spiridon's insistent questions about my mother-in-law.

"A woman of striking beauty, don't you think? You see, I knew her when she was finishing her medical studies. We were quite young."

At the end of each sentence, Spiridon paused in a brief silence that could be interpreted in many ways, but his distant smile and careful choice of words made his meaning perfectly clear. With a strange gesture, as if brushing away a fly on a summer afternoon, Spiridon broke free of that past to speak to me about his current preoccupation: his arboreal project.

"I have two books in mind. The first, which could be entitled *Trees of France*, would be a deluxe survey of the principal species of our nation. The second, *Trees of the World*, would follow the same format but on a planetary scale. The attraction of these works would of course lie in the illustrative treatment, in the excellence of the photographs. I would like true portraits of each tree, with careful consideration given to the lighting, the angle of the shot, the perspective. Jean has shown me your work and it's exactly what I'm looking for. Nowadays most photographers can take action photos in a thousandth of a second. Very few, on the other hand, have the eye or the ability to illuminate the beauty of immobility."

"Who selects the trees?"

"You do. There's a lot of research involved. Getting leads. Traveling. And then you'll have to play around with the seasons, the evergreen and deciduous varieties. When you're working on a species, you'll have to spend days seeking the specimen that stands out from all the others, the one that will suddenly strike you as exceptional. Each time you will have to find the tree that in itself encompasses and eclipses the forest. And when you have finally found that rare pearl, its surroundings must set off our marvel to perfection. I won't mislead you: this project will be a long labor, requiring patience and exacting care. What do you think?"

To be paid for looking at the world. Speaking to no one. Living in the solitude of the woods. Learning from the trees and the earth. I could not imagine anything closer to perfect liberation. As Spiridon was talking to me, I was already at the foot of a cedar I knew, framing the shot, studying the light.

"For both these works, the editorial approach must be clear and inviolable: one tree per page, full bleed, in its natural setting. No tricks, no artificial lighting. Please understand me, Monsieur Blick, this project is much more than a commercial undertaking. I want everyone who opens these books to feel something indefinable, a primordial emotion that revives the connection that once bound us to the world of plant life, a bond we no longer remember today."

Life was offering me a magnificent gift: a year's salary to live in peace among trees. I had lucked into my goal: professional work unhampered by schedules, supervision, or supervisory responsibilities. As soon as I got back from Paris, I decided to acquire a Hasselblad 6 x 6 to complement the excellent and reliable photographic equipment I'd inherited from my father: a twin-lens Rolleiflex, two Nikon F cameras with 20mm, 35mm, 50mm, and 105mm lenses, and a Leitz Focomat IIc enlarger.

Anna was very supportive of me but dubious about a project she felt was doomed to commercial failure.

"I'm just delighted for you. But you have to agree that this whole thing hasn't got a leg to stand on! A venture so poorly worked out, based on a vague feeling and intuition, would be ripped to shreds by any sane banker. You wouldn't get to square one in the real world."

Anna's *real* world was the business world: a competently managed universe where hiring was done in dribs and drabs and firing in great swaths, thus cleverly transforming work into a commodity as rare as cobalt, and indoctrinating an entire generation into the humiliating act of kowtowing.

I began my work a few days before the Greenpeace Affair hit the news. Flitting from tree to tree, I heard on the car radio about the murderous underwater adventures of a handful of the French Republic's scuba divers sent halfway around the world to Auckland to satisfy the ego of some Socialist zealot by blowing up the *Rainbow Warrior,* a Greenpeace vessel protesting the French nuclear testing program at Moruroa Atoll. Fernando Pereira, a Portuguese photographer, was killed in the explosion.

Luckily, I had my trees. It was as if they had been waiting for me forever. As if they had pushed all the other trees away to provide me with beautiful perspectives and clear shots of their solitary splendor. Nature was bursting with showy specimens. A stroll around a forest or through a valley was enough to spot them. I would come back later, when the shadows began to lengthen and the light was turning to gold, or early the next morning, when the world still seemed to float in the anonymity of night. Species after species, week after week, I filled my gigantic arboreal portfolio. I drove all over the country looking for weeping willows, cedars, plane trees, elms, magnolias, oaks, chestnuts, birches, hazel trees, beeches, cypresses, maples, walnuts, hackberries, yews, mulberries, parasol pines, firs, poplars, palms, pear trees, lindens, olives, peach trees, acacias, cherry trees—every sort that grew on French soil.

As Spiridon had so presciently advised, there would inevitably be one tree embodying all the majesty and particularity of its species, one that would "eclipse" the rest of the forest. I had only to position my tripod, screw on the Hasselblad, and wait for the right moment. I often worked that way: selecting my tree by noon, I would set up nearby. By the time the lovely late-afternoon light arrived, the tree and I had gotten to know each other, in a way. The tree doubtless envied my mobility, whereas I admired the patience and perseverance that enabled it to remain rooted to its spot for centuries. The toughest among them—oaks, beeches, chestnuts, yews, olive trees—merrily lasted more than a thousand years. There were two-thousand-year-old olives at Roquebrune-Cap-Martin, in the *département* of Alpes-Maritimes, as well as in the Haute-Garonne, quite close to Toulouse. Six-hundred-year-old yews were still living in the *départements* of Corrèze and Calvados. Some chestnut trees had been growing in the Finistère for fifteen hundred years. And in the Var, there were countless cork oaks more than a thousand years old.

During those long waits I would imagine that these trees must have a memory somewhere, one doubtless quite different from our own, but capable of recording the history of their meadows, and the chatty frequencies of distant cities. I was absolutely certain that they also possessed an understanding of the world just as subtle as ours. Like us, they had a mission: to build their destiny from nothing, from a combination of chance and necessity, from a simple seed borne by a bird or the wind, and then to adapt themselves to the rain and to the salt of the earth.

Like agitated ants, we strive to find a place in this world. The trees must not understand our species at all. Small aggressive mammals with meager life expectancies, we struggle constantly and fall inexorably at their feet without ever taking root anywhere. We never seem to learn anything lasting from our mistakes, despite our genius for inventing fizzy drinks and wireless telephones.

Meditating beneath the trees changed me. Frequenting them so faithfully that I almost came to speak their language, I realized that I would hereafter find it practically impossible to photograph human beings. Whenever the wind blew through the forest, it was as if a sudden equinoctial tide were beating in the heart of the woods, as if the forges of the sea were roaring close by. I spent hours listening to the chorus of those phantom waves.

The Hasselblad took superb pictures, exceptional in their clarity of detail. The 6 x 6 was truly a grand format—small wonder that this Swedish camera was selected by NASA to record the images of the astronauts taking their first steps on the moon. As my pictures piled up by the hundreds in boxes, my eye grew expert at discerning the personality of each tree. There were those who took things lightly, ready to frolic at the slightest breeze. Grown accustomed to their poor soil, the austere trees had learned to make every effort count. The true arboreal fortresses were unshakable, plunging into the earth right down to the kingdom of the dead. The coddled trees, the progeny of fertile soil, reveled in the richness of their luxuriant greenery. The slender dreamers with their heads always in the clouds were not really of this world. The knotty, nervous ones were tortured and twisted by their age-old doubts. The aristocrats, ramrod straight, betrayed a subtle disdain through their slightly haughty demeanor. The generous trees offered their abundant branches and shade without a second thought. All lined up, the toilers worked tirelessly to hold the earth in place. I spent hours in the darkroom succumbing to this pathetic fallacy, ascribing every shade of temperament to my subjects. Two photos in particular, however, remained impossible to define, and they never failed to affect everyone who saw them. I couldn't say why, but both those trees seemed so alive in their portraits that you felt they were looking at you, and not the other way around.

The first picture had been taken south of La Montagne Noire—Black Mountain—between Mazamet and Carcassonne. It was a winter evening. That day the earth was dusted with snow and girdled waist-high with mist, but the air above was crystalline, with a limpid, eerie luminosity. At the summit of the hill, set well apart from the forest and dominating the plain, was an araucaria, a conifer native to Chile, a kind of fir tree with stiff prickle-tipped leaves and intricately ramifying branches like those of a huge chandelier. It looked like a Viking ship floating in the fog, a green sentinel at the outposts of the world, a figuration of solitude and exile. For a while I stood face-to-face with that tree, and throughout our encounter I felt myself somehow an intruder, sensed that my presence disturbed the araucaria, which did not hesitate moreover to tell me so by staring back at me through the camera lens. The photo faithfully captures that malaise. Anyone studying the image can feel the araucaria's challenge: "You have no business being here."

The second photo was quite different. I took it in a clearing in a forest in the Landes on a stormy day when the sea winds were gusting at more than sixty miles an hour. Because of the weather, I hadn't intended to take any pictures, I was simply scouting. And then I spotted it. An immense pine alone in an open corridor through which the wind was pouring like an avalanche. The tree was a colossus, head and shoulders above the other pines, and buffeted by the gale, it flung itself about in every direction as if trying to escape from invisible flames. You could hear it crack and groan, too, as the wind played it like a pipe. The tree seemed to be waging solitary battle against the tempest, as vanguard of the forest, attempting to blunt the attack all by itself. Knowing that I would never again have the chance to capture such a struggle, I took the picture. There is something astounding about that image, and terrifying, too. The entire tree is fighting: braced on its roots, it clings to the belly of the earth, dramatically embodying the often abstract idea people have of "the rage to live." The next day, when I returned to the forest to take some more pictures, the mighty pine tree had been laid low. Uprooted, vanquished.

Begun during the summer of 1985 while the wishy-washy Social-Democrat Laurent Fabius was in office, *Trees of France* was finished two months after Jacques Chirac had replaced him as prime minister. The uneasy "cohabitation" of a Socialist president and a more right-leaning prime minister allowed the country and the whole Ship of Fools of State to scratch that little eczema patch that passed for national life until it bled, and some old conservatives now shared the power previously monopolized by the reformers. As for the president of the Republic, the impassive pharaoh from the Morvan region in central France, he was supervising the construction of his vainglorious pyramid at the Louvre.

To say that *Trees of France* was a success is an understatement. The book was one of the year's best sellers, acclaimed by both the press and the general public. Television, radio, and newspaper reviewers praised it extravagantly, all finding something to suit their own editorial interests and particular audiences. The mainstream settled on "the beauty and majesty of the photographs," while the higher-brow magazines analyzed "the stunning simplicity of a concept carried rigorously to its logical end, without pandering to cheap thrills or the empty esthetics of a coffee-table book." Louis Spiridon was ecstatic. He accompanied me on every radio or TV program that invited me. And whenever someone asked how I'd come up with such a simple and lovely idea, I always pointed out that I was merely the cameraman carrying out a project for which my editor deserved all the credit. Whenever I paid him homage like that, and I did so many times, Spiridon became giddy from his adorably effervescent little sin of pride.

Even with our publicity tour in full swing, Spiridon was already telling everyone that he would soon be publishing *Trees of the World*, putting the idea of that sumptuous global sequel into the heads of journalists and booksellers, describing species he didn't even know existed. I would be the photographer, of course—and just wait until they saw what I would bring back this time!

The tidal wave of sales had instantly made me very rich. With the press now calling me "the Weegee of the plant world," my status at home had changed as well. Success, it seemed, had made me sexier, and Anna was seeing me in a new light. Back when I handled the household chores, she would fuck me sporadically with the perfunctory generosity usually reserved for the presentation of holiday tips. Now that I had sold more than three hundred thousand copies, she treated me like some important Japanese buyer who could without a second thought order a hundred of her dreadful Jacuzzis. I'm convinced that the mere idea excited her. In her eyes, I was a new man, one of those fashionable types you see on TV who one day will inevitably wind up buying a hot tub.

As for the children, they always seemed surprised to see me talking on a prerecorded TV program even as I was changing the broken plug on the vacuum cleaner. Although they had no problem dealing with such distortion in time and space where a stranger was concerned, they were at a loss to understand the illusory ubiquity apparently enjoyed by this father who was both everywhere and nowhere. For the bond between my children and me had been broken. Vincent and Marie had forgotten all the life we had shared during their earliest years, and they remembered only my—to them—inexcusable absences of recent months. They were not hostile to me, but treated me with indifference, making me pay dearly for having abandoned my post. Their mother had regained control of them through Jeanne, the nanny she had hired.

The person most impressed by my brief media exposure was unquestionably Martine Villandreux. A few TV programs were enough to endow me in her haughty eyes with the aura of a sort of latter-day Napoleon. Now whenever the Blicks and Villandreuxs dined together, she hung on my every word. To be anointed by television was to her the sanctification of modern times; anyone so honored deserved gold, incense, and—why not?—myrrh. When I had pursued my tree photography without either recognition or compensation, I'd been grudgingly allowed to sit at the family table with humbly downcast eyes while dreaming about the derrière of the mistress of the house; now that same backside, previously so intimidating, was positively quivering with happiness at the mere thought of my crossing her threshold.

This development effectively short-circuited my incestuous fantasies; I now considered Martine Villandreux's charms on a par with the famous beef roast of David Rochas. So I will never know if, had my feelings not changed, she would have allowed her newly glamorous son-in-law to slip a hand beneath her violet cashmere to knead her admirable bosom to his heart's content.

The only two who couldn't have cared less about my celebrity were Jean Villandreux, to whom I was still "a guy with a good eye," and my mother, who would consider me, millionaire or not, "Vincent's little brother" until the day she died.

Before I set out again to work on the second book, Anna demanded that we buy a house; the children, she argued, should now enjoy the advantages of a yard. I sensed that her real reason was keeping up appearances, building a little principality to compete with the maternal duchy. I had always underestimated the rather primitive rivalry that set Anna against her mother, an antagonism that sometimes surfaced in unexpected and barely decipherable ways. Anna wanted to show her that she could handle everything, whether it was swimming pools, Jacuzzis, children, a new house, or that laconic tree portraitist everyone was talking about on television.

When I think back to that time, I see a lost man, in a daze of his own indolence, sucking an insipid happiness from a tired tit. I no longer really liked the people around me, but I didn't hate them enough to have the courage to leave them. I was working to earn money I no longer needed. I drove a 1969 Volkswagen Cabriolet to enjoy the luxury and amusement of dreading mechanical breakdowns. I continued to screw Laure Milo now and then, and to dine twice a month with her husband, François. He still talked about his planes, Anna would discuss her hot tubs, and Laure kept fondling me discreetly between courses. Michel Campion's surgical anecdotes interested no one, apart from the fact that they were salacious. As for his wife, Brigitte, she was still consulting all sorts of beauty experts without ever managing to improve her plain face or lumpen figure.

Our new home was probably two hundred years old, and with its walls of pink brick and Garonne pebble, modest tiled eaves, stone front steps and windowsills, the building seemed like a fat cat dozing in the sun. The color of the façade gave a golden tint to the daylight and a permanent late-afternoon atmosphere to the terraces. A superb house—to look at. Because you had to be completely insane to buy such a thing and hope to feel at home inside it, to raise children, make love, sometimes stay in bed sick, grow old within its walls, and of course, eventually, die there. To make the slightest impression on a house that had seen so much, to fill all those rooms with the reassuring shouts and laughter of life required a good dozen hefty humans, and we were only four unhappy castaways, wandering its endless halls. Living in a house that is too big quickly instills a feeling of chronic anxiety. The unoccupied space becomes a hostile zone of silent reproof. At first, when I came home, I would feel myself being swallowed by a gigantic stomach that would slowly digest me throughout the evening and night, finally excreting me when morning arrived. It took a long time to get rid of the feeling of going through a demeaning daily cloacal cycle.

When I confided my unease to Anna, she replied, "Now that, that's going beyond interior design and right on into psychoanalysis."

"Listen, I'm serious! The house really bothers me, I'm not comfortable here."

"You'll get used to it, comrade. It's just your guilty left-wing conscience that's getting to you."

"What are you talking about?"

"It's the truth! Unconsciously, you don't accept what's happening to you—either the money, or the book, or this nice house. According to your logic, you have to refuse these things because they make you a petty bourgeois, a middle-class guy like all the rest, just a cog working inside the system you've programmed yourself to consider evil."

"That's ridiculous."

"I don't think so. Actually, my dear, I'm afraid happiness has caught up with you, and that's why you're panicking."

She was not being disingenuous. Anna's idea of happiness required two things: a seven-figure bank account and a very large house. Ignoring my protests, she had bought that place not to live in it, but to show it off as the repository of unimaginable treasures. She didn't care that the four of us dragged around inside it like souls in torment.

Every once in a while I'd go have lunch with my mother, who, ever since François Mitterrand had been elected, now swore only by the Socialists. Her unconditional admiration for the president was enough to blot out all the incompetence and treachery of his friends. She experienced the "cohabitation" as a slow crucifixion, and likened Prime Minister Chirac to a painfully tight pair of hiking boots that impeded the triumphant progress of the Great Strider. The house had not suffered too much from my father's disappearance, and although the garden had reverted to a wilder state, it kept its indefinable charm. Anyway, the place was still welcoming and familiar, and I found it restful and comforting to be there. It was there I felt at home. This is not to say that my mother had any sympathy for my feeling that I was living in Anna's house like a stowaway huddled inside the immense vault of a tanker. My mother would listen to me politely, and abruptly cut me off with a little toss of her head: "You're too spoiled."

I never learned what my mother really thought of Anna. Whether she felt true affection for her. Whether she appreciated her undeniable business acumen or, on the contrary, despised her love of lucre. When they were together, Anna and my mother each became opaque, unreadable. Their relationship was one of astonishing neutrality, and any feelings they may have had for each other were concealed in the froth of their chatter. My mother never once asked me if I was happy with Anna. The frequency of my visits and my aversion to the tanker, however, doubtless told her all she cared to know.

Whenever I returned home from visiting my mother and walked up the long path through the garden in the darkness, I felt like an insect flitting instinctively toward the light. Like all insects, I would hesitate for a moment at a window before entering, to see what awaited me inside.

Was I too spoiled, as my mother kept telling me? Probably. But I also had good reason to wonder about the evolution of my own life and my ability to control it effectively. Having always prided myself on resisting the temptations and pressures of the ruthlessly seductive or subtly authoritarian social contract, I discovered that like everyone else I had been carried away by its kinetic energy. Step by step, I had undergone all the phases of indoctrination into middle-class citizenship without even realizing it. A student in pursuit of his diplomas, a libertarian after his amusements, an intermittent libertine when adventure required, then respectably married, proudly paternal, and finally, remarkably rich. In the end, I had proved a good pupil. Instead of thrashing me or bringing me to heel, the system, like Anna's house, had decided to digest me. Actually, I went like a lamb.

I think it was around this time (with a push from AIDS) that monogamous love resurfaced as a fashionable preoccupation. Given the logic of evolution and its indelible conditioning, I thus seemed condemned, eventually, to experiment once more with that emotion, though I no longer cherished any illusions. I considered love a kind of belief, a form of religion with a human face. Instead of believing in God, one had faith in the other person, but in reality this other person did not exist any more than God did. The other person was only the deceptive reflection of oneself, the mirror assigned to calm the terror of unfathomable loneliness. We are all weak enough to believe that every love story is unique and exceptional. The simple truth could not be more banal: all our heartfelt feelings are identical, reproducible, predictable. Following the initial excitement, the long days of habit arrive to usher in the endless tyranny of boredom. All of that is programmed deep inside our hearts. The rhythm and intensity of the sequence depend solely on our individual share of hormones, the mood of our molecules, and the speed of our synapses. Our education—our obedience training, I should say—takes care of the rest, making us believe that a one-track mind, a pounding heart, and a stiff erection are the happy signs of who knows what divine or supernatural grace granted to us mortals on a case-by-case basis. Love is one of those sophisticated emotions that we have learned to foster, one of those narcotic diversions that help us await death patiently.

I never talked about such things with Anna or her friends. None of them would have even considered—much less shared—such a mechanistic point of view. The only person I trusted enough to broach the subject with was Marie. We had talked a few times about this human tendency to embellish and misrepresent our love affairs, in conformity with the strictures of head-over-heels bliss, the template of Eros. The more I think back on it, the more I tell myself that Marie was probably the only woman I've known who never hesitated to look life squarely in the face and deal with it for what it is. When we were sleeping together, I would sometimes glimpse the faint gleam of her eyes in the darkness, and whenever I asked her if something was wrong, she would simply say, "I'm thinking." With that same unflinching gaze, she took the true measure of love.

. . .

I hardly felt like dealing with emotions, preoccupied as I was with preparations for my long trip from continent to continent in search of my arboreal models. The day of my departure, the children went off to school without kissing me or even saying good-bye, and Anna simply waved as though I were going to the post office. Despite all my mechanistic theories about the cold truth of emotions, their behavior broke my heart.

But then began the most magical and mysterious period of my life. Even today it's hard to talk about it, to describe that almost unbroken series of amazing experiences that changed my perception of the world as I went from place to place, from tree to tree. Traveling light, nomadically, unburdened by responsibility, like an aerial sprite, I delved into the infinite beauty of the plant kingdom.

I encountered extreme heat, fought fierce winds, trudged through raging storms and torrential downpours, all to see a tree, one tree, and take its picture. I saw sempervirent sequoias and Douglas firs well over a hundred meters tall swaying in the breezes of northern California and British Columbia; giant saguaros towering in the Arizona desert; nonchalant coconut palms in the Bahamas; portly baobabs in Kenya; the sweet-sapped sugar maples of Quebec and the heveas of Malaysia; cryptomerias, the *Larix leptolepis* with its drooping lower branches, and maples with seven-lobed palmate leaves, all three living in Japan; striking palms in Morocco; the generous coffee trees of Colombia; indestructible ironwoods in South Africa; the precious spurge olive, worth its weight in gold in Thailand; the flamboyant Hinoki cypress of Taiwan; austere Montezuma cypresses in Oaxaca; immortal three-thousand-year-old chestnut trees in Sicily; massive oaks in the Sherwood Forest of Robin Hood; the giant eucalyptuses of Tasmania; and in Calcutta, unbelievable banyans with their myriad trunks—three hundred and fifty big ones, three thousand little ones—whose total circumference exceeded four hundred meters. Branch after branch, species after species, they just kept coming, and each was more elegant and spectacular than the next. I knew I would never get to the end of them. In all my portraits I concentrated compulsively on the tiniest details of each specimen's bark. Time was no object, and before long my lists fell by the wayside, along with my schedule. I hadn't the slightest idea what I was seeking, succumbing at last to that absurd, mad quest for perfection, completeness, and even purity. Always alone, I would walk. For hours and hours. Until I saw it. Until I understood that it was for this tree that I had come all this way. Then, finding the right angle, I had only to wait for the light. I had learned to accept bad weather, to integrate it into the scheme, no longer stymied in my work by rain or overcast skies, by gusts of wind or snow. Deep in certain tropical regions, I sometimes witnessed storms worthy of Dante, echoing with a thousand bombardments, shaking the earth's crust so violently I was moved to imagine the very creation of the world. On my solitary walks, I often found myself thinking about my father's garden, and the silent labors of my mother, whose father I still remembered, standing on the summit of his pass, lost in amazement at the beauty of his mountains. In periods of rest and waiting I studied the leaves of my models. I examined their blades, their veins, their petioles, and I classified them into families according to their outlines: palmatisect, digitate, pinnate, pinnatilobed, sinuate, thorny, dentate, pinnatisect, sheathing, peltate, palmatilobate, or palmatifid. Almost without realizing it, I was penetrating deeper every day into a universe that was becoming more spectral, more ethereal. It was near Colombo that my voyage, which might have lasted a lifetime, came to an abrupt end, on an evening when my mind and body conspired to lay me low as I returned from photographing some tea trees in the mountains of Sri Lanka.

I was staying in a little wooden hotel on the beach. Night fell early, and I usually ate supper outside on the terrace by the light of an oil lamp. That evening everything began when I started shivering. Then came the fever, nausea, and violent diarrhea. I felt I was expelling liters of water and vomiting handfuls of fishhooks. My guts were engaged in a ferocious battle; my body was on fire and quaked uncontrollably. I stuffed the hem of my bedsheet into my mouth to keep my teeth from chattering. Then I would get up—and the hell would start all over again. I kept thinking of something I had once read about Sri Lanka: "If someday you come to Ceylon, make the trip for good reasons, or no matter how strong you are, you will die there."

By day the fever and intestinal symptoms vanished as if by enchantment, but I was so exhausted that I was bedridden; when night fell, the fever and gut-wrenching symptoms would return like an inexorable tide.

During those nocturnal episodes, I couldn't tell anymore if I was delirious or having nightmares. Sometimes all the trees I had photographed appeared at my bedside, bending over me and slowly covering me with their dead leaves; sometimes my brother, Vincent, would silently enter the room and with his Brownie Flash take picture after picture of me in my sweat-drenched sheets. I begged him to help me, to get me out of there, but he went methodically about his task.

After a week I was completely helpless. The owner of the hotel would bring me rice, vegetables, and a bit of fish that I barely touched. I also vaguely remember the visit of a local doctor who prescribed for me, as I later learned, a decoction of herbs and other plants. I slept all day long, until the return of the tormenting devils at twilight. Every night I would throw up, crouched in front of an old portrait of the queen of England dating from the colonial period. It never even occurred to me to have myself taken to a hospital. The owner of the hotel hadn't thought of that either; he was used to seeing his Western guests tossing and turning and vomiting into his toilets. He had faith in time, which he believed should be allowed to do its work. I knew that in those parts, when poor people had exhausted their strength, they would lie down and die in the streets. In the morning men hired to check the sidewalks would collect the bodies and pile them into a cart. But whatever was Vincent going to do with all those photos?

When things were really bad at night, just before I went under I would wind the strap of my camera bag around my wrist and gather my films and cameras into my arms. I never did figure out if I was hoping to protect them from some danger that way or if I was trying somehow to comfort myself. Sometimes blood would gush from my nose and my gums would bleed. Breathless with anxiety, I would feel an icy chill flow slowly through my body.

During my illness I bowed down, but I never prayed. Not even in the worst of my pain and fear, not even when I saw my strength draining from my belly. From my bed I could smell the incense burning in a nearby temple, and those sickly sweet fumes of supplication only added to my disgust.

I have always been an atheist who finds any and all religions inadmissible. I had seen the vermin of faith and belief gnaw away at human beings everywhere, humiliating them, demeaning them, driving them mad, and reducing them to the state of caged animals. God is the worst thing that man ever invented: I consider it a useless, unwarranted idea. A species coaxed by evolution to stand on its hind legs should not give in so swiftly to the temptation to sink back to its knees out of fear of the void and invent its own master, animal trainer, guru, accountant, entrusting him with life and death, the soul and its eternity. When my fever was at its height, when I was nauseated by the incense, even on the brink of losing consciousness, I never prayed to anyone. I simply clung to the reality around me, finding comfort in the company of my cameras, my pictures, and, above all, my trees.

One morning after the usual nocturnal scouring, I managed to find the energy to break that infernal day-and-night cycle: I got dressed and took a taxi to the airport.

The ride seemed endless, as if we were driving through every suburb in the world. The dizziness that had dogged me constantly for a week made this road trip feel rather like a storm at sea. The floor of the taxi—an old Hillman, I think—was rusted through in places so that I could see the pavement rushing past beneath my feet. Once more I was strapped to my most precious possession: my camera bag, and especially my trees, which I dreaded to see vanish into that yawning gap. Halfway to the airport, it began to rain, and water started splashing into the vehicle through the holes in its chassis. Making no effort to avoid potholes or any animals crossing the road, the driver simply leaned on his horn, and when he ran down a dog, we barely felt the impact, but for an instant I saw the animal's body pass below me before it snagged by the jaw on the side frame of the taxi. Was I still in the hotel, enveloped in my infected sheets and the putrid limbo of my bad dreams, or were we driving in a monsoon downpour to the Colombo International Airport dragging along a dead dog?

As soon as the stewardess stowed my bag in the overhead compartment and offered to assist me to my seat, I had the physical sensation that all the devils that had been infesting my belly for three weeks were deciding not to come along with me on the flight. I really felt them desert me. As the Boeing 747 gained altitude, I closed my eyes, reassured and at peace, and slipped without fear into a night I now knew would heal me.

Anna came to fetch me at the airport in Blagnac. When she caught sight of me, she drew back in dismay.

"What happened to you?"

"I was sick."

"With what?"

"I don't know; diarrhea, fever, vertigo . . ."

"Did you see a doctor?"

"I think so. I don't remember anymore."

"You're so pale and thin it's frightening. Are you on medication?"

"No."

"You can't come back to the house in this state."

"Why not?"

"What if you have something serious and contagious? Where did you fly in from?"

"Sri Lanka."

"That's it: I'm taking you to the clinic. You have to think of the children. Look at you, you can hardly walk. Give me your bag."

"No, I'm holding on to it."

I spent four days in a center for the treatment of contagious tropical diseases. I don't remember ever sleeping as soundly as I did during that short hospital stay. Hooked up to an IV, rehydrated, transfigured thanks to some kind of therapeutic cocktail, I went home thoroughly rested and serene in body and spirit.

And for the first time, I was glad to enter that house. After what I had just gone through, I could no longer imagine my home devouring me and shitting me out. I wasn't afraid of the house anymore. In spite of its grand airs, I knew it could not approach the carnivorousness of my hotel room in Sri Lanka.

I had been gone for six months and by chance had returned a few days before my son Vincent's birthday, which that year happened to coincide with the crash of 1987 on Wall Street. Stocks lost 30 percent of their value after the announcement of America's gargantuan foreign trade deficit. For reasons that I did not yet understand, Anna followed these developments with dramatic intensity. I later learned that the crisis had seriously damaged her portfolio, but for the moment, indifferent to this financial earthquake, I was feeling the effects of a much more intimate disturbance: Vincent was almost an adolescent, and with the exception of his earliest years, I had barely seen him grow up. All the regret in the world couldn't change that.

Vincent's features still showed the smooth grace of childhood, but he already displayed his mother's self-assurance and determination. I'm sure he had a David Rochas among his friends, some kid bold and knowing enough to teach him, much better than I could, the secrets— rather basic, after all—of masculinity.

Since my return, I had noticed that my daughter, Marie, was keeping a certain distance and not speaking to me much. And when I was reading, she sometimes came to sit in a nearby armchair and studied me silently. This insistent, searching examination, in which I sensed a mute reproach, made me so uneasy that I occasionally went somewhere else.

In my darkroom I had begun developing my films and printing the first pictures in black-and-white. The definition of the images was so precise that the texture of the tree trunks seemed three-dimensional. Spending my days shut up like that with my trees, I never spoke and saw no one. Now I felt as though a pane of glass had been installed between me and my family. Whenever I tried to reach Anna by showing her some of my pictures, she would glance through them distractedly and say, "You're lucky you can earn a living so easily." The bitter edge to her voice implied that for her, success demanded constant vigilance, and survival was a never-ending struggle. She gave me to understand that the jungle of the marketplace was a lot more dangerous than photographic safaris through the plant kingdom. Watching for her slightest slipup, predators were waiting to pounce on her and make off with her business. I nodded my agreement with an affectionate smile, wondering how much competition there could possibly be for the production of ugly Jacuzzis in unspeakable colors.

"I'm tired, you know. Sick of all this."

It was the first time I'd ever heard Anna admit such a thing. "All this" was the family business to which she had devoted her time, the better part of her youth and energy, a firm she had modernized and that provided a livelihood for almost a hundred employees, an enterprise devoted entirely to the trivial mission of selling little bubbly pools to people who already had running water.

"Things aren't going well. I'm going to have to lay people off."

Anna's eyes were dulled by exhaustion and, for the first time I could remember, the shadow of defeat. Her voice, which could range over every tone of authority, now seemed to quaver.

"This collapse is real, and naturally we're the first ones to feel it."

"But why?"

"All those guys who've lost a bundle were our potential customers, the ones who support the luxury and leisure industries. We straddle those two categories. Our orders have gone down by sixty-five percent."

"How many people are you going to let go?"

"A third of them, to start with. A few in every department."

"If it can help you, take the money you need from my royalties."

"That's sweet of you, but it wouldn't help at all. Maybe it would delay things a little, but it's not a question of getting over a hump. The party's over and we may have to live with that for a good long while."

"Have you discussed this with your father?"

"My father? Since he left Atoll he hasn't once set foot in the office. He's obsessed with that magazine. The magazine and my mother."

"Your mother?"

"He's convinced she's got a lover. He's becoming impossible."

"Still, you should talk things over with him before you let anyone go."

"For God's sake, can't you understand? It isn't a problem of competition, or modernization, or productivity. There are no more orders, no
more buyers, that's it, period. People have things they need a lot more
than Jacuzzis. I'm tired of fighting all alone. It's not enough that the
banks are breathing down my neck, now I have to deal with the unions
and meet with all those people to tell them that I can't pay them anymore. I've never done that before in my life."

Anna curled up on the sofa and laid her cheek against my thigh. She
closed her eyes like a little girl who is fast asleep. You could barely tell
that she was breathing. I thought about the helpless distress of all the
Adam Smiths of this world, and the absurdity of the free market, and as
I softly stroked Anna's hair, I saw a tear trickle slowly down her cheek
to the corner of her mouth.

The tribulations of modern times ceased at my darkroom door. There
I worked in the old-fashioned way, with time-honored materials: silver
salts, hypo, photo paper, and, above all, patience, meticulous care, neat-
ness, and the silence that finally upholstered every square inch of that
room. Spiridon was after me to send him my camera-ready black-and-
whites as soon as possible, while the distributors and bookstores were
still excited about *Trees of France*. Everyone, it seems, expected big
things from *Trees of the World*. But I continued to take my time obsess-
ing over each image. Having decided to go with strongly contrasting
tonalities, I was constantly using my Exaphot automatic integrator to
adjust the light, and I also used my hands to dodge parts of the print,
highlighting a lovely cloudy sky or sections of a trunk that were too
dark.

As I was pulling my trees one by one from the night, working as
slowly as a taxidermist, Laure Milo came twice to see me. The first time
was about ten days after my return, and the visit was cut short when
Laure saw how thin I was. My drawn face, the circles under my eyes,
and that pasty complexion one often sees with liver trouble dispelled
every glint of desire from Laure's eyes, which promptly filled with the
solicitous compassion appropriate at the bedside of invalids. Our second meeting took place two or three weeks later, after I had recovered
my strength and my face looked human again. Laure had slunk into the

darkroom as though trailed by the cops. She looked quite tan in the light of my sodium lamp, and I couldn't make out the precise shade of her blouse, but I definitely recognized the light summer skirt I had lifted up a few times before. Laure was on pins and needles, shifting from one foot to the other, glancing at a few photos, coughing gently, tossing back her hair, crossing and uncrossing her arms, clearing her throat again, watching me pull a print, then going off to fiddle with some implement or other.

"Can you listen to me for a moment?"

"I'm all ears."

"No, I mean I'd like us to have a serious conversation. I've got a major problem."

"I'm listening."

"I've met someone. A little over a year ago. It began six or eight months before you left. He's only a bit older than I am, and he's wonderful."

"Hmm."

"Are you shocked?"

"Not at all. I'm just trying to figure out what the problem is."

"The problem is that we love each other, but he's married, and I'm pregnant."

"By him?"

"Yes."

"You're sure?"

"Absolutely. François was in Germany at the time. In any case, with him, it's every three months. Believe me, there's no doubt about the father."

"What are you going to do?"

"That's it, I don't know. I would have liked to go live with Simon and keep the baby, but it's impossible, there are way too many complications. Simon, my friend, is . . . what I mean is, he's a rabbi."

It was inconsiderate of me, given Laure's predicament, but I burst out laughing anyway.

"I knew you'd react like that! You're the last person I should have come to for help."

"I'm sorry, it was just so unexpected—a rabbi?"

"I'm completely lost, Paul. Some evenings I'm on the verge of telling François everything, if only to bring him back down to earth, so he'd forget his fucking planes for two lousy minutes!"

"Why can't you live with this other man?"

"Simon? Are you crazy? In the first place, I'm not Jewish. And really—can you see him, the pillar of morality in his community, the rabbi who performs marriages, leaving his wife and children overnight to go live with a shiksa he got pregnant? Promise me you won't ever tell anyone about this!"

"Of course. And François?"

"As always, on another planet. If I were to tell him all this tonight, he would smile like an idiot, tell me that's great, and get right back to work on his computer. I don't give a shit about François."

"And your rabbi?"

"Him? He gets furious when I tell him that I want to keep the child. The only thing he's worried about is that the news might get around."

"If I understand correctly, he's more of a rabbi than a lover."

"I don't care! I can't do without him, do you understand? He drives me mad, I've never known anything like it."

"Known what?"

"I'm not going to draw you a picture!"

Then Laure told me something I never thought to hear on this earth.

"You see, Paul, I think two men have truly touched me in my life. You, because in a way you were the nicest, and Simon, because he was the only one who ever made me come."

I had just turned thirty-eight years old. I was living among my trees. My children didn't trust me. My mother-in-law had a lover. My mother had voted for a bourgeois in Socialist's clothing. My wife was preparing to put dozens of people out of work. And Laure had discovered orgasm in the arms of a debauched but conservative rabbi.

The absurdity of Laure's predicament kept me from sympathizing sincerely with her emotional problems, but I was nevertheless grateful to her for all the trouble she'd taken in faking—for years, and in that very room—ecstatic climaxes.

Was François Milo really a flaming asshole?

And even if he was, did he deserve to raise a rabbi's child?

By what miracle did an idiot like that manage to keep planes up in the air?

I wondered about these questions and a lot more, holed up in the silence of my retreat and the glow of my sodium lamp. Meanwhile, François Mitterrand was campaigning for a second term. In the last seven years, he had spoken in public seventeen hundred times. He had also—as his staff had just revealed—taken one hundred and fifty-four trips abroad. His political travels broke down this way: sixty official visits to fifty-five countries; seventy day trips; eighteen European Union councils, and six European summits.

Reading this, I reflected that if you judged the seriousness and competence of anyone running for the presidency of the French Republic by the breadth of his international peregrinations, then the publication of my globe-girdling itinerary would make me a highly qualified candidate.

FRANÇOIS MITTERRAND (II)

(May 8, 1988–May 17, 1995)

THE success of *Trees of the World* was way beyond Louis Spiridon's wildest expectations. By mid-December bookshops and department stores were out of stock. The book was the top buy for the end-of-the-year holidays and was still heading the best-seller lists at the beginning of the summer. It was such a phenomenon that several weeklies featured articles by sociologists and behavioral analysts considering why consumers might be so infatuated with a simple catalog of exotic trees. Most experts explained this craze as the visible sign that society was acquiring a deepening awareness of planetary ecology.

Once, perhaps, I would have railed against that silly academic habit of sifting the meaningless froth of daily life to obtain a trivial residue, but the sociologist in me had long ago given way to the "tree man," as I'd been baptized by a reviewer in the book section of *Libération*.

I must say that the book's reproductions and design were magnificent. Spiridon had published, in an appendix, my close-ups of the bark of every tree. Printed four to a page, these looked like the painstaking work of a Japanese calligrapher or the abstract paintings of some wild, self-taught artist.

Spiridon continued signing new contracts with distributors and foreign publishers, and the book was wending its way all over the world:

Sydney, Bombay, Montreal, Lima, Moscow. Spiridon was so happy about this that he hadn't been the least bit angry with me when I'd told him that I would not be helping to promote the book. Already overwhelmed by orders, he had smiled at me knowingly and shrugged as if to say, It's not serious—I don't think we're going to need any help.

When spring rolled around, my children's school asked me if I would give a talk there on a date of my choosing. After consulting Vincent and Marie, who supported the idea enthusiastically, I accepted the invitation. I was to speak on the afternoon of May 9, 1988.

Mitterrand's share of the vote in the battle against Chirac in the second round of the presidential election was 54.01 percent. I spent part of that election day evening with my mother, who welcomed the results with juvenile exuberance. I can still see her joyfully pounding her little fists on the armrests of her chair. François had been elected. (She called him François, now.)

She did not understand my misgivings about the man who had given new stature, life, and even a mission to the entire left wing. My presence inspired her with a missionary zeal, and she deployed a full range of propaganda tactics. In addition to the sheer volume of Mitterrand's verbal output, my mother—as an expert—admired the way in which he handled language. "He always chooses the judicious word, the felicitous turn of phrase. His conjugations are perfect, and he observes the proper sequence of tenses. In fact, he is the only candidate who speaks French correctly, as opposed to someone like that right-winger Le Pen, who gets carried away with his hodgepodge of dog Latin, some imperfect subjunctives, and bloated words like 'palinodes' or 'myrmidons' that just show how pompous he is."

The day after the election, at the appointed hour, I went off to my children's school feeling the same uneasiness that had dogged me throughout my education. That fear of not being good enough, of being evaluated, compared, judged. The principal welcomed me as if I were a distinguished guest, a member of an eminent ministry or prominent academy. He insisted on introducing me to most of the teaching staff before leading me to the auditorium packed with several hundred people.

I was compared to the cine-ethnographer Jean Rouch and the polar adventurer Paul-Émile Victor as "a respectful explorer searching for the eternal traces of the timeless world of plants."

While the principal was talking about all that, I was trying to find my children's faces among the crowd. Even though our relationship had been rocky for some time, I knew that at this moment their hearts must be beating a little faster than everyone else's.

I spotted them. They were not alone. They were seated between Anna and my mother-in-law, as if for a family photograph. The sight of those two Villandreux women unnerved me so much that I was tempted to leave the stage. I'm sure I was overreacting, but their unexpected presence struck me as a show of hostility, a gesture of defiance. I felt that they had come to oppose me, to publicly humiliate me, glaring at me with their pitiless eyes. This wave of paranoia subsided only when it was time for me to speak, and I began, in a placid tone, to plunge into the complicated story of my transcontinental tree safari. I talked about the music of the Asian winds caressing the rough bark of firs; the crackling patter of American raindrops on the fleshy leaves of catalpas; the thousands of odors the earth gives off in India; those aimless walks that always wind up somewhere, unlike the inner wandering that leads you nowhere. I spoke of the fragile beauty of this planet, whose trees are both its hardy lungs and unrecognized heart. I spoke of afternoons spent waiting for beautiful light while listening to the never-ending rustle of life going about its business; of the mysteries of those long voyages that end by hijacking your itinerary and directing your steps. I spoke of chance, of luck, of misfortune that brushes by you, narrow escapes, the rapture of heights, and run-over dogs. I talked about all those little things, so ordinary, inconsistent, unimportant. Finally, I talked about Vincent's Brownie Flash, my father's Leitz enlarger and magic developing baths, and that miraculous moment when an image comes out of nowhere. I said nothing, on the other hand, about the splendid buttocks of Laure Milo.

At the end, when my mouth had run out of words, children and parents stood up and applauded as if I had just won the election. When I saw my family waving to me out in the audience, I had the strange feeling that I was going on a trip, that I was standing on some sort of departure platform.

As I left the school together with the students, I wondered where among all those well brought-up adolescents might lurk a David Rochas, who when he got home would head straight for the fridge and the embrace of the family roast.

Back at the house, Marie and Vincent welcomed me with unusual warmth, proudly reporting that their friends had found me "really cool," which seemed to position me at the top of a scale of values between, let's say, the Clash and the Police. Anna had brought the children home without stopping by Atoll. When I asked her why she had shown up unexpectedly at school, she took a deep breath that sounded like a sigh.

"I sent out more than thirty layoff letters this morning, so, frankly, I didn't have the courage to stay in the office. I called Mama, and since she was free, we decided to come. You were very good."

"Thirty layoffs?"

"Thirty-six, to be precise."

"Good Lord, but why didn't you come to me? I don't spend money, and besides, the books keep selling. We could have figured something out."

"That's good of you, but we've already had this conversation. If I want to keep the business solvent, my only course is a substantial reduction of overhead, including labor."

"Did you warn all those people that you were letting them go?"

"Of course. I met with them one by one."

"And how did they take it?"

"Paul, please . . ."

Anna's eyes filled slowly with tears. Standing motionless in front of her, stunned by what she had just told me, I wondered if my wife was feeling sorry for herself, or if she was showing any compassion for the thirty-six men and women she was abandoning by the side of the road.

"I think that Mama is going to leave my father. She says she can't stand him anymore," murmured Anna, holding back a sob. "I didn't dare ask her if she had someone else. Why does all this have to happen at the same time?"

The next day I went to *Sports Illustrés*. Jean Villandreux was standing before the bay window in his office, gazing down into the street with his hands clasped behind his back. When he had left his swimming pools to go work at the magazine, he had hoped to experience every day the kind of electric thrill he felt when he first passed through the editorial department once or twice a week to sign papers or attend meetings. Now he had discovered how boring the daily routine at a sports weekly could be. The editorial staff only really came alive on weekends, but Villandreux, psychologically attuned to the standard workweek, never came to the office on Saturday and Sunday, not even on those spring weekends when the final phases of most competitions and their always dramatic epilogues took place.

"Paul, how are you?"

"I've come to see you about Anna. Has she spoken to you about her problems at Atoll?"

"I know about them, naturally."

"I was wondering if you couldn't try to deal with this, to see, with your experience, if there might be another way to address the situation."

"You can be sure that if Anna is letting people go, it's because she has to. She's taking this very hard, you know. I phoned the accountant, he gave me the figures. They're catastrophic. Orders have been plummeting for months now."

"You wouldn't want to try taking a closer look?"

"Actually, no. I'll tell you the truth, Paul. I don't give a damn about the problems at Atoll. That business no longer means a thing to me. I'd like to say that I feel guilty about those thirty or so people who'll wind up unemployed, but that's just not so. Some guys screw up on Wall Street, and the next day here in Toulouse we can't sell Jacuzzis anymore. I no longer understand a thing about this shitty world. Did Anna talk to you about her mother?"

"Her mother?"

"Yes, her mother, my wife, you remember!"

"No, what about?"

"Martine's lost it. Off the deep end. Oh, while I think of it, La-gache asked me whether he could have one of your books with an inscription—would you mind?"

Jean Villandreux said nothing more about his domestic worries, but everything about his bearing reflected an anxious man facing loneliness on the threshold of old age. Meanwhile, Mitterrand (trained, in youth, by the Marist fathers) had appointed as prime minister Michel Rocard, his best enemy (this one, a man suckled at the breast of Protestant scout-masters, whom he had served under the nickname of "the Learned Hamster"). And so, priest-ridden into the ground, France was in good hands.

When the time came, as she had said she would, Laure Milo kept her child, giving all paternal credit to her husband, and continued her episodic relationship with her priapic rabbi. Whenever I reflected upon the emotional and sexual contortions we put ourselves through, I now envied the impassiveness of the giant sequoias, ignorant of the wretched torments of temptation, swaying but gently in the breeze and the mists of the Pacific.

Ever since returning from my trip, I'd felt time passing more slowly. The days dragged on, and they all seemed alike. While Anna was strug-gling with her business, bringing files home every evening and working on weekends, I was living like a crossing guard still assigned to an aban-doned railroad line. I took care of the garden, trimmed the shrubs, cut off dead branches, ran the lawn mower. And I cooked. Complicated, sometimes exotic dishes, all of them swiftly ingested by Anna and the children, who wasted little time or interest on earthly nourishment. Occasionally I found myself thinking nostalgically of Laure's vigorous derrière. Or Marie's imposing shoulders. I had called her one afternoon at Hoover's office. She still worked with him but continued to live in her own apartment. I'd told her that I would like to see her again, but she very gently declined my offer, explaining that she no longer wanted to complicate her life with "extraneous" relationships. That expression was a new one to me. Since when and by what criteria could a relation-ship be so classified, and on what basis, inversely, could one establish that another relationship was vital? I could spend hours mulling over such puzzles, especially since, according to what Spiridon told me every week, my "trees" kept on sprouting in the far corners of the world.

In the spring of 1989, thanks to new and cheaper manufactures in Southeast Asia, the Jacuzzi order books began to bubble once again. Anna didn't rehire a single extra employee, however, claiming that overhead remained too high and the firm's economic health was still quite fragile. My wife had regained her authority. To see her in action, you might think that nothing had ever happened, that the crisis was an artificial phantom of the marketplace and that in fact she'd never had to fire a third of her personnel only a few months earlier. I was even convinced that coming through the bad patch had strengthened her convictions, and that to her the current rebound was proof that she had made the right choice. A responsible company president, she kept saying, was someone who had the courage, when the crunch came, to cut off a limb to save the life of the business. But as for those severed limbs, they too were phantoms now.

Things had also settled down between Martine and Jean Villandreux. Tired of her friend (unless it had been the other way around), my mother-in-law had finally made up with her husband, who, for his part, had gone on a diet and now exercised daily. In addition, thanks to the technology of discreet and progressive hair coloring, a capilliculturalist regularly restored his locks, sadly tarnished by age, to their former glory. Once a month, Jean Villandreux took his wife for the weekend to a great European city: Venice, London, Geneva, Madrid, Florence, Stockholm, Vienna, Copenhagen, Amsterdam.

Villandreux was no longer the same man. He was like those battle-field survivors who have heard the whine of passing bullets, and now savor each second of their lives as though it were their last.

Things were gradually working themselves out. Except for me and Salman Rushdie. We were both living as recluses. I, in my mental prison, hemmed in by boredom and depression; he, more prosaically, sharing an apartment with a fatwa. Foolish as it may seem, at the time I often envied him his life as a fugitive, and dreamed of clandestinity: fake beards, bodyguards, Walther P38s, sudden midnight flits, gorgeous girls lurking in corridors, journalists praising his art and his courage, threats, escapes in cars with tinted windows—in short, that absurdly virile existence scented with sweat and adrenaline. There was only one hitch in Salman Rushdie's setup: his face. No hero ever had such a face. Rushdie looked like a wily roughneck with criminal tendencies. With his slightly undershot jaw and his fakir's eyes, hooded and vaguely menacing, he seemed to be constantly plotting villainous schemes. He was to my eye the felonious Indian in the Tintin comic book *Cigars of the Pharaoh*.

Idleness and solitude finally flipped me out. I could fixate on anything that I didn't really give a rat's ass about—Rushdie, for example—and chew on it for days, running it through infinite pointless permutations as if it were a Rubik's Cube in a single color.

I do think I was at a low point in those debilitating pastimes when shortly before Christmas the phone roused me from one of those compulsive naps that usually accompany slow nervous breakdowns. It was Michel Campion. There was something disagreeably upbeat, a kind of annoyingly affected heartiness in the way he spoke.

"Hi, there, friend! How's life?"

"The usual."

"Were you asleep? You sound like you've just woken up."

"No, don't be silly."

"Here's the thing: What would you think of coming on a mission with me?"

"What kind of a mission?"

"For Doctors of the World; I'm headed for Romania."

The first shots of the revolution had rung out two or three days before, and now crates of medicine would be dispatched with a team of doctors to evaluate the needs of the main hospital in Timisoara. Michel had been working for the NGO for a long time and had already taken part in several humanitarian operations, most notably after earthquakes in Turkey, Armenia, and other central European countries.

"Me? What would I do on a mission like that?"

"Nothing, you'd come with me, that's all. And you could take photographs, I guess, if we need any."

"Photos of what?"

"How would I know until we get there? We're taking off in a special charter at around six p.m. from Blagnac. There'll be four of us: me, another doctor, a nurse, and you, if you're up for it."

The sky, the moon, and all the wandering asteroids had just fallen on my head. There I was paddling around in the benevolent muck of a deluxe depression and the next moment an acquaintance was proposing to carry me off to the front lines of a conflict he himself believed would end in a bloodbath.

"You're a man of action, after all," continued Michel, "and didn't you once tell me that you'd like to see what a mission was like?"

I had absolutely no memory of spouting or even thinking such nonsense. My profession was chasing around the world after lotus trees in twilight, not dodging the bullets of furious Transylvanians and other hysterical Walachians. Everything sensible in me was refusing Michel's proposal outright, yet I heard myself reply that yes, I would be, with my passport, at the appointed time, at the airport.

The old Boeing had been stripped of most of its seats and filled with several tons of emergency medicines and bandages. At the rear were ten rather unprepossessing passengers all looking exactly alike: built like stevedores, as rugged as marine commandos, with military brush cuts.

We landed in Budapest, where two trucks in the colors of Doctors of the World were waiting on the tarmac. The ten samurais helped unload the medical cargo before disappearing like a puff of smoke.

We had to drive the two vehicles to the city of Szeged, on the border with Romania, before descending toward the frozen plains of Timisoara. I was driving one of the trucks with Michel, and the other van was piloted by Dominique Pérez, the second doctor, and Françoise Duras, the nurse. At customs in Szeged, some Hungarian officials bluntly advised us to turn back. Romania, to hear them tell it, was both in flames and awash in blood, thanks to furious rioters and the savage reprisals of Ceauşescu's Securitate.

As soon as we'd crossed the border (with a handwritten and

extremely dubious "driving permit"), some soldiers still loyal to the dictator inspected each truck and extorted from us, for some spurious visas, an amount in dollars that must have represented three or four times their monthly salaries.

Dawn seemed like sundown. Snow blanketed the fields and road-sides. We were stopped repeatedly at barricades by armed men in mis-matched uniforms assembled from Adidas tracksuits and muddy hunting jackets. Most of these militiamen had the faces of dog thieves, and their manner was no more pleasant. Traumatized by the Hungari-ans' warnings, Michel had sunk down into the passenger seat. When-ever we were stopped, he would raise one hand, jiggle a stethoscope in the other, and shout to all and sundry in English, "French doctors! French doctors!" We had no way of telling which side they were on, those shady-looking irregulars who searched us, patting us down and practically sniffing us head to toe so many times that it took us most of the day to reach the hospital in Timisoara.

The place looked like an abandoned barracks. A few ground-floor windows were broken, doors without latches let the cold in more or less everywhere, and some tipped-over gurneys were lying around the courtyard, but this disorder seemed more like general sloppiness than the sign of any recent looting. A few idle male nurses were smoking and warming themselves at a wood-burning stove.

"French doctors!" Michel kept saying, still waving his stethoscope. Before we entered the city, he had made us stop by the roadside to attach some enormous NGO badges to the backs of our anoraks. As I was fixing one of these blue circles about sixteen inches in diameter to my Gore-Tex jacket, I imagined how tempting this round and incredi-bly visible target would be to a sniper.

A young doctor emerged warily from his office in the hospital and came to meet us.

"French doctors! French doctors!"

"Roman Podilescu. I understand French quite well; I earned my medical degree in Montpellier. And you are . . . ?"

When Michel introduced himself and explained our mission, Podilescu seemed dumbfounded, but he followed us politely to the trucks. Like a magician about to pull rabbits from his hat, Michel Campion opened the rear doors of the vans and made that silly little wave the magician's female assistant always does by way of a presentation. Podilescu just stood there in front of those boxes of wound dressings, crêpe bandages, disinfectants, and God knows what other condiments that are usually sprinkled on the wounded.

"That's very kind of you, and we're grateful for the support of your country, but we don't need all this."

"But of course you do, for the emergency treatment of your casualties."

"We have no casualties."

Michel looked as if he'd been slapped. He was speechless.

"The Swiss and the Germans were here this morning. They'd brought a surgical unit and a mobile emergency room. I told them the same thing I'm telling you: thanks, but we have no victims. Not even any corpses. The few bodies we were keeping in the hospital morgue were carried off by soldiers, who buried them in a suburb of the city to try and create a mass grave."

Michel Campion looked at Dominique Pérez, who offered a light to Françoise Duras, who blew a cloud of smoke straight up into the air like a prayer borne aloft with helium.

"But I still have to give you all this," said Michel almost plaintively. Podilescu rounded up the gang of male nurses, who rolled up their sleeves and attacked the shipments as if they really were urgently required.

"So I suppose my assignment to evaluate your needs is not necessary."

"Well, if you're talking about aid in response to the current revolutionary disturbances, then no. On the other hand, if your organization wants to contribute here for the long term, to support us in our everyday work, then yes, our needs are immense. We lack lots of things: equipment, surgical instruments, radiology supplies. That's what I explained this morning to the Germans."

The fact that the Germans had beaten him to the sacred site of a false emergency was one more humiliation for Michel. This mission was a complete fiasco for him.

"But then everything they're saying on the television about the casualties, and all that . . ."

Podilescu smiled evasively.

"In Bucharest, perhaps . . . Here, we hear gunshots, especially at night. There's been a rumor ever since yesterday that we're going to be attacked by agents from the Securitate, who'll come to finish off the wounded, but as I said we have practically no wounded. So I don't know. A lot of those news bulletins come from the Yugoslavian press agencies, and the Yugoslavians, well . . ."

I had never in my life seen such a sinister and terrifying building. The ancient globes of dull glass illuminating the hallways gave off a sallow light that seemed to ooze down walls made greasy by time. As Michel and his friends inquired further about the situation in the city, I wandered upstairs. Sporadic gunfire rattled off in the distance.

The hospital director, a Ceauşescu appointee, had fled his post and doubtless Timisoara to escape the settling of scores that would inevitably shake up every administration in the country. His office was typical of a provincial apparatchik. The walls still bore the telltale marks where portraits of the *Conducător* had been prudently removed after the initial riots and piled on top of the imposing bookcase, behind the glass-fronted doors of which there wasn't a single book. There were, however, a hundred bottles of the great wines of Bordeaux, arranged by vineyard and by château, along with jars of potted salmi of dove, jugged hare, duck breast, and foie gras.

The desk, of cheap institutional wood, flaunted its dictatorial proportions. Sitting behind such a desk, one must feel credibly protected from many things, safely out of reach. Three old telephones, a lamp with an aluminum shade, a letter opener with a leather-sheathed handle—and nothing else. Not so much as a single file folder or note.

Hardly had I seated myself on the throne of this small kingdom when two men carrying weapons and wearing some kind of armband entered without knocking. Seeing me lounging in the boss's chair gave them a terrible fright: they literally recoiled in fear, remaining frozen for a moment in that ridiculous posture before getting a grip on themselves. Then they saluted me, let out what seemed like a war cry, and vanished back into the hallway, down which I could hear them running for a long time.

On the ground floor, Podilescu was doing his utmost to show courtesy to his guests.

"You can sleep in the hospital: here you won't be a target for snipers. We have some empty beds."

I was ready to cross a minefield under heavy fire rather than spend another hour in that hellhole. A half hour later, escorted by an army tank, we left the hospital in our trucks. During the drive to our hotel, the tank's machine gun sprayed the façades of houses and apartment buildings, even though no one was shooting at us.

Night and an icy chill had fallen over Timisoara. The public rooms of the Hotel Continental were swarming with reporters who had arrived that very day from all over Europe, while in the lobby, Kalashnikovs in hand, uniformed soldiers were guarding the establishment against a possible attack by the Securitate. I shared Room 501 with Michel, while Pérez and his nurse stayed in 502. We had neither heat nor hot water, and the restaurant kitchens, deprived of gas, were no longer serving anything but improvised cold meals.

At every table in the dining room, journalists were talking about nothing but a recently discovered mass grave, with its freshly turned earth and all those bodies lined up, filmed by the television cameramen. That same evening the whole world had eaten supper in the company of images of that massacre attributed to Ceauşescu's brigades.

If I had managed to inform those reporters about what Podilescu had told us regarding the bodies stolen from the morgue, the subsequent setting of the stage, and the fantastic allegations of the Yugoslavians, none of them would have believed me, much less agreed to amend the impeccable dramatic effects of a revolution written, we would later learn, by the screenwriters of the CIA.

The meal was cold, but the looks exchanged by Dr. Pérez and Nurse Duras were not. When an insurgent came dashing into the hotel at around ten p.m. shouting "Securitate! Securitate!," the soldiers on guard turned off all the lights and began to machine-gun the street. When the shooting started, diners of all nationalities did their best to hunker down on the floor, but Pérez and Duras, ignoring the surrounding chaos, were kissing in the darkness, deaf to the Walachian din.

With no heat, our room was freezing. Fully clothed and wrapped in the blankets and bedspread, Michel and I tried to get some sleep despite the gunfire echoing throughout the city.

"Podilescu says it's insurgents pretending to be Securitate who shoot up the buildings at night to stir up the people's hatred."

Michel spoke in the dark in a monotonous voice tinged with fatigue and discouragement. He was a mission leader who no longer had a mission. A Doctor of the World whom the world did not need. He had barely finished his sentence when we began to hear noises from the neighboring room that left no doubt about the nature of the skirmish going on in there. Pérez and Duras were going at it in the time-honored twelve-tone mode, and in addition to this dainty dodecaphonic music, there was also some percussion on the headboard, rhythmically thumping the wall. With each hip thrust, Pérez would grunt his basso, while Duras ran through a short series of high notes. The end of the first movement was breathtaking. Stamped with a joyous animal savagery, it reminded us all, in that icy and inhuman setting, of our humble origins.

"Nothing like this has ever happened to me before!" Michel said in despair.

His musings cut short by a series of gunshots out in the street, or perhaps in the hotel lobby, he then asked softly in an almost childish voice, "Did you lock the door to the room?"

The battering ram started up again next door. I couldn't wait for that night to be over.

In the morning, turning on the television, we discovered the hallucinatory trial of Nicolae and Elena Ceauşescu, broadcast live and in Romanian. There was something unreal about seeing that tyrannical and omnipotent couple handcuffed and shoved around by young conscripts, who were probably much more affected by the drama than they seemed. Obviously, I couldn't understand any of what was said, but the judges, whom we never saw, were clearly leveling accusations that the Ceauşescus found unbearable and which they denied with a canine rage. With her coat and knotted kerchief, and his fur hat and big gold watch, the two of them resembled a couple of prosperous shopkeepers who had rushed to file a complaint after an attempted mugging. They were full of the ill-concealed exasperation of the self-important when they don't immediately receive special treatment at the clinic or the police station.

The following day Romanian national television broadcast edited images of the couple's execution. When I saw the body of Nicolae Ceaușescu, only one question occurred to me: What had happened to his watch?

Freed from all professional preoccupations, Pérez and Duras continued their honeymoon. Michel seemed deeply dismayed by this idyll.

"And he's married. . . ."

"What does that change?"

"Nothing. I suppose I'm simply old-fashioned."

"And Duras?"

"What about Duras?"

"Is she married?"

"I've no idea, I don't know her. This is our first time on a mission together. But Pérez seemed to know whom he'd be traveling with."

I spent the afternoon walking around Timisoara, a city as charming as a toolshed. With its uncertain architecture and its old trams with their aboveground rails, the downtown area looked as if it were under construction. What had looked simply unfinished a few days before was now also bullet-ridden. The inhabitants were scurrying about their business, showing studied contempt for the nightly street skirmishes. Spotting the limbs of an old oak in the corner of a garden, I realized that not once since my arrival in this country had I used the little Nikon I'd brought along. The day after that walk, without really understanding what we had come to do in that city, we left by truck for Szeged, and then Budapest, where the sight of a McDonald's made me think that a revolution was under way there, too, one probably more discreet but infinitely more unsettling.

Before checking out of the Hotel Continental in Timisoara, I'd done something strange that I can't explain even today. As Michel settled our bill, I'd stayed in the bathroom for a moment to stop up the drains in the sink and the bathtub. Then I opened the faucets full tap and waited for the water to overflow. Getting out my camera for the first time, I then took several pictures of these domestic waterfalls pouring from the bathroom fixtures, slowly soaking the carpets with ice-cold water.

I spent several days in Budapest before going home. Along the Danube, I photographed a few solitary trees. The air was frigid. People were preparing to celebrate their first New Year after the fall of the Berlin Wall two months earlier. Looking at that city, I tried to imagine life there in the time of the Warsaw Pact, and what sort of economic festivities the new Crusaders from the West would inflict upon Pest.

Anna's parents invited us for lunch on New Year's Day and questioned me at length about my Romanian escapade. Ordinarily indifferent to popular movements, they had been completely swept up this time in the scenario of that revolution. My mother-in-law was even stunned to discover that I hadn't had the presence of mind or even the desire, in the belly of the beast, to take a single photo.

"Sometimes, Paul, I ask myself what world you're living in. And you haven't a thing to show for your daring adventure?"

I had, actually: the key to Room 501, a banknote for *una sută lei* from the Banca Nationalä a Republicii Romänia, and another for *szäz forint* issued by the Magyar Nemzeki Bank.

Far from sharing her mother's disappointment, Anna had been highly amused by the story of that pathetic expedition, concluding with the unexpected nocturnal excesses of Dr. Pérez, whose pelvic exploits delighted her, especially since she had known—and disliked—his wife for a long time.

It was not long afterward that Laure had her baby. Of course, I was the only one who knew who the real father was, which sometimes put me in an awkward position, as when François, taking a short vacation here on earth from his Airbus stratosphere, would say, rocking the infant in his arms, "Look at that Milo chin."

I sometimes had trouble understanding Laure's decision. Having a third child at forty years old with a married rabbi, the father of a large family, and saddling an absent husband with this paternity did not seem to me like a particularly wise course of action. Having made that choice, however, she now had no alternative but to keep silent forever. Under these circumstances, I became the keeper of a true secret, an accessory to a breach of genital faith. So I could only hope that no genetic customs officer would ever compare the chromosomal charts of the son and his supposed father.

Laure, for her part, seemed oblivious to the situation, luxuriating in the role of fulfilled mother and beloved wife. She was in complete denial. Except when our eyes met, when hers would fill with mute supplication and just a hint of menace. Since Laure never did anything by halves, she named her child after the rabbi: Simon Milo.

According to Laure, that tender consideration had deeply moved the saintly man, although not enough for him even to consider any alteration of his double life. Their relationship would therefore continue offstage, in the wings, leaving them to juggle all the accessories of long-term adultery: children constantly underfoot, improvised sexual encounters, perpetual deception, lots of religion, and planes, always more planes.

A world away from these hysterical schedules, I had returned to my own domestic routines.

It was late May 1990, and the voice on the telephone said, "Good morning! I am calling from the office of the secretary to the president of the Republic."

The man's name was Auvert or Aubert and he was calling me, he said, on behalf of François Mitterrand.

"The president particularly admired your last book. He would like you to photograph him in front of some of his favorite trees in Paris, Latché, and in the Morvan region."

"*What* are you talking about?"

"I'm completely serious, Monsieur Blick. You are surely aware how much the president enjoys the company of trees. He has never made a secret of his fondness for them. What he would like is for you to take his portrait next to his trees."

"Why are you calling me?"

"As I said, because of your book. The president can't say enough how much he likes it. Would you like a moment to get your date book?"

"I'm very sorry."

"Excuse me?"

"I cannot accept this commission."

"I can well understand the demands on your schedule, Monsieur Blick; we would certainly . . ."

"I'm sorry."

"Fine. Well, let's say that your response is . . . unexpected. I will inform the president of your decision."

The man's voice had indeed had that high gloss of professional detachment so characteristic of the lackeys of important officials, but I still found it hard to take this Auvert/Aubert seriously. Even if the president of the French Republic did have a pronounced penchant for plants, could one seriously imagine him devoting three or four days of his agenda to posing in front of tree trunks? The whole thing seemed so absurd that I never even mentioned it to Anna.

Three days later Auvert/Aubert called me back early in the afternoon. A few rays of sunshine filtering through the chestnut leaves floated islands of light across the wide blond planks in the parquet of the front hall, where I was vacuuming.

"Monsieur Blick? I'm calling from the office of the secretary to the president; I have the president of the Republic on the line."

Auvert/Aubert hadn't even asked me how I was, or whether he was disturbing me. He didn't care whether I was vacuuming in a flood of perspiration or busy meticulously printing an image on a sheet of twenty-four-by-thirty glossy.

"This is François Mitterrand speaking. How are you, Monsieur Blick?"

"Fine, thank you."

"Good, good. I hope that you were told how much I admired the beauty of the photographs in *Trees of the World*. You've created a remarkable work managing to represent, with a completely new vision, the majesty of an eternal world. . . . Are you there?"

"Yes, yes, of course."

"So you have explored all the continents."

"Yes."

"Which one astonished you the most?"

"Perhaps Australia."

"Really! Is the flora there that dazzling, or were you under the spell of the Coriolis force?"

"I couldn't say."

"Well . . . well. Now, you are doubtless aware that I share your passion for woods and forests. I can only say therefore that I was taken aback when informed that you did not want to participate in my project. It was doubtless poorly explained to you. Permit me please to clarify it: I have a certain number of mascot trees—in Paris, in the Morvan, and especially in the Landes, below Bordeaux—next to which it would give me great pleasure to be photographed. Something quite simple, intimate, for my personal collection . . . Are you there?"

"Yes."

"No lighting or makeup. A total of, I would presume, let's say, about thirty pictures. Before the arrival of autumn. I would be the one to schedule the appointments. Let's be clear that this is a personal commission. Are you there?"

"I'm here."

"So that's it. Very simple shots, in black and white. As in your book, you see. Just a tree, and me next to it. Just you, me, and the tree. I am sure that you will do a splendid job."

"I don't think so."

"But why not?"

"I never photograph human beings."

"My opponents would tell you that I am becoming less and less human," he said with practiced jocularity.

"I'm sorry."

"You do not like human beings in general, or do you detest me in particular, Monsieur Blick? I must say I am disappointed. I would have liked those photos. I think they would have been good for me, perhaps even good for you. But let's not carry on with a pointless discussion. It's as simple as that. Good afternoon, Monsieur Blick."

The line went dead at the end of his sentence, and it took me a few seconds to realize that the president of the Republic had just hung up on me. His high-handed behavior and capricious, imperious demands left me fuming with republican wrath. I felt like calling Auvert/Aubert back to tell him what I thought of this Socialist in royal purple raised by the Marist brothers, a former member of the Vichyist Volontaires Nationaux, who through crass self-interest had wavered throughout his career between a lackluster left and various opportunistic right-wing parties. I hadn't the slightest desire to photograph François Mitterrand. Or his trees.

When I told Anna about the conversation that evening, she reacted with some surprise.

"I'm not sure that it was a good thing to have refused."

"What do you mean?"

"I don't know—it would have been an experience. Plus I find his idea rather creative, even touching."

"But after all, I have the right to refuse a job, even if the president of the Republic taps his foot impatiently while he commands me to accept it."

"You have every right. Including the right to put *your* foot in it when you're blinded by your foul temper and your old left-wing reflexes."

"With two books I have earned enough money to live three lifetimes doing nothing, and you want me to crawl off to satisfy the whims of a former stooge of the Volontaires Nationaux?"

"That's none of my business. I think you handled it badly, that's all. And while I think of it: I ran into Laure today. She has something she's doing tomorrow afternoon and wants to know if you can look after little Simon."

"Absolutely not."

She could just park him with the rabbi. Unless it was precisely with him that she planned on doing that "something." I'd just suffered an indignity inflicted by the president of the Republic; there was no way I would now be used by a former mistress who had the nerve to ask my wife for my babysitting services while she trotted off to bed the father, a first-class Pharisaic phony, who of course required less than an hour to give her what I'd never managed in years to provide: pleasure.

I thought I'd seen the end of the Mitterrand "affair."

I hadn't counted on the shopkeeper's soul of my mother-in-law and my own mother's Socialist fixations.

Barely two days after my conversation with the president, Martine Villandreux, doubtless briefed by her daughter, stopped by the house to see me late in the afternoon. She was no longer the same woman. She was suddenly showing her age: her once radiant face had lost all charm, and her flesh now seemed a boneless, doughy mass.

"Paul, have you lost your mind, or what? Do you want to get us audited?"

"What are you talking about?"

"Don't be a fool, everyone knows how it works."

"How what works?"

"What Socialists do when you cross them!"

"And what would that be?"

"They sic the taxmen on you, of course! Would it really have been so much trouble for you to take a few damn pictures?"

"Wait a minute. Even if you're right about tax auditors, then I should be the one to worry, not you."

"There's no guarantee of that at all. Must I remind you that in your marriage, husband and wife own everything in common?"

"So?"

"So, my poor friend, if the locusts swarm down on you, they'll attack Anna's business, too. Sometimes I wonder what you've got between your ears. Even Jean, who always defends you, can't figure you out this time. Just last night he asked me, 'But after all, Paul's a leftist, isn't he?' "

The fluctuations in the French stock market caused by Iraq's invasion of Kuwait at the beginning of August soon refocused my in-laws' financial preoccupations. But then on one of those stifling summer days when I had given in and gone to have lunch with her, my mother had her say. Before I'd even had time to unfold my napkin, my mother—usually so calm, so composed—lit into me as I'd never seen her go after anyone before.

"I think I must have a lunatic for a son. Don't give me that bewildered look! You're out of your mind!"

"What's gotten into you?"

"What's gotten into me is that for several weeks I've been holding my tongue, telling myself that it's not my business, but now, when I see you in front of me, I can't tell you how angry I am! How could you!"

"How could I *what?*"

"Say no to the president, refuse that beautiful offer he made to you! When I think that we had you do Latin and Greek . . ."

That was a refrain I had often heard in my life. My mother used it whenever I had deeply disappointed her. She did not understand how a man suckled on those twin breasts of civilization could have remained so impervious to the wisdom of the ages. The way she figured it, just as I had been protected from tuberculosis by a vaccine, my lycée courses in Latin and Greek (an eminently cultured strain) should have protected me from errors of judgment and improper conduct. By refusing the presidential commission, however, I had revealed the vaccine's impotence on defective characters like my own.

"You behaved like a hooligan. What must that man think of us Blicks!"

"Not a thing, I'm sure. All this fuss because I refused to take some photos!"

"Some photos? My poor boy, they were *the* photos of your life. And may I ask what excuse you gave the president?"

"I simply said that I did not photograph human beings."

"Paul, you didn't say that. That's unbelievably rude. That's completely disrespectful and contemptuous!"

"Mama . . ."

"An elderly man, who chose you from among thousands of others so that you could simply take pictures of him with the trees of his life, an intelligent, dignified man with an unrivaled command of and respect for language—and you, you reply, 'I don't photograph human beings.' Just who do you think you are, Paul Blick?! I can tell you that what you've done will follow you all your life. And it will have repercussions even on your work, believe me."

"But, Mama, I don't work. I've practically never worked—I've just earned money by accident."

"You were too spoiled. And that's what spoiled your judgment and common sense."

My mother wasn't completely wrong. The miraculous sales of my two books had allowed me to live on the margin of the world, my family, and sometimes myself. I was never involved in anything, never shared any project with anyone else. I sometimes felt like the unique representative of a caste that interested no one and took an interest in no one. Was this a life—photographing silent and motionless trees, taking scrupulous care that no human being should ever enter the frame? It had taken the sale of my pictures throughout the world for me to realize that I had almost never photographed my children, Vincent and Marie, or Anna or my mother, either. The only portraits my mother had of my father had been taken by strangers at the garage. I had crisscrossed the globe searching for tree trunks, neglecting the family life taking place all around me, on my own doorstep. Now forty years old, I felt as though I had just left the university. I had barely seen my children grow up, and my son was already wearing size twelve shoes. Although I had never had a serious job, for a long time now I had been shielded from want. Without desiring this, and quite in spite of myself, I was the pure product of an unscrupulous and ferociously opportunistic time, when work had worth only for those who were worthless.

Shortly after that unpleasant conversation, my mother had a stroke that paralyzed part of her face and crippled one of her hands for a good three months. For a long time, I worried that her circulatory problem had been provoked by her intense irritation at my behavior toward the president. During one of my frequent visits during her convalescence, she blindsided me with a strange request.

"You know what I'd like? For you to take, *you,* a photo of Mitterrand. A photo for me."

At the time the idea seemed amusing to me, even if I immediately thought of asking one or another of the press photographers I knew to slip me a portrait of the president. But given the way my mother had emphasized that *you*, I didn't have the heart for this stratagem. In her frailty and her illness, she was ruthlessly exercising her power over me. I felt that she wanted to test me, to punish me in a way that might both make up for my supposed impudence and draw me closer to the presidential three-ring big top.

"Would you do that for me?"

How could I say no—to an old lady with a half-frozen face and one paralyzed hand? How could I not promise that, yes, I would do that for her? Even though I had no idea *how* to do it.

After considering other options, I finally decided to buy a telephoto lens and a small camera with a motor drive to try grabbing a shot of the president during one of his public appearances. Autistic plant photographer that I was, I felt surges of panic at the idea of this conversion. Overnight my mother had turned me into a vulgar paparazzo. Farewell to the beautiful light and the afternoons spent waiting with my Hasselblad on its tripod. From now on I would live to the rhythm of a 35mm Nikon, lying ignobly in ambush, grubbing stressfully with the rest.

It was impossible for me to obtain a press pass, so I had to stake out public places frequented by the president during his official and private outings. A magazine photographer had gotten me a copy of the presidential schedule from the Élysée Palace. Early in 1991 there were a few inaugurations in Paris and two provincial visits. My window of opportunity was limited. I had to make my move during the brief period when the president had left his car but not yet vanished behind the walls of whatever institution was welcoming him. I had to succeed in isolating my subject from the crowd and his bodyguards, then pray for the light to be good, for the president to smile, for him to look in my direction, and for me to be alert enough to react in an instant. After that, the shot would depend on whether or not luck would decide to get behind the viewfinder with me. I was ready for my first attempt: an official presidential appearance on January 18, 1991, in Paris.

The first Gulf War broke out on the seventeenth. All official sorties from the Élysée Palace were canceled, of course. So, like the rest of the nation, I sat in front of my television and watched America bamboozle the world. Alteration of reality. Semantic malfeasance. Falsification of motives. Exaggeration of results. False testimonies. Counterfeit proofs. Mission creep. Dissimulation of suffering. Concealment of the dead. Those people across the Atlantic embodied the civilized version of savagery. Manipulators of conscience, exterminators of thought, inseminators of predatory ideas, they had turned images into lying mirrors that they could deform at will to suit their purposes, with the complicity of hired mouthpieces. In the future, if necessary, war—like peace, moreover—could be waged in a teacup.

Life did not return to normal until early April, at the end of the war. The French stock market settled down and my mother-in-law recovered her smile. Me, I got my hands on a new presidential schedule and set out at the first opportunity on the trail of he who was to become, as the weeks went by, my white whale. Like the cetacean that haunted Ahab, Mitterrand obsessed me, possessed me, an elusive moving target, a sort of ectoplasmic entity that left no impression even on film. After three attempts in one month, I didn't have one decent picture. I had missed every shot. Either the president was hidden by a member of his security detail, or a door was swallowing him up before I'd even managed to press the button. He was slipping through my fingers. To my cost, I was proving the truth of my own claim: I really didn't photograph human beings. Some eerie combination of incompetence and an evil spell was preventing me from capturing that man's face. After three botched attempts, I decided to change my approach, abandoning the telephoto lens for a 50mm that would oblige me to mingle with the crowd and work within a few steps of my target. There wasn't anything extraordinary about that. At each of his appearances, thousands of French citizens crowded up against the barricades to take pictures of their president. I was probably the only one among them, however, who believed himself marked amid the throng as the killjoy who had refused a modest harmless request from the chief of state. At the height of my paranoia, I imagined that Mitterrand would recognize me between two handshakes, come over, and with sly arrogance say to me, "How strange to see you here, Blick, photographing human beings!"

My first series of 50mm films, shot in the late spring during a presidential trip to the provinces, was another failure. This time, though, I had gotten in close. He had passed within a few feet of me, and the Nikon had run through two frames a second—still without giving me an acceptable picture, alas. A fuzzy profile. A close-up of a shoulder. The back of his neck. The back of his neck from about every possible angle. As if, sensing my presence, the president had suddenly turned away, sticking me with a shot of his contemptuous nape. Strange though it may seem, as soon as Mitterrand appeared in my viewfinder, I went blind. The frame would go dark and I really couldn't see what I was shooting anymore. As time passed, and one unproductive trip followed another, I realized how utterly ridiculous my predicament was. Here was a man whom I had refused to photograph, under optimal conditions and at his own request, and to satisfy a maternal whim I was now stalking him, and to no avail. I was consumed with two perfectly complementary emotions: shame and rage.

In a weak moment, I'd talked about my project to Anna, who'd been much amused by my adventures.

"You really have deluxe problems, and the hobbies of a spoiled child."

"I told you why I'm doing this."

"I know, but still. If only it would at least make you think about your own fecklessness!"

"My character has got nothing to do with it."

"Paul, you have a singular gift for getting bogged down in impossible predicaments. You spend your life trying to salvage situations you yourself have taken pains to screw up."

"I didn't screw anything up, it was a series of—"

"In any case, even the children think you're being silly, posing as a paparazzo. Just yesterday Marie asked me why you didn't simply give your mother a press photograph. And why did you go and tell that story to the children? Do you really want the whole lycée to know how crazy you are?"

No. I absolutely did not want that. I was so ashamed of the fix I'd gotten myself into that I would have paid any price to obtain the silence of my children and their friends.

At last, at the end of my seventh trip, I found what I was looking for: a sequence of portraits taken from the crowd, one or two yards from the president while he was moving toward the pyramid of the Louvre. The light, the exposure, the definition—everything was perfect. In most of the shots, François Mitterrand wore a relaxed little smile that one hardly ever saw upon his face. Those photos were technically impeccable, even if the president sometimes appeared with his eyes closed, mummified at the instant of blinking by the blind operation of the shutter. On the other hand, one image was truly unique. In it, François Mitterrand was turning and looking straight at me with a mixture of surprise and irritation. It was as if, through the play of lenses, he were trying to stare me down. When I saw this unfriendly face, I heard him say to me, "Seven trips for this? You're ridiculous, Blick." No doubt, *Monsieur le Président,* but when I saw my mother's face light up as she unwrapped the object of her passion, framed in blond wood, I realized that although I truly didn't have any talent for photographing human beings, I could sometimes, through my stubbornness, manage to offer them a little bit of happiness under glass.

My mother had recovered from her disability, but old age was tightening its grip, tormenting her, warping her body. Aside from her *raptus mitterrandiens,* however, her mind was as clear as ever, and she continued in her retirement to point out the spoken and written linguistic errors of her compatriots. My mother had no mercy on journalists, TV announcers, or government ministers. She prophesied that Édith Cresson, our prime minister at the time, would not last long, done in by her poor manners and worse diction.

A few months before the lady was sent packing, the Élysée Palace revealed to the press that François Mitterrand had just been operated upon for cancer. My mother reacted as if one of her own family had been stricken with the disease, and she was scandalized by the ensuing awkward controversy: Was the president still capable of managing the affairs of the nation? I need hardly add that the appointment of the Gaullist Édouard Balladur as prime minister, after the defeat of the Left in the parliamentary elections of 1993, reminded my mother of the dark hours of the first "cohabitation," memories that pained her as grievously as rheumatic twinges. Unfortunately for Balladur, in addition to his outrageously right-wing policies, the poor man was burdened with an undeniable Bourbon profile. And it was for that double chin, that little jabot of the pompous aristocrat, I believe, that my mother never forgave him.

So the future of my son, who was about to turn seventeen, was entrusted to that former boss of a subsidiary of the Compagnie Générale d'Électricité, who in his spare time wrote such indispensable liberal tracts as "I Believe in Man More Than in the State," "Passion and Patience," "Twelve Letters to Rouse Complacent Frenchmen," and "On Intellectual Fashions and Convictions."

Seventeen. It seems that all men are alike: they grow old without even noticing that their sons have grown up. Until the day when, in the bathroom, they run into a tall guy with a buff body, someone who vaguely resembles them and whose voice reminds them of something. And without warning their inner world implodes, and they feel an icy chill. They think that it isn't possible, it was just yesterday that—then the clock stops abruptly inside them, a coiled spring relaxes . . . and in the ensuing silence, they do some rapid mental arithmetic: yesterday, they realize, was seventeen years ago.

I was like all those other men, blind to that growth, deaf to the murmurs of time going by. By way of extenuating circumstances, I'd be tempted to point out that my son and daughter grew like grass in the springtime, without any serious illnesses or special problems in school. That both of them seemed to follow the course of a peaceful river flowing through every millrace over all those years. Yes, I could say that.

At that time I was foolish enough to think that as a father I was available, present, close to them. I was sure that I knew them intimately. That I shared the essential things in their lives. In reality, they considered me a sort of social misfit, an embarrassing anomaly, violating boundaries, living off-schedule, without plans or goals, perversely playing househusband, living weeks of Sundays and going off on long trips. It was only much later that I understood that children hate that kind of eccentric confusion, those free-form existences, those floating characters. Marie and Vincent wanted a normal father, one who set out for the office and came home at set times, who followed their schooling, knew their teachers, took the family away on the occasional weekend, and spent a month at the seashore with them every summer. Parents who were a pair of solid, trusty guardrails, always in the same place, to which they could cling in case of need. Instead of which, and for differing reasons, their mother and I had provided them with wobbly banisters, slippery steps, doors that were there one day, gone the next. Without my even noticing it, my children had moved away from me to draw closer to life. Now they were on the other side of the river. On the shore of untroublesome people. Where the fathers belong to parent-teacher committees.

Trying to reassure myself, I sometimes decided that I was good at taking care of babies, not at rearing children. But those pathetic thoughts neither dispelled my remorse nor won me back my children's trust. So I made a difficult choice: not to try to make up for lost time or pretend to recover what was gone forever. Although the distance that Vincent and Marie had put between us was painful, I would respect it. As for everything else, since the very idea of involvement with official institutions had always disturbed me, I was not about to be converted to the politics of PTA membership in the Balladurian era.

Anna came home one evening with the news, saying simply, "I can't believe it! François dumped Laure." I had immediately concluded that he'd suspected something or that she'd told him the truth about the rabbi and the boy, Simon. I was way off. The king of planes had left home for the least lofty of reasons: he had simply fallen in love with a twenty-four-year-old woman who had led him back to certain long-forgotten pleasures. Announcing his decision to his wife upon his return from work, he packed his bag and an hour later, without further explanation or commentary, walked out on his whole world.

"Can you imagine . . ."

Nadia was a pretty, sensual brunette who appeared to have an opinion about everything. She had inherited her smooth skin from a North African mother, and her blue eyes, it seemed, from her father, a native of Luxembourg. As for her flashing smile, it was hers alone. Shortly after leaving Laure, François had phoned me to engage in that ritual observed by all men in such circumstances: self-justification to a friend of the family, followed by a recital of the particulars of his new happiness, which, for a forty-five-year-old man married for twenty years, comes down to three basic things: fucking twice a day, taking up sports again, and watching stupid movies with the beloved.

As is often the case, François had met Nadia at work. He had only to lay eyes on her, and it was all over for his family life, his indifferent wife, his invasive children. He had swiftly invited Mam'zelle to lunch and had found her incredibly mature for twenty-four. She had confided that she found boys her own age "too superficial," and that she preferred the company of experienced men—especially when they oversaw an aerodynamics design department. He'd fretted for days trying to invent a plausible alibi for attending a weekend seminar in Frankfurt, so the two delinquents could flee to a seaside hotel where, a titan reborn, François had made love to her for two days. The sylph, minding her manners, had of course poured on a little extra to make him happy. And feeling revived, rejuvenated, restored, he was led to wonder how he'd managed to screw up his life for so long. Back home, he'd found Laure dull, faded, common, uninteresting, and his children ill-bred. Still, he took some time before reaching a decision, considering above all the financial ramifications of a separation. But Nadia was more and more attractive, available, loving, independent, free, intelligent, young, athletic, firm, and arousing. She was the first to be informed about the new world order and to show her gratitude blew him on the spot. He went home, made his announcement, and left without a thought or a backward glance for the weeping woman in his wake. Then, of course, it was all wine and roses for some time. But after a while, he started to miss his children, and, well, he'd gotten so used to his wife. . . . The *other* woman began to reproach him for not taking her out more, for always staying home, for never inviting anyone over. And so he felt himself grow old again, only now with the vague feeling that he'd made a foolish mistake, and that it was too late to do anything about it. But things gradually returned to normal and, as everyone does, he capitulated to the requirements of recombinant families, giving his new young wife a baby who actually resembled him this time around. Then he went back to designing the wings and asses of planes, while waiting for retirement in the company of his lovely young brunette who would also, when the time was right, go looking for a more vigorous partner.

In those days, whenever I ran into François, he was in the glowing phase of his transformation, relieved of familial burdens, intoxicated by the wine of recaptured youth.

"You can't imagine—Nadia has really brought me back to life. It's never happened to me!"

"You never had an affair before?"

"Two or three years after I married Laure, I met a girl at a party while I was on a business trip. We'd both had a lot to drink, and we wound up in my hotel room. I don't know what happened after that, but I can tell you that when I woke up the next morning, she was gone. There was a note on the night table. And you know what she wrote? 'I've known men who fell asleep before, and some who fell asleep right after, but you're the first to drop off during.' I swear it's true. I don't know where I put it, but I kept that note."

In his new guise as a liberated and conquering lover, François seemed totally different to me. Where before he was bathed in the austere odor of trigonometry, he now gave off the feral scent of youth and vitality. Women, even the basic Mam'zelle-Twenty-Four-Year-Old kind, have that incredible power of transfiguring men, plumping their souls up with spiritual collagen and mysteriously rejuvenating their glands.

"You know, I'd forgotten how good it could be. With Laure, that passion had been over for a long time."

I could have done without hearing that confession, which gave me a hot flash that momentarily short-circuited my conscience. I thought back to the afternoons when I'd seen Laure's splendid buttocks in the amber glow of the safe light. Simultaneously, however—and that partly attenuated, I suppose, both my embarrassment and my offense—I reflected that, in spite of our valiant efforts, I had been incapable of bringing Madame Milo to climax even once.

"Have you seen Laure again since I left?"

That innocent question sounded to me like breaking glass. There was too much hidden meaning in the words *seen again*. No, I had not *seen Laure again* for quite a while, but naturally another Lothario was *seeing* her regularly in my place. François seemed to be the only one who was still blind to all those people who kept buzzing endlessly around his wife.

"I'll be compelled to get a divorce."

"What do you mean 'compelled'?"

"Nadia wants a child. Not right away, of course, but she really wants one."

"And you?"

"Me? I don't know. It's too much for me to deal with all at one time. For the moment, I'll work on the divorce. It'll cost me a fortune. I know Laure; she'll bleed me dry."

Flashing her toothy smile, enter Nadia: a pretty princess, way too young to hang around men of our age. She said that François often talked about me. Then she sat on the sofa and spent a good half hour crossing and uncrossing her legs. She was clearly in need of exercise. When she walked me to the door I studied her appearance, and while she certainly had all the charms of youth (suppleness, freshness, and firmness), she lacked the knowledge, the patina, the cultivated sensuality of women over forty. I didn't tell François, but leaving Laure's derrière for this little schoolyard backside was sheer madness.

So François was happy, and his planes were selling better and better. As for me, on the advice of Spiridon I had gone back to work, this time doing macrophotography of nature in its minutiae. Mosses, lichens, buds, tadpoles, insects—unseen and precious ecosystems, all minuscule forms of life. I accumulated prints without really knowing what I wanted to do with them, but the work had a point at least: to give an iota of meaning to my days and allow me to pass the time.

It was around then that Pierre Bérégovoy committed suicide. I heard the news on the radio in my darkroom. That day I was developing a series on click beetles, busy little insects, coleoptera of the family Elateridae, also called spring beetles or skipjacks. The news stunned me. Not that I'd been a great admirer of his (he'd been shuffled out of the prime minister's office in just under a year), but the end of his life—and the way he had ended it—were so sad that the news hung on me like a sodden overcoat. I know why I remember that moment so well.

It has to do with the click beetle. Insignificant though it may be, that insect has one peculiarity. When it finds itself on its back and in peril, it flips itself abruptly into the air like a spring and lands somewhere else, in what it obviously hopes will be a better world. Pierre Bérégovoy's suicide made me think of the click beetle's reflex. Humiliated, laid low, perhaps in his own way he had tried to eject himself, to escape the wretched fate he had been handed. It was not at all by chance that this former workingman committed suicide on the first of May. The indifference with which the Socialists and Mitterrand himself had treated him after his dismissal had been roundly criticized at the time. A man from the lower classes, accused of corruption, burdened with defeat, Bérégovoy was no longer welcome in the imperial court. So the click beetle found himself back in the darkness of his tunnels. In the sadness of that end, in the story of that abandonment, was all the cruelty I sometimes discovered through my viewfinder in that miniature world where, driven by who knows what impulse, the insects would begin suddenly to vivisect one another. Five months after the suicide of his former prime minister, when François Mitterrand faced the mob that demanded an explanation of his own past and his disgraceful ties with René Bousquet (who as minister of police in Vichy France had overseen the infamous mass arrests of Paris's Jews), I spared a thought for Pierre Bérégovoy, and, I swear, the high value he placed upon his honor. Him, yes, click beetle though he was—I would have liked very much to have taken a picture of him, standing next to some trees.

Inaugurated in the intoxication of its campaign promises, endowed with a certain grandiloquent majesty, the Mitterrand era came to an end somewhat politically and morally adrift, leaving behind on the drapes and tapestries of the Republic a grime so typical of the end of a reign.

The financial scandals just kept coming; political officials, former government ministers, elders of the ruling elite were going to prison; a close associate of Mitterrand's killed himself in the Élysée Palace itself; and everyone was talking about Bousquet again, plus the affair of the HIV-contaminated national blood supply, the phone taps the president had ordered, his secret family, his illegitimate daughter, and the progress of his illness.

Wishing to preserve her faith in socialism, my mother refused to deal with the reality of that monarchical Republic, which had left state ethics and the public welfare in a prehistoric condition. However serious the crimes imputed to Mitterrand, he remained, for her, the great helmsman, the elegant duelist, the ultimate protector of arts, letters, and, of course, grammar. One day when we were looking through the magnifying glass at photo enlargements of bark beetles, she said, "You ought to do a book on insects. Find the strangest and most frightening ones and photograph them from close up, like these, turning them into real monsters. I'm sure that people would love that. People love monsters."

My mother's house had become a reassuring haven for me, welcoming and peaceful. There one felt sheltered from most of life's unpleasantness, even though the garden and the bushes were doing just as they pleased.

"I must tell you something," she murmured from behind her magnifying glass, never looking up from the photos. "Come closer, sit down over here."

I felt a confession coming on, a disclosure, even some uneasiness. She took off her glasses, gathered together all the photos, stacking them in a neat little pile. Then she looked out at the garden.

"François Mitterrand came to see me last night."

"Excuse me?"

"I have to tell you this. It was a dream, naturally, but it was so intense that it's been bothering me ever since, the way you can't shake off a nightmare sometimes."

"Was it a dream or a nightmare?"

"Decide for yourself. I am asleep in my room and I hear the bell at the little gate in the garden. I get up and go to the window, where I see

Mitterrand coming in with his hat, coat, and scarf on. He walks up the path and into the house. And then, calmly, as if nothing were happening, I go back to bed. He comes up the stairs, comes into the bedroom, and without saying a word takes off his fedora and loden coat and puts them on the armchair. Then he turns to me and quietly gets undressed."

"Completely?"

"Completely. He comes over to the bed, pulls back the sheets, sits down on the edge, takes off his wristwatch, places it on the night table, and lies down next to me. And do you know what I told him then—you know what your mother said to the president of the Republic? 'Don't even think about it: your feet are too cold.' "

I laughed like a kid, and my mother laughed, too, holding her hand in front of her mouth like a little girl hiding her embarrassment.

"Then what?"

"Then I don't remember anymore."

I adored my mother's dream. I also suspected that it hadn't ended there and that she remembered perfectly well what happened next, something that truly upset her, since to all appearances she had just betrayed my late father for the first time—with an elderly Socialist president who was a braggart, a liar, a mountebank, a deceiver, and who, to top it all off, had frigid feet.

Perhaps it was a consequence of that short night spent in his company, but in the days that followed the demise of the president, my mother put on the face of a grieving widow.

She found the funeral ceremony, with the two families—the legitimate and the illegitimate—united around the coffin, quite dignified. A few days later, though, her mourning done, she said something curious to me.

"We keep telling Africans that bigamy is illegal in France. I wonder what they must have thought when they saw the president of this country buried in public before his two wives and all their children."

JACQUES CHIRAC (I)

(May 17, 1995–May 5, 2002)

I N THE summer of 1994, without telling anyone, I had begun seeing a psychoanalyst every week. His name was Jacques-André Baudoin-Lartigue. Quite a long name for a short man who—you realized at once—would have surrendered all his Freud and Lacan just to be a few centimeters taller. He gave the uncomfortable impression of stretching upward to grasp a hypothetical object on an invisible shelf. I had been driven to Baudoin-Lartigue's doorstep by a profound feeling of loneliness. Anna devoted all her time to her resurgent business; my children were busy with their lives; François was attending to Mam'zelle Twenty-Four and her childbearing aspirations; Laure divided her days between her interminable divorce and her rabbinical recreation; Brigitte Campion shuttled between Botox sessions and collagen seminars; her husband, Michel, opened and closed human hearts. As for my mother's heart, it was gradually weakening, which made it increasingly difficult for her to get around.

All that made me feel as if I were living on a peninsula at the end of the world. I spent whole days without speaking to anyone, cooped up in the unnerving world of insects. Baudoin-Lartigue was probably not the companion of my dreams, but for the price of two full tanks of gas I could at least hope to stabilize my general condition with his help.

How do you explain to an impartial listener that you are encumbered by yourself, that through negligence and complaisance you have wound up at a complete loss as to what to do with your life? Oddly, Baudoin-Lartigue seemed disconcerted by our discussions. He had no idea that I expected nothing from his treatment, that I was visiting him and paying him for his time simply so that I could chat, trade opinions with him on sports, politics, or television. I could tell he would have preferred that I open other doors for him, the portals on intimate worlds with which he was more familiar: the death of a brother, the theft of a silvery coach, a father's discretion, a mother's transparency, a wife's silences, a mother-in-law's bust, a friend's wife's buttocks, a boyhood friend's family roast, a president's trees, the parable of the click beetle—all those little things that make a man, helping him to stand up on his hind legs for a while, and bringing him low at the same time. Occasionally Baudoin-Lartigue tried to impose a more abstract, conceptual tenor on our conversations, but I invariably brought things back to the banality of my days and the company of my insects. We could just as well have discussed all that in a café smoking cigarettes, instead of which, I lay on a kind of couch upholstered in a dreadful rep while he sat at his listening post, which from my angle looked something like a dentist's or a barber's chair.

Over time, Baudoin-Lartigue accepted our sessions more as therapeutic chitchat than a talking cure. We had discovered a common passion: rugby. We usually saw each other on Wednesdays, an ideal day, midweek, allowing us both to comment on the previous weekend's match and speculate about the game our mutual team, Stade Toulousain, would play that coming Saturday or Sunday. Our main concern was not whether Stade would win, but by how much. We both agreed that our club played the handsomest game in Europe, displaying verve and style worthy of its hundred years on the field, and that we were lucky to have such a model of strength and elegance in our own hometown.

Whenever he felt that we were infringing too blatantly upon clinical ethics, Baudoin-Lartigue would make a show of getting back to business and firming up the boundaries of the treatment. His next sentence would always begin with "In fact," even though his question would never have the slightest connection to what we'd been discussing.

"In fact, Monsieur Blick, at the very beginning of our sessions, when you first came to see me, you briefly mentioned the death of your older brother, I believe. Shall we examine that episode in your life?"

"I don't see any need for that."

"Or the death of your father?"

You could never accuse Baudoin-Lartigue of neglecting to put on his big Freudian wooden shoes and periodically clomp a sinister pas de deux around the profession's prize chestnuts. Like a fly-fisherman, he sometimes used rather tacky lures, casting them into the lively waters of hackneyed streams teeming with the dangerous little things that nibble endlessly on our psyches. After two or three fruitless castings, Baudoin-Lartigue would give up, put away his rod and reel, and take up where we had left off—Stade's powerful forward five. We had even (an unthinkable professional lapse) gone to see two championship matches together. Blick and his shrink, side by side, amid a crowd chanting its joy. And the spicy scent of cigarillos. Out in the sunshine. Happy and in cahoots. A thousand leagues from the psychoanalytic regimen. Simply admiring those tests of strength, those displays of speed, those moments of courage. Baudoin-Lartigue would forget his short stature, and I, my enveloping solitude. We were just two guys from the same city, cheering our hearts out for the home team to which we both secretly looked for a bit of happiness and life. I'd almost be tempted to say that for a short while, Baudoin-Lartigue was close to me, someone I paid to be my friend. Given the nature and the evolution of our relationship, moreover, he had lately been having trouble accepting payment. I'd had to insist, practically putting the money into his pocket myself.

As far as I can remember, only once did Baudoin-Lartigue and I strongly disagree about something. It was between the two electoral rounds of the 1995 presidential election won by Jacques Chirac. I quickly realized that I'd teamed up with the only right-wing psychoanalyst in France. He shamelessly championed the candidacy of this former mayor of Paris, whose chief merit, he admitted, was to have risen from the political dead to beat out Balladur by a nose for the nomination. I think it was mostly that outsider pose, that come-from-behind dash that Baudoin-Lartigue admired. Still, I just couldn't understand how any man of my generation, especially someone licensed to tinker with brains, could support that boor, who in 1962 was already handling infrastructure, construction, and transportation in Pompidou's cabinet. Baudoin-Lartigue's theory was simple: voting for Chirac meant breaking completely with the era of base behavior, of Machiavellianism raised to the level of a fine art by the Socialists, an era of sinecures, lies, deception, and scandals. Voting for Chirac meant entrusting the country to a guy who hadn't invented twelve-tone music, perhaps, but who was going to urge France forward by leaning on the horn, a bit like Vittorio Gassman at the wheel of the Lancia cabriolet in *The Easy Life*. Actually, I think the one and only intrinsic merit Baudoin-Lartigue saw in Chirac was that he wasn't a leftist. As it happened, most of the country felt the same way, and instead of the undeniably erudite and refined Mitterrand, they installed as chief of state a man who could pen a book called *The Gleam of Hope: An Evening Reflection for the Morning*.

It was 1995 already. During the rare conversations she granted me, I got the impression that Anna's business was going well, even though shipments to Spain were steadily declining. The children were spending less and less time at home, which they treated as one more element of the service sector: a hotel-restaurant-laundromat. To my surprise, Louis Spiridon had not seemed pleased by my proposals for a book on insects, and he had politely put off the project several times. And so it was that at forty-five years old, I found that my only friend was my psychoanalyst. I could probably have endured that situation for a few more years, but a tragedy ended our relationship. The small happiness we gleaned from each other's company must have weighed but lightly in the balance when Jacques-André Baudoin-Lartigue was faced with a truly dreadful decision.

It was on a Wednesday. A Wednesday in November. The previous week we had made plans to go together to see Stade Bourgoin or Stade Narbonne, I can't remember which anymore. We really enjoyed the atmosphere of those autumn games, the crisp air and humid earth that muddies jerseys, so different from the spring matches, when the terrain never seems large enough to contain the kinetic energy of the players as they race up and down the field. In cold weather they try to keep the ball warm, all those big guys sticking together, drawing on their inner reserves, counting on the power and heft of the herd. That's the kind of game we were expecting to see the following Sunday.

Instead, that morning I arrived at Baudoin-Lartigue's apartment building to find a crowd and the police at the entrance. Three ambulances with their doors open blocked a side street off the Boulevard de Strasbourg. When I tried to enter the lobby, a police sergeant asked me if I lived there. I replied that I was going to see Monsieur Baudoin-Lartigue. Then he tipped his kepi—just barely—to me and with a doubtful grimace made an incredible remark: "You won't be seeing him today."

Indeed, I never saw Jacques-André Baudoin-Lartigue again. No one did. At around ten o'clock that morning the psychoanalyst had left his office and returned to his apartment, which was on the same floor. There, with a gun he fetched from his bedroom, he had killed his wife and two children, shooting them in the head. Then he had gone back to his office, placed the barrel of the revolver in his mouth, and pulled the trigger. He left no explanation for his actions.

Perhaps his personal life was a disaster? Had he learned something that he shouldn't have? Or had his children stopped speaking to him? Was his wife seeing someone else? Was he ill, or despondent? Had he lost his older brother when he was a child? Unless it was his patients, all poisoning him one after another, day after day, with our doses of toxic personal misery? I had probably overlooked what was right in front of my eyes: I was calling for help from a man who was himself slowly drowning. I was so upset that the next day I tried to talk to Anna. I'd barely begun my story when she lashed out at me.

"You've been seeing a shrink for more than a year and you never told me?"

"But Anna, why would I talk to you about that when we never talk about anything?"

"Do me a favor, don't start that again. Have you noticed the hours I keep? And the state I'm in when I finally get home in the evening?"

"Have you noticed the state *we've* been in for *years*? We're not even a family anymore, let alone a couple. We share lodgings, and we're all so alone it's frightening."

"*You're* alone. Me, I see people all day long, I talk to them, I share something with them. I'm in the real world, you see—the real world! You're trying to make me feel guilty, but you forget the most important thing: you and you alone shut yourself up every day in your steam bath, preferring the company of trees and bugs to human beings!"

"That's not what I'm talking about."

"Of course it is. You like that fossilized universe. What do you expect to find there? You've never really worked, you don't know what it's like to live by the clock. The worst thing that ever happened to you was selling all those damn books."

"Anna, I don't give a fuck about the books, or work, or any of that. What I'm trying to tell you is that I was so alone, here, with you, in this house, that I was reduced to paying that man to talk to me, you understand, paying someone just so he would listen to me!"

Anna did not reply. For long seconds of silence, the only sound was the clanking of the radiators as the heat came on. We must have looked like two mummies frozen solid in a glacier. How could we have paid so little attention to each other for all those years? We never even helped each other anymore, each simply carrying out a strict personal share of domestic duties. Why—even if love was lost—hadn't we preserved even the reflex of mutual support? Why had I been reduced to ringing Baudoin-Lartigue's office doorbell to enjoy some simple table talk?

Anna walked over to the window and stood with her back to me (that elegant, eloquent back), gazing out into the night.

"The children called; they won't be home for supper," she said. "If you're hungry, fix yourself something—I'm too tired to cook."

"Do you want me to make you some fish?"

"No, I'm going to bed."

"That shrink I've been seeing—he killed himself this morning. He put a bullet in his head after killing his wife and two children."

"I'm very sorry. . . . Good night."

I was sitting at the kitchen table. At the other end of the house, Anna was lying awake in her bed, staring up at the ceiling. We hadn't been happy, separately or together, for ages, and the fact that we were think-ing the same thing at the same time didn't bring us one bit closer.

I spent an hour or two in the darkroom developing close-ups of some of the ugliest insects in creation. No one could ever hope to find the slightest hint of fellow feeling among them, for they all embodied a mechanical, autistic, authentically egotistical perception of the world. From birth to death, their every action was one of necessity governed by chance or by the instinct for survival, and they knew nothing of joy, sorrow, fear, or love.

Thinking about my life and Anna's, I reflected that a not too obser-vant ethnologist might put us in the same category.

Late that night I went to Anna's bedroom. Like Mitterrand visiting my mother, I undressed completely and lay down in that bed as cold as the grave. When I slipped my arm around Anna's shoulders, she hesi-tated for a second before shrugging free the way one throws off the covers on a warm night. I missed Baudoin-Lartigue already.

In the months that followed, Anna had more problems at Atoll and practically moved into her office, coming home only to go directly to her room, where she collapsed in exhaustion. Her sole diversion was to have dinner with her parents, where she gulped her food and fulminated against the Left, the tax authorities, and especially the trade unions, which she considered a true plague on society.

"Let me tell you something: when they see our labor laws, the coun-tries in Southeast Asia can't believe their own luck."

Martine and Jean Villandreux pretended to hang on their daughter's every word, but at heart they were disillusioned old folks who really didn't care, preoccupied as they were with monitoring their own creep-ing senescence.

"I mean, their latest-model Jacuzzis, sold in France with fourteen water jets and all the trimmings, are cheaper than my basic models. Besides which, for two years now the Confédération Générale du Tra-vail and the other big unions have been pressing for a thirty-five-hour workweek. How can we possibly manage? Everything's turned upside down."

At *Sports Illustrés*, Jean Villandreux had no complaints: the seasons changed, but the sales figures remained gratifyingly steady. Sports in general—soccer and rugby in particular—were unbelievably impervious to the capricious instability of markets and the influence of political conflicts; although increasingly dominated by the power of money, ball games survived financial crashes and the worst wars. Whatever the ups and downs of geopolitics or economic forecasting, the readers of *Sports Illustrés* faithfully purchased their weekly fix of muscular heroics. Jean Villandreux used to say that it was "a magazine that ran on automatic pilot." And privately, he congratulated himself on having gotten rid of his swimming-pool business at the right moment, even though he now felt some remorse at seeing his daughter struggling to keep the firm afloat.

Millions of French people marched in the streets against the harsh reform of social security proposed by Alain Juppé, the prime minister whose elitist arrogance captivated my mother-in-law. "We don't deserve him," she kept saying, watching the waves of discontent break against his stony intransigence.

Although I was hardly a model citizen, thanks to my feeble interest in the ballot box and my ignorance of what Anna called "real life," my gloomy mood and pulverized morale did rather faithfully reflect the disenchantment, dejection, even the aging of this nation. With every day came a delivery of fresh manure: corruption, breach of trust, misuse of public funds, embezzlement, indictments, racism, poverty, contempt, unemployment. All these factors conspired to breed their own viruses that were resistant to all therapy and led to chronic malignancies, with cycles of remission and sudden relapse.

Whether considering my own life or the nation's destiny, I saw no way out, no light, not the slightest reason for hope or relief.

To escape this family neurosis, my son, Vincent, left home soon after his twentieth birthday. While not excellent, his grades in secondary school had been quite satisfactory, and he had decided to earn a degree in languages with the intention of obtaining a master's in technical English. He had always been close to his paternal grandmother, and had been won over, I believe, by the way she worked peacefully in the seclusion of her home. Diplomas in hand, he would then start a small business translating scientific documents as well as more literary texts. François Milo had in fact strongly encouraged him in this direction, promising him some subcontracting work, various administrative and technical catalogs and schedules from Airbus Industrie. Vincent had also studied Japanese, which he seemed to assimilate without too much difficulty, with the help of his friend Yuko.

Two years older than he was, Yuko Tsuburaya worked at the Centre National d'Études Spatiales as an exchange student in space research from Kyoto University. Both Yuko and Vincent were quiet and even-tempered: no raised voices, no exuberance, never the slightest show of anger. The thermostat for their moods and emotions seemed to have been set permanently at room temperature. With them, both joy and sorrow appeared to be filtered and purified to produce a single drop of concentrated extract that irrigated all their intimate receptors. I admired their serenity, and their placid relationship. When they came to lunch at the house, I often wondered how such a couple could evolve over time. I imagined their granitic exteriors, their mineral surfaces preserving them from the erosion of the passing years. From whom had my son inherited that remarkable Oriental wisdom? Not from his mother or myself, in any case, since it was obvious that our particular genetic combination probably represented the most spiteful biological inheritance any parents could bequeath their descendants.

Yuko, on the other hand, had impressive ancestry. She was the daughter of Kikuzo Tsuburaya and, more important, the niece of Koki-chi Tsuburaya. Who still remembers that man who flashed across our television screens one day without really attracting our attention? When Yuko first related the story of her uncle's life, several days passed before I could stop thinking about what she had told me.

Kokichi Tsuburaya loved to run. During his childhood and adolescence, he had run along every path and road in the prefecture of Sai-tama, to the north of Tokyo, with a tireless enthusiasm that caught the eye of athletic club recruiters, who saw in him the makings of an exceptional runner. With rigorous training, the young man swiftly became an excellent athlete, and when Japan hosted the Olympic Games in 1964,

Tsuburaya was chosen to represent his country in the marathon. During the year before that footrace over 42 kilometers and 195 meters, Kokichi had run up mountains and across plains, galloping through mud and snow, sunshine and rain, buffeted by every wind. He ran during the day, but also sometimes at night, always cutting imaginary corners tightly, unleashing tactical bursts of speed at the fourteenth, twenty-seventh, and thirty-eighth kilometers to shake off phantom rivals, and launching a sprint for the finish in the last kilometer to pull away from any tenacious pursuers in the hope of entering the Olympic stadium on his own to receive the ovation of seventy thousand spectators. Tsuburaya had run this race thousands of times in his head, boosting his courage and the capacity of his superbly conditioned heart with every stride.

When he rose at dawn on that great day in 1964, he drank a glass of tea and quietly got ready as usual. A few seconds before the race began, he realized that the entire country was watching him, and he felt a thrill of pride. At the signal, Tsuburaya took off, and his legs, so often maltreated to accustom them to harsh conditions, now raced toward the wonderful goal he had promised them. The other runners had a hard time matching the pace set by this human locomotive and one by one they all fell back. Halfway through the race, there was Kokichi, with the rest of the field trailing behind him. Ten kilometers before the finish line, the Japanese runner seemed to have the victory sewn up. One man, however, was gradually closing in on him, quickening his pace and lengthening his stride. His name was Abebe Bikila, and he came from the other side of the world. Three kilometers from the stadium, at the very place where, in his dreams, he left all challengers in his dust, Tsuburaya saw Bikila pass him, followed by another runner. For a moment he did try to catch them, but this time his legs, his muscles, his bones and heart—the entire machine he thought he had trained perfectly—refused the extra burden.

Kokichi Tsuburaya stood upon the third step of the podium. While Bikila beamed, Tsuburaya sank into the shadows. After the ceremony to award the medals, Tsuburaya spoke to reporters to ask forgiveness of the Japanese people for not having won the race. He said that he deeply regretted the humiliation thus inflicted on his country and he promised to redeem himself at the coming games in Mexico City.

The day after the Olympics ended, Kokichi laced up his running shoes again, put on his windbreaker, and went back out along the paths and roads he had run so many times before. And months passed. And still more seasons. The man kept running, but the distances he covered began to shrink. As if every passing day were stealing a little bit of strength and courage from him. Rarely, I think, has a man gone to the very end of himself like that, and it seems that what he found at the bottom of that exhausted soul robbed him of all desire to go any further.

Kokichi Tsuburaya did not leave his home one morning. Or the next morning, or the one after that. No one noticed this modest change in the neighborhood's routines. What could be more ordinary than a man who runs? His older brother, Kikuzo, Yuko's father, telephoned Kokichi several times without reaching him. Kikuzo rang his brother's doorbell, but no one came to open it. Then a locksmith was summoned to open the door. Inside, Kokichi's visitors found his running clothes carefully folded and placed on the ground next to the shoes he had worn in the marathon. The runner himself was lying on the rug in a pool of blood, facing Tokyo Bay. He had slashed his wrists with the razor blade still clutched in his hand. On the table lay a curt note written in blue ink: "I am tired. I do not want to run anymore."

After she told me that story, I no longer saw Yuko without remembering that man, that stranger who would forever keep running through my mind.

Although I had never thought of her as deeply maternal, Anna took her son's departure very hard. Her sadness was probably exacerbated by the party I threw to celebrate this new phase in Vincent's life. Our children had invited their friends; François Milo came with Mam'zelle Twenty-Four-and-Counting; Michel Campion arrived with Brigitte, who was enameled in makeup and Botoxed nearly to death. At the last minute, Anna had invited a few of her circle, supposedly to add some luster and liveliness to our gathering of about twenty couples. I had spent two days preparing the meal: Greek and Lebanese salads, shellfish, sushi, cooked fish, and stir-fried vegetables. All my efforts were in vain, however, as the evening slowly foundered. First, Mam'zelle picked an incomprehensible fight with François, accusing him—if I understood correctly—of having "the uptight tastes of an old man." Anna burst into tears when the woman sitting next to her asked if she now dreaded dealing with "the empty nest syndrome" ("half-empty," at any rate, since Marie would still be living with us). There was a phone call from a babysitter informing one of the young couples that their baby had a high fever. Then Michel Campion subjected the entire table to a blow-by-blow account of one of his heart surgeries, rather sickening in detail and of no interest to anyone except the surgeon himself. Finally, in the middle of the meal, one of Yuko's friends began vomiting violently, which she blamed on a bad oyster.

Upset by all these mishaps, I fled to the kitchen, where I remained until the last guest had left. Then I went to find Anna in her room. She was sitting slumped on the edge of her bed, resting her elbows on her knees in a vaguely masculine way that made her face look particularly tired. My wife seemed like a man who'd had a long, hard day.

"I didn't think that Vincent's leaving would affect you so much."

"What *did* you expect? That I'd want to celebrate?"

"I don't know—I'm simply surprised, that's all."

"At what? You're realizing that I love my son—is that what you're trying to tell me?"

"That's not it. I thought you were tougher, less sentimental."

"What, are you angry with me for crying at the party?"

"Absolutely not, quite the opposite—I thought it was sweet of you."

"It's not sweet at all, it's sad, Paul, just sad. Vincent is going away, and that's an important change for our family. Until this moment, we've always lived together. From now on, we'll grow old separately. And that's quite different. Especially for a woman."

"I think you're being a little dramatic. Your son will be living ten minutes from here—it isn't as if he were moving to Japan!"

"Vincent will go to Japan."

"There's nothing to indicate that he'll be spending his life with Yuko."

"He'll spend his life with her and move to Japan. You have to realize that. One day he'll go there. And anyway, what difference does it make? You try to reassure yourself by remembering that he'll be close by, but that doesn't mean anything. Your son has left, do you understand that? And he won't ever come back."

Anna had barely finished speaking when she broke down, sobbing. Everything she'd said had hit home, leaving me stunned at the gloomy prospect of our son crossing Asian landscapes to run away from us forever.

I would have liked to take Anna in my arms and tell her that she had me, and Marie, and that we would grow old, of course, but gently, letting time come to us. I said nothing, though, and left the room, knowing that when she was in that state, Anna Blick stood behind a wall so smooth that there was no reaching her.

I telephoned Yuko the next day and under some pretext or other got her to talk about her work at the space research center. Through my little investigation I learned that she was going to remain at the center for four more years. Unlike Anna, I was now certain that my son was not preparing to leave Toulouse. That very evening I proudly told my wife the news.

"I don't want to talk about this anymore, Paul. I've already explained to you that for me, Vincent has left us. Whether he's right next door or in Kyoto doesn't change a thing."

"Does this have anything to do with what you think of Yuko?"

"I don't think anything about Yuko, just as I'm sure that she hasn't the slightest opinion about me. She is there, so am I. We respect that distance, that's all."

"That's a bit restrictive, don't you think?"

"If it's any help to you, I think exactly the same thing about our son. I have never found out who he really is, what he wants, or what he hopes to do with his life. Which has never prevented me from loving him."

"What you're telling me seems accurate, and at the same time, so . . . harsh."

"Paul, I'm going to be fifty years old soon. And I'm not mellowing with age."

Even though Anna was two years older than I was, to me she was still the young woman I had craftily stolen from Grégoire Elias. She had kept the same beauty that used to bring tears to my eyes. Life had worn us down, sometimes roughly, but to me she had emerged intact from that long crossing, even though she seemed to be revealing that her heart was bruised all over.

"Do you think Vincent is happy?"

"Paul, you're unbelievable. How can you expect me to answer that question?"

"I don't know. You're his mother. . . ."

"And you're his father. You've lived twenty years under the same roof with him, and you had eyes to see with, like me. You have never spoken with your son—and you've waited until he's no longer here to ask me the essential question you should have asked him."

"I didn't see how time was slipping by."

"Dear God, why do men always have the same problem with time? So you don't see, you don't *feel* that we're getting older every day?"

"But that's it—I was just thinking that you don't change, that you've hardly changed at all the whole time I've known you!"

"Cut the crap."

Anna always had a problem with compliments. Especially one relating to her appearance. She had a somewhat gruff and mannish way of rebuffing anyone who praised her.

"Paul, I think we should never have had children."

"How can you say that?"

"I don't know . . . I feel as if we haven't given them everything they had a right to expect, as if we loved them from too far away, and only off and on. I've often felt that. And then I'd always tell myself that I'd make up for lost time, that I'd come home earlier from the office to be with them, or else that I'd take them somewhere for the weekend. But I was always so tired, and cowardly, too, so I never did any of that. Today they're going away, and I realize that I've spent most of my life dealing with Jacuzzis and diatomite swimming-pool filters instead of taking the time to be with them."

I understood perfectly what Anna meant; I also felt that same clammy culpability, so long repressed. An autumn thunderstorm was in the air: great gusts of wind were whipping the trees around, making them whistle and groan. Standing at her bedroom window, Anna watched their trunks and branches sway in the tempest of the night. I went over and placed my hands on her shoulders. We were alone in that huge house. I heard her say, without turning around, "Fuck me."

I had a pretty good idea what Anna wanted at that instant: a moment of relief, some breathing space stolen from the numbing routine of everyday life—a burst of sex without the frills, something primitive. She knew that afterward things would be no better than they'd been before, that we would wretchedly remain what we'd always been. But that wasn't important, since Anna wanted only one thing: to be simply in the present. Although sex couldn't transcend or restore anything between us, it still allowed us to take a kind of break, relief from the burdensome weight of our bodies. To cling to the frayed fabric of existence. Not that our couplings weren't pleasurable. On the contrary: stripped of its Judeo-Christian trimmings, our sex recovered a certain instinctive integrity, as we each made the other one pay for the mistake of having lost touch with ourselves.

It can be instructive to return like that to the origins of our species and rediscover what we're really made of, and recover that desire to survive, to see another sunrise no matter what the day will bring. On that stormy night, while the wind raged outside, I think Anna wanted us to survive. And so did I. Together or separately. Whenever I thought about us, I was frightened by how far apart our lives were. She, day and night, the Queen of Jacuzzis, the Holy Mother of Swimming Pools. I, an ex-photographer of trees, still out on a limb.

After 1997, Anna's business situation grew more and more grim. Her moods followed those of the market, and as her financial difficulties increased, relations with her personnel deteriorated. Just before

Chirac's self-defeating dissolution in April of an essentially conservative Assemblée Nationale (which led to the unexpected triumph of the
Left in the June elections), the unions at Atoll went on strike for more
than a month, right in the middle of the electoral campaigns. This
earned them a certain amount of local press coverage and even the
encouragement of the leftist candidates who later went on to win. Their
support outraged Anna, who fulminated against the "irresponsibility"
and "demagoguery" of the Socialists while at the same time excoriating
the incompetence of "that other huge asshole," Jacques Chirac, whom
she would never forgive for having upset the apple cart just for the hormonal hell of it. As a rule, the business world loathes instability and
sudden change. And that goes double for the swimming-pool game.
Having heard this repeated a hundred times, I can say that they operate
at the most vulnerable level of the economy, among the first to suffer in
a slump or crisis. To Anna, embroiled as she was in a labor dispute, the
replacement of Alain Juppé, our former right-wing prime minister
from Mont-de-Marsan, by Lionel Jospin, a Socialist from Meudon, was
a veritable October Revolution. Beside herself with fury, Anna capitulated on all fronts and gave the unions the wage increases they
demanded. On the evening after the agreements were signed, she spent
more than three hours on the phone with her parents and then with a
reporter from a business magazine. Marie and I could hear the echo of
this tumult while we ate dinner in the next room.

"Well, of course . . . Everything fell apart when the Assemblée
Nationale was dissolved. . . . What do you expect, they felt they had
wide support, obviously. . . . I told them: we're heading straight for
disaster. . . . A business can't survive paying what you're asking. . . .
Well, they couldn't have cared less, egged on by their agitators. . . . But,
Papa, no, that's all changed, the relationship isn't what it was in your
time. . . . There's nothing more to be said. . . . And what's worse, to hear
the press spin it you'd believe that unionism is dead and that the bosses
have a free hand. . . . Don't kid yourself—after this, the bank is going to
rake all the accounts, and they'll call us on every overdraft. . . . Things
have simply gone too far, and all because of that flaming asshole. . . ."

All that managerial moaning seemed to upset Marie, who was as shy and reserved as her brother, and whose sympathies, I knew, lay with the non-Communist Left. She did not relish hearing her own mother spouting such resolutely right-wing capitalist propaganda, and was now torn between her own nascent political militancy and her love for Anna. I, more prosaically, was thinking of the "flaming asshole," his burlesque destiny, and the incredible Teflon resistance to ridicule that had enabled him to sail on—as if nothing had happened!—after personally sinking his entire fleet. And if it hadn't been for the five centuries that separated them, you might have thought that the Italian poet Ludovico Ariosto had assiduously studied the author of that mind-blowing legislative dissolution and all its consequences before penning his own definition of stupidity: "The vulgar imbecile always hankers after great events, whatever they may be, without foreseeing whether they will prove useful or harmful to him, for the vulgar imbecile is moved solely by his own curiosity."

As for me, since fortune had already smiled on me once and for all, I lived off my royalties while I continued my work on insects, to which pursuit I added plans for a book on television sets. Unlike my monograph on Pseudoneuroptera and other Hymenoptera, my idea of photographing the historical and esthetic evolution of those magic lanterns (in black-and-white, against a gray background) positively enchanted Spiridon, who immediately opened a line of credit for me to cover my research and travel expenses. Before going anywhere, I examined the most beautiful examples I could find in archives and catalogs. This project suited me. Especially since I didn't have to take pictures of human beings, that restless species constantly slipping out of focus.

I was not able to research my new idea for very long. On the day before the World Cup final, my mother had a second stroke, this time a serious one, affecting not only her motor functions but also her outlook on life. Although she did not talk much about it, she knew that from then on, every night, death would be sleeping in her bed.

When she came home after two long months of rehabilitation, she entered her own house as if it were some luxurious Oriental palace. She was rediscovering a world she had thought lost forever and finding all its familiar objects patiently waiting for her.

In addition to installing an electric hospital bed, we arranged for a physical therapist to visit my mother and for a nurse to come twice a day to wash and dress her when she got up and put her to bed at night. Every morning a municipal service brought her hot meals that tasted like hospital food.

To my mother's great delight, I quickly canceled those deliveries and took over the preparation of her meals myself. The improvement restored her taste for life, and my daily visits soon became routine and indispensable. Within a few months, of course, my life was turned upside down. Without my really wishing it, or even noticing it, I had become my mother's cook, accountant, gardener, butler, and confidant. Months passed during which I sometimes spent more time in her house than in my own. Some evenings I went home exhausted, demoralized, and prematurely aged.

I could no longer retreat: trapped in a tangle of emotions, I had to continue what I had started or break the tacit contract between us, abandoning my fragile mother to her crippled loneliness. Every day she told me how grateful and happy she was to be able to live at home until the end. The end: she probably saw it so clearly that she could touch it, and so she spoke about it with familiarity, with a lightness and detachment that were new for her. So silent and discreet all her life, my mother now did not hesitate to share her thoughts and feelings with me, as if all the dikes of restraint that had dammed up her emotions had been swept away when the hemorrhage filled her brain. Although she was half paralyzed, I had never seen my mother so alert.

I would accompany her down that long tunnel for four years, years for me ever more painful and sad. Some evenings, I left her house like a miner coming up for air. It wasn't the work that overwhelmed me, but everything else—that heartrending spectacle of illness and old age. And then I began to notice certain shameful feelings in myself: I started resenting my mother for stealing my time, for blackmailing me emotionally, for taking advantage of the situation, for complaining without trying to help herself. All these reproaches, I knew, were completely unfair, yet I felt them.

In that autumn of 1998, I had indefinitely delayed my book projects.

For some time now, when she came home in the evening, Anna had seemed calmer, more relaxed than in the past. She spoke of her worries and difficulties as if Atoll were some troublesome subsidiary of a greater enterprise. No longer at constant loggerheads with the unions, she had been practicing laissez-faire for months. She was concentrating on a new scheme: setting up a production facility for Jacuzzis in Catalonia and slowly transferring the assets of Atoll to Barcelona. This relocation plan was top secret, and there was no question of letting the employees in Toulouse get wind of their impending dismissal. I thought this was terribly treacherous, but what could I do except go denounce my own wife to the unions, and, frankly, I just didn't see myself doing that.

Anna made more and more trips to Barcelona. Every week she was off to negotiate contracts and visit prospective sites, returning each time with more optimism and trust in her lucky star. Labor, she said, was cheaper in Barcelona than in Toulouse, and the province of Catalonia, wishing to attract new entrepreneurs, was aggressively helpful to her efforts.

As I felt myself crawling day after day through a winding tunnel I myself had dug, Anna, on the other hand, seemed to be returning to life, as if she had resolved her business problems through a decision that was brutal, admittedly, and undeniably selfish, but bluntly effective. Without the slightest scruple, she continued to run Atoll as though nothing were going on. When I came home in the evening, I often found her relaxing on the sofa in the living room, her legs stretched out on the cushion, having a drink and chatting with Marie. Sometimes I tried to talk things over with her.

"Anna, do you really have to move so quickly on this Barcelona project?"

"So, you're taking a sudden interest in my business now?"

"Actually I'm thinking of the business of a hundred or so people who are going to find themselves out of a job overnight."

"And they'll have done everything in their power to ensure that."

"Why don't you just tell them the truth?"

"How?"

"I don't know—tell them that the company's in trouble, that you've got real problems. And that it's better to earn a little less for a while than to risk losing their jobs."

"What a child you are, Paul. You think the union officials will give a shit about the company's troubles, or mine?"

"I'm not talking about them—why not speak to the workers directly?"

"They hate me even more than the union bosses. You don't seem to understand: the game is lost. We can't compete anymore. The move to Barcelona alone saves me thirty percent of overhead."

"What does your father say?"

"My father? Believe me, he's light-years away from all this. Ever since he started on Viagra, his mind has been on other things."

"How do you know that?"

"How do you think I know it—my mother told me!"

"You talk about that with your mother?"

"I can't believe how uptight you can be."

"How old is your father?"

"Seventy-eight or -nine, I forget."

"And your mother, what does she say about it?"

"Two minutes ago you were scandalized that my mother and I talked about my father's sex life, and now you want details about their relationship!"

"No, no—I simply wondered how your mother was reacting to this development, that's all."

"You know what? Call her up and ask her yourself."

"Seriously, you ought to talk to your father about this whole business—it just seems like madness to me. Please think it over."

"I have thought it over, sweetheart."

"You called me 'sweetheart'?"

"Sorry, it just slipped out."

To illustrate the spontaneity of her remark, Anna made a sort of twirling motion with her hand over her head. Usually so serious and even stern, Anna had for some time now been adopting a tone and certain mannerisms that sometimes truly puzzled me. And I'd also noticed that she was paying much more attention to her clothes, even when she went off to lock horns with some official of the Confédération Générale du Travail. Another change I would have been hard put to criticize was that Anna had regained her former sexual appetite. Catalonia definitely had strange metabolic effects, capable of stimulating a woman simultaneously to ruin and make love to her fellow man.

And so a very full—and strange—year went by: during the day, I was the dutiful son, spoon-feeding my mother, while by night I was an obedient lover, climbing atop the satin-smooth belly of a wife suddenly reenamored. In addition to some trifling perversities I'd never noticed in her before, Anna, a longtime devotee of silent couplings, was now speaking up: she would give me a short series of clear directions that sounded to me like encouragement. For a while now my wife had also been bringing a certain bluntness to our encounters. Just before I came, for example, she would now command me to "Look down!" And she would repeat those same words, louder and louder, until—no matter what my position—I had in fact lowered my head. It gave me a peculiar feeling, and I never figured out whether it improved or degraded the quality of my pleasure. In any case, there seemed to be no comparison between Anna's present pleasure and her orgasms throughout our long life together. Now when her eyes would half close and her head tip slightly back, I could almost feel the invisible currents penetrating and shocking her body. The veins in her throat stood out like a faintly blue collar, almost as if she were strangling herself. Then deliciously coarse bedroom obscenities would burst from Anna's lips like embers, tiny droplets of lava thrown off by her soul at the moment of eruption.

I admit that for a while I was intrigued by all these developments and even suspected that Anna, like Laure before her, was faking her orgasms. However, it wasn't really in character for her to indulge in such deceptions or to bother shoring up the fragile ego of an unsatisfactory partner. No, for some months I had generally felt that we'd grown closer not only in body but also in spirit, a feeling that grew stronger when Vincent told us that he and Yuko were expecting a baby. Once we had recovered from our initial surprise, we felt a bond form between us at the prospect of this stimulating although as yet abstract project: taking care of our children's children. Vincent and Yuko's baby was due in February or March of 2000. To hear us discussing this near future made it clear that we were a couple again. Unfortunately, appearances often lull fools into complacency, and life, exasperated by this idiotic confidence, promptly washes such poor souls overboard.

The new millennium was only a few months away, and the West, in a fever of consumerism, was treating itself to the luxury of a few technological scares. In addition to imminent stock-market meltdowns, various scatterbrained visionaries were promising us a cataclysm of viruses and other computer disasters. Preoccupied by my mother's health and by the turn my life was taking, I was paying scant attention to the daily ravings of these Cassandras. I had no idea that I was about to jump the gun a bit and find out for myself how true all those malicious millenarian prophecies could be.

My personal little Armageddon began late on the afternoon of Thursday, November 25, 1999, with a call from the police in Carcassonne. I didn't understand what the man on the phone was telling me. His voice was uncertain, his explanations confused, and he spoke with the strong accent of Corbières. Darkness had already fallen, and it was raining.

"You need to come identify the body."

It was the third time he had said that. Identify the body. Come identify the body of Anna Blick. She had died in a plane crash. I kept pointing out to him that this was impossible, that Anna had left that very morning to drive to Barcelona, but he insisted, apologetically: come identify the body. That was all he wanted. For me to say yes. And then he would hang up.

Without telling anyone or informing my son and daughter, I drove to Carcassonne. I remember driving without any real haste or anguish, in a quite neutral state, letting all sorts of emotions float around inside me. I neither felt nor foresaw anything. Experienced no speculations, jumped to no logical conclusions. Raindrops smashed into the windshield; the wipers swept them away. I drove along to the rhythm of those squeegees trying to keep my coast clear and illuminate the gloomy vision I might have of the world around me.

The body had been washed, but there were still spangles of coagulated blood at the roots of the hair. There were deep wounds in the chest and the legs. The left foot had been severed above the ankle, and the right breast sliced through the middle. Although discolored and deformed by bruising, the face retained a certain beauty, and despite all the damage, one could still see the delicacy of the features. I looked at her the way one discovers the end of the world, when there is nothing left after evil has laid waste to everything. I looked at the woman to whom I had said good-bye that very morning, a woman in her usual hurry, radiant with energy and trailing whiffs of freshly applied perfume. I looked at the former lover of Grégoire Elias, the mother of Vincent and Marie, the daughter of Martine and Jean, but I could not bring myself to believe that this battered corpse was also the wife of Paul Blick.

I was there and I looked at her. I was waiting for something to happen inside me, an event that would have stirred me and made me understand what I was living through, which was beyond me.

"Do you recognize your wife?"

All I had to do was say yes for Anna to die, for them to shut the sliding refrigerator drawer, for her death to be recorded in the police log, for everything to be different, for telephones to begin ringing, and people, all of a sudden, to start crying.

" . . . Excuse me. . . . Do you recognize Madame Anna Blick?"

How shall I put it? It was she and at the same time someone else. A sort of older sister with a face hardened by age, the survivor of a bloody nightmare, slowly recuperating on an icy couch. Yes, a sister knocked down by a bad dream, and who never left home without her Kodak Brownie Flash or her silver coach, whose parents had always preferred her because she was the livelier and more intelligent of the two. A sister who later through some mistake married a boy whose brother was dead, a boy named Block or Blick, who used to say that he had earned his living once and for all and who lowered his head when he reached orgasm.

"I'm sorry, but I must insist. . . ."

I turned toward the policeman. I saw a man tired by his workday, doubtless in a hurry to go home to his family and let the red mark left on his forehead every day by the edge of his kepi fade slowly away. It was the man on the telephone, the one who spoke with the accent of Corbières. He was sorry to insist but did not hesitate to repeat his question. And he would repeat it as often as he had to until he obtained his answer and could assign a name to this dead woman.

"Was this your wife?"

Hearing the policeman speak of Anna in the past made me break down in tears. He had just forced me to understand that Anna was no longer of this world. I replied that yes, she had been my wife for almost twenty-five years.

The policeman shut his notebook and quickly signaled to an employee of the morgue. The man came over, covered Anna with a sheet, and, after discreetly seeking my permission, carefully pushed the drawer, which slowly slipped away with Anna into the void.

At that instant, I wanted only one thing: to take my children in my arms and cling to them, never letting them go, protecting them from men and planes, keeping them near me, watching over them as I had for so long when we were still such a young family. The policeman asked me to come to his office so that he could give me some information about the accident.

"Tomorrow . . . not tonight . . ."

"I understand. When you're ready."

"Where did it happen?"

"In the foothills of La Montagne Noire."

"It was a commercial airline?"

"Ah, no: a small single-engine plane, a tandem—a Jodel, I think."

The drive back to Toulouse took forever. I felt as though I were steering a small craft buffeted by contrary winds and treacherous currents. The car would pass through solid curtains of rain, and each time I drove through them, they seemed to open onto worlds of increasing darkness. The fury of the downpour matched the chaos of my emotions. At times a kind of terror overwhelmed me, the idea that I would never hear Anna's voice again. At other moments, my thoughts revolved around the circumstances and the very nature of that plane crash. Questions of simple logic gradually occurred to me. How could

Anna, who had set out in her car that morning for Barcelona, have died a few hours later in a two-seater plane in the middle of that mountain forest? What was she doing in that tiny Jodel? Where was the plane going? Where had it come from?

I reached home at around ten o'clock. It took me some time to find the courage to get out of the car. The rain was hammering the roof of the automobile, and through the trees I glimpsed the lights of the den, where my daughter liked to spend her evenings when she wasn't going out. She was probably watching television, listening to music, or talking on the phone, curled up on the couch, with no idea that she was sitting on the edge of a chasm into which she would fall as soon as I came through the front door.

How can a father tell his daughter that her mother is dead? Are there some words that are less painful than others, any sentences that are less wounding? It was the first time I had entered my own house bearing such a burden. I could hear the familiar jabbering of the TV, the invisible, torrential chatter of that unreal world that never slept or died. I would tell Marie the news and nothing would change on the screen, where everyone would survive to spout their clichés in their walk-on parts.

I must have looked like a timid burglar: stiff and chilled, my face dripping with rain, I took a few hesitant steps toward Marie, who was watching a film with subtitles. I remember which film: Atom Egoyan's *The Sweet Hereafter*. I remember Ian Holm as the father, telephoning from his car to his daughter, who lived hundreds of miles away; I remember the sadness in his eyes, and his forlorn words: "I don't know who I'm talking to right now."

I remember Marie turning to look at me, the sudden fear in her eyes, her hand reaching out to grasp the edge of the couch.

I remember looking down and, unable to hold back my tears any longer, hearing myself say, "Your mama is dead."

Marie didn't ask me anything, didn't say a single word. Huddling there on the couch, she seemed to shrink before my eyes, as if to disappear and thus escape the tragedy. Cold tears slipped down her cheeks. She was crying with her eyes wide open.

I had to phone Vincent. His first reflex was to bombard me with questions that I obviously could not answer. He wanted to know everything—the time, the place, the circumstances, the cause of the accident. He kept asking those questions over and over, trying to keep from giving in to overwhelming sorrow.

He arrived at the house at a little past eleven with Yuko and found Marie and me sitting at opposite ends of the sofa. We must have looked like a couple of strangers parked in a waiting room. Marie went over to her brother, I followed her, and the three of us wound up hugging one another, clinging to that little knot of family we had left. I was standing in the middle of the room with my children in my arms. In the doorway, Yuko Tsuburaya and her big belly were clearly waiting for a sign to join our circle, but none of us had the presence of mind to make that gesture.

That same evening I had to tell Anna's parents. Tell them the little that I knew. The Jodel. La Montagne Noire. Carcassonne. The police station. Strangely, the Villandreuxs seemed to accept very quickly the idea that they would never see their only daughter again, and they questioned me endlessly about material and practical details we would have to take care of. We all had our own ways of forestalling grief, I suppose.

That evening, I decided to spare my mother, to let her have another night of peace. There was no hurry. Tomorrow, perhaps, when it was daylight.

In the morning the rain was still pummeling the earth and glistening on the trunks of the plane trees. At nine o'clock I was in the police station in Carcassonne in a freezing office that smelled of bleach.

"It's a little early for definite answers, but we think that the accident was caused by the weather. Conditions yesterday were particularly bad over La Montagne Noire."

The policeman handed me photos of a small single-engine plane so crumpled that you could barely distinguish the ghostly silhouette of the cockpit.

"What was my wife doing in that plane?"

"That's what I was going to ask you."

"Anna left the house yesterday to drive to Barcelona. That is all I can tell you."

"Do you know Monsieur Xavier Girardin?"

"No."

"He was the owner and pilot of the plane."

"A professional pilot?"

"No. He had his license, of course, but flew for his own pleasure. He was a lawyer in Toulouse. By the way, what kind of car did your wife drive?"

"A Volvo."

"A dark gray S70 sedan?"

"That's right."

"We found it in the parking lot of the Lasbordes Flight Club in Toulouse."

"The plane was coming from Barcelona?"

"According to the flight plan, the Jodel was simply making a round-trip between Toulouse and Béziers. The name Girardin really means nothing to you? May I show you a photo?"

In the picture Xavier Girardin looked like a happy man, smiling and confident. His face was strong and appealing, with something of the masculinity of a more refined Nick Nolte. I had never seen Xavier Girardin in my life, or heard of him either.

"Why was your wife traveling to Barcelona?"

"For her work. She had been going there more or less once a week for a year now. She was busy with a business project there."

"Do you know if she sometimes traveled there by plane?"

"Never. She always made the trip by car."

"And yesterday nothing suggested to you that she had decided to fly there in the Jodel with Monsieur Girardin?"

"No."

"May I ask you what your profession is?"

"I take photographs."

That interview left me quite perplexed. What little I'd just found out from the policeman had led me into a morass of questions without any rational answers. In the days ahead, however, I would learn much more than I would ever have wanted to.

First of all, there was the unexpected atmosphere at Anna's funeral.

My wife had often mentioned how deeply the entire workforce at Atoll hated her, so I was surprised when the firm closed its doors to observe a day of mourning, and every employee, without exception, came to the funeral. The most puzzling thing was that all those people seemed truly upset. Wherever I looked in that crowd, I saw only sad faces and sympathetic looks. How could anyone hate a boss so much and mourn her loss so unaffectedly?

A few days later I went to Atoll to see Bernard Bidault, Anna's right-hand man, a reserved and thoroughly businesslike fellow who knew everything there was to know about the firm. He handled the accounts as well as all fledgling or full-blown projects, and he knew all the employees by their first names and their positions in the company.

"I'm so sorry to bother you at this very painful time, but I absolutely had to see you. I did try to contact Monsieur Villandreux, but his wife told me that he was too upset to be able to deal with things at Atoll."

"There are problems?"

"In fact, Monsieur Blick, I believe the firm will have to . . . shut down."

"What do you mean, shut down?"

"We're six months behind in our social security taxes and a whole year behind in other accounts payable. We're overdrawn on all our accounts, we have taken out loans we can never hope to repay, we owe a fortune in back taxes, and we have a payroll of more than two million francs to meet by the end of the month."

"Anna never told me about all this."

"She didn't tell me all of it either, Monsieur Blick. She handled almost everything herself, and dealt with problems on a day-to-day basis. In her own way, with her own methods. We in management sometimes had some trouble following what she was doing."

I didn't understand any of what Bidault was telling me. Everything was going wrong—his story, the numbers, the outlook for Atoll, and above all the truth about Anna, which grew more and more confused.

Back at the house, I decided to search her business files for financial records regarding the firm's future move to Barcelona. Nothing. Not the slightest memo, not a single dossier. Spain? Nowhere.

Then something took hold of me, a kind of compulsion, a rage to find answers to all of my questions. I was going to rummage through the private papers of a dead woman, snoop into every corner of her life, unpack everything, haul it all out into the open.

First, Barcelona. Several phone calls to the chamber of commerce in the autonomous government of Catalonia revealed that Anna had never sent them any applications regarding the relocation of Atoll or any requests for subsidies, nor had she ever contacted any provincial representatives. Her name did not appear in any file or official appointment book. Besides which, her credit card statements did not show a single charge in Spain throughout the past year.

Anna had never gone to Barcelona. Nor had she ever considered relocating Atoll to Catalonia. It was all some bizarre trumped-up story that seemed to have no rhyme or reason.

A few days after that discovery, Vincent and I drove to the parking lot of the flying club to pick up Anna's Volvo. While I was waiting among the cars, a club mechanic came over to me, thinking that I was interested in renting a plane.

"No, I'm a relative of the lady who died in the crash."

"Please excuse me. What a terrible thing—we still haven't gotten over it here. Just imagine, in one of our planes . . . I'd checked it over only two days earlier. We can't figure it out. They say it was the weather, but I find that hard to believe. Monsieur Girardin was the most experienced pilot in the club. That trip to Béziers? He could have flown it with his eyes closed. Did you know Monsieur Girardin?"

"A little, yes."

"He had a house over by Sète, on the seashore. Perhaps you've been there yourself. He and the lady used to hop over there every week. So, you can imagine, he must have filed that flight plan hundreds of times. I can't believe he'd let himself get tricked by the weather. Do you fly?"

"Never."

I felt as if each day were taking a wicked pleasure in humiliating me, while the nights kept busy stirring up this vile mess. My pathetic subterfuges and degrading little investigations were upsetting me as much as my discoveries were. My son and daughter kept asking me what their mother was doing in that plane in the middle of the week with a lawyer who defended people accused of organized crime, but what could I tell them? I could only silently shrug and feign ignorance.

When I wasn't ferreting around, I was back taking care of my mother, who had been much affected by Anna's death. In fact not a single day went by without her praising Anna's courage and determination.

"It can't be said that you helped her much. She paddled her canoe all by herself. It can't always have been easy for her, you know, what with the children, the business, and you off on your trips."

Fortunately, counterbalancing my inadequacies I had the Jodel, Barcelona, and the Mafia mouthpiece. To tell the truth, I wasn't mad at Anna for lying to me. I was simply dumbfounded by her talents as an actress and the intricacy of her cover story. What surprised me the most was not that she'd had a lover, but that she'd abandoned her firm precisely when she knew that it was on the edge of bankruptcy. I had always taken Anna for a conscientious company director, so I probably found it hard to imagine her in the frivolous role of a mistress. Obviously, as in so many things, I had been mistaken. Barcelona had had nothing to do with the renewed intimacy Anna and I had experienced over the past year. I actually owed that sunny interlude to Monsieur Xavier Girardin, her clever suitor, who had discovered how to reawaken the sleeping memory within my wife's body. How had he done it? Had he immediately divined where Anna enjoyed being touched? Did she love his skin, his smell, his voice, the shape of his genitals? Did he tell her things she loved to hear, dirty talk that drove her wild? Did he know that after offering herself to him all afternoon, she would ask me to make love to her in the evening? Was he the one who invented the song and dance about relocating to Barcelona? Was he a money-grubbing bastard or simply a lowlife who preferred taking his pleasure with other men's wives?

None of that was really important. Anna had had her reasons for living as she did. Death had surprised her before she'd had the chance to tidy up the closets of her existence. The Jodel had revealed that private disorder. Every day carried me further away from my wife, yet closer to her, too. I would have loved to talk about Béziers, Catalonia, and

Girardin with her, listen to her trot out her cock-and-bull stories. How exciting it would have been to see her the way I'd never seen her before. Take the time to recognize her lies and evasions, and then one evening, surprise her by taking her to dinner in Barcelona.

The year 1999 was running out, drained and disillusioned, which was just how I felt. Ministers, mayors, administrators, and deputies of our incorrigible Republic had been summoned—sometimes in handcuffs—before judges to account for their countless villainies. On New Year's Eve, when the millennium would end and my little world would collapse, I was sitting in front of my drowsing mother, thinking about all those rogues and rascals whose cases Xavier Girardin, that estimable attorney, might have taken on. Yes, the lawyer to brigands, the porter, the chamberlain, the Gatsby of gangsters had definitely vanished too soon, missing his chance.

Fresh developments arrived with the New Year. On January 2, the lawyer dealing with Anna's estate told me that our house was mortgaged to the hilt and already belonged, so to speak, to the banks.

"By thus divesting herself piecemeal of her assets, your wife was trying to shore up Atoll, which firm you may now consider bankrupt. Last week I met with one of their managers, Monsieur Bidault, whom I believe you know. He referred to the company as 'a flatliner.' "

"Bluntly put, that leaves me in what position?"

"Bluntly put, a hole. You inherit enormous debts and your house may be sold out from under you at any moment. Madame Blick could not have disappeared at a worse moment."

"I'll leave you to do the best you can with all this."

"There is no 'best,' Monsieur Blick. Prepare for the worst."

Three days later two tax officials showed up at Atoll to audit the firm's books. I was informed of their arrival by Bidault, who advised me to go see them as soon as possible in the office he had placed at their disposal. I found two nice strapping young men, smiling and athletic. They looked more like a couple of pole vaulters than a pair of punctilious financial examiners, but spread out in front of them were the account books, bank statements, bills, and two laptops into which they were constantly entering data. They welcomed me so warmly into their lair that I was rather disconcerted. Were they putting into practice some new "behaviorist" guidelines concocted by the income tax authorities, or were they simply good-natured executioners, for whom cutting off heads was strictly business, nothing personal? They had me sit down beside them, poured me a cup of hot coffee from a thermos, and then, almost with remorse, began to ask me questions that were no doubt elementary but that I was unable to answer.

"You don't appear anywhere on the organization chart of the company, Monsieur Blick. May we ask what your position is?"

"I have none. I had never set foot here until recently."

"What do you mean?"

"I don't work here."

"Then why have you come to see us?"

"The company belonged to my wife. She died about ten days ago."

"We're very sorry to hear that . . . we had no idea. The inspection notice was sent here a month ago. This is all most unfortunate, obviously we've come at a terrible time."

"Please, do what you have to do."

"It's just that . . . Monsieur Blick, I'm afraid that we have more bad news for you. Atoll's financial state is quite dire."

"The lawyer has already spoken to me about it."

"Did he outline the company's financial liabilities?"

"No, he simply said the firm was 'terminally ill' or 'brain-dead'—something like that."

"We've only had time for a quick look at the accounts, but it already seems clear that the back taxes, not to mention the social security payments you owe, amount to several million francs. If your assets are in the same state, I'm afraid your lawyer's analysis might be correct."

"What can I do?"

"We're here to verify your fiscal situation and estimate the arrears owed the state. We are not authorized to give advice."

"I understand. But what usually happens to companies that find themselves in this position?"

"May I speak frankly? The business goes into liquidation and bankruptcy."

"That means all the employees are laid off?"

"Yes."

"There's no way to avoid that?"

"That's something to discuss with your managing director, Monsieur Blick, not us. This is not easy to say, but you must understand. We are civil servants; we are not here to help you. We're here only to assess the extent of your financial improprieties and any possible fraud."

"You think there's been fraud?"

"Regarding the past year alone, we have discovered operations that are suspicious, to say the least."

"Suspicious in what way?"

"Substantial withdrawals of cash every month. At a time when the company was supposedly in difficulty. Regular transfers to a bank account under the name of Girardin, accounted simply as 'managerial consulting.' Without a single report received from this consultant, no notes, much less any invoices. We're truly sorry. Especially at such a time. All this must be very difficult for you. But perhaps things will work out for the best."

How could they, when the very mission of those men was to withdraw, one by one, the few props still keeping the company alive?

After losing their only daughter, the Villandreuxs now saw an entire era of their professional lives collapse before their eyes. Atoll, which had for decades been the flagship of the family business interests, was sinking. Faced with the wreck, despite the repeated pleas of Bidault, Jean Villandreux—architect of the enterprise, now a broken old man—stubbornly refused to return to the company he had nurtured for so long, not even to speak to the personnel, explain the situation, and prepare them for the inevitable.

That arrived right on schedule at the end of March, after the company had been expeditiously liquidated: the firm closed its doors and dismissed everyone. Under the terms of various statutes, obscure regulations, and a marriage contract that turned out to have been poorly drafted, a large part of my personal savings was seized by the tax authorities and the bankruptcy court to honor numerous debts and loans incurred by Anna, whose legal partner I remained until the end.

The small fortune my trees had brought me vanished as suddenly as it had appeared. My life of leisure was over. At the age of fifty, I now had to become an office worker and live by the clock, but first I had to find a job—I, whose last real paycheck dated back to the mid-seventies.

Strangely, I wasn't at all angry at Anna for causing my misfortune. By supporting our family, she had allowed me to live as I pleased, to watch the children grow up, and even, for years, to fuck her best friend with impunity while she was off at work.

I had seen Laure again at Anna's funeral. She had come alone, and at the end of the service she gave me a sympathetic hug. We hardly said a word to each other, and I had no idea what her life was like or whether the rabbi was still a part of it. When we said good-bye she promised to call me, and of course she never did.

As for my grandson, he came into the world in the midst of that enveloping financial and familial crisis. With the most perfect discretion, he landed his seven pounds four and a half ounces gently upon this earth. From the moment I first held him in my arms, I felt the unbelievable, the inestimable weight of his life. That child was instantly mine. How can I explain it? I adopted him at first sight; I loved him without a second thought. That he was my son's son had nothing to do with our relationship. He and I were linked by something much more important, more intimate than the blood tie we shared. From then on I carried that child in my heart, and he possessed me, as an integral part of my being. Wherever he went, I would be. I would protect him. And when he was older, I would offer him a silver coach. And a Kodak Brownie Flash. And I would initiate him in the magic of safe lights and the smell of hypo. And then we would stroll around the world simply to learn the names of trees and see their branches reaching out into the lovely light.

Louis-Toshiro and I.

It was Yuko who chose the baby's name. She called him Louis. Louis-Toshiro Blick. It sounded like a household appliance company or a respectable Katsushika consortium of machine tools. Louis-Toshiro Blick. The family name, in any case, inspired confidence and loyalty, and betokened prosperity. Unlike "Girardin," of course, that two-bit yakuza of the Jacuzzis.

I couldn't wait for that child to grow up enough for me to see if he would look at all Japanese. For the moment it was impossible to tell for sure, even if his dark, smooth hair suggested the beginnings of a Nipponese mop.

Shortly after Louis-Toshiro's birth, the three banks that held mortgages on the house informed me that I had one year to settle those debts. After that, they intended to seize the property and put it up for sale. That's the way of the world. Given the large sums involved, I hadn't the remotest chance of repaying what I owed. I could only wait while trying to find some honorable course of action. I will never forget the condescending smile one of those bankers flashed me as he was leaving the house: "Don't worry, Monsieur Blick, I'm sure you still have that Midas touch."

At around that time, laboring in the Socialist vineyards, Lionel Jospin thought he was doing just fine when in reality he was busily digging his own grave. Meanwhile the treasurer of the Gaullist Party, Jean-Claude Méry, in a detailed account videotaped before his death, accused the president of the Republic of being a kind of pickpocket of public contracts. A backroom swindler. A common crook. After the Giscardian diamonds and the Mitterrandian bribes, we had entered the era of Chiracian cutpurses. No doubt about it: our monarchs had flabby ethics, and they were growing brazenly vulgar in their light-fingeredness.

As for my prospects, they were singularly disadvantageous. Spiridon finally told me that he couldn't take on my last project: I had dawdled too long, he said, in completing it. Priorities had changed. My moment had passed.

Anna was right: I had lived too long outside the real world, ignoring the new imperatives to work fast, be flexible, react quickly. Styles and fads changed so swiftly that neither man nor machine could afford to take a breather on the assembly line. Accumulation was the name of the game, a desperate attempt to fill an ontological void, to close an existential gap.

When I presented myself at the Agence Nationale pour l'Emploi, I sensed right away that things would not go well for me.

"You're looking for a job in what field?"

"Photography, if possible."

"Have you had professional experience?"

"Yes."

"Did you bring a list of your employers?"

"Actually, I've never had any; I've always been self-employed."

"You had a business?"

"No, no. I did books."

"Books of what?"

"Photographs, I told you."

"What kind of photographs?"

"Of trees. I took pictures of the most beautiful trees in the world."

"Wait a minute—you mean to say that your only job was photographing trees?"

"That's right. Well, I also photographed bark, plants, and insects."

Perplexed, my interviewer looked at me as though I were an exotic seashell, an amphora, some singular object that vaguely reminded him of a vacation abroad.

"So you have never had any employers. And these photos of trees: What did you do with them?"

"An editor published them."

"You've been doing this for how long?"

"Twenty-five years."

"And you published how many books?"

"Two."

"In twenty-five years?"

"Right."

"Do you mind my asking, did you have other sources of income?"

"No."

"Monsieur Blick. If I understand correctly, you published two books about trees that allowed you to live without any livelihood for twenty-five years. Is that right?"

"Yes."

"I'm sorry to say I have no similar situation on file here, whether in journalism, studio photography, or even wedding pictures. Do you have any computer skills?"

"No."

"Aha. Your situation does seem rather unpromising."

"What would you advise?"

"A training program. To reorient you toward fields where labor is in demand: the building trades for one, perhaps the food service industries. Assuming you don't waste any time, you might still find something at your age."

What he was trying to tell me with such touching solicitude was that, given the state of the world and my particular curriculum vitae, I was a goner.

"May I ask you a question? During those twenty-five years, aside from your trees, you really never took pictures of anything else? No news events, no sports, or fashion shows?"

"No. I've never worked with human subjects."

"I forgot to ask you: Do you have any degrees?"

"Yes, in sociology."

"Never mind."

He closed his notebook and handed me some forms that I had to fill out as soon as possible if I wished to take advantage of any training and assistance offered by various obscurely named agencies. If I had informed my interviewer that besides spending my life in the company of trees, I had actually been within an inch of becoming the personal photographer of François Mitterrand, I think his view of the world in general and of human resources in particular would have changed forever.

A few weeks after that meeting, realizing that my survival depended on keeping clear of all such institutions, I decided to set myself up as a gardener and to invest some of my last savings in landscaping equipment: a manual lawn mower, a power mower, a brush cutter, a leaf blower, a chain saw, pruning shears, a soil aerator, a wood chipper, and an old Toyota pickup to lug all that around. My little business really began to take off in the early spring of 2001. My appointment book was filling nicely, and as soon as I got started, I had the reassuring feeling that I'd been doing the job all my life. This physical work out in the fresh air suited me wonderfully. I had practically no contact with the owners of the yards in which I worked, so I could do as I pleased, applying the precepts inculcated in me by my father, that great sachem of lawns and bushes, with particular attention to those geometric rules governing the cutting of grass, which laws he had handed down to me like divine tablets. My wages were nothing like my former royalties, of course, but I earned enough to support myself and my daughter, who was still living with me.

Ever since Anna's death, Marie had changed. Of us all, she had the most trouble dealing with the loss. My mother did mortal combat with her illness and its handicaps, Louis-Toshiro filled Vincent's days and nights with fatherly cares, and I had to concentrate on my new work, a labor that strengthened me in both mind and body. Saddled merely with her own existence, however, and idly pursuing her nonchalant studies, Marie had remained frozen in her wintry pose, staring at the icy film that had ironically promised, on that night, *The Sweet Hereafter.*

Marie had taken our expulsion from Anna's house very hard. The move had been a miserable experience, since the banks had not granted us the slightest reprieve. With relentless officiousness, we had received the requisite summonses and notices of foreclosure leading up to the drumroll of eviction. For me, leaving that house, which I had never liked, was a kind of emancipation. For my daughter, though, the departure from her childhood haunts meant the disappearance of a world, the definitive dismemberment of a family hounded from its home, a home that Marie had intimately associated with her mother—she always called it "Mama's house"—and that she'd thought of as a kind of memorial after Anna's death.

Since the state of my own mother's health was deteriorating, I proposed to Marie that we go live in a wing of her grandmother's house. This initiative both reassured and delighted Claire Blick. Although the nursing routines had not changed, the house was large enough for the three of us to live our own lives, independently of one another. After I got home from work, I still prepared my mother's meals, while nurses, doctors, and physical therapists provided their usual care at the appointed times.

At the end of the evening, with my back and shoulders aching with fatigue and my hands swollen from toil in intransigent gardens, I sometimes dozed off for a moment before supper. Then I would feel as if I were plunging into a bottle of ink, or a chasm so deep and dark that neither dreams nor any living creature could survive there. Awakening to find myself back in my family's house, newly widowed, already a grandfather, chained to the bedside of my mother, three-quarters impoverished, and a part-time gardener, I would measure how far and how fast life could propel us from positions we'd been naive enough to think impregnable. A simple private plane crashing into a mountainside had sufficed to knock us from our cloud castles and exile us from our little dominion. What is true of the destiny of men holds for the fate of nations. In that month of September 2001, three airplanes would remind a hitherto untouchable America of those dictates of uncertainty. And ten days after that, those same laws, with the same consequences, would again prove their effect, this time in Toulouse.

An explosion that seemed to come from the center of the earth. The feeling that the sky would suddenly split in two. The ground beginning to shake—followed almost immediately by a deadly blast that lacerated lungs. The dead, the wounded, the shredded cars, the twisted buildings sheared apart, the collapsed ceilings, the walls and windows and roofs blown to pieces. And the stupor. And then the silence . . .

On that evening of September 21, Vincent, Yuko, Louis-Toshiro, Marie, and I spontaneously felt the need to gather in our extended family home. Far from the site of the explosion, it had suffered only a few cracks in the ceilings on the second floor, but Anna's house, which now belonged to the banks, had felt the force all across its façade. The windows had been blown out, and in places the roof looked as if it had been clawed by a giant bird. The building was unrecognizable. Although it was still standing, the structure remaining intact, it now seemed like an abandoned ruin, brought low by war or the ravages of time.

Gathered around my mother, we followed the news of this invisible bombardment on the radio and television. And we saw pictures of the AZF fertilizer production plant owned by Grande Paroisse, a subsidiary of the fourth-largest oil company in the world. We saw the gaping hole, that still smoking volcanic crater. This time the evil had not come from the sky, but from the bowels of the earth. The same laws of uncertainty and imminence applied, however: suicide planes or ammonium nitrate, Manhattan or Grande Paroisse—the unexpected lay murderously in wait for us everywhere. Side by side on the sofa, at either end of life and the world, facing images of the apocalypse, my mother and Louis-Toshiro had fallen asleep. Holding hands.

Like many with greater reason, I remember that autumn as a season in hell, a stormy time of relentless hostility, of blind, savage days. Two weeks after the explosion at AZF, returning home late in the afternoon, I found my mother lying on the floor, moaning in pain. Trying to stand up, she had tripped over a few steps an hour or two earlier, breaking a hip and her collarbone. One month in the hospital and two of rehabilitation. The rest of the story was written in her face, that old book with dog-eared pages: the tired eyes, the growing discouragement, the temptation not to press on, to let that broken body rest in peace. Elsewhere, and in a different way. Death was an incessant refrain on my mother's lips, not like one of those tidbits of senility chewed over by someone harping on days gone by, but as a future so close that if you listened carefully, you might almost hear its footsteps.

By day I hacked at bushes, and in the evening I fed my mother, whose right arm and shoulder were still immobilized in a splint. When she came home from the hospital, she had tried to feed herself with her left hand, but her stroke-damaged brain could not manage even such simple movements. Feeding my mother every day, cutting up her food, carrying it to her mouth, waiting patiently for her to chew, to swallow, then wiping her lips with a napkin, giving her a drink—all these actions brought us back to basics, to those distant, forgotten beginnings when children cannot survive without help, without maternal care and assistance. Those arms and hands, now crippled, had put in their time, carried out their duties, and sometimes even moved small mountains. Now it was my turn. From then on, my job was not to give her the will to live, but to lead her gently to the limits of her exhaustion, the mortal frontier that in many ways terrified us both.

JACQUES CHIRAC (II)

(May 5, 2002–?)

Y MOTHER was now so thin that she reminded me of Gérard Macé's description of ancient Incan mummies: "poor things with their false eyeballs and stuffed cheeks, their bodies grown so light that a mere child could have carried these former kings."

Marie found it increasingly difficult to keep her grandmother company and in her presence would become agitated, never sitting down to chat, but staying on her feet, coming and going like a nervous farm dog, with a look in her eye both searching and evasive. Perhaps she had a premonition.

Lionel Jospin had never replaced François Mitterrand in my mother's affections. She had not appreciated his vaunted right to "pick and choose": Just who was this presumptuous former Trotskyite who dared revise the flawless work of the Little Father of the People, Uniter of Leftist Splinters? Such audacity—even contempt—was not something Claire Blick could forgive. Nevertheless, Jospin, although not of the purest water, was a leftist. Despite her heart attacks, recurrent edemata, limited mobility, and quite modest life expectancy, my mother followed the 2002 election campaign with more interest and attention than most people who had every expectation of lasting through the victor's five-year term.

Whenever I saw her, she gave me an exhaustive summary of everything she'd heard reported on the radio. From reveille to lights out, its antenna fully deployed, her transistor radio never left her side. It had become her last link to this world and this life she so loved. I remember how annoyed she was upon learning that her candidate had criticized the age and weariness of his opponent. "That's extremely rude. One doesn't attack someone for his physical infirmities. It's not acceptable, just not done." There was something not quite right about this entire campaign—at least that's what my mother kept saying. She wasn't at all pleased by the wide diversity of choices, which, experience showed, was always damaging to the Left. Too many candidates from the Workers' Struggle, the Revolutionary Communist League, the Greens, and even the Chevènementists, a French nationalist party founded by Jospin's former minister of the interior. You didn't know whether you ought to team up with them or take to your heels.

"The Left needs a real leader. Mitterrand would never have permitted these dribs and drabs of candidacies scattered all over. Crumbs, plus crumbs, plus more crumbs won't add up to a loaf on election day."

"Shall I fix you some fish?"

"Are you listening to me?"

"Yes, of course I am, but I'd like to get some supper into you before the nurse arrives to put you to bed."

"Something's going to happen. I've no idea what, but I don't have a good feeling about this election."

I let my mother rattle on. I had no doubt that Lionel Jospin would be the future president of the Republic. Distrusted on all sides, hounded by judges, despised even in his own ranks, ridiculed by the press, his opponent, Chirac, hadn't a chance. Although my mother hated the slightest suggestion that her physical deterioration had affected her intellectual faculties, age and illness had unquestionably diminished Claire Blick's lucidity. During her hospitalization and rehabilitation, she would bridle whenever a nurse or caretaker greeted her with a condescending "And how are we today, my dear?" I can still hear her curt correction of the innocent offender: "My name is Blick, Claire Blick."

During the last week of the campaign, at each meal she would nag me to go to the polls on April 21.

"Your vote won't be wasted. Otherwise, I'm telling you, you'll see, Jospin won't make it to the second round."

The Socialist candidate's elimination in the first round of the presidential election had become her daily mantra, her permanent fixation. Through what perverse or deficient neuronal pathway could that absurdity have lodged itself in her brain?

"You think I've lost my mind, is that it?"

"No, come on. It's just that you spend too much time listening to the radio."

"You really think that I'm going gaga because I'm stuck in this chair and being spoon-fed? You think my brain doesn't work anymore, that I can't listen to the radio and draw my own conclusions? I'm telling you today, on Saturday, April 20, and listen closely, that Jospin will not make it to the second round."

"We'll see about that tomorrow."

"We certainly will."

When the astonished TV announcers broke the news, for all her warnings, I felt poleaxed. The Other Guy, the right-wing nationalist Le Pen, was in the second round. Jospin was not.

Strange though it may seem, that April 21 will always symbolize for me not the defeat of the Left, but the unbelievable, glorious victory of my dying mother. Helpless, isolated, holed up in her last refuge, that woman had managed to sense the bad vibes of a nation even before it had decided to pick two vile unworthies for the last electoral round. Like everyone else, Claire Blick spent the evening in front of the television, watching and listening. She was moved but also quite shocked when Lionel Jospin announced his retirement from political life.

"Mitterrand would never have done that."

I couldn't tell from her tone whether her remark was in praise of the nobility of the first man or the careerist tenacity of the second.

The Fifth Republic could not sink lower. That evening, contrary to what they were saying on television, there were two big winners: the Other Guy and above all, my mother.

I am struck by how that whole episode allowed me to measure the futility of the modern world, that outrageously busy universe bristling with sensors, charging blindly at the phantoms of its certainties, deleting its mistakes as if they were mere glitches, never thinking twice, disdaining deliberation, forgetful, amnesic, and loutish. Loutish to the core, not through a love or knowledge of evil, but simply by nature.

So the winner, who wasn't much, beat the Other Guy, who was even less, and I had no hand in it, absolutely none. My mother never asked me whether I had voted. I would have said yes, of course, to avoid upsetting her. She probably wanted to spare her irreligious son from lying yet again, and on account of something that was pointless anyway.

At the end of May, increasing heart problems and fluid retention were drowning my mother's lungs. The doctor came almost daily to do what little he could, saying those comforting or at best harmless words that allow us to make it through another day. Something in my mother's eyes, however, had changed. She seemed to see. To see what was now approaching. In the same way that she had sensed the dereliction of the French electorate, she smelled the uncanny odor of that animal now closing in for the kill. She was dying on full alert. Ears pricked, eyes peeled, watchful, she intended to be fully present for this encounter she had been expecting and dreading for so long.

I tried to talk to my mother, to listen, to absorb, to record the sound of her voice, and to notice how a pale green film seemed to dull her large brown eyes. Most of all, I tried to show her how proud I was to be her son. We had come so far together, and now I would have to go on by myself. In spite of everything, I could not truly believe that this woman would soon cease to speak and breathe, and see, and live, and love.

On the eve of the last day, she asked me simply to cremate her body and place her ashes next to my father's coffin. And then, as if we were on vacation at the seashore, she spoke to me with the gentleness and lightness old age had given her.

"I don't know if you can comprehend this, but at the end of my life, I can't manage to accept, still less understand, that I am old. I have almost no more arms, or legs, or heart, or lungs, or anything, yet when I look within, I see myself at eighteen, eager to discover everything and rush toward life. It's awful to die thinking such things. The years go by too quickly. Your brother, your father, and Anna, they all went too soon."

Then something passed before her eyes—a shadow, a thought, the reflection of some pain—and her face changed. She turned toward me and clutched my hand.

"I'm afraid, you know," she murmured. "So afraid . . ."

The next day, in the middle of the afternoon, serous fluid invaded her lungs. The outer edges of her lips turned blue as she fought harder and harder to breathe. While we were waiting for the ambulance, Claire Blick made the most terrible request a mother can make of her son. Squeezing my hand, she said, "Paul, please, do something, help me to breathe. . . ."

Until my last moment, I will be haunted by that frightened face, begging to be saved from suffocation. When the ambulance took my mother away, her condition had improved: intubated with oxygen, revived by the spectacular powers of a tiny aerosol pump, soothed by the solicitude of the doctors who had taken charge of her, she seemed to have weathered this crisis. When I arrived at the clinic an hour and a half later, I found Claire Blick sitting up in bed, joking with a nurse and a cardiologist, but asking mainly about how soon she could go home, now that she felt so much better.

Once again her face had changed dramatically. Gone were the tremors of anguish and the vagal pallor. My mother, like an infirm mountain climber clamped to the side of a cliff, had caught her breath and tightened her grip on life. We talked until it was dark, and when we said good night, she flashed me a big smile and said, "When you come tomorrow, don't forget to bring my radio."

But there would be no tomorrow. Or radio. At around four in the morning, the clinic called to tell me that my mother had just died of a heart attack. When I entered the room where her body lay, a doctor showed up right away to explain various irrelevant things concerning her cardiac arrest. No doubt tired from a night spent trying to resuscitate the dead, the doctor was clearly doing his duty under the International Organization for Standardization rules, which the clinic had agreed to observe.

I passed my hand over the face of Claire Blick. Already imprisoned by death, it was pale and cold, nothing but absence. I stayed for a long time with her, the bearer of a personal and essential question that would remain forever unanswered.

My mother was reduced to ashes in a quarter of an hour, and when they handed the container to me, still warm, I was amazed that such a life, so much intelligence and kindness, would fit into so small an urn. Claire Blick was as light as a summer breeze.

Little Louis-Toshiro, who had proudly celebrated his second birthday and whose face now reflected the essence of his two worlds, ran up and down the shady lanes of the crematorium. Watching him come and go like that, with his elbows held close to his torso, I wondered if his Olympian ancestor had bequeathed him his tireless heart and legs of steel. My mother, well, she had been content to offer the child the sweetness of her simple presence. Louis-Toshiro had just lost his napping companion, next to whom he had fallen asleep so many times, while she softly caressed the back of his neck before dozing off herself.

After the ceremony, we returned to the house. As soon as we stepped into the front hall, Louis-Toshiro began to dash about everywhere, looking and calling for my mother in every room.

After Vincent and his family had left and Marie, quite done in, had gone to her room, I went out into the garden. The foliage of the elms, the chestnuts, and the tall cedar formed a vault so dense that it seemed liquid, like a great wave immobilized in the arc of its omnipotence. Far indeed from that peaceful seaside image, I reflected that our family had been struggling in a relentless storm for two years. Accident, illness, mourning, explosion, eviction, bankruptcy—we had experienced a good range of the indignities of the human condition. I could only hope that things would now calm down, that we would each be able, at last, to return to the peaceful progress of our lives.

A few weeks after my mother's death, Marie fell into a deep depression that even today keeps her sequestered from the world. Already profoundly disturbed by Anna's death and the strange circumstances surrounding it, Marie could not manage to accept the agony and death of her grandmother. The loss of those two women left her helpless, and deprived her of almost all her will to live.

Coming home from work, I would often find her sitting on the sofa, staring vacantly at the trees outside. She hardly ever spoke, never went out, and had dropped out of college. I noticed that she had taken to wearing her mother's clothes, which she had insisted on keeping. Whenever I asked her why, she would shrug lightly, affectionately, to indicate that I shouldn't pay much attention to such haphazard details. Some evenings, however, when I caught sight of my daughter, it was Anna I seemed to see walking through the living room. I came to regard Marie's behavior as both painful and unhealthy.

"What's so strange about them? They're only clothes. . . ."

"That's just it, Marie, they aren't. They're the skirts and blouses of your mother."

"So?"

"You should wear your own clothes, don't you understand? You have to stop living in the past and hiding away with the dead, that's not normal."

With a look of disapproval I'd never seen from her before, Marie merely said, "And you think it's normal at your age to live in your parents' house?"

I didn't know what to say to that. She was perfectly right. I was living between my father's gardening bench and my mother's grammar books. I knew that I was in no position to lecture Marie on proper mourning rituals, given that I had poured a handful of my mother's ashes into one of her perfume bottles, which I kept in plain view on a little shelf above my desk.

Shrouded in her dead mother's clothes, Marie began to lose weight, plunging into an inexplicable fast from which nothing and no one could deter her. She practically stopped speaking, became inactive, and at last would not leave her room. Two visits from our family doctor had no effect. She seemed locked shut from the inside. Marie had closed all the windows of her life and imprisoned herself alive. I no longer dared go to work and leave her alone in that state of withdrawal. Her face was thin, her arms skeletal, and the outline of her jaws began to show through her sunken cheeks.

At my request she was taken to a psychiatric clinic, where she was immediately put on intravenous nutrition to restore her bodily health before any attempt was made to diagnose the illness of her soul. Located about thirty kilometers from Toulouse, the Résidence des Oliviers was a rather unusual private care institution resembling a large resort hotel. Like a big cat stretched out in the sunshine, the large farmhouse rambled along the airy crest of a hill in the Lauragais region. There the dramatis personae of the psychiatric floor show— flyweights or heavy hitters, light comedians or tragedians—gathered and mingled. Broken-down wage earners, messy alcoholics, stupefied Alzheimer's victims, the chronically suicidal, the occasionally depressive, natural-born schizophrenics, everyday anorexics, all strolled the grounds along paths surrounding a swimming pool, the use of which was strictly controlled. Aside from the main house, there was also a smaller building about which nothing was known except that it was locked and that cries were sometimes heard within, cries that did not always sound human.

After she emerged from her first sleep cure, Marie looked like a small pet half-paralyzed by arthritis. She took tiny steps and her movement was incredibly slow. A rather disconcerting artificial serenity had replaced all anxiety in her expression. During my daily visits, I often found Marie lying on her back, studying the ceiling. I would sit down next to her and caress her face for a long time, the way I used to send her to sleep when she was little. She showed absolutely no awareness of my presence. I talked to her occasionally about this and that, about what had happened during my day or some furniture I'd rearranged at home. She never spoke. One evening, however, when I was leaving her room and murmured automatically, "Sleep well, sweetheart," I heard her reply, "I'm already asleep, I always sleep with my eyes open." Her words made me shiver: I felt as if some sort of ghost were speaking to me from beyond the shadows. I left the room without answering her, as if she hadn't said anything, and I hadn't heard.

The doctor taking care of my daughter was a rather conventional woman who seemed to me lacking in both modesty and intellectual flexibility. She studied her patients' cases according to textbook criteria indicating a range of standard therapies. Dr. Brossard had already met with me several times but always said more or less the same thing:

"Your daughter is suffering from a pathology of the schizophrenic variety, with a strong dysphoric tendency." Françoise Brossard addressed me while looking over the top of the glasses perched on the end of her nose. She also asked me many personal and occasionally indiscreet questions.

"Have you been seeing anyone since your wife's death?"

"No."

"So no sexual relations for two years."

"What does that have to do with Marie?"

"Everything is illuminating, Monsieur Blick. Sometimes the light comes from unexpected places. To continue: Are you observing the traditional restrictions of widowerhood, or are you simply lacking in opportunities?"

"I have no answer to that."

"Did your daughter have a boyfriend before she was hospitalized?"

"I don't know."

"Has Marie ever introduced you to a fiancé, or brought anyone home with her?"

"No."

"You have another child, I believe."

"Yes, a boy."

"Does he live with you?"

"No, he's married."

"Did your daughter ever happen to see you engaged in sexual relations with her mother?"

"No. But I should like to point out that Marie has come here after the painful loss of two close relatives, not because of any problems with her libido."

"Who knows, dear sir. Sex often hides behind death, and vice versa."

I felt something like despair in the face of Brossard's clumsiness and pedantry, but whenever I asked other people what they thought about her doctor, they always warmly recommended her.

Vincent had no more success than I did. He bumped up constantly against the vacant gaze of an uncommunicative stranger, plied with drugs, who sometimes took a minute to cover the few meters between her bed and the bathroom. The rest of the time, as Marie had once explained to me, she slept with her eyes open. Vincent confessed to me that he could never sleep after visiting Marie. He couldn't stand the idea of that nauseating illness preying on his sister's mind.

How, in only a few months, had our souls fallen into such dark despair? What would happen now? Who was next on the list? During my bouts of uncertainty and despair, I was obsessed with Louis-Toshiro—his health, his life, his happiness, his peace of mind. Why did Brossard never ask me about him? Was he an insignificant part of the family puzzle that seemed to intrigue her so much?

Brossard. She was also often in my thoughts. She was more and more pompous, and less and less effective. For no objective reason, I wound up holding her responsible for Marie's condition. Our meetings became increasingly combative. I found her extremely aggressive, for a doctor, and too liable to fly off the handle. When she came at me with her unpleasant questions, she reminded me of those undisciplined terriers that dive into every burrow they find. To take some of the wind out of her sails and remind her how fragile certain appearances can be, I had told her about my experience with Baudoin-Lartigue and how everything had turned out, with his tragic suicide. At which point she had lost her composure and launched into a long diatribe that ended, as I recall, with a disquieting claim that "there's about as much likeness between psychiatry and psychoanalysis as there is between a policeman and a thief!"

Day after day Marie moved farther away from us. Casting off all lines, carried along by an invisible current, she was drifting out to sea. No matter what Brossard said, I was well aware of that fact. So I decided to end my painful and useless meetings with the doctor. I simply came by every evening after work to see my daughter and spoke to her quite naturally about everyday things, as parents do with children locked in persistent comas. I learned to avoid all interrogative forms and to phrase things in such a way that Marie need never reply. I was trying to play for her the role once filled by that precious transistor radio in my mother's life.

I would take Marie's hand and bring her news of her family and the world, of the magnificent progress of Louis-Toshiro, and the optimistic aphorisms of a certain Raffarin, a conservative burgomaster from Poitiers who became prime minister under Chirac. I also tried to describe to her the international disorder caused by the war that began in Iraq in March 2003, and the Christian, imperialist, fanatic, and stock-marketed America that had started it all. At moments Marie's fingers would lightly clasp mine, and each time I wanted to see in that reflex a sign of awareness, presence, approval, and perhaps even affection.

Knowing Marie and the sincerity of her youthful convictions, I was sure that if she hadn't been imprisoned in that psychiatric cell, she would have joined the millions of people marching in the streets against the absurdity of an oil crusade, a war for the fun of it. I'd gotten Brossard to agree to have Marie's radio turned on every day so that even if she didn't listen to the noon and evening news bulletins, she could at least hear them. I secretly hoped that those broadcasts would bridge the gap between her universe and what was left of ours. Marie had always been interested in current affairs. Inspired, no doubt, by the ecstatic socialism of my mother, she'd cultivated her own political consciousness and had naturally found her niche among the radical Greens and the altermondialist movements. At an age when most of her girlfriends were putting up posters of the Spice Girls or Boyzone on their bedroom walls, my daughter preferred to hang over her desk a small framed transcription of an exchange recorded in 1995 between Canadian authorities and the United States Navy. This authentic document, which said more about America than ten thousand books ever could, had been sent to her by a friend whose father worked in a ministry in Quebec.

This is the transcript of an actual conversation between the Canadian authorities and a U.S. naval ship off the coast of Newfoundland in October 1995.

> CANADIANS: Please divert your course 15 degrees to the
> south to avoid a collision.

AMERICANS: Recommend you divert your course
    15 degrees to the north.
CANADIANS: Negative. You will have to divert your course
    15 degrees to the south to avoid a collision.
AMERICANS: This is the captain of a U.S. Navy ship. I say
    again, divert YOUR course.
CANADIANS: No. I say again, divert YOUR course.
AMERICANS: THIS IS THE AIRCRAFT CARRIER
    USS *LINCOLN*, THE SECOND LARGEST SHIP IN
    THE UNITED STATES ATLANTIC FLEET. WE
    ARE ACCOMPANIED BY THREE DESTROYERS,
    THREE CRUISERS, AND NUMEROUS SUPPORT
    VESSELS. I DEMAND THAT YOU CHANGE
    YOUR COURSE 15 DEGREES NORTH . . . I SAY
    AGAIN . . . THAT'S ONE-FIVE DEGREES
    NORTH . . . OR COUNTERMEASURES WILL BE
    UNDERTAKEN TO ENSURE THE SAFETY OF
    THIS SHIP.
CANADIANS: We are a lighthouse. Your call.

I was proud of the way my daughter reacted to injustices and brutality. She had never been fooled by worldly machinations, and her mind always tried to look beyond the obvious, to see through the window dressing, to understand "the wheels behind the wheels." That was why I had asked Brossard to turn on the radio, to leave that door ajar, the way one does to reassure children who are afraid of the dark. And because I could not accept the possibility that my daughter was imprisoned for life inside that mental cage.

Martine and Jean Villandreux had never come to see their granddaughter since her hospitalization. They had apologized to me for this on several occasions, confessing that they could not endure such an ordeal. For my part, I visited them only rarely.

Every year since the death of their daughter, however, I did make a point of bringing them a bouquet of flowers on her birthday. Jean was always quite touched by this gesture. At our last meeting, I'd found him even more sad and weary than usual.

"I'm miserable about what's happened to Marie. That child was so sweet, so gentle. Have they seen any improvement?"

"No, there's been no change."

"Have you ever thought about it? Everything started with Anna, with that accident. I still don't understand."

"Understand what?"

"Life turning upside down from one day to the next . . . And that guy in the plane, that Girardin. You never told me about it, but I learned what the tax auditors discovered: the money paid out, month after month. . . . It just doesn't seem like my daughter."

"Forget all that, it's in the past."

"As long as we don't know the truth, as long as little Marie is locked up in that hospital, you know it'll be impossible to forget. It won't ever be over. . . ."

"But it is over, Jean. There isn't any truth to be learned, there's nothing to know."

"You say that, but I'm certain that deep down you think otherwise. That lawyer and all those payments must keep prowling around in your head, I'm sure of it. And it's those mysteries, those shadowy areas no one ever cleared up that have destroyed Marie."

"We don't know any such thing."

"Yes, I do. She came here to ask me a whole bunch of questions a few months after her mother died. We spent the afternoon together, talking about lots of things. Before she left, I remember that she kissed me and said, 'You know, Grampa, we might not talk together again for a long time, the two of us.' "

"She never came back?"

"Never."

Jean got up from the sofa, took my bouquet, and placed the flowers one by one in a vase, arranging them with the delicate gestures of an old woman. Watching him, no one would ever have imagined that he was the head honcho of *Sports Illustrés,* one of the most manly magazines on the face of the earth.

"Paul, I don't understand this world anymore. I feel as if someone changed the rules on us without any warning."

During the summer of 2003, an endless heat wave settled over the country. In Toulouse we were being broiled alive. Trees shed their desiccated leaves, and the stifling night air did nothing to cool off brick walls that had absorbed so much heat during the day. My father-in-law and I hadn't spoken for months, but when he invited me to spend the weekend sailing with him, I accepted. He kept a little boat in the port of Sète, and every year, as soon as the weather turned fine, Jean Villandreux began sailing. Martine hated anything even remotely related to floating objects and rarely accompanied him on his outings.

Even though it was probably pointless, and I didn't even know if she could hear me anymore, I stopped by the clinic to tell Marie that I was going sailing for two days with her grandfather. Villandreux was now an elderly man, twenty-three or -four years older than I was, and increasingly hampered by arthritis, but as soon as he stepped onto the deck of his boat he became young again, setting out to conquer the waves, darting around with strength and agility to set a sail or make some adjustment. Out on the water, the fresh breeze swept all care from his face, leaving it relaxed and smooth.

As we left the land behind, I felt a weight lifting from my chest, relief from anxieties that had accumulated for years. Nodding exuberantly to me as he manned the tiller, Jean shared that feeling of lightness. The sea gleamed like one of my father's new cars and our eager boat seemed determined to leave its mark. For the first time in a long while I was rediscovering, in that salt air, the scent and spindrift exhilaration of happiness. Nothing had really changed, yet everything was suddenly different. I wouldn't have been at all surprised to hear that back on land, Anna was at that moment on her way to Barcelona, my mother was listening to her radio, and Marie was getting dressed to go out.

When the wind dropped a little, Jean lowered the sails, and the boat slowly glided to a stop. The light faded, and for the first time in my life, I saw night fall out at sea. The silence was broken only by an occasional wave lapping softly against the hull. In the distance, off to the south, we saw the lights of a vessel whose size and shape were lost in the darkness.

Jean, who never cooked at home, prepared a salad of calamari while keeping an eye on a large shrimp omelet. From my seaside-resort point of view, the boat was like a cozy summer terrace at dinnertime, when the air carries the aromas of garlic, cooking fish, and hot olive oil.

While we ate we talked about Yuko, Vincent, and little Louis-Toshiro. I told Jean how his great-grandson had lately become inordinately fond of both dinosaurs and the solar system, and had announced to his mother that later on he wished to work in the sky as well as on land, practicing the rather unlikely profession of astro-paleontology. Whenever he became unruly or behaved badly, he would come back to Yuko right after she had scolded him and tell her, "I don't know what's gotten into my brain at the moment, but it just keeps making me do silly things." He also offered priceless questions, as at Easter, for example, when he'd asked his mother how hens managed to lay chocolate eggs "and wrap them up in tinfoil."

Jean began to speak of Anna, of her childhood and youth. Fueled by several glasses of Gigondas, the father had the power to bring his daughter back to life, without any sadness or nostalgia. Jean's evocation was sometimes so intense that it was as if he were describing not the past, but some time in the near future, clear, fresh, and peaceful.

As the alcohol wore off, that artificial enthusiasm waned. Then silence fell, and Jean closed his eyes. We stayed a long time like that, motionless, forgetful of headings and currents.

"You know, Paul, there are things that can be said only at sea, things that would probably never come up back in Toulouse. Do you follow me?"

I was willing to believe, yes, that the open sea did release our emotions and made them more navigable.

"I've done a lot of thinking since Anna died. And the result is that now I have nothing left to hold on to. I don't believe anymore, Paul, not at all. Religion never brought me anything. On the contrary, it made me regress. It taught me to kneel, that's all. To put my two fucking knees on the ground. And for a long time I paid no attention to the value and importance of each day. I resigned myself to a whole heap of things, accepted others through cowardice, grew old, and one morning I realized that there was nothing—not ahead of me, not behind me, nothing in my life, nothing in any church, and that it was too late."

A hot wind from the south was starting to hum through the rigging, while a few wavelets began periodically slapping the hull. Although I didn't completely understand what Jean was driving at, I certainly saw what he'd meant about the sea's power to tease out men's secrets.

"Nothing is worse, at my age, than to end up facing such emptiness. Now I'm angry at the whole world. And I don't even understand why. You know, Paul, those damned religions and their wretched idea of God have made us a stupid and servile race, some kind of genuflexible insects. . . . Is that a word, 'genuflexible'?"

Occasional gusts of wind, laden with humidity, were prodding the boat. We even began noticing the rocking of a steady swell. Half a day's sailing from shore, we were heartily insulting the gods. They were about to make us pay for that.

I was sleeping in my bunk when a loud noise awakened me. It was the waves pounding the hull. With each impact, the sailboat rose, then fell back with the sound of a slamming door. It was not quite four o'clock in the morning. Jean was no longer in his cabin. I noticed that he had closed all the portlights. When I came up on deck, a storm was violently sweeping the sea. Attached to a lifeline, Jean was at the tiller, trying to keep his boat aligned on invisible rails. I don't know how tempests are rated according to degrees of fury, but the one we were in terrified me more than anything I had ever experienced. The sea was as black as the sky, eliminating even the perspective line of the horizon, which was revitalized only now and then in the void by distant lightning.

"I think we're in for a blow!" shouted Jean in a strangely cheerful voice.

This coming squall of his worried me enormously, since I felt it was already blowing *quite* enough. I hooked up my own tether and headed for a narrow bench next to the tiller, but I'd hardly sat down when the boat reared up practically on its haunches, almost tossing me overboard. For a moment I thought we'd been bumped by a surfacing whale, but it was only a wave—the modest vanguard of the monsters now bearing down on us. Facing this onslaught of battering water, Jean seemed incredibly serene. As if he were setting out on vacation in a little sports car. While I was flung about in all directions, Jean, on his old legs, was anticipating, absorbing, weathering every blow.

Now rain joined the wind, like walls of water collapsing on us. Under bare poles, the sailboat climbed white-crested mountainous seas. In less than half an hour, the world had run amok, and the velvet of a peaceful night sky had given way to the hysterical attacks of waves bent on chewing the boat to bits.

The wild gyrations of the craft and the violence of the waves were making it harder and harder to keep our balance. Despite my paralyzing fear, I was discovering my father-in-law's true nature, his sangfroid, his ability to sort out problems and deal with them according to their urgency. From utter darkness, we had gone to the blinding and icy glare of lightning bolts that arrived in sequence to illuminate the raging sea. We could take stock of our surroundings, and estimate the size of the leviathans frolicking around us. Waves several meters high crashed onto our deck, picking up speed as they swept astern to try to bowl us overboard. We were clinging to life by two thin cords of blue nylon attached to our safety harnesses.

Jean shouted orders at me; the wind blew them away. Deafening thunder reverberated off the sea like a drumbeat. Then I felt the boat rise in a strange way into the air and incline so far on her beam-ends that the mast struck the surface of the water. Unseated, Jean dangled at the end of his tether, while I tried to hang on to what I thought were the chrome bars of the rails. For a long moment, cracking in all its joints, the craft seemed to hesitate between the temptation to sink and the instinct to float. A wave no doubt more kindly disposed than the rest struck the keel, which was just breaking the surface, and the boat righted itself as abruptly as it had tipped over. The impact had shattered two portlights, and we were now taking on water. Entangled in his safety line and slicker, struggling with the tiller, Jean yelled at me to go below and plug up the broken portlights.

Inside the cabin, the mess was even more impressive than the mayhem on deck. Things would hurtle to starboard, only to be flung back to port by an invisible hand. Whenever the hull stopped groaning, the pounding was so ferocious that you could only fear the worst.

I tried to get used to the idea that the hull would give way in the end and the boat would sink, taking us with her. It was summertime, and we were going to die. I stuffed the gaping portlights with foam rubber cushions, which turned out to be excellent compresses. Hardly had I applied these emergency bandages when my stomach keeled over as well, dropping me to my knees, where I threw up even my innermost thoughts.

When I went back on deck to rejoin Jean astern, dawn was just beginning to glimmer off to our left. I would never have believed the Mediterranean capable of such chaos. I'd thought these storms were reserved for the professional maniacs who braved the Atlantic in mid-winter and calmly radioed home their horrific news. If I had been able to send a message, what would it have been? I probably would have screamed that the boat had been pushed to the breaking point, all the portlights were blown out, the cabin was trashed, and the deck lockers had been swept away. I thought I heard Jean call to me, "Things should calm down at daybreak," and just when I was turning around, a sly wave whipped my feet out from under me and laid me flat on deck. The warmth of the water washing over me somewhat relieved the frightening impression of submersion and suffocation as I slid down a seemingly endless slope without—strangely enough—trying to stop myself. In that frothy confusion, I hit a few things with my shoulders or head, but I felt no pain at the time. When I reached the far end of the deck, a second mass of water fell on me and this time, I went overboard. Instantly, I had a kind of peripheral vision of my situation, panoramic images that might have been filmed by a camera a few yards above my head: I was alone in the water, surrounded by death, from which I could escape only by that single thin cord of rough nylon tying me to Louis-Toshiro Blick. So my grandson became my winch, and after a long naval battle, I hauled myself back on board. Busy keeping the boat alive, Jean signaled me to take shelter in a corner of the cockpit, and it was there, curled up like a traumatized animal, that I rode out the tempest.

When the storm finally ended, I had no idea what time it was. I remember only that the sun began to break up the clouds, and that the sea, once its fit had passed, was slowly recovering the calm we associate with the Creation. Jean, whom I had most prematurely written off as an old man, had captained his vessel with the elegant ease of one who, although he believes in nothing, no longer has much to fear. We sailed into the harbor at Sète in the early afternoon. The interior of the boat appeared to have suffered a pirate attack, and a jumble of objects still floated on the water sloshing around the cabin. Before leaving his boat, Jean surveyed the damage one last time. Placing a hand on my arm, he said, "This one, I think, was a narrow escape."

We were about halfway home when Jean asked me to drive him to Marie's clinic. He wanted to see her. The front courtyard was an inferno. The very air was on fire. All around, the countryside of Le Lauragais, usually so flourishing, had been charred by the drought. Not a drop of rain had fallen in two months. Thanks to the thickness of the walls, the inside of the clinic seemed relatively cool. Marie was in her room, sitting in her chair, facing the window. The bright summer sunshine was filtered by the branches of a chestnut tree that shaded her window.

We went over to Marie and kissed her in greeting. Back on land, Jean now looked his age again, and standing before his granddaughter, he seemed dumbfounded. She, as usual, remained impassive and silent, as still as a statue.

"We've just been out sailing. I felt like visiting you. Can you hear me, sweetheart? It's your grandfather. Do you recognize me? Marie?"

The old man who had brought us both back from hell, the man who had fearlessly defied the wind and waves, collapsed on his knees before his granddaughter and began to cry, clasping his hands like a supplicant deep in prayer. I knew that this prayer was addressed to no one, and that in this misleading posture, Jean was simply begging life to be a little less cruel. I tried to help him up, but he refused my aid and clung to the arm of his granddaughter, covering it with tears and kisses for a long time.

A few weeks after that visit, Dr. Brossard summoned me to her office. As we began our conversation, I had the feeling that the heat wave had shaken her self-confidence. The deaths of three elderly patients in the locked ward—all due to the fierce temperatures—had had something to do with this transformation. Brossard spoke about both the latest evaluations of Marie's condition and a new treatment she hoped would prove helpful.

"I also wanted to ask you something. Two or three days ago, Marie spoke for the first time in a long while."

"What did she say?"

Brossard set her little glasses on the end of her nose and read from a piece of paper.

" 'Jean came yesterday.' Can you tell me who Jean is?"

"Her grandfather. He did in fact come to see her two or three weeks ago. It's a good sign that she reacted, isn't it?"

"Time will tell."

"Do you think we should try another visit from Jean?"

"Why not?"

The next day, feeling optimistic, I returned with Jean. He sat a long time, holding his granddaughter's hand. And he held her hand again the next day. And the next. And again, all week long. We waited for a word, a gesture, something that would have allowed us to keep up hope. But months passed, and Marie would never mention Jean again. Or anyone else.

When autumn came, and it was time to rake leaves, I went from yard to yard, performing my tiring and repetitive labors. This silent and solitary work was now the image of my life: I saw no one and hardly spoke to anyone anymore. Sometimes I let myself believe that Marie and her madness lay a world away from me; at other moments, when I considered things more objectively, I had to admit that I had never before felt so close to my daughter. This impression was confirmed in an embarrassing way one November evening, I think it was, when I was finishing work in a client's yard. I had collected and shredded some leaves for compost, but many remained, and I decided to burn them. While I was tending the fire, the sun sank slowly from the sky. The yard then took on an aura of harmony, like a little territory not of this world. The garden wasn't particularly orderly or elegant, but a few simple bushes, emerging from the billowing smoke, gave a pretty good idea of what the bare bones of happiness would be, once stripped of the weight of humanity.

I was so absorbed in the contemplation of this soothing tableau that the owner of the property surprised me sitting motionless on my toolbox, oblivious to the late hour and chilly air. This episode made me very uneasy. Back at the house, I took a long, hot shower and tried symbolically to strip off the crust that I could sense was gradually hardening on me. Psychiatry was drawing me into its vortex. I tended to get too close to that mysterious wormhole that whisked us into another universe, that place of anguish where Marie lived, along with all those at the clinic who struggled in the toils of madness.

Whenever I thought of my daughter, I imagined her sitting in the paralyzing beauty of the garden where I had myself forgotten what time was. I liked to think that she was there, enchanted by a spell, lost in a peaceful daze, but the cries of fright and anger I sometimes heard escaping from the locked ward led me sadly to believe that the realm of madness was far more terrifying.

To relieve my boredom in the evening, I sometimes sorted through my music collection: about a thousand records and two hundred and fifty CDs. This activity was both a ritual and an unsolvable puzzle. I was loath to organize the collection by genre (which is never convenient for quickly locating an artist) or in alphabetical order (a choice that offers the advantage of simplicity, but is singularly lacking in style). Most of the time, I opted for a hybrid, irrational taxonomy, in which I grouped artists together for obscure idiographic reasons. Although there was a certain logic to placing Tom Waits with Rickie Lee Jones, or putting Herbie Hancock, Jeff Beck, and Chick Corea together, one might well puzzle over my grouping of Jimi Hendrix, Johnny "Guitar" Watson, Stevie Ray Vaughan, and Stevie Wonder. In this rational disorder, I set up little clumps of my favorite musicians or current interests: thus Curtis Mayfield, Keith Jarrett, Bill Evans, Chet Baker, Miles Davis, and Charlie Hayden rubbed shoulders with Chico DeBarge, Tony Rich, Babyface, Maxwell, and D'Angelo. In my more lucid moments, I felt unnerved by this compulsive behavior, these old man's manias, and I figured that I probably spent more time arranging and rearranging my music than I did listening to it.

I didn't mind my solitude, even though I did occasionally realize that it was disassembling the basic elements of my life. I could feel it taking me apart piece by piece from the inside, removing the components I supposedly didn't need anymore. And so feelings like joy, pleasure, happiness, longing, desire, hope—they were all disconnected, one by one.

I had not had sex with anyone since Anna's death. I can't say that I really missed it. I deplored the widower's well-known predicament, of course, but in an abstract, theoretical way, as one might regret the long-gone excitements of one's salad days. The idea of desire was still alive in me, and I entertained the possibility of being attracted to a woman one day, but without having to endure the searing torture of deprivation.

Around Christmastime, probably to perk up a particularly depressing evening, I telephoned Laure, whom I hadn't seen since Anna's funeral. I called her without any expectations whatsoever. Frankly, finding out what she'd been up to interested me about as much as checking the weather reports for a country I had no intention of visiting.

Still, we fell into conversation as naturally as if we'd last spoken together only the day before.

"How old is your baby now?"

"My baby? My baby, as you call him, just turned twelve years old."

"I can't believe it. What's his name?"

"Simon. Simon Charcot. He has my last name, because François and I divorced, you know."

"Do you still see the father, the famous rabbi?"

"Hardly. The rabbi vanished forever with the first contractions. I never saw anyone so frightened for his reputation. The day he left me he begged me on his knees and in tears, I'm not kidding, never to tell anyone about the child and our affair."

"And François?"

"He takes the kid every other weekend and for half the holidays."

"Have you ever said anything to him?"

"Are you joking! He's never had the slightest suspicion, and a good thing, too, because this way at least I get some decent alimony."

"Who does the boy look like?"

"Who do you think? He's the spit and image of the rabbi. But you know François—resemblances and so forth, that stuff goes right over his head."

"He's still living with his sweetie?"

"Absolutely. I even think she's pregnant again. And you, are you seeing anyone?"

"No."

"Really, no one?"

"No one."

My answer surprised Laure, who for one awkward moment just couldn't think what to say. Recovering quickly, she told me about her life and her complicated relationship with a divorced police detective. She went on and on, pouring out anecdotes, details, digressions. Listening to her lively and remarkably candid monologue, I concluded that no matter what she claimed, she, too, was feeling the pinch of loneliness. As we said good-bye, she wished me a Merry Christmas, which I thought was perfectly normal and, at the same time, completely uncalled for.

Nothing is worse than Christmas Eve in a psychiatric clinic, when night falls and the institution turns on its pathetic strings of holiday lights. Even the holiday meal they make a point of serving to their patients has a dreary air about it. The trays, the food, all reeking of that hospital cafeteria smell, mingling the aroma of meat with the fumes of camphor and rubbing alcohol. Marie was at her post, sitting in the dark, facing the window. The radio was bringing her news of a world coasting along toward Christmas dinner. I kissed her face, took her hand, and sat with her until a nurse came in much later and announced that Christmas Eve or not, it was time for my daughter to go to bed.

I spent that night sitting on my sofa looking at the photographs in *Trees of the World,* reliving each of those days when my sole concern, my unique preoccupation, had been waiting for a breeze and the perfect light to caress the dappled branches of a tamarisk.

On New Year's Eve, as I was leaving Marie's room, I encountered a patient whom I saw every day in the clinic halls or on the paths through the grounds. He came toward me, shook my hand warmly, and wished me a Happy New Year.

"You know, when you arrived here, you weren't in good shape, I could see that right away. Now things are different: you're a new man. They've cheered you up, they really have. They cheer us all up here— we're getting better and better!"

Shortly before midnight, I was awakened by the telephone. Vincent and Yuko were calling from Japan, where they had gone to spend ten days or so with the Tsuburaya family. Yuko wished me a Happy New Year in Japanese, and Louis-Toshiro explained to me in French that he had seen an enormous scaly dragon breathing fire.

For a long while after we'd hung up, I thought about my grandson's great-uncle Kokichi. I felt as if I were experiencing the same weariness he must have known at the end of his life. Like him, I'd had enough of running after a vanished world, a past that was long gone, and ghosts I could never catch up with.

But on that December 31, my phone call from the ends of the earth had come from the only family I had left. And that made me incredibly happy.

With spring came the season of lawn care, and the telephone was ringing off the hook. I was cutting grass all day long, always following the geometric precepts I'd learned from my father. Every day, like a stubborn navigator, I sailed up and down those green seas, measuring my way with a sextant through the heart of my gardens, leaving in my wake the illusion of a pacified world, where nature had been tamed and life held no surprises.

In April, hounded by the judicial system, a discredited President Chirac (whose right-hand man, Alain Juppé, had just been convicted in a court of law) reappointed as prime minister the very man who had been swept out of office in our recent elections: Raffarin. *Absolutely* impolitic. *Flagrantly* undemocratic. There was a Vichyist–banana republic aspect to this petty neighborhood fascism. The country had been handed over to crooks whom my father would not have allowed even to enter his dealership. Kokichi Tsuburaya's slightest stride deserved more respect than the interminable careers of those parasites. After their crushing defeats, you could rest assured that they'd never consider taking the honorable way out.

Marie never stopped "sleeping with her eyes open." Sitting beside her, sometimes I would get up the courage to tell her what was going on in the world: the cabinet-shuffling adventures of Raffarin (episodes 1, 2, 3), the torture in Iraq, the American quagmire. On some evenings, visiting her after work was a real ordeal, so difficult that I was unable to show her the slightest sign of affection. I would sit down next to her and join her in staring silently toward the window. I was angry with her for not being like the others, for not clinging to the blue nylon cord when she needed to, for causing me such worry and pain. At other times, I would enter her room and hug her tightly like a father returning from a long trip. At such moments I was convinced that it would all be over one day, that I simply had to be patient, letting time do its work. My job was to hold her hand and squeeze it to let her know that I was there, that I would never let go, not now, not ever.

Losing a child, even little by little, is a torment. A daily trial beyond the understanding of gods and men. Torture that never lets up, a weight that doesn't burden your back but crushes you more insidiously, wringing the life out of your heart.

At the end of May, Louis-Toshiro informed me that he had won a medal for improvement at his judo club. I was quite surprised to learn that children so young could learn the rudiments of the sport, but the bubbling joy and pride my grandson displayed as he showed me his modest trophy overcame my misgivings.

Every time Louis-Toshiro and his parents had come to see me during the past few months, I'd dreaded that it was to tell me that when Yuko's contract expired, the family would be moving to Japan. I had never forgotten Anna's solemn prediction of that exile. To dispel my fears, I could only remind myself of the many translation contracts Vincent had signed with major companies like Motorola and Airbus Industrie, contracts that kept him in Toulouse, at least for the time being. In any case, I was not going to ask him about his plans. The news, good or bad, would arrive in its own time. I had grown accustomed to letting things do as they pleased and happen when they liked. I had no idea what lay ahead of me or what would become of Marie. During the day I mowed lawns, and at night I slept in my parents' house, surrounded by their furniture. At times I felt that they were watching over me. At other moments, I had the uneasy feeling that they were simply watching me. On a shelf over my desk, the perfume bottle of my mother's ashes sat next to Vincent's chrome-plated coach.

I sometimes saw Anna's death mask in my dreams, and woke still seeing the vision of her swollen face. For a long while I tried to drive those images away, until I realized that they were part of me and would remain with me all my life.

On July 3, Marie's birthday, I arrived at the clinic bright and early. Taking my daughter by the arm, I escorted her out the big front door.

Instead of taking her for a walk in the grounds, I settled Marie inside my car and we drove off, heading south, toward the foothills of the Pyrenees.

My daughter and I were retracing the journey I had made with my grandfather forty years before. He had returned to those mountains a few weeks before his death and had showed me his pastures, where everything had begun. The sheepfold, the mountain peaks, the silence. For a moment he had forgotten his own ghosts and had opened himself to the beauty of the world that had once been his home.

The road grew winding and increasingly narrow, just as I remembered, until it stopped abruptly right below the summit of the pass.

My daughter, who had not moved during the ride, stared straight ahead of her. I couldn't tell what she saw, or felt, or understood of this journey.

The air was astonishingly crisp. I helped Marie out of the car and put a warm jacket on her. I took her arm, and we began to walk up the path to the peaks.

The sky was overcast, and a few low-lying clouds occasionally clung to the flank of the mountain. The surrounding silence was so pure that it seemed to have been filtered, distilled, and dissolved into the crystalline transparency of the air.

Without my help, Marie climbed the slope with surprising agility. When there was room on the path, she stayed at my side, forging ahead when the way up became too narrow. Who, seeing her then, could possibly have guessed her condition? To the surrounding landscape, she was simply a woman like any other, walking toward the sunset.

The view from the summit was exalting. The mountain plunged steeply toward Spain, while a few scruffy meadows and clumps of snow descended haphazardly on the French side.

Blowing up from the bottom of the cliff, an icy wind ruffled Marie's hair now and then, giving her face an illusion of life.

We had come to the end of our long walk.

I put my arms around my daughter. I felt as though I were hugging a dead tree. She stared straight ahead. We were at the edge of the void, balancing on the top of the world.

I thought about all my friends and family. In that moment of doubt, when so many things depended on me, they were no help, of no comfort. That didn't surprise me: life, I knew, was nothing more than an illusory strand connecting us to others and leading us to believe, for a brief time we find meaningful, that we are something after all, and not just nothing.

A Note About the Author

Jean-Paul Dubois was born in 1950 in Toulouse, where he still lives today. The author of many novels and collections of travel writing, he is also a reporter for *Le Nouvel Observateur*.

A Note on the Type

This book was set in Fournier, a typeface named for Pierre Simon Fournier fils (1712–1768), a celebrated French type designer. Fournier was an extraordinarily prolific designer of typefaces and of typographic ornaments. He was also the author of the *Manuel typographique* (1764–1766), in which he attempted to work out a system standardizing type measurement in points, a system that is still in use internationally.

Composed by Creative Graphics, Allentown, Pennsylvania
Printed and bound by Berryville Graphics,
Berryville, Virginia
Designed by Anthea Lingeman